The Charter of Oswy and Leoflede

A Fenland Mystery Set in the Twelfth Century

by Diane Calton Smith

Published by New Generation Publishing in 2023

Copyright © Diane Calton Smith 2023

First Edition

The author asserts the moral right under the Copyright, Designs and Patents Act 1988 to be identified as the author of this work.

All Rights reserved. No part of this publication may be reproduced, stored in a retrieval system or transmitted, in any form or by any means without the prior consent of the author, nor be otherwise circulated in any form of binding or cover other than that which it is published and without a similar condition being imposed on the subsequent purchaser.

ISBN: 978-1-80369-739-0

www.newgeneration-publishing.com
New Generation Publishing

In memory of Auntie Christine, whose laughter and kindness I will always remember

The front cover image is used with the kind permission of St Peter and Paul's Church. It shows detail of stained glass in the north east chapel.

Also by Diane Calton Smith:

Fenland Histories:

A Georgian House on the Brink (2015)

(Winner of a Cambridgeshire Association for Local History [CALH] Award)

Webbed Feet and Wildfowlers (2017)

Plague, Flood and Gewgaws (2019)

Fenland Mysteries:

Quiet While Dollie Sings (2016)

The Quayside Poet (2018)

In The Wash (2020)

The Lazar House (2021)

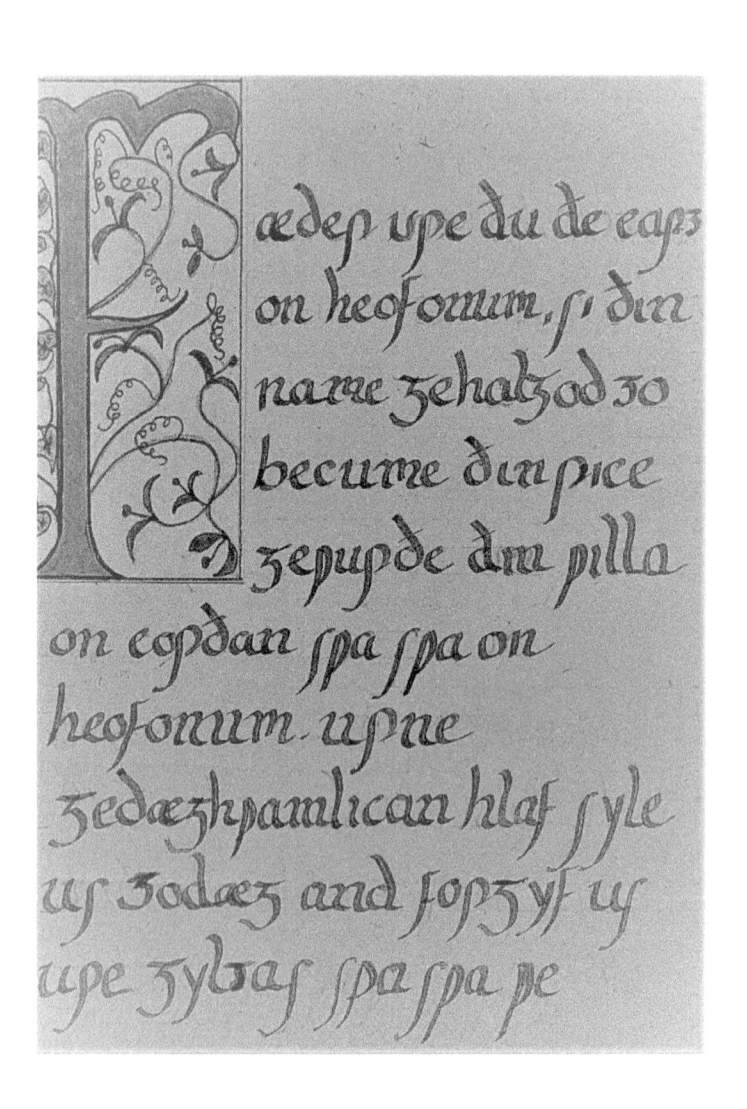

Fæder ure þu þe eart on heofonum, si þin nama gehalgod to becume ðin rice gewurðe ðin willa on eorðan swa swa on heofonum. urne gedæghwamlican hlaf syle us todæg and forgyf us ure gyltas swa swa we

ONE

Feast of St Perpetua and Felicitas; Wednesday 7th March 1190

The young Sir John of Tilneye came to a halt and stared.

The rider entering the bailey from the gatehouse was sitting his horse like a sack of turnips, though he had about him an air of precocious confidence. He was dressed in the usual long, faded tunic and shapeless hose of all peasant folk, and the hem of his dark cloak was thickly plastered with mud.

He looked completely out of place, thought Sir John, and the horse was clearly more used to pulling a cart than being ridden. He wondered idly what had brought such a poor excuse for a rider to the great castle of Wisbech Barton.

Sir John continued on his way to the chaplain's office. There were messages his father needed to be sent to the bishop in Ely and John, as the only son and future lord of the manor of Marshmeade, was invariably the one entrusted with such tasks. He could quite easily have written the letters himself, having benefitted from a good education. Learning had always come quickly to him, though he had often resented spending so much of his youth in study. Anything that took him away from riding and being outside in the open air had always been something of a bore for him and that attitude had not changed with the years. Even now, a trip to the castle and finding someone else to write his letters was preferable by far.

'Who's that fellow that just rode in, sitting his horse like a jester on a mule?' asked John as he reached the chaplain's office. Eric de Bourne grinned.

'Someone with an inflated sense of his own importance, I'd wager. I saw him as I came in just now. The chaplain's gone to St Peter's, but I'm quite sure I can manage your letters myself. A letter to my lord bishop, is it? Why don't you write it yourself? You always were an idle good for nothing.'

'Very true, but I think Bishop William de Longchamp would appreciate your efforts more than mine. You'll make a far better job of it.'

Eric shrugged good naturedly, accepting the compliment with the task. He drew a clean sheet of ready trimmed parchment towards him and settled it on the steep slope of his writing desk.

He and John had studied together as boys, learning Latin, French and numeracy from an elderly priest in Elm. They had even studied the almost abandoned language of the Saxons, the Old English that few spoke or cared to understand anymore. Neither boy was descended from Saxon families; their roots, like most families of note these days, were well and truly Norman. Their tutor, however, was insistent that his pupils had some understanding of the old language of the country in which they thrived, before the knowledge was lost forever.

Eric had always been diligent and hard working, while John had never seemed to make any effort at all. He simply soaked up information like an irritating sponge, cutting corners wherever he liked. In the end, Eric's hard work and John's natural brightness had brought both boys to the required standard. After that, John had departed to serve a neighbouring lord as a squire on his way to knighthood.

That too, he had managed with baffling ease. It seemed that anything attempted by the newly knighted Sir John of Tilneye was achieved with hardly any bother at all.

Despite the differences in the boys' characters, they had remained friends. While John had ridden off to acquire knightly qualities, Eric had buried his nose happily in his books, eventually going to work at the castle as one of the chaplain's clerks. It was worthy employment and Eric was justly proud of it.

He was writing quickly now as John dictated. His lettering was admirably neat and he made no errors.

'You always did pen a good note, Eric,' John acknowledged. 'Thank you. My lettering always resembles the trail of a drunken spider staggering across the page.'

'More like,' grinned Eric, 'the death throes of a sick caterpillar.'

By the time John had left the chaplain's office, the sun had come out. Its brightness flickered uncertainly at first, as if not quite sure of itself, but it slowly spread its light across the thatched buildings grouped around the great castle keep. It was too early yet to think of spring; snow often made its return at Eastertide, plunging folk back into winter and all the uncertainty and perils that accompanied it.

As John walked towards the stables, he was afforded another glimpse of the visitor he had noticed earlier. The man was making his way up the steps towards the castle forebuilding, the structure that served as the entrance to the keep itself. He climbed as badly as he rode. He was tall, but did not carry his height well, slouching and splaying his feet out to the sides. There was something about him that John found faintly disturbing, though he could not have said why.

He frowned and went to find his horse, Albanac.

TWO

Simon de Gardyn

The last thing Sir Simon de Gardyn, deputy constable of Wisbech Castle, needed that morning was to be interrupted again. The day had started badly and he was now trying to concentrate on composing a very difficult report. Yet he just kept being disturbed.

Only that morning, one of the castle's prisoners, one who was awaiting trial at the next Assizes, had tried to escape. Such attempts were not uncommon and fortunately this one had been particularly clumsy and quickly thwarted. In the dark of early morning, the prisoner had taken advantage of a rare occasion on which the cell door had to be opened. He had landed the guard a mighty blow to the head and bolted down the passage. His freedom had been pitifully short, his progress blocked by another guard, and he was now safely back in custody, nursing his bruises.

The prisoners held at Wisbech Castle pending the next Assizes were generally of the most dangerous sort, men charged with murder or treason. Since the Assizes were held but twice a year, some of the prisoners had to endure a long, hopeless and miserable wait for their trial and the almost inevitable guilty verdict and hanging.

Though that morning's attempted escape had been speedily dealt with, it had left Simon feeling troubled. Whenever the constable was away, on this occasion on business in Whittlesey and Thorney, his deputy was determined that things should run smoothly. They rarely did, however. This morning's events had been another reminder of the enormous responsibility of running Wisbech Castle, the legal and administrative hub for the whole of the Isle of Ely.

And now he was being subjected to another interruption. The visitor had been admitted to the office, but Simon kept him waiting for as long as possible, aware of the man's bristling impatience. At last, he looked up from his work and regarded the visitor with an appraising eye. The young man was clean shaven and his clothing was simple but in generally good repair. His cloak, which was mud stained and faded from its original black, had a clerical look about it. He was about as unkempt as anyone who claimed to have ridden from Ely ought to be, and his face was still smeared with dirt from forehead to chin. He had clearly not bothered to smarten himself up before entering the keep.

It was not so much the youth's appearance that roused the deputy's suspicions, however, as something far more subtle. Simon had seen hundreds of messengers during his time at the castle and something about this individual was wrong. Whether it was his speech or the overbold manner in which he regarded him, the deputy was immediately on his guard, and he listened with scepticism to what the messenger had to say.

'You are requesting that I hand over one of our oldest charters?' queried Simon incredulously.

'The request comes from the bishop himself, my lord.'

'Then where is my lord bishop's written mandate?'

'Regretfully, I have none, my lord. This is a verbal message which I have been entrusted to deliver to you.'

'What utter nonsense! Such requests are always written down. And besides, all charters relating to the Isle of Ely are held by the bishop himself. Why would his grace need to see our copy of this document?'

'I am given to understand, my lord, that the document long held in Ely cannot be found. A matter has arisen for which sight of the document is needed, and so my lord bishop would take into his keeping the copy held in Wisbech.'

'And might I know what that matter is?'

The messenger did not reply at once, appearing to be collecting his thoughts.

'There is a small manor in Walpole, my lord,' he said at last, 'one that takes its name from the town of Ely itself. It was gifted to Ely Abbey in Saxon times by means of the same charter which granted Wisbech and other manors to the Church. However, it appears that the people of that small manor in Walpole have become resentful of the rents which they are duty bound to pay to the bishop. They demand to see evidence of their manor's ties to Ely. They wish to see the charter itself. They are threatening to withhold their rent until they have proof of this unwanted allegiance.'

Simon looked steadily at the youth, disbelief written all over his face.

'I have never known the good people of Ely Manor in Walpole to cause trouble. What has occurred to bring about this sudden rebelliousness?'

'I do not know, sir. I am merely aware that the bishop is greatly concerned about the matter.'

'And so my lord bishop requests that you take away our copy of the charter in order to solve this problem?'

'That is so, my lord.'

The deputy rose from his seat and turned away from the messenger for a moment, taking a step towards the pair of long, narrow windows behind his seat. He took a deep breath of the fresh spring air that wafted liberally through the unshuttered windows. He rested his chin on the high sill and peered out to watch the activity in the bailey below. It was late in the afternoon now and the place was quiet. Just a few men-at-arms, cooks and clerks crossed the wide court, making their way between offices, workshops and stables.

'Go and find yourself refreshment in the great hall,' he said to the messenger. 'Supper will soon be served and I shall send word to you when I have had time to think about this.'

The youth bowed awkwardly and made his exit.

Left alone, Simon crossed the room towards the huge, iron bound oaken chest that sat against the north wall. Above the chest hung one of the castle's finest tapestries. It was richly woven, its colours vibrant, but neither the constable nor his deputy had ever thought highly of its design. It was meant to depict the First Crusade, but was far from convincing. A group of puzzled and puny crusaders, accompanied by a horse with a bad squint, was being led along by a painfully thin, yet jolly looking hermit. Some chance, the constable and his deputy had sometimes remarked, of a clueless army like that ever capturing Jerusalem.

The deputy unhooked the bunch of keys from the long girdle tied around his waist and selected one of the smaller keys. He fitted it into the lock of the chest and turned it carefully. After the usual resistance, a hidden part of the old mechanism turned, allowing Simon to open the lock and lift the chest lid.

It was in this chest that the town's charters and most important documents were stored. They were all in scrolled form and were arranged neatly across the bottom of the trunk. It took Simon but a few seconds to locate the one he was looking for and he lifted it from the trunk, holding it reverently in his hands. It was ancient and yellowed, faded and frayed, but it was safe.

The Charter of Oswy and Leoflede dated from well before the coming of the Normans and the document in Simon's hands was one of only two known copies. The other was supposed to be in Ely but, according to the messenger, it was missing.

Simon unrolled the charter and glanced at it briefly, as if to reassure himself, before replacing it in the trunk. He locked it again and rose to his feet, going to the door and hailing the guard in the passageway.

'Send word to the messenger who was here just now. He will be in the great hall. Tell him that the document cannot be found. He must carry my apologies back to Ely.'

The man barked his assent and passed the order to other guards further along the passageway, who left to do the deputy's bidding.

Perhaps, thought Simon, he would come to regret his decision. It might turn out that he was wrong in sending the youth away, but he had to trust his instincts.

Because there was just something very dubious indeed about the messenger.

THREE

Feast of St Maud; Wednesday 14th March 1190
Morning

Sir Alexander de Astonne, constable of Wisbech Castle, returned after an absence of ten days. He was glad to be back; his journey by boat to the fen islands of Whittlesey and Thorney had been tediously long and his business there had been drawn out and almost as wearisome as the travelling.

Now comfortably reinstalled in his office in the keep, Alexander had been joined by his deputy and Sir Nicholas Drenge, the bishop's seneschal and keeper of the peace in the Isle of Ely. The deputy was delivering his report and Alexander listened attentively, lifting his hand every now and then to scratch his chin beneath its new, fashionably short and pointed beard.

The constable was a handsome man, his dark hair only just starting to show touches of grey even though he was approaching his middle years. The experience gained from ten years in the most senior position at the castle had given him an air of unshakable confidence, but he used his authority wisely and was known for his good judgement.

Simon, his deputy, was a much younger man, tall, fair haired and pale skinned, his beard skimpy and his neck rather long with a prominent Adam's apple. He was delivering his report in an efficient manner, explaining his actions over the last ten days with proper attention to detail. Alexander nodded as he reached the end.

'All would appear well, then. The attempted escape from the cells was swiftly dealt with, by the sound of it. Regarding that other curious matter, you reacted in the only sensible way. Handing over the charter without a written and sealed mandate from the bishop would have been foolish indeed. Do not concern yourself, Simon. If it turns out that the man truly represented my lord bishop, I shall send my apologies along with the charter to Ely. I doubt any such action will be necessary, however.'

'Perhaps,' ventured the seneschal, 'you could give me a little background on the matter?'

Having spent less than a year in the post of bishop's seneschal, Sir Nicholas Drenge was still keen and energetic. Unlike Alexander, he had rarely been described as handsome. Despite his youth, he had already lost most of his hair, the only remaining tufts of it hugging his large ears. His long face showed intelligence and his blue eyes shone with curiosity from otherwise indifferent features.

'Of course, Nicholas,' replied the constable. 'Some sixty or seventy years before the Conqueror's people arrived in these parts, a noble couple by the names of Oswy and Leoflede gifted some of their manors to the abbey in Ely. They did so, I believe, to mark the occasion of their young son Ailwine's admission to the monastery. Leoflede was the daughter of Brythnoth, the first abbot of Ely, and it would appear that this greatness ran in the family because Ailwine eventually became a bishop himself. The Bishop of Elmham, I believe it was.'

'Ah, yes,' replied the seneschal, 'I seem to remember hearing about that gift. It was very generous, I believe.'

'Generous indeed,' agreed Alexander. 'A number of significant Suffolk manors went to the abbey, as did our own Wisbech and some small settlements in Walpole, one of which is known as Ely Manor.'

'And, we are told,' added Simon, the deputy constable, 'it is in that manor of Ely in Walpole that there lies a problem. According to the messenger who came here, the people there are objecting to the payment of rents due to the bishop. Apparently, they dispute this obligation and demand to see the charter. The whole tale is ridiculous, of course. I doubt that anyone there could read the document, even if they saw it.'

'I agree,' said the seneschal, 'and as far as I know, there has never been anything but peace and law abiding from the people of Walpole. I think I should go and see for myself what is going on there. I am not due back in Ely for a day or two and a ride to Walpole will take little of my time. I shall let you both know how I find things there.'

Sir Nicholas Drenge left the office and strode along the narrow passageway to the spiral stairway. He descended cautiously, his large feet feeling for the widest part of each stone step, and made his way outside.

As he stepped out into the bailey, a gust of cold wind tore at his cloak and almost succeeded in lifting the cap from his head. The day was thickly overcast, the dense, grey mass of cloud moving with lowering intent across the sky. Everywhere in the open court, castle serfs were doing their best to ignore the cold, persisting with their work. A group of labourers was spreading straw from a cart, adding another layer to soak up the mud on the main thoroughfare. It was a job that was never completed to anyone's satisfaction. The mud and straw were constantly trodden and churned by the boots of hundreds of clerks, soldiers, churchmen, officials and visitors that walked across it every day.

The men, heads covered with hoods, had rolled up the sleeves of their loose, dun coloured tunics as they laboured. The mule, still hitched to the cart, was drinking peacefully from a large bucket, readying himself for the next trip to fetch hay. He looked more content with his lot in life than did the serfs, who kept their eyes lowered, not even glancing at the seneschal as he crossed the yard in front of them.

Nicholas found Brithun and Ordgar, his two men-at-arms, seated outside the stables. Having brushed down the horses and left them to feed, they were enjoying some refreshment of their own. Slumped on a weather beaten bench, they were drinking ale from horn cups. Between them on the bench were a chipped earthenware jug and a basket of bread. When they caught sight of Nicholas, they sprang hastily to their feet.

'Finish your ale,' he said dismissively. 'In fact, I'll join you if there's enough for three. We have a short journey to make this afternoon, but nothing will be lost by taking time for a little bread and ale.'

The two men settled themselves back on the bench, making room for the seneschal. They were aware of the honour of working for Sir Nicholas; his rank as seneschal was equal to that of High Sheriff in any other shire, his responsibilities as great. As the keeper of the peace for the Isle of Ely, he had been appointed by the bishop himself. It was an arrangement which had been in place since the founding of the Liberty of Ely in the time of King Edgar, many centuries earlier.

Sir Nicholas Drenge could be a demanding master at times, but for all his expectations, he was fair. As Ordgar and Brithun often remarked to each other, that was as much as any man could hope for.

FOUR

Afternoon
Piggery

The wind had soared to shrieking pitch as Sir Nicholas Drenge and his two men-at-arms set out from Wisbech along the eastern bank of the Wash estuary.

The Wash reached inland as far as Wisbech, bringing great benefits for trade but also a perennial threat from sea flooding. High tides, enhanced by the ferocity of winter and spring storms, all too often brought terrible floods in their wake. Time and time again, people, livestock, homes and crops had been lost to these inundations. Had it not been for the high sea banks that lined the edge of the Wash, the situation would have been far worse.

The banks had been built long ago to protect the surrounding flat land, and in many places roads ran along their tops, raising travellers to a position of relative safety. The road to Walpole was one such route and its exposed situation gave the riders no relief from the wind. They were facing straight into the teeth of it for most of the journey and the view that stretched before them did nothing to lift their spirits.

The tide was out, leaving a bleak landscape of smooth mud flats and deep gulleys that meandered across the sea bed. Even the sedge, eel grass and sea lavender that grew close to the banks looked desolate, forced into supplication by the wind and recovering between gusts only to shiver in anticipation of the next.

At least the road was in a passable state for the time of year; there had been no rain for a week or more and the wind was playing its part in drying out the surface. No one spoke much as they rode along, though now and then Nicholas heard Ordgar mumbling one of his earthier curses. His men had no love for this wild coastal country with its high winds and lamenting seagulls. Brithun and Ordgar were men of the Black Fen, the boggy land around Witchford in the south of the shire, where the sea was a distant thing and the water that lay everywhere was habitually still, dark and quiet.

Nicholas reached up with his right hand to adjust his cap, trying to pull it further down over his ears. The cap was a smart and fashionable item of richly dyed blue wool, but was scarcely warm enough to cover his head in weather such as this. He wished, as he often did, that he had been more generously blessed with hair and that his smart travelling cloak had been supplied with a hood.

His men had no such problem. The hooded cloaks that covered their coats of mail and tunics were of heavy wool and lined with rabbit fur. They were unimpressed by the fashionable elegance of Nicholas's clothing, though it was fitting for his knightly status. His green tunic was long and well tailored, its skirt split at the front for ease of movement and horse riding. The sleeves flared out from the waist like a gull's wing and narrowed to an elaborate cuff at the wrist. The leather girdle that encircled his waist was ornately buckled and jewelled, one end of it hanging neatly down the front.

Nicholas was indifferent to his men's opinion. It was only when exposed to the elements like this, when the wind rattled his teeth and the gulls that wheeled overhead seemed to cackle with mirth at his adherence to fashion, that he questioned the wisdom of it himself.

At last, the first modest dwellings of Corpus Christie, the closest of the Walpole manors, came into view. Walpole consisted of eight manors that were dotted across the flat landscape hugging the eastern bank of the estuary. A track led the riders down from the high bank road and on to a winding lane, where at last there was some shelter from the wind. They rode through a spinney of stunted willows and elders and were soon entering the village with its modest manor house.

The lord of the manor of Corpus Christie, as far as the strangers could see, held dominion over a well ordered settlement. Signs of springtime activity could be seen everywhere and in the faces of folk engaged in their labours the seneschal saw no cause for alarm. There were no covert glances, no underhand behaviour, nothing at all to suggest a brewing rebellion against their lord. If trouble existed in Walpole, it had not spread to the manor of Corpus Christie.

In a distant field, villeins were working with a pair of oxen and a heavy plough, preparing the land for the early sowing of wheat. Closer by, men were loading a small cart with turf for the fire. Some of them lifted their heads and stared at the strangers as they rode by on their fine horses, but it was with idle curiosity, nothing more. The seneschal's party did not stop to speak to anyone until almost out of the village, when they came across a villein leading a mule along the track. The man greeted them with a bow and readily told them what they wished to know, that the Manor of Ely was no more than two or three miles further along the road.

The first thing that greeted the riders as they entered the small manor of Ely was its silence. The bustle so evident in Corpus Christie was notable here only by its absence, and the scarcity of folk in the lanes and outside the houses filled the village with an uncomfortable stillness. The settlement had no manor house as such since, like Wisbech, it belonged to the Episcopal see and its manorial lord was the bishop himself. There was, however, a steward, the officer responsible for keeping things in order on behalf of the bishop.

The steward's house was in no way imposing, set apart from the others only by the tall palisade fence which encircled it. The house was modest in size, though its thatch was higher than the norm and a small stable and pig sty were set to the side of it.

The seneschal and his men dismounted and tethered their horses under the stable eaves where the animals could drink from a water trough. There was no evidence of grooms or servants. No one at all, in fact, emerged from the house to greet them. The steward's house, like the village, was eerily quiet.

The seneschal's men-at-arms stayed back while Nicholas approached the house. He raised his hand to knock on the plain board door, but just as he did so, it flew wildly open. A very large pig burst through it, almost knocking the seneschal from his feet. The animal was followed by a heavily perspiring man, his cap askew, who was trying to steer the pig from behind. His plain, undyed woollen tunic had ridden up and was covered in straw and other debris.

'Excuse me, sir,' he uttered with a breathless effort, 'but she will keep coming in. Prefers my fireside to her piggery.'

Nicholas watched in bemusement as the man attempted to guide the sow across the yard to the pen in front of the sty. Eventually, and not without a great deal of trouble, the steward managed to secure the animal inside the pen. He closed the gate behind him, brushing down his tunic and straightening his cap.

'She won't stay there,' he said philosophically as he approached the seneschal. 'I need to put a better catch on that gate. My wife objects to having pigs inside with us, for some reason.'

'Perhaps the threshold is a little low,' said Nicholas as he regarded the house. There was no step up to the door. It simply opened straight on to the yard, allowing the snow and flood water of winter, as well as all creatures, free and unchallenged access.

'You could be right, sir. Please accept my apologies for keeping you waiting. How may I help you?'

'I am Nicholas Drenge, the bishop's seneschal. There is a matter which I need to discuss with you.'

The man looked perplexed, but hastily smoothed his tunic again and made sure his cap was set straight on his bushy hair. It was far from an everyday event when the seneschal paid a visit.

'Come inside, my lord seneschal, and take some wine with me. It's not bad stuff at all; the bishop is good enough to send me a cask every now and then. Usually on feast days. Would your men prefer ale? I shall have some sent out to them.'

Nicholas followed the steward into the house, ducking his head as he passed through the low doorway. The room inside was large and surprisingly clean, considering that it had so recently played host to the pig. The floor was covered with fresh rushes and a cheery fire burned within a ring of hearthstones in the centre. The air was smoky but the warmth was inviting and Nicholas settled himself comfortably, at the steward's invitation, on one of the long benches around the fire. A servant appeared through a small door from the back of the house. He was carrying a tray with a large, well potted and green glazed jug and two cups.

Silently, he set the tray down on a trestle table in the corner and poured wine into the cups before withdrawing with an awkward bow.

'Thank you,' said Nicholas as he took a few appreciative sips. 'The abbey's vineyards can always be trusted to produce a good vintage.'

The steward smiled in agreement.

'This seems a very quiet manor,' the seneschal went on after a pause. 'In fact, I saw very few of its inhabitants as I arrived. Is anything amiss?'

'Amiss? No, my lord, nothing,' said the steward with some surprise. 'All is well. We have no more than ten families living here and the men are busy, away in the far fields. There is so much to do at this time of year, as you know, sir, with the spring ploughing and sowing. My lord bishop has but a modest acreage of land in demesne here, but as his steward I ensure that it is profitably tended. The women, I expect, are busy inside their homes with their household tasks. My wife tells me that a woman's work is never done, and a sensible man always takes notice of his wife.'

The seneschal smiled. He had heard his own wife make similar remarks many a time.

'And the rents due to the bishop? Are they sent on time? Do you have trouble in paying them?'

'No, my lord!' The steward sounded shocked, even a little offended, by the question. 'The manor is thriving and our dues are paid on time. There is always enough to go round. Our villeins and serfs are well treated and in return they are hard working...'

His last words were drowned out by the excitable and deafening barking of a large, long haired dog who ran boisterously in through the back door. Swishing his great hairy tail and thrusting his nose against his master's, he proceeded to wash the man's face with his huge tongue.

'Down, boy! What have I told you? Excuse me, my lord seneschal, but this great fool of a dog insists on greeting me whenever he pleases. I really should use a little more discipline, but...'

Nicholas could not help smiling.

'And do the payments to the bishop cause any resentment amongst your people?'

The steward looked at the seneschal in puzzlement as he stroked the big dog's ears. Nicholas could have sworn that the animal was grinning.

'Resentment, sir? Of course not. Such things are normal. Why would any of us object? Might I ask why you are making these enquiries?'

'A suggestion has recently reached the ears of the castle constable in Wisbech that the people of this manor were making a stand against the bishop's manorial rights.'

The steward looked affronted. Even the dog looked vaguely insulted.

'But that is not true, sir. I do not understand how any such rumour came about.'

The seneschal nodded and finished his wine. There was no cause for concern in this small manor of Ely. He rose to his feet with some reluctance. He had enjoyed the warmth of this man's hearth and the friendly, if somewhat eccentric, hospitality.

'Then I am sorry to have caused you concern. Think no more of it. Thank you for the excellent wine; I shall leave you in peace now.'

The steward and his dog stood and watched as the seneschal and his men rode away. From her pen, the huge sow was keeping an eye on everyone, doubtless planning her next escape.

Nicholas was still smiling from the encounter. And at least on their journey home they would have their backs to the wind.

FIVE

Thursday 15th March
Alexander de Astonne

These truly were troubling times.

The constable, Sir Alexander de Astonne, laid down his pen and heaved a sigh, rubbing his tired eyes. Before him on the desk was a pile of scrolled documents, all of them awaiting his attention. Some were urgent; missives from the bishop and reports detailing the latest intake of prisoners to the castle gaol. Others he could afford to leave for a day or two; these were mainly updates from the dyke reeve on the state of the manor's river banks and drainage channels, accompanied by the usual requests for repairs. Then there was a miscellany of more trivial matters, all of which demanded the constable's approval or action.

He felt restless, in no mood to tackle any of the work in front of him. Placing his seal on a pile of documents would resolve nothing about the state of the country, the land for which its new king seemed to care nothing. King Richard, it appeared, had abandoned England for the greater glory of a crusade in the Holy Land. Since his coronation the previous year, Richard had spent a mere four months in England and had left the country in the hands of a few worthy individuals including his chancellor, William de Longchamp, the Bishop of Ely himself. However deserving of such an honour the bishop might be, it was high time that the king returned and fulfilled his duty to England.

King Richard had, despite his apparent indifference to his people, taken the time to bestow favour on some of his more ordinary subjects. The Manor of Wisbech Barton had done particularly well. Only that year, Richard had granted its inhabitants exemption from tolls on all its markets and fairs. This was a considerable boon. The weekly market and annual fair were where most of the local trade took place, making these events a handsome source of revenue for the monarch. Bestowing the right for the town to keep this income in future was generous indeed.

The constable's uneasiness stemmed from more than just the absentee monarch, however. More local matters played on his mind. He pushed the pile of documents aside and scraped back his heavy chair. He went, as he often did when thinking, to the pair of high lancet windows behind his desk and peered out at the bailey below. He could see the seneschal, mounted now on his fine palfrey, the horse he had named Micah. The palfrey raised its handsome brown head for a moment, perhaps alerted by a sudden movement in the castle grounds. Then, in no time at all, the horse and rider and two men-at-arms had disappeared from view, riding out through the gatehouse on their way back to Ely.

It was the news which the seneschal had just brought that was the real source of the constable's discomfort. On the face of it, all was well. It appeared that, despite previous news to the contrary, there was no rebellion brewing in Walpole. It had been nothing but a ruse, a lie to give the trickster posing as the bishop's messenger access to the old charter. Thankfully, it had not demanded many of the deputy constable's wits to see through the story and the charter was still safe. It remained locked in the documents chest where it had been for a century at least.

And so, the obvious question had to be asked; why would anyone be interested in such an old document? It was unlikely that the messenger, even if blessed with a modicum of education, could have read it, since it was written in the Old English of the Saxons. Few folk learned the old language these days.

Even if anyone managed to read it, the Charter of Oswy and Leoflede was unlikely to keep them interested for long. It consisted of nothing more than detailed descriptions of the manors and land gifted to Ely Abbey in around the year 1000. Later, in 1109 when the Episcopal see had been created, the first bishop had taken over the lordship of the manors in the abbey's possession from the abbot. Those manors included Wisbech, or to give the town its full name, Wisbech Barton.

From what Alexander remembered about the charter, it was long and wordy, as all such documents were. He could not imagine it being desirable to anyone. Yet someone had wanted it badly enough to come to Wisbech with an ill conceived story in an attempt to take it. Perhaps in time their reason for doing so would come to light, but for now all the constable could do was to stay on his guard and get on with other matters.

He sat down at his desk once more and pulled the first document towards him.

SIX

Thursday, 15th March
Weland

Weland had never really liked books. It was a great pity because he worked in one of the most prestigious monastic libraries in the Isle of Ely and its neighbouring shires.

Every day he saw how reverently the Benedictine brothers handled the great tomes, almost as if they were holy relics, but he had never understood their devotion. As a boy, he had been fortunate enough to learn to read and write. It was a rare privilege for the son of a freeman, but his father Godmund had wanted to make sure that Weland had the best start in life. It was his wish that his son would one day take over the family's carpentry business and develop it into something of significance in the town.

When the chance came, he had sent Weland to work in the great abbey as a monastic servant. Such proximity to learning, he hoped, would give the boy a good grounding. The discipline would not go amiss either; Godmund was fully aware of his son's wayward character.

And so, Weland had cut his dark hair very short and shaved off his beard, donning the black robes of a Benedictine servant. There was no danger of him ever being mistaken for a monk, his father thought privately, not with his heavy features and semi-permanent belligerent expression.

The monks hardly knew what to make of him. He showed no interest in the documents that he helped to store away on the high shelves of the library and scriptorium. He was, however, hard working and strong. He could carry a massive pile of books with as much ease as some of the punier brothers lifted a stack of parchment.

Sometimes, when he was left with a little time on his hands, he peered over the shoulders of the monks working in the scriptorium. He was fascinated by their dedication. Day after day and for long hours at a time, they sat at their high, sloping writing desks, painstakingly copying on to fresh parchment every word of some of the most highly regarded books in the library. Eventually, their work would result in a full copy of the book, but weeks, months, even years stretched ahead of them before the task would be completed. Weland often shook his head in disbelief. He could not imagine labouring at something so utterly pointless and unrewarding.

About the only time he found the monks' efforts truly interesting was when they made mistakes, though he was careful never to say so. He made an effort to be polite and to keep his opinions to himself because he had no wish to lose this job with the brothers of Ely. Such a loss would result in having to work as a carpenter for his father, and that was the last thing he wanted. For now, this work suited him. Something better would come along eventually.

When one of the monks made an error it was a matter of great consternation for them. The armarius, the monk responsible for all the work carried out in the library and scriptorium, would tut and fuss and mutter endlessly about the waste of good parchment. Some mistakes could be scratched away with a knife, but others were harder to remedy. Occasionally, a scribe who had been working for hours on a page would realise with horror that he had missed out an entire line of script. In such situations, the fussing and tutting of the armarius would become even more fretful, though a clever way of adding the missing line was usually agreed to in the end.

Despite Weland's general lack of interest in the work, he could not help but admire the creativity that went into dealing with these errors. On one occasion, he had watched Brother Michael as he worked to correct one such mistake. The monk had added the previously omitted line of writing along the bottom margin of the page. He had then drawn an elongated loop of bright red ink around the words.

'What are you going to do with that?' Weland had asked.

'You watch,' the monk had smiled.

He had then added detail to the red loop to make it look like rope, extending the end of the rope like a pointer to the place in the text where the line belonged. And then, intriguingly, he had begun to draw in the left hand margin.

'It's a man!' Weland had remarked as the drawing took shape and coloured inks were used to form the character's face, tunic and hose. One of the miniature hands was reaching out, Weland noticed, to grasp the red rope, and Weland had found himself smiling in admiration. The tiny man even had a look of deviousness on his face. He looked real.

'You've made it look like the man is pulling the missing line back into place with a rope! Won't the armarius be angry with what you've done?'

'He will not be angry. He has a sense of humour, or have you been too busy with your surliness to notice?'

That exchange had surprised Weland. He had never realised before that beneath the monks' industriousness and seriousness very often lay humour and kindness. The brethren were not living their lives in resentfulness or regret, but in calm acceptance, and that peace of mind meant that they laughed as often as other men. They were just careful to do so at more appropriate times.

After that, Brother Michael had begun to tell Weland about some of the books he was working on. Perhaps he hoped to educate the boy, to bring out something hidden beneath all that rough arrogance. He was wasting his time, but Weland was clever enough to humour him. It might, he thought, bring some sort of benefit. And in a way it had.

It was through Brother Michael's teaching that Weland had learned about the charter. There was a legend attached to it, the monk had explained, though no one gave it any credit these days. Weland was intrigued, asking whenever he could about the charter and its legend. Most of the time, Brother Michael laughed it off and spoke instead about some yawningly tedious work of history or science. Weland had, however, been able to discover from these discussions that the legend involved treasure.

Apparently, the key to that treasure lay somewhere within the charter. After finding that out, all Weland could think about was how he could take a look at the old document. He was never able to, though. The small anteroom where all the scrolled documents were kept was always locked. On the rare occasions when its great carved oaken door was left open, there was always a monk in attendance.

Weland had become increasingly frustrated, but then he had come up with a plan. Brother Michael had told him that another copy of the charter was held at Wisbech Castle. Unfortunately, his plan to recover that document had failed and he had returned from Wisbech empty handed. Since then, however, another possibility had opened up and he felt a new glimmer of hope. He was not ready to give up yet.

He was still thinking about the charter as he arrived home from the abbey that evening. His father greeted him with his usual disappointed look and even the elderly servant, who had helped in the house since Weland was a boy, scowled at him. He ignored her as she handed him a dish of mashed and salted turnip. He kept his head down as he scooped up the vegetable with his spoon and chewed his way through a large platter of bread. It was simple yet tasty fare, but Weland did not trouble himself to thank the servant as she withdrew from the room and left the carpenter and his son to eat.

'I don't know what your game is lately, lad,' Godmund began, his voice harsh with frustration, 'the way you keep disappearing. And I'll thank you not to take my horse whenever the fancy takes you. How am I supposed to make my deliveries to customers? The cart will not pull itself. And what about your work at the abbey? The good brothers will not continue to put up with your absences. What are you up to? Knowing you, it's trouble and you'll be caught if you're not careful. Then what will happen to us? I have made a good name for myself in this town. I am a worthy enough carpenter, but folk will withdraw their business if you abuse your position at the abbey.'

'What position? I'm the lowliest of the low at that abbey. A servant to the abbot and the brethren! That miserable old armarius and his dull-witted monks give me the creeps.'

'Don't be so disrespectful, boy. Brother armarius is a good and learned man. He has been entrusted for years to look after all the books and documents in the abbey library. You're fortunate that he still gives you a chance. I assure you, there are far harder ways to earn your bread. You could be breaking your back with dyke digging or labouring behind a plough. Or, of course, you could be helping me in the family business, earning a position of trust in the community, as well as the status which my grandfather and father built up and which I am proud to continue...'

'All right, all right! Don't get started on the family pride thing again. I shall show you. I know what I'm doing.'

'Do you, though, lad?' Godmund's voice had softened slightly and he looked sad rather than angry now. 'I truly wonder if you do. I hate to think what your poor mother would think.'

'Don't bring mother into this. She is dead and gone. And who knows? One day I might even give her cause to be proud of me.'

'Well, whatever it is you are playing at, take care, because if you're caught no one will be able to save you.'

Weland waved a large piece of bread in the air dismissively and smirked.

'You sound more and more like a silly old woman every day, father. Do your cronies in the ale house tell you that? You just need to trust me. I am working on something.'

'What sort of something?'

'Too soon to talk about it yet. But it is promising. Have no fear.'

Godmund the carpenter left the table, leaving his son to finish his meal and his plotting. It was all very well for Weland in his arrogance to tell his father not to fear, but the boy's remarks did nothing to reassure him. At times like these, the lad truly worried him.

SEVEN

Saturday 7th April
Baldwin

The last days of March that year were bitterly cold. Snow had fallen heavily again, followed by dark days of biting frost. With the arrival of April, however, the spring seemed at last to be claiming a tentative hold on the land. In the hedgerows, the first small buds were bursting with life and the birdsong that sounded from every bush and copse was building steadily into a chorus of hope.

The constable's sergeant-at-arms had that morning been sent to a house in the New Market. There had been a report of a break-in and an injured household servant. The sergeant, a solidly built and heavily bearded officer going by the name of Baldwin, made his way across the market place towards the house.

It was Saturday, and the market square was filled with a merry disorder of booths and awnings, stalls selling everything that the good folk of Wisbech could possibly have need of. A ruddy faced brewer was pouring ale from a roughly potted jug into the cups of a few early customers who lined up on a bench under a faded awning. At the next stall, the miller's boy was selling flour in a variety of differently sized sacks, his young voice almost drowned out by the pie man who yelled endlessly about the quality of his rabbit and boiled fowl delicacies.

The authority of the sergeant-at-arms was well respected in the town. As he strode through the market place dressed in his hauberk, the long mail shirt he wore over a padded undergarment, his sword hanging at his side, folk turned to nod deferentially.

The house Baldwin sought was a modest dwelling on the northern side of the square, one which was badly in need of repair. The thatch was green with moss and one of the window shutters drooped from a single hinge, the timber having rotted away at the top. In spite of its run down appearance, the house, being slightly wider than its neighbours, had the air of old respectability about it. A narrow passageway ran down the side, perhaps leading to a back entrance and a stable, but Baldwin strode to the front door and knocked.

The door was opened cautiously by an elderly widow. Her hair and neck were completely covered by a veil and wimple of undyed linen, the wimple tucked into the round neck of her plain, faded gown. Like her house, her clothing was respectable but well past its best. The face which regarded the sergeant looked care worn, as if she were very weary of the world.

'I do not understand it,' she said as the sergeant entered and started to look around the large room with its central hearth. 'Why would anyone choose to break in here? We have nothing worth taking and indeed nothing seems to be missing, but they've messed everything up and hurt poor Oswent. I don't think they realised he was there, sleeping in the shadows.'

Oswent, the only household servant, looked as frail as the widow herself. Baldwin found him sitting on a sagging bench in the small pantry that backed on to the house. He was holding a moistened rag to the back of his head where traces of blood still showed amongst the thinning strands of his grey hair. By his side was a crudely fashioned wooden cup containing weak ale.

'Tell me what happened,' said the sergeant, his voice gruffer than he intended it to be.

'I didn't hear him come in,' the man replied. 'I was asleep by the fire. He must have broken in through the back of the house. The door bolt is broken there and some of the timber is rotten, and he was very quiet. The first thing I knew about it was a boot kicking me in the back, though I don't think he meant to do that. The fire had died right down and it would have been hard to see me lying there in the straw. There was no point in waking me and I think he was as surprised as I was. I hollered out and when I tried to get up he hit me hard over the head. I must have passed out because the next thing I knew, he had gone.

'The widow must have heard the disturbance because she came to help me. As soon as it was light, we saw that everything in the house had been turned upside down. The poor widow has little left to her name, but most of her pots were smashed and the lock on the chest in the main room was broken. We checked through the chest and nothing seemed to be missing, though its contents had been disturbed as if our unwelcome visitor had been searching for something. I doubt he'd have been interested in the widow's winter gown and woollen cloak, though. Why did he come here, sergeant? What did he want with us?'

'You're sure it was just one man?'

'I believe so. I was only aware of one, but since he knocked me out, I cannot be sure.'

The sergeant nodded and left the man to his ale. Back in the main room, the elderly woman was kneeling by the hearth, checking the contents of an earthenware cooking pot that was nestled among the glowing embers. A pleasant, herby aroma was beginning to fill the room.

'We have done what we could to tidy up,' she said as she rose stiffly from her knees, 'and I am thankful that the devil left my cooking pot in one piece. But who would do this to us? Will you ever find out, sergeant?'

'I shall certainly do my best,' Baldwin replied. He could not help feeling extremely sorry for this widow and her old servant. The break-in made no sense at all.

He left the house and made his way back towards the castle. He would report the incident to the constable, but doubted whether the perpetrator of this pointless crime would ever be found. Such people rarely were.

EIGHT

John of Tilneye

The young Sir John of Tilneye was returning from another errand for his father. He had been to check on some of Marshmeade's land to the north of Wisbech, fields held in demesne and tended on behalf of the manorial lord. Tasks like this could at times be tedious, but they were part of his training for the role that would one day be his; the lordship of the manor of Marshmeade.

Thankfully, today's visit had been straight forward and it had given John the opportunity to ride at a gallop along some of the few decent roads in the vicinity. The marshy Fenland, criss-crossed by the muddy tracks that passed for roads, rarely offered much scope for keen riders.

The morning had been cloudy but pleasant enough as he set out. His horse had relished the fresh April air and had needed no encouragement to fly when the opportunity presented itself. It was only as they turned for home that the weather had showed signs of change. By the time they reached the first scattered dwellings on the outskirts of Wisbech, the sky had darkened considerably and John urged his horse on. They passed quickly through the Old Market and over the sluggish Wysbeck, turning towards the castle and the road to Marshmeade.

As they passed the castle gatehouse, the first cold drops of rain began to fall, rapidly turning into hail that hammered down on horse and rider like a storm of blunt arrows. John made the decision to turn into the market square and seek shelter. It was not for his personal comfort; he would have put up with the hail without much bother, but Albanac was another matter. The highly strung palfrey had never been able to tolerate storms. As a foal he had shied away from them in panic, and even now he was showing signs of distress.

'Easy, lad,' John coaxed, but it was no good. Albanac was tossing his head and his eyes had a wild look about them. John dismounted and led the horse along the lane towards the market. Everywhere he looked, people were hurrying to take their merchandise into the shelter of their workshops. A couple of well dressed merchants trotted with inelegant haste towards a riverside warehouse, slamming the door behind them. Humbler folk were left to huddle in doorways, leaving no room for an extra man or horse. Ahead, John could see the first canvas awnings of the market stalls and he hurried his horse towards them.

He sought shelter beneath the first awning he came to, bestowing a smiling apology on the girl who was in the middle of selling a bolt of cloth to a heavily jowled goodwife. Both women were speaking loudly to make themselves heard over the drumming of hail on the canvas cover of the market stall. The girl looked up and returned John's smile. Her eyes lingered on him, but the customer threw him a black look, pursing her lips and pointedly pressing on with the negotiation.

John of Tilneye had come to understand that, although he was not particularly handsome, young women tended to look favourably upon him. His hair was a fiery shade of red and his complexion was rather too ruddy for his liking, but his blue eyes shone with good humour.

Albanac was calmer now that he was sheltered from the elements. The barrage of hail stones seemed at last to be abating but John continued to speak soothingly to the horse. He failed to notice at first that the customer had completed her purchase and, raising a heavy hood to cover her skimpy veil, was leaving the market stall.

Finally sensing that the girl was looking at him, John turned to speak to her.

'I must apologise for my intrusion,' he said courteously, 'but my horse took fright. He has never liked storms.'

'No apology is necessary sir,' smiled the girl. 'The sky is clearing now, so I suppose you must be on your way.'

'And the sooner the better,' boomed a voice from behind them. Baldwin, the sergeant-of-arms, had ducked under the awning and stood there, as immovable as a church tower. 'Take care, young Ida. Your mother will be along soon to see how her cloth is selling and will not take kindly to your dalliance with a ne'er do well like this one.'

John cursed under his breath.

'Baldwin, I'll thank you to...' but then he grinned, acknowledging defeat. There would be other opportunities to renew his acquaintance with Ida. Other girls too. There were always plenty of girls.

'Thank you for the shelter,' said John with a wink at the girl. 'As you say, I must be on my way. I wish you good fortune with business today.'

Albanac was perfectly calm as his master led him between the market stalls with the sergeant towards the castle.

'What brings you to this part of town,' asked John, 'apart from the need to check up on my conduct, that is?'

'A break-in,' Baldwin replied. 'A miscreant who stole nothing yet destroyed what he could of the home of poor folks.'

'Perhaps he was disturbed before he managed to take anything.'

'In truth, Sir John, those poor souls had nothing worth stealing. I despair sometimes. In spite of all our Church does to relieve suffering, there are always folk beyond help who would rather steal, kill and hide away than live like honest people.'

'Just the way of the world, I suppose.'

'A strange world too. During my time of peace keeping in this town, I have seen many senseless things.'

'It seems that strange things go on everywhere,' replied John. 'According to what someone told father, King Arthur's grave has been found at last. Over in Glastonbury. Did you hear about that?'

'King Arthur's grave? After, what? Seven hundred years or more?'

'Apparently so. It seems the monks of Glastonbury have found the remains of the old boy stuffed inside a hollow oak tree.'

Baldwin raised his eyebrows.

'Are you taking me for a fool, young Sir John? Who would bury a king standing up inside an oak tree? '

John laughed.

'That's what they're saying, and the monks, as God's servants, must be telling the truth.'

Baldwin looked quizzically at John and then they both began to laugh. Their boisterous guffawing earned them a few curious looks from passersby and disturbed a cage of hens on the corner. The elderly goodwife who stood guard over the birds gave the men a hard glare.

'Well, sergeant, I must be on my way,' said John as they reached the castle dyke. 'My stomach tells me it is almost dinner time.'

'Be off with you, then, Sir John, and keep away from the women.'

John of Tilneye laughed as he placed his foot in the stirrup. In no time at all, horse and rider had disappeared from view.

NINE

Feast of St George; Monday 23rd April

The Old Market was generally a peaceful place. Nothing much happened in that part of town, the ancient Saxon quarter situated on the far side of the sluggish Wysbeck River. Well away from the noise and bustle of the New Market, the creaking timbers of its aging buildings slumbered beneath their mouldering thatch. It was an unfashionable, rather shabby area that no one of consequence gave much thought to.

It had once, however, been the very centre of things. Before the Normans had come, claiming the country with their thuggery and theft, the Old Market had been at the midst of Wisbech itself. But then the invaders had built their castle and the part of Wisbech that mattered had shifted to a new site across the river. The Old Market had slipped into the shadows beyond the Wysbeck and no one who remained there minded very much.

It was because so little disturbed its peace these days, that when something out of the ordinary occurred, people noticed, and noticed quickly.

Burdo the basket maker had lived in the dwelling that was both workshop and home all his life. It overlooked the small square of the Old Market, and though modest, supplied all he needed from life.

He had reached his middle years and, having lost his wife some time ago and never having been blessed with children, lived alone. He had learned the trade of basket making at an early age, soon becoming skilled at working willow into all sorts of forms and sizes to create the essential items needed for everyday life. He produced baskets for bread, storage, laundry and fishing. Burdo's baskets were used too for the gathering of fruit and nuts from the countryside, harvests that were used to dye cloth as well as for cooking. His wares were well made and sought after, and by day they were always displayed outside his workshop, on a stand beneath the window.

On the feast day of St George, as always, his baskets had been brought inside before dark. Nothing in particular disturbed Burdo's peace that evening, yet when night came he was unable to sleep. The moon was full and its silvery light was so bright that it pierced the gap between the window shutters, frustrating all his attempts to sleep. He seemed hardly to have drifted off at all before he was abruptly awoken. His dog was barking; an insistent alarm of the type he rarely troubled his master with. Burdo gave a groan as he eased himself up from his bedstraw mattress by the banked up fire.

'What is it, Foxtail?' he called, reaching out to the dog in the darkness and laying his hand gently on the animal's back. Foxtail's barking, however, only grew louder, reaching a volume that could not be ignored. Burdo went to the door and listened before opening it cautiously, peering out at the empty square. From the neighbour's stable he could hear the restless sounds of panicking horses and from somewhere perilously close drifted the distinctive smell of smoke.

Then there was a man, a stranger, hurtling across the square, running as fast as his legs would carry him. He was hooded, but Burdo caught a fleeting glimpse of his face and the wild eyes that reflected the moonlight. He was heading for the river, looking neither right nor left as he climbed the bank and disappeared from view. Burdo could hear the faint splash of water as the man waded across the Wysbeck at high tide. The water would hardly slow him down at all. Even at its fullest, the river never reached higher than a man's waist and could be crossed by anyone unafraid of a wetting.

Other doors around the square were beginning to open; a few curious voices raised in confusion were answered with bafflement. But it was not long before everything became clear.

There was smoke, one of the neighbours remarked, thick, billowing smoke coming through the roof of the Big House. As the people watched, sparks became visible, bright points of light that intensified to become flames which spread across the ancient thatch. In hardly any time at all, the flames had grown in fury, stunning the watchers in the square and rendering them incapable of anything more than emitting a chorus of dismay. They seemed to be gripped by the inability to move or do anything to stop the horror.

The door of the Big House was thrown suddenly open, releasing a mighty cloud of black smoke. Burdo reached inside his dwelling and felt for a piece of sack cloth that lay beside his work bench. His fingers closing around it, he ran towards the burning house just as two men staggered out through the door and collapsed on to their knees in an agonising fit of coughing.

'Aelfric?' Burdo demanded of them. 'Where is Aelfric?'

'We tried,' gasped one of the men. 'It is like hell itself in there.'

Burdo covered his mouth and nose with the sack cloth and made his way blindly in through the door. It was hellish indeed. Thick smoke filled the main hall of the house, but the side room, the smaller one where Aelfric slept, had become a chamber of roaring flame. No one could have survived such an inferno.

Hopelessly, Burdo staggered outside and helped the two men to their feet. He knew them well. They were Aelfric's only two remaining servants and were known for their loyalty. If anyone could have saved their master, it would have been them.

The neighbours had broken out of their trance by then and were out in the square, having formed a raggedy line from the river to the Big House. Just about any shape and condition of containers, from buckets to cooking pots, were being filled with water and passed hand to hand along the line of men, women and children. This feeble yet persistent supply of water was then thrown on to the flames by the men closest to the fire. They could not hope to save the house, but they had to try to prevent the fire spreading to the other buildings in the square. With their old thatch, crumbling timbers and walls of woven willow, they would be no match at all for the flames.

The people who fought the fire had one thing in their favour; the night was practically wind still. With determination and unceasing endeavour, the number of buildings destroyed by the fire could at least be kept to a minimum.

Burdo helped the two servants into his workshop before joining the line of fire fighters. They worked for what remained of the night, but were unable to save the two small dwellings that neighboured the Big House on the northern side of the square.

No more lives were lost, neither of man nor beast, but however hard anyone worked, it was too late for Aelfric.

TEN

Tuesday, 24th April; early morning
Norman Devils

By the time the fire in the Old Market was finally put out, all that remained of the Big House was a heap of charred roof timbers and smoking debris. The first glimmers of daylight revealed a truly bleak sight. Where the northern side of the square had been, there remained nothing but smouldering ashes and the stench of destruction.

The alarm had been raised just after midnight, bringing the constable's sergeant-at-arms and his men to join the fire fighting.

The tenants of the smaller houses lost in the fire were, like Aelfric's servants, now being cared for by their neighbours. The horses, mules, pigs and goats from the burned stables, pens and sties had also been rescued and were lodged for the time being close by.

Aelfric's body had been recovered from the ashes of his home and taken on a litter to the church. Already, word had spread around the town about Aelfric's death and there were many who came to the Old Market to express their sorrow. The burial would take place in a few days' time and many of the townspeople would attend it. Aelfric's two servants would be among those mourners, but for now they were huddled in their cloaks by the fireside in Burdo the basket maker's workshop.

Baldwin, the sergeant-at-arms, had also found his weary way to the workshop once there was no more to be done in the square. He had dismissed his men and was now sitting on a stool by Burdo's work bench. The basket maker had disappeared to fetch bread and ale for his guests from the small lean-to at the back of the single roomed building.

'How did the fire start?' the sergeant enquired of Aelfric's servants in a tired voice. It was the first opportunity he had had to ask this obvious question.

'We do not know,' confessed the man called Magan, the taller of the two peasants. 'It happened so quickly. I was awoken by the smoke. We were sleeping where we always do, by the fireside in the main hall, and the house was filled with smoke. I got up quickly and could hear Leof rising too. I couldn't even see him by then; the smoke was so thick. I could scarcely breathe but went straight to our master's chamber. It's to the side of the hall, the room where he always slept, but I couldn't reach him.'

'No,' agreed Leof, the other servant, 'our master's chamber was on fire and the heat was terrible, sir. We could not go in. We could not save him.'

'And you have no idea how the fire started?' persisted the sergeant.

'No sir,' continued Leof miserably, 'except that it must have been in the master's chamber. Perhaps some of the floor rushes were pushed on to the fire. It had been banked up for the night, of course. We always make sure that the two fires, in the main hall and in the master's chamber, are safely banked up for the night, but if the rushes get too close...'

'It is very likely,' agreed the sergeant. 'It happens all too often.'

'And now our master is gone. He was a good and proud man,' lamented Magan. He looked utterly lost and bewildered. As a tied peasant of Aelfric's old manor, he knew nothing but serfdom and following his lord's commands. With that world reduced to ashes, he was left without a clue as to how he might fend for himself.

'There was no one like him,' agreed Leof. 'He liked to tell us about his ancestors. His family went right back to the time of the Saxons, you know. Times when life was good. Our master's family once owned many manors, but that was when our country was still a bountiful place to live in.'

'Before the Norman devils came,' added Magan.

'Steady on,' grinned Burdo as he returned with a generous supply of rye bread, sheep's cheese and ale. 'I'm one of those Norman devils, and so is the sergeant here, and I can tell you we're not all bad.'

'Of course not, sir,' admitted Magan hastily as he started to help himself to food and ale. 'I apologise for my poor choice of words. When our master spoke of the Normans, he was talking about the time when the Conqueror's soldiers first came here and stole all the land they desired. They tortured and murdered good men to get what they wanted. Those times still live in men's memories.'

'Don't be a fool, man,' snapped the sergeant. 'All that happened more than a century ago.'

'Very true, sir, but the memories are handed down, father to son, and are still very much alive,' Magan insisted.

'Before the invasion,' Leof said, taking over the narrative from Magan, 'our master's ancestors were wealthy, with manors and land all over the shire, some even in Norfolk and Suffolk. Then the Conqueror's men came and drove our master's noble ancestors into poverty. They treated many others like that too. Their land was seized and given to men loyal to the new Norman king. The only land the incomers left was of the poorer sort, yielding little in the way of crops. It wasn't long before our master's ancestors were scarcely able to feed themselves or graze their few remaining animals. By my lord Aelfric's time, things were really bad. He had to leave his last manor in the shire because it was in such a poor state, and he came to live in what folk call the Big House in the Old Market.'

Leof accepted a cup of ale from Burdo and took a small piece of bread from the board in front of him, wrapping it around a piece of cheese.

'Which is now reduced to ash,' said Magan, continuing from Leof's words. He had been helping himself to food and his mouth was full of bread, so was speaking with some difficulty.

'And were you Aelfric's only two remaining peasants?' asked the sergeant as he leaned forward to refill his cup from the heavy earthenware jug. He had quickly downed his first cupful of ale, his thirst too keen from a night's fire fighting to be satisfied by sipping.

'Yes sir,' replied Leof. 'Sickness reduced our numbers greatly and it was just the two of us who came here with the master a few years ago. The Big House was just a simple dwelling the family had kept in the town. Perhaps it reminded our master of grander times past. It became his refuge when all else was lost.'

'So, where shall we go now?' asked Magan forlornly.

'Aelfric had a daughter, I believe,' replied the sergeant.

'He did,' confirmed Burdo, who was sitting on a bench by his fire and chewing a large mouthful of bread. 'She married well. Her husband holds several manors in the north of the shire and in Lincolnshire.'

'A Norman,' stated Leof bleakly. 'How can we go to a Norman? And what else was there for our poor master than to accept a Norman as a husband for his beloved daughter? She has wealth now through her marriage, but her lineage has come to mean nothing.'

'Well, that's nonsense!' retorted Burdo the basket maker. 'The Norman, as you call him, married Rowena *because* of her noble lineage. It has not been forgotten at all. My lord Mortimer de Hurste is not a bad man and I am sure you will be able to join his household and serve Lady Rowena. She will not see you homeless.'

The two men grunted something unintelligible and helped themselves to more cheese. It seemed there was nothing more the sergeant-at-arms could learn from them, so he thanked Burdo for his hospitality and left the house. He trudged back to the castle, knowing that before he could take any rest, he would have to make another report to the constable.

ELEVEN

Tuesday 24th April; late Morning
Ancestors

The constable's office was situated on the first floor of the keep, but to Baldwin that morning it felt much higher up. He found the narrow spiral stairway harder to climb than usual and by the time he reached the top he had to stand and catch his breath.

The night's fire fighting had left him longing for his bed and he wondered, not for the first time, whether his youth had abandoned him for good. In his younger days he had been able to go without sleep and work for long periods at a time, but those days had long gone. He seemed to be gaining weight too. His muscular frame, which had always made folk think twice about challenging his authority, was becoming a little flabby these days.

He made his way along the passage and rapped with his knuckles on the heavy oak of the office door. Hearing a curt consent, he entered the room.

Sir Alexander de Astonne and his deputy, Sir Simon de Gardyn, were seated on high backed chairs beneath a pair of tall windows. Before them, spread across the broad desk, was a large document. The deputy had paused in the middle of making a statement and his mouth was still forming a small 'O' shape.

'The fire in the Old Market, my lords,' stated Baldwin, getting straight to the point, 'has been put out, but has destroyed the northern end of the square. Aelfric appears to have been the only casualty, however, so things could have been far worse.'

'The bishop will not be pleased,' responded the constable with a heavy sigh, 'but as our manorial lord he must be informed immediately. I shall go to the square myself later and see what needs to be done to put things right. The ruined buildings will have to be closed off from the rest of the Old Market, until rebuilding can start.'

'I'll see to that, sir,' offered Simon.

'Thank you,' replied Alexander before turning to the sergeant. 'What about the folk who have lost their homes? Are they safe? What about their animals?'

'All safe and well, sir,' confirmed the sergeant. 'The families made homeless are lodging with their neighbours and their horses and other livestock have been moved to safety. Aelfric's two remaining servants are staying with the basket maker until their future is decided on.'

'Two remaining servants?' echoed Alexander ponderously. 'It seems tragic to me that a man descended from such a noble family should have been reduced to living in that mouldering old house. And with just two servants.'

'Elderly ones too,' added Baldwin. 'I doubt they are capable of much these days.'

'Aelfric had a daughter,' pointed out Simon. 'I expect she will send for them. It's not too much of a walk for them to Tydd St Giles, which is where I believe she lives now. She married well; to one of Norman stock.'

'That is true,' agreed the constable. 'Sir Mortimer de Hurste, a wealthy man with a great deal of land. I am sure he can find work for two more villeins, elderly or not. He will take care of Aelfric's estate, small though it is.'

'Small?' the deputy scoffed. 'Any smaller and it would disappear altogether.'

'Which is what has just occurred,' pointed out Alexander reprovingly. 'Sir Mortimer will not have forgotten that it was Aelfric's ancestors, Oswy and Leoflede, who gifted this manor of Wisbech to the Church of Ely. He will not have forgotten that his wife's family were once people of consequence.'

'So, it was Aelfric's ancestors who did that?' queried Baldwin. 'I didn't know.'

'Yes,' replied Alexander with a knowledgeable and lofty expression. 'It was they who granted land by charter to the abbot long ago, before the time of the Conqueror. In fact,' he added with a frown, 'was it not that same charter which some rogue tried to get his hands on, a month or so ago? Did he not come here and spin some ridiculous tale of rebellion in Walpole?'

'Yes, sir,' confirmed Simon, 'but it came to nothing and he went away empty handed.'

'Yet now, the descendant of the family which granted that charter has died in a fire and his home has been destroyed. It seems rather a coincidence.'

'But, my lord,' objected Baldwin the sergeant, 'the fire was started by accident.'

'Of course it was,' agreed Simon. 'House fires are hardly rare occurrences. I can see no connection between the two incidents. As you say, sir, it is simply a coincidence.'

'But I do not like coincidences. Aelfric is dead as a result of this fire. The seneschal might be interested to hear about this. When I notify the bishop of the fire, I shall request the seneschal's opinion. Perhaps, if he can spare the time, he may choose to pay us a visit.'

'He will not thank us for wasting his time,' said Simon.

'Perhaps not, but I feel it is my duty to report the situation to him. It is up to him whether or not he follows it up. Like me, I believe, the seneschal does not like coincidences.'

TWELVE

Wednesday 25th April
Aswig

The deputy constable saw to it himself that work started immediately on screening off the ruins of the houses from the rest of the Old Market. A team of villeins from the castle was quickly set to work and Simon settled himself to watch their progress. He found a comfortable spot on the grassy river bank and sipped ale from his flask.

Usually, Simon would have left the men to work while he concentrated on other matters, but this situation appeared to warrant extra attention. The constable was concerned, suspecting perhaps that something more than carelessness had resulted in this fire. He had even mentioned bringing in the seneschal. In Simon's opinion, the constable was over reacting. As he had stated at the meeting, house fires were far from uncommon. The construction of most dwellings relied heavily on timber and thatch, materials which were easy prey for errant sparks from cooking fires, reed lights and candles.

The constable always insisted on having any buildings damaged by fire and other catastrophes closed off from the surrounding area as soon as possible. It was done to prevent looting from the sites while rebuilding was being organised, and Simon was used to overseeing the work.

The place on the bank where he sat was partly hidden from the square by a large blackthorn bush and he was confident that few people would be able to see him. He still had a good view, though, between the branches of blackthorn, and was able to watch the workmen at the far end of the square as they moved tall panels of woven willow into place.

A few people had come out to stand in the square and watch. Among them Simon could see the cobbler, a most unsavoury character in his opinion. Even from a distance, Simon could see that he was laughing. The man's round, sweaty face was split into a malicious grin, though what he found amusing about fire and death defied imagination. Two youths joined him, boys who from their body shapes and ugly expressions Simon guessed to be the cobbler's sons. A sharp faced woman walked towards them, shouting and pointing her finger. She was jabbing it into the well fleshed chest of one of the boys.

Simon replaced his flask in his scrip, the small satchel attached to the girdle tied around his waist. He rose from the bank and approached the group. The cobbler and his sons looked him sneeringly up and down before realising who he was and hurrying sheepishly away. They disappeared into the Ship, a tumble-down shack of an ale house that backed on to the riverside. The woman who had been arguing with them watched them go with a disgusted look on her face.

'You want to watch that pair, my lord,' she informed the deputy constable. 'Shifty, they are. Always have been. I'd lay any wager on that family starting that fire, that I would.'

'Is that so? Goodwife...'

'Aswig. Goodwife Aswig. Aelfric was a nice old gentleman. Nobility he was, too. None of the muck we usually have to put up with around here. You want to have a word with that cobbler, that you do.'

Simon nodded coolly. His reaction seemed to frustrate her and sharpen her determination to make her point.

'I tell you, sir. They did it!'

'Do you know that for sure, Goodwife Aswig, or are you just relying on your low opinion of them?'

'Both, sir. I don't see how there's much difference.'

Simon bestowed another of his cool nods upon her and made his way over to the high woven panels that were gradually shielding the ruined buildings. He walked through one of the gaps between the panels and stared at the heap of broken, blackened timbers. This debris was all that remained of Aelfric's house and it was pitiful. Some of the wood was still smoking and the pungent smell of burning hung in the air.

The constable's insistence on fencing off ruins to keep looters at bay was well meant, Simon admitted. It was, however, hard to see the point in this case. There was simply nothing left to take.

Even so, he stood for a while, surveying the mess.

Behind him, the work went on.

THIRTEEN

Feast of St Athanasius; Wednesday 2nd May

As things turned out, the seneschal had no decision to make about the constable's message, because by the time he received it he was already on his way to Wisbech.

Sir Nicholas Drenge, riding his bay palfrey Micah and accompanied by his two men-at-arms, arrived at the castle early on the Feast of St Athanasius, to begin work on the imminent Hundred Court hearings.

These hearings, held regularly in the Mote Hall of Wisbech Castle, dealt with a multitude of minor crimes and disputes arising in the Witchford Hundred. The shire of the Isle of Ely was divided into smaller administrative regions called hundreds, each of which held its own regular courts presided over by a senior official of the Isle. In the case of the Witchford Hundred, the presiding officer was generally the seneschal himself, and he dealt with cases from all over the hundred. Besides Wisbech, this included villages such as Doddington, Leverington, Newton in the Isle, Tydd St Giles, Elm, Welle, Welney and Thorney.

Neither the constable nor his deputy was there to greet Sir Nicholas when he arrived at the castle that morning. They were not expected back until the afternoon, so the seneschal went straight to his office in the Mote Hall to start his work there. The hall stood next to the gatehouse and still had a look of newness about it. Having been built only a few decades earlier to accommodate the new Assize courts, its walls of Barnack limestone glowed a pale honey colour against the greyer background of the more aged parts of the castle. This softer colouring, however, hardly offset the menace of its massive walls and uncompromisingly narrow window slits. The Mote Hall could put the fear of God into anyone whose fate was to be decided within its walls.

Nicholas's office was tucked into one corner of the building, between the main entrance and the high neighbouring wall of the castle gatehouse. It was a very small room, but generally adequate for the seneschal's needs.

The Hundred Courts were part of the old justice system that had existed in England before King Henry II's legal reforms of the 1160s. Henry had introduced a new type of court; Assizes, which were held twice yearly to deal with the most serious cases, such as murder or treason. These courts were presided over by a Justice and required a jury of twelve men. Gradually, this new, far better regulated justice system was replacing the old world of Baron Courts and their questionable idea of justice. There was now one set of laws which all courts had to abide by; the Common Law of England. For now, though, the Hundred Courts continued to operate alongside the Assizes, dealing with matters of less severity.

Nicholas settled himself into the familiar, modest dimensions of his office. He made himself comfortable on the bulky chair behind his desk before selecting one of the documents placed there for his attention. It was a list of cases to be heard that month, and he ran his eye down the columns of names, offences and grievances. It was the usual medley of assault, robbery and complaint of neighbour against neighbour. As always, many cases involved the obstruction of drainage ditches or the wrongful removal of trees or hedges.

Some complaints seemed hardly worthy of his attention. In one case, a woman was charged with putting 'dung and other defilements' on the road outside her house. Two other women were accused of being scolds, women considered too loud and opinionated for their own good, who had worn out the patience of their long suffering husbands. There was also a complaint against an Elm man who had received payment for a number of sacks of rye from a Wisbech man, but who had refused to hand over half of the sacks. That case, thought Nicholas, might take up more time than most, but many of the others would result in nothing more than a good telling off and an amercement of a penny or two to be paid by the guilty party.

However trivial many of the cases appeared to be, Nicholas would give them all his full attention and fairest judgement. He would have to carry out the usual preparations for the hearings and familiarise himself with all the cases, but none of that had to be done today. There was time in plenty before the hearings began in ten days' time.

He stood up and stretched his back, becoming aware of his hunger. It was dinner time, the main meal of the day which was usually served around noon. He left the office and made his way through the bailey towards the great hall. The bailey was as busy as usual with folk gathering to depart or to meet and exchange news. He caught snatches of conversation as he walked. Trade seemed to be the main topic, but anyone not boasting about their wool yields or hopes of good harvests to come, spoke of the weather. It was always so. Now that May had arrived, fears of the winter's cold had been put away for another year, but still people spoke of their relief. Survival of another winter of freezing temperatures, deep snow and hunger very often felt like a major achievement, especially for poorer folk.

By the time Nicholas had eaten his fill in the hall, the constable had returned to his office and so the seneschal made his way up to the first floor of the keep. Sir Alexander de Astonne, it appeared, had concerns about a recent fire in the Old Market and he spent some time in bringing the seneschal up to date.

'It just seems very curious to me, Nicholas,' Alexander said as he reached his conclusion, 'that the fire destroyed the home of the descendant of the family who granted that charter. That very same charter which a trickster tried to take from us and whose lies led you on a wild goose chase to the manor of Ely in Walsoken.'

Nicholas smiled wryly, remembering the steward's struggles with his sow and dog.

'It does sound interesting,' he agreed, 'and certainly merits some attention. I have time this afternoon, so I might as well go to the Old Market and see what I can discover.'

'Thank you, Nicholas. My sergeant is looking after things there, so he'll show you the damage. No doubt you will reach your own conclusions, so perhaps we could speak again tomorrow?'

Nicholas left the constable's office in no great hurry to poke around in the ashes of a house fire in the Old Market. Despite his youth, his recent lack of sleep was catching up with him. His journey from Ely, with only a few hours' rest under canvas to break it up, had kept him on the road since early the previous day.

Rather than venturing straight outside, he made his way up to his rooms.

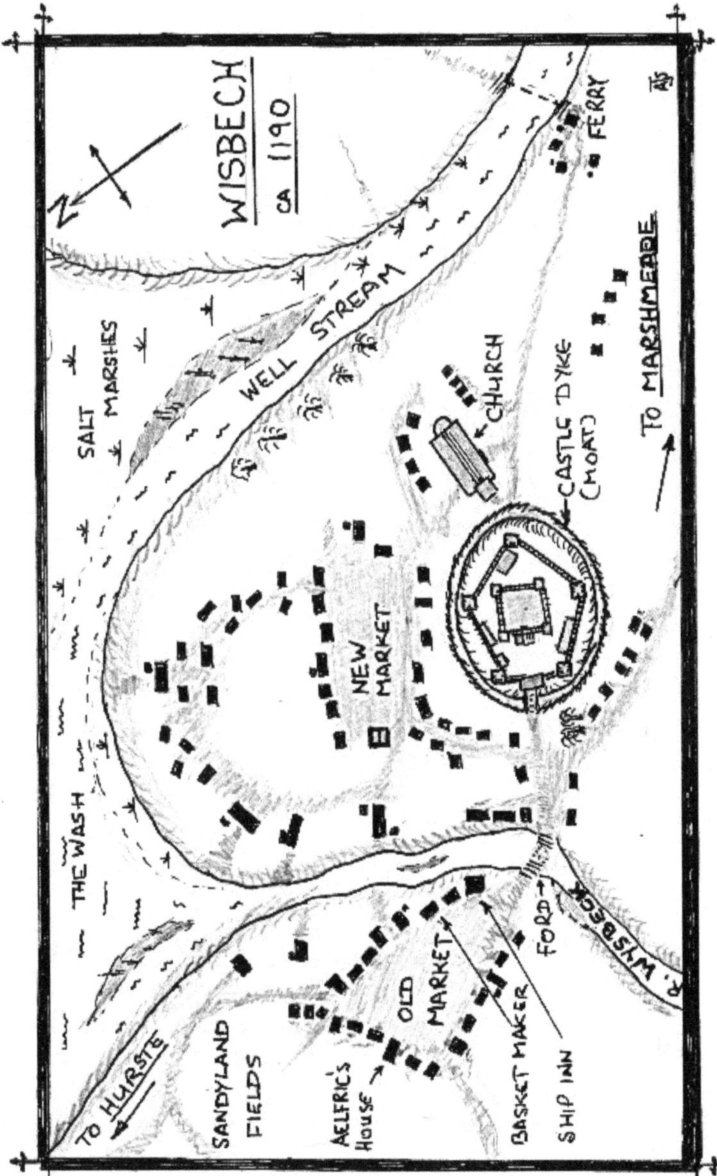
WISBECH
CA 1190
N
WELL STREAM
SALT MARSHES
THE WASH
TO HURSTE
SANDYLAND FIELDS
AELFRIC'S HOUSE
OLD MARKET
BASKET MAKER
SHIP INN
FORD
R. WYSBECK
NEW MARKET
CHURCH
CASTLE DYKE (MOAT)
TO MARSHMEADE
FERRY

FOURTEEN

The Old Market

Sir Nicholas Drenge's quarters on the second floor of the keep were nowhere so grand as those kept for the bishop and other visiting elite, but they were certainly fine enough. The rendered and lime washed walls were painted with a bold floral pattern in shades of red and yellow ochre and the floor was covered with fresh rushes and sweet smelling herbs. The shutters on the south facing windows had been thrown wide open to air the room in anticipation of his arrival. The May breeze that billowed in, however, stirring the folds of his travelling cloak which he had hung in the garderobe, was a little too fresh for comfort. He reached up to close the shutters and lay down on the hard bed in the darkened room, closing his eyes to rest.

By the time he awoke, he could tell from the thinning crowds in the bailey below that the afternoon was well advanced. Standing and stretching, and feeling considerably better after his short sleep, he put on his cloak and was soon making his way down the two flights of stairs to the great hall. Brithun and Ordgar, his men-at-arms, were still there, bantering with two of the castle men. He did not interrupt them. He had no immediate need of their services, but once the Hundred Courts began there would be more than enough for them to do.

Once through the bailey, he walked across the bridge that straddled the castle dyke and carried on towards the Wysbeck. The tide was almost fully out and the flat stones marking the fording place were clearly visible beneath a shallow depth. He wetted his boots and hose as little as possible, though his boots still squelched uncomfortably as he climbed the river bank on the far side. He stood for a while on the top of the bank, observing the Old Market.

The sight was a sorry one. The entire northern end of the square had been closed off behind tall screens. The buildings closest to the screens were darkened with soot, their poor state having become bleaker and more obvious overnight. Even the houses and workshops untouched by smoke were in a sad condition. Most of the thatch was tired and old, green with moss and heavily patched, and in many cases the walls sagged through rot and wear. The whole square, in Nicholas's opinion, needed to be demolished and rebuilt.

It was now more than a week since the fire, but preliminary work was still in progress. Baldwin, the constable's sergeant-at-arms, was supervising the fitting of a gate between the screens and looked less than happy about it. He was red in the face and venting his frustration on two workmen who struggled to attach a heavy hinge to the new gate.

'Good day, my lord seneschal,' he said as Nicholas approached. 'We shall soon be finished here. The debris will be cleared from the site and then rebuilding can begin. Some of the buildings lost to the fire had workshops behind them and the tenants need to start working again.'

'And a roof over their heads, presumably.'

'Yes, sir, though the tenants and their livestock are safe enough with their neighbours for the time being.'

Nicholas nodded and waited patiently for the villeins to finish fitting the hinge. Once he was able to, he stepped through the gap to look at the ruined buildings. There was hardly anything left, nothing even to indicate where one structure had ended and the neighbouring house began. Only a few split timbers reached from the rubble like gesturing fingers, their blackened ends jagged and distorted.

How was it possible to tell whether a fire like this had been started by accident or by deliberate intent? Although he agreed with the constable, that two incidents connected to the old charter occurring within a few weeks should not be dismissed, he did not see what he could do. This fire had happened more than a week ago. If anyone had deliberately started it, they would be long gone by now, their tracks well covered.

He sighed heavily. He ought at least to try. There was a whole week in which to prepare for the Hundred Court hearings, and that was more than enough. He might as well spend his spare time usefully.

'We need to speak to everyone whose home overlooks this square,' he informed the sergeant who was standing expectantly by his side. 'While you begin making enquiries at each house, starting in the western corner closest to the screens, I shall visit the basket maker and Aelfric's two servants.'

'That's the place over there, sir,' said Baldwin, indicating the basket maker's workshop. 'I did speak to them just after the fire, but they didn't seem to know much.'

'But that, I presume, was before there was any suspicion of foul play. What I need to know now is whether anyone noticed anything out of the ordinary, either before or after the fire, and whether they noticed any strangers. Use your wits, sergeant. Talk to everyone and we shall speak again later.'

The house and workshop occupied by Burdo the basket maker, Nicholas noticed, was one of the best maintained in the square. Though it was tiny, its door and single window taking up almost the full width of the building, the walls were freshly covered in daub and the thatch was in decent repair. Beneath the window was a stand on which were displayed examples of Burdo's basket ware. Nicholas knocked on the door and waited.

The man who welcomed him into the workshop was of average height and middle aged, slightly stooped, but with clear, intelligent eyes. The seneschal was invited into the single room which served as both workshop and home. A work bench was positioned beneath the window and was covered with all manner of tools and equipment. A sharp knife lay beside the half-finished basket Burdo had been working on and sheaves of willow withies were stacked on the floor, leaning against the end of the bench.

'Please sit, my lord seneschal, and I shall fetch you some ale,' said Burdo with a good natured smile. Nicholas perched himself on the end of the bench beside the central fire and watched the two elderly peasants who were busying themselves over a cooking pot nestled among the embers. Aelfric's servants, he assumed.

Both men looked up and gave him a deferential bow of the head before returning to their labours. One was making hard work of chopping a turnip, most likely one of the last from the winter store, using a knife on a wooden board. The other servant added sliced onion to the pot before picking up a wooden spoon and ponderously stirring the pot's contents.

Burdo returned without delay, carrying a small tray with a jug and four cups. He settled the tray on the end of the bench and proceeded to fill the cups, handing one first to the seneschal and then one each to the servants. Nicholas, who was not used to seeing a freeman pouring ale for his underlings, looked surprised.

'It's something of a novelty for me to have company in the house,' said Burdo, seeing the seneschal's look. 'I shall be sorry to see these two fellows leave. They're a good help to me and it is pleasant to have them to talk to.'

The taller of the men, the one who was stirring the pottage, rewarded Burdo with a grateful look and went back to his work.

'I need to speak to you about the night of the fire,' Nicholas began, addressing Burdo.

'A dreadful night,' the man replied.

'Your workshop overlooks the square. Did you notice any activity, anything remarkable at all, when you first became aware of the fire?'

'Well, yes, sir, I suppose I did. I was awoken by the barking of my dog, Foxtail. It's unusual for him to make a fuss, so I knew something was wrong. I went to the door and looked outside and after a while I saw smoke. Just smoke at first, but then the first flames broke through the old thatch of Aelfric's house. But before any of that, before I really knew what was happening, I saw a man running across the square towards the ford.'

Nicholas leaned forward on the bench.

'What did he look like, this man?'

'Hard to say, sir, since he was hooded, as most folk are, but my impression was that he was tall and thin. I had the briefest glimpse of his face. Quite heavy featured, you could say, with a broad nose.'

'Had you ever seen him before?'

'No, sir, never. He was certainly not from the Old Market. Not even from the wider town. I am well used to all the faces around here and I know I had never seen this man before.'

'And have you seen him since? Anywhere in the town?'

'No, sir.'

'Thank you,' said Nicholas after a slight pause. 'Is there anything else that comes to mind about that night?'

'Other than running to the burning house and finding these two poor souls outside, no. I tried to enter the building because Aelfric was still inside, but it was hopeless. There was so much smoke and part of the house was in flames by then. It was impossible to save him.'

'Part of the house?' prompted Nicholas. 'Which part?'

'Aelfric's chamber,' clarified Burdo.

'Presumably, then,' said the seneschal, 'that was where the fire started. You did well to help these poor wretches and must feel no guilt or regret about their master. You did your best and no man can do more than that. I'd like now to speak to Aelfric's servants.'

'Of course, sir. The taller one goes by the name of Magan, the shorter one Leof. Come up here, fellows,' Burdo added, raising his voice slightly to address the servants. 'Rest your bones and sit on this bench while the seneschal speaks to you. I shall go into the back and busy myself there.'

The two men slowly raised themselves from their crouching positions amongst the floor rushes. The taller one winced with pain as he stood and the smaller man looked no more agile.

'Tell me about Aelfric,' Nicholas began once they were finally settled on the bench beside him. 'What sort of master was he?'

'He was the very best,' replied Magan sorrowfully. 'We have been with his family all our lives. He was a good man.'

'How well was he liked in the town? Did you know anyone to hold a grudge against him, or dislike him for any reason?'

'No, sir,' continued the same villein. 'I doubt anyone disliked him. He was good and kindly to all. He had lost all his wealth and so lived plainly and troubled no one. He rarely left the house in his last years; his rheumatics were very bad by then.'

'Yes,' agreed Leof. 'He lived simply, but there was that box. We used to wonder, did we not, Magan, why he didn't just sell a piece or two from it and make his life a little more comfortable. Ours too, coming to that.'

'A box?' queried the seneschal.

'Yes,' continued Leof. 'He kept it in the attic above the main hall, where the apples, pears and winter vegetables were stored. He used to fetch it down sometimes when he thought we were asleep. We always slept on the floor rushes by the fire, and the ladder he used to reach the attic had to be positioned close to my feet, so sometimes he woke me by accident. Usually, he carried the box into his own chamber, but sometimes he just sat on the bench near us, thinking we were sleeping, of course. Then he would open the box. I could never see much in the darkness, but I'm sure by the way he moved the contents around that there were treasures or coins in there. I could hear the clink of metal.'

'Our master would not appreciate us saying this,' said Magan reprovingly.

'Perhaps not,' said the seneschal, 'but if I am to discover who was responsible for the fire and your master's death...'

'But the fire was an accident, sir! The sergeant said so!' interrupted Leof.

'It is far from certain yet what happened,' replied the seneschal patiently. 'In order for me to discover the truth, it is important that you tell me all you know. It cannot hurt Aelfric now. Is it possible that other folk knew about this box? Did you ever hear your master telling other people about it?'

'No, sir,' replied Leof. 'My lord Aelfric was very secretive about it. I am certain that he never knew we'd seen it. I suppose the only people who knew about that box were his family.'

'Do you mean his daughter? I understand she is his only living relative.'

'That is correct, sir. She is wed to a Norman by the name of Sir Mortimer de Hurste, a proud and haughty man,' said Magan with more than a hint of chilly disapproval.

'A man for whom you have little admiration, it seems,' added Nicholas with a slight smile.

'It is not our place either to admire him or not,' replied Magan self righteously, 'especially since it appears that he will be our new master.'

'So, you will both be going to his manor near Tydd St Giles?'

'Yes, sir, to Hurste Manor. The Lady Rowena called to see us when she came to arrange her father's burial. She said we must go to her, that there would be work found for us on the manor. We shall be sorry to go. Burdo has been good to us and we would rather stay here, but we have no choice.

We must be at Hurste by tomorrow evening. We shall set out early tomorrow and hope to be there before supper.'

Nicholas regarded them both. Neither looked capable of walking very quickly or for very long at a time. They had spoken about Aelfric's rheumatics but had not mentioned their own. Both of them were stooped and bent and their joints were clearly painful. As the seneschal took his leave, he felt heartily sorry for them both.

FIFTEEN

The Cobbler

The sergeant-at-arms began with the homes closest to the sectioned off northern end of the square. Some of the stables behind these dwellings had been lost to the fire and the tenants Baldwin spoke to were grateful that the houses themselves had been spared.

'Did I see anything suspicious?' shrieked one of the first to answer a door, in reply to the sergeant's question. The woman was clearly not cowed by his mail shirted and helmeted presence, nor by the sword that hung from his belt. 'No I did not! We were too busy trying to save the animals to gawp at what was going on in the square. You should ask that lot outside the Ship. Never have anything better to do than hang around on that bench, belching and staring at folks.'

Presumably though, thought Baldwin as the door was shut in his face, the Ship's regular drinkers had not been outside, belching and staring, at night. He could understand the woman's impatience with his questioning. The fire had come close to taking everything these people had, and all they cared about now was repairing the damage and making new shelters for their animals. The authorities, and what they probably saw as pointless questions, were far from welcome.

The further Baldwin progressed along the western side of the square, and the further away from the fire damage, the more he found residents willing to speak to him. That, unfortunately, did not mean they had anything useful to say. Most people reported being awoken by the smoke and commotion, going to their doors and looking out. In most cases, by that time flames were already destroying the thatch of the Big House. No one had seen anything that might be described as suspicious.

There was one woman, however, who was more than happy to share her views with him. It seemed to the sergeant that this woman had been part of the Old Market forever, as much a part of its ancient fabric as the groaning timbers themselves. Goodwife Aswig was not elderly, but her pursed lips and the lines that creased her thin face told of years of disapproval of the world at large. Her pale hair was held back from her face by a barbette, a linen strip which passed under her chin and was fastened with a pin on the top of her head. Its severity only enhanced her judgemental appearance. She leaned against her doorpost and folded her arms as she delivered her wisdom.

'No,' she began in a shrill voice, 'I saw nothing, apart from the fire of course, but if you're looking for who's to blame, I can save you a lot of time and effort. Go and see the cobbler. He's a mean old devil, if ever there was one. He would do his own mother down, he would. And those two sons of his are even worse, that they are. I often saw the pair of them sneaking around Aelfric's house. Before it burned down, of course. Up to no good, that's for sure. Trouble is with them, they don't know what hard work is. Far too much time on their hands, and that's a fact. Their father can't control them and in my opinion...'

'Why do you think they were sneaking around Aelfric's house?' interrupted the sergeant at last, taking advantage of the woman's need to take a breath.

'Who can tell with that lot? I sent my husband over to sort them out. Gave them a thick ear, he did. Nobody argues with my husband when he's on the war path, and that's a fact. There's been many a time...'

'Thank you, Goodwife Aswig. Have no fear; I shall speak to the cobbler and his sons.'

'You do that, sergeant, and then come back here and tell me what he says. I'd wager any day of the week that he...'

The sergeant gave her a brief nod and departed, leaving her standing in her doorway, still venting her anger to thin air. He continued along the row of houses and workshops, but learned nothing of use. The last remaining building on that side of the square was the cobbler's workshop, but before he called there he decided to transfer his attention to the eastern side of the Old Market.

The buildings there backed on to the river and much of that side of the square was taken up by a sizeable warehouse. There was no sign of life when the sergeant hammered on the splintered old door, but he was not concerned. It was unlikely that anyone worked at the warehouse at night or had witnessed the fire. Next door was the basket maker's small premises and a few houses down was the Ship.

The door of the tumbledown hostelry stood open and Baldwin walked straight in, passing the bench of regulars who habitually drank outside. They had obviously been there for most of the day. A couple of them were dozing, their heads leaning against the ale house wall with their mouths open. The others were engaged in a noisy, belligerent exchange and would doubtless soon receive a reprimand from one of the ale house's neighbours.

Baldwin knew it would be pointless to ask the drunks anything, and the hostelry keeper was unlikely to be much better. He had known the man for years, but not for good reasons.

'Ah, so it's the sergeant again, is it, come to lock me up have you?' the man said distastefully as Baldwin entered the building.

The place stank. No wonder, thought the sergeant, that the Ship's most loyal patrons chose to drink outside. Judging by the filthy state of the floor rushes, the rank odour was probably the result of a few dead rodents and the daily spills of food, ale, urine and worse.

'That won't be necessary if you learn to keep better order,' he replied.

'What do you want this time?'

'You may have noticed the fire just over a week ago?'

'Hard not to. Aelfric's gone, then. I'm not wasting any time feeling sorry for him. A miserable old skinflint who never set foot in here. Place wasn't good enough for the likes of him.'

'Did you see anything out of the ordinary going on in the square, either before or during the fire?'

The man laughed, showing a fine set of stubby brown teeth.

'If you knew what a day's work was, sergeant, you'd understand that I was fast asleep by the time that fire started. All my customers were long gone and the place was shut. To make it clear, so that you clear off and leave me in peace, no I did not. I never saw nothing.'

Baldwin left. He had known it would be a waste of time. Even if he had information worth knowing, the hostelry keeper was unlikely to tell him. He was no friend of the law, especially since that night he had spent in the town lock-up, along with the rowdiest of his customers, on Baldwin's orders.

As Baldwin emerged from the hostelry, the seneschal was leaving the basket maker's workshop.

'Anything?' Nicholas asked him.

Baldwin told him what Goodwife Aswig had had to say about the cobbler. In turn, he heard what the seneschal had learned from Burdo. The sergeant listened intently, especially when it came to Burdo's sighting of the stranger fleeing the square just after the fire had started.

'Hooded?' grunted Baldwin. 'That applies to most of the men in Wisbech. Some of the women too.'

'Very true, but at least we have a description.'

What was more, added Nicholas to himself, Burdo's description, however scanty, matched the deputy constable's account of the false messenger who had tried to take the charter from the castle. It was likely that the same individual had been involved in both incidences.

They went to the cobbler's workshop on the square's south-west corner, close to the ford. Behind the shop, an untidy sprawl of outbuildings lined the narrow track that led out of town along the river. The seneschal knocked on the scruffy, patched up door and waited. The sound of mumbled cursing came from inside, but no one opened the door. Nicholas hammered more loudly. The cursing became more explicit, but still the door remained shut.

'Open up!' hollered the sergeant. 'The seneschal of the Isle of Ely demands it!'

Another barrage of cursing brought one of the occupants at last to the door. The cobbler was unshaven, his corpulent, round face sweaty and smeared with dirt.

'The *seneschal* had better come in then,' he sneered, 'but he can probably see that I am *busy* and have no time for idle chatter. There are boots I need to repair by tomorrow and my good for nothing sons do nothing to help.'

'I need very little of your time,' said Nicholas as he moved into the workshop. A wooden last stood on a very untidy workbench beneath the window. One old boot was stretched over the last, ready to be worked on, and next to it a pile of leather scraps and a jumble of old footwear in varying states of decrepitude vied for space.

'You'll be here about the fire, then,' stated the cobbler as he seated himself back at his bench. The sergeant and seneschal remained standing, since there was nowhere in the workshop, with its sparse floor rushes and lazily smoking hearth fire, to sit. 'Well, before you ask, we saw nothing and heard nothing. By the time we looked out to see what all the shouting was about, that old miser's house was in flames.'

'We?' queried the seneschal.

'Me and the two boys.'

'I would like to speak to them.'

The man tutted loudly, slumped his shoulders in exaggerated resignation, and bellowed.

'Get yourselves down here!'

The seneschal did not expect an immediate response from the man's sons and there was plenty he needed to ask while he waited.

'It sounds like you had little liking for Aelfric.'

'Your ears are working right, then. As you put it so genteelly, no, I had *little liking* for him. He was always telling folk about his grand family and how once they owned all the land around here. Well, that was then and this is now. I was sick of his airs and graces. He was fond of getting honest folk to do jobs for him, but he never paid them. He still owes me for the last lot of boot repairs I did for him and his servants. I shall never be paid now and I can't live on fresh air. He owed all the tradespeople around here money. Did you know that? While that dozy old basket maker talks of *dear Aelfric*, I'll wager he never mentioned how much he owed him. Aelfric placed orders with all the swagger of the lord of the manor, but he had nothing to pay any of us with. I'm not the only one who was sick of him, but I'm the only one honest enough to tell you.'

While Nicholas listened, the cobbler's two sons made their lazy way down the ladder from the attic and stood there with matching vacant expressions on their faces.

'Come here and talk to the man,' the cobbler growled at his sons. 'He won't have you hanged just yet, though it'd teach the pair of you a lesson if he did.' His huge face creased with laughter. His joke seemed to have cheered him up.

'I understand,' began Nicholas, addressing the adolescents, 'that you went to Aelfric's house on regular occasions. You were seen there by people who live close by.'

'Yeah, that's right,' muttered one of them. Both lads had round faces like their father's, with tiny snub noses that were almost engulfed by their fleshy cheeks. The one who was speaking had an angry rash of spots on his chin. Both boys looked in need of a good wash. 'That old baggage up the other end sent her husband over, asked me what I was up to once. Cut me lip, he did.'

'Why were you there?'

'Why?' demanded his father. 'Why? Because we were trying to get the money the old man owed us. That's why!'

'Yeah, that's right,' said the other lad. He paused to scratch his rear end before continuing. 'And before you ask, no we never tried nothing heavy on him. We just used to go to the door and ask for the money. He always gave us a reason why he couldn't pay.'

'Reasons in plenty,' continued the first lad, 'but never any money. It was always "next week" or "on St Agnes' Day" or some other faraway date.'

'People have seen you poking about at the house,' persisted Nicholas.

'Maybe we did a bit,' admitted the same boy. 'Thought we might find something round the back when we'd given up hope of being paid. You know, something we could sell...'

'And did you?'

'That's a laugh! The old man had nothing! Nothing! Almost felt sorry for him in the end,' replied the other lad. He was giggling at the memory.

'All right,' said Nicholas. 'Did you start the fire? Did you take your revenge on an old man who could not pay you?'

'They did not!' bellowed the father. 'How could we ever hope to be paid if the old man's house was burned? We are honest folk, my lord seneschal, *despite* what folks say about us. We only wanted to be paid for our work and now we shall have to go without.'

The seneschal and the sergeant were glad to leave the workshop. Outside it was beginning to rain and the air smelled fresh, a welcome relief from the smoky squalor of the cobbler's shop.

'Burdo the basket maker described a man running towards the ford and wading across the river,' said Nicholas. 'That might arguably have been one of those lads. Not the father;

I doubt he could run. Burdo, however, said the man he saw was tall and thin with heavy features and a broad nose. Neither of the cobbler's sons remotely fits that description, and anyway, Burdo said the man was a stranger. He'd hardly fail to recognise one of his own neighbours.'

'Can't imagine either of that pair doing much running either,' replied the sergeant, 'and their explanation for their visits to the Big House sounded likely enough.'

'Yes, but I shall not discount them yet. Come on, let's speak to everyone else in the square and compare our findings later.'

They split up again and continued to go from house to house. The rain picked up its pace and began to fall with stronger intent. Both men were glad when their house calls were finished and they could return to the castle.

SIXTEEN

Supper

It was still raining when the seneschal and sergeant forded the river again on their way back to the castle. The seneschal had spent longer than expected in the Old Market and the tide in the Wash estuary had risen considerably, swelling the usually meek Wysbeck. There was no ferry serving this part of the river and so the men were obliged to wade thigh deep across.

Nicholas crossed quickly and impatiently, frustrated by the knowledge that it was almost certainly too late to catch the arsonist. He hardly gave his wet clothing a thought as he climbed the river bank on the castle side. The man Burdo had seen running away from the fire would be long gone by now. Any effort made to trace him would probably be a waste of time, but still Nicholas had to try. He needed to speak to the constable, and the sooner the better.

The sergeant, as he followed the seneschal across the river, was less indifferent to a soaking. He cursed with ribald frequency as he reached the far bank. His duties were far from over for the day, and he had a particular dislike of walking around in wet clothing.

Nicholas, who was completely oblivious to the sergeant's discomfort, left him to his grumbling at the gatehouse. He strode across the bailey, the soaked leather of his boots gathering coatings of mud from the damp ground. The bailey was very quiet, as was usual for late afternoon, with most of the castle personnel being at supper in the great hall. Only a lone seagull, sweeping low to feast on dropped bread crumbs outside the bake house, paused to regard the seneschal from one beady eye, before taking off in hurried flight as the man crossed its path.

Having failed to find the constable in the great hall, the seneschal continued along the passage towards the spiral stairway. He had only climbed a few steps when he met Alexander hurrying down. The two men almost collided.

'Nicholas! What ails you?'

'My apologies, Alexander. Might I have a word?'

'Of course, but let it be over supper. Judging by the state of you, though,' Alexander added as he stared at the seneschal's wet clothing and mud-caked boots, 'you would benefit from a change of hose before honouring the great hall with your presence. Still, if you don't mind, neither do I. You *are* dragging in rather a lot of mud, though.'

Nicholas glanced down at his boots as if noticing the state of them for the first time. With their thick coating of mud, they looked more like blocks of peat than footwear. Looking back at the stone steps he had already climbed, he saw the trail of wet mud he had left behind and frowned distractedly. Alexander's reference to supper had at least made some impression on him, reminding him of his own hunger, and he agreed to accompany the constable to the great hall.

They made their way to the high table on the dais which was still unoccupied. The deputy constable was away on business in March and there were no guests that evening of sufficient importance to join the constable at his table. Alexander lowered himself into the high backed and heavily carved oaken chair at the centre of the long table and gestured for Nicholas to be seated next to him.

With impressive speed, one of the senior cooks arrived before them. With a formal bow and a flourish, he began to place cups, an elegantly potted jug and large platters of pastries and other delights on the table. From behind him appeared a second cook who poured wine into two of the cups, passing them with immaculate courtesy to the constable and seneschal.

'Have some of these, Nicholas,' Alexander said, ignoring the wine and biting into a pastry filled with honey. Its contents dribbled from the corner of his mouth and he wiped it cheerfully away with a linen napkin. Nicholas reached for one of the delicacies and held it between his fingers.

'I believe you are right,' began the seneschal, 'to have suspicions about the fire that killed Aelfric. Though so far there is nothing certain to connect the fire with the attempted theft of the charter, it seems the fire was not started by a domestic accident. One of the square's tenants, the basket maker...'

'Ah, yes,' interrupted the constable. 'Burdo; a good man.'

'He told me that he saw a man running across the square just after the fire would have broken out. The man wore a hood, of course, but the description Burdo gave me was as good as anyone could hope for under the circumstances.'

'I see, but that was more than a week ago. Whoever it was will have fled long ago.'

'I fear so. No one else in the square mentioned seeing the man, but I have no reason to doubt Burdo's word. He did not recognise the person he saw, so it's unlikely we are looking for a Wisbech man. Though it is probably too late to find him, we cannot be sure he has left town. He may be holed up somewhere nearby, so the town should be searched.'

'I agree,' said the constable after a brief pause. 'I shall see to it that my sergeant organises a thorough search of the town. I have twenty or thirty men who could be spared for the task.'

Nicholas thanked him, biting at last into the pastry that was rapidly disintegrating between his fingers. It was very good; filled with honey and sticky sweetness. There was the usual supper fare on offer too; good bread and creamy cheese, and the wine was excellent. He sipped it slowly in appreciation. Even supper, usually such a modest meal anywhere else, was always good at the castle.

'While the search goes on, I would like to visit Aelfric's daughter, Lady Rowena. I am told I shall find her at Hurste manor, close to Tydd St Giles.'

'That's correct,' confirmed the constable as he took a sip of wine. 'She is the wife of Sir Mortimer de Hurste, a proud man of no particular Norman breeding but with plenty of land. He wedded himself to the last of a noble Saxon family.'

'That was the impression I had from Aelfric's servants,' nodded Nicholas. 'They are to go to Lady Rowena tomorrow. It is possible that the lady might shed some light on why anyone would do her father harm. The servants mentioned a box which their late master had in his possession, one which they believed to contain items of value. They may be wrong, of course. The box they saw might have contained nothing much at all, but if they are right, Aelfric may have been wealthier than generally believed. Though he was apparently very secretive about the box, others could still have found out about it, which would make theft a likely motive for the break-in. Whether or not the intruder stole anything, he might have started the fire by accident.'

'The fact that the servants knew about the box means they could be guilty themselves. '

'That is true, but if they had stolen the box, why would they tell me of its existence?'

'A good point,' acknowledged Alexander, 'but if they *are* guilty, their walk to Tydd would be the perfect opportunity for escape, to make a life for themselves elsewhere. It will be interesting to see when you reach Hurste Manor whether the pair has arrived.'

Nicholas nodded in agreement.

'I intend to ride over there tomorrow. I'll take my men-at-arms; it's about time they earned their keep.'

'And my sergeant will begin the town search immediately. Perhaps between us we shall have some success.'

Nicholas thanked him again and rose from the high table, walking through the crowded hall and out into the cool May evening. The rain had stopped at last.

His hose were slowly drying and the mud covering his boots was gradually flaking away to reveal the wet and filthy leather beneath. There was no point in changing them, he considered, not now that it was so late in the day.

No one in the town's hostelries was likely to care about a bit of mud on a man's shoes. He decided to walk over to the Mitre in the New Market for an ale or two before retiring to his chambers for the night. He had to curb his impatience about the investigation he had just begun. He had done all he could do for now and everything, as he was learning in this role as the bishop's seneschal, would happen in its own time. A few ales would help him to remember that.

SEVENTEEN

Friday 4th May
Hurste

The seneschal's visit to Hurste Manor could not take place, as he had hoped, the following day, because of other pressing matters. The Hundred Court hearings were due to begin in just over a week's time, on the Feast of St Pancras, and Nicholas had to spend most of Thursday in preparation for them. The weather had taken a turn for the worse, heavy rain falling from dawn to dusk, so he was not altogether sorry about the delay.

The next morning was fair and bright from the start, the mud and wide puddles that covered every road surface the only reminders of the previous day's rain. The constable's men were beginning their second day of house to house searches and the mood in the town was already dampened because of it. People seemed to cower in the armed men's shadow as they made their way through the New Market, questioning and disturbing, probing every attic, outbuilding and workshop.

Nicholas left them to it, setting out cheerfully on his bay horse Micah and enjoying the warm May air. Brithun and Ordgar, his two men-at-arms, rode beside him on rounceys, good, capable horses but without the finer breeding of the seneschal's palfrey. They passed through the Old Market where guards were stationed by the screened off remains of the burned houses. Nicholas had given orders for the square to be kept under continuous observation. It was unknown whether the felon had found what he was looking for when he had broken into the Big House and it was possible that he would return to search the ruins. The box of valuables Aelfric's servants had mentioned, however, had never been found.

The road out of town rose to run along the top of the high bank that framed the western edge of the Wash estuary. The road was in a poor state, the recent heavy rain having softened it to a slippery sludge, and progress for the seneschal and his men was frustratingly slow. Fortunately, they did not have far to go before turning away from the estuary and following the narrow track towards the village of Tydd St Giles.

The track took them past the small stone built church dedicated to St Giles. Its new, honeyed stones were cloaked in the peaceful shade of mature yew trees and a neat path, devoid of weeds and planted with young hollies and apple saplings, led to a door of stout, pale oak. The whole church looked so fresh and new that it might have been built from Barnack stone only yesterday. Perhaps, considered Nicholas as he rode by, it had. He seemed to remember a far simpler timber-built church standing there in times past.

Gathered around the church were a few simple homes, barns and workshops, all of them wearing a hazy, sunlit halo of smoke above their thatch. The manor of Tydd St Giles, like Wisbech, was held by the Bishop of Ely. The much smaller settlement belonging to Sir Mortimer de Hurste lay further along the road and the riders reached it soon after leaving Tydd. The two manors were close together, allowing a traveller to see before him the rooftops of Hurste before turning to glance back across the flat landscape at the smoke from Tydd's hearth fires.

For all its reputed wealth, Hurste was small. It had no church of its own, so its lord, his family and peasants were obliged to make the short journey into the larger village of Tydd St Giles each Sunday. Nicholas, as he and his men entered Hurste, found the village's modest size surprising. He reminded himself that Sir Mortimer de Hurste held several other manors in neighbouring Lincolnshire and much more land besides. The quality of his pasture and fertility of his fields were said to keep this Norman knight in great comfort and to assure him of considerable standing in the shire.

It was not difficult to locate the manor house. Its range of timber buildings was neatly enclosed by a high, imposing fence. The gates stood fully open, inviting the travellers in. Mature cherry and plum trees shaded the southern side of the courtyard, around which the manor house's buildings were arranged. Dappled sunlight, filtered through the gently stirring green of the fruit trees, settled warmly on the front of the great hall and gave the place a welcoming, pleasant appearance.

A couple of villeins emerged from the stables to take the horses as soon as Nicholas and his men-at-arms had dismounted. The men took the reins and led the horses away, leaving the three visitors standing alone in the deserted courtyard. No one appeared, either at the door or at the windows, though workers' voices could be heard through the open shutters of the bake house and the kitchen to the right of the great hall. Undeterred, Nicholas strode towards the huge door set to one side of the main buildings and knocked loudly.

The door was disproportionately large for the size of the wall in which it was set, giving the impression that the builder had tried to compensate for the understated dimensions of the manor house he had been engaged to construct. Nicholas was not left long to think about this, though, because the door was quickly opened by a balding servant of short stature. Inclining his head respectfully to acknowledge the seneschal's status and request, he stood back to let him enter, leaving Brithun and Ordgar outside. They expected nothing more and went to the stables to check on the horses.

The seneschal was led straight into the great hall. Smoke from the large central hearth hung in the air, clouding his view of the men who sprawled on benches or leaned against the timber pillars which supported the heavy roof timbers. A hum of male voices filled the hall, punctuated now and then by the clicking of dice or a cough. At the far end of the hall, on the raised platform of the dais, sat a group of ladies and the seneschal made his way towards them.

There were four women in all. The higher level of the dais allowed all who occupied the chairs positioned there to sit just above the level of the smoke that settled like a low fog over the rest of the hall. This provided the ladies with considerably more comfort than any of the other occupants of the hall, though anyone observing their facial expressions might be forgiven for believing otherwise. Their looks of sourness and disapproval expressed a general dissatisfaction with life and, though none of them appeared particularly engrossed in their needlework, not one of them looked up as the seneschal approached.

As he drew closer, Nicholas was able to work out which of the group was the matriarch. Her pale face, with its tightly pursed lips and deep wrinkles, was framed by an uncompromising wimple and veil which hid her hair and any finer features she might have possessed. The other three women, who Nicholas guessed were in their middle years, were less severely veiled and wimpled, allowing at least a glimpse of hair to show at the forehead.

Nicholas bowed as he reached the dais, but was obliged to wait before any of the women acknowledged his presence.

One of the middle aged ladies finally appeared to notice him, but was frowning, screwing up her eyes in an effort to see him properly. She scowled, casting her embroidery aside with an ill tempered gesture.

'I am Nicholas Drenge,' he announced, 'seneschal for the Isle of Ely. I am looking for Lady Rowena de Hurste'

'Then it would appear, my lord,' said the woman coldly, 'that you have found her. What do you want from me?'

'Lady Rowena,' Nicholas continued undeterred, 'may I offer my condolences on the death of your father?'

'You may,' she sighed. One of the other middle aged women tutted loudly, but Rowena ignored her. 'It was an unfortunate occurrence, one which could have been prevented. He was to come here. It was all arranged, but he changed his mind at the last moment. He had become wilful and stubborn in his old age.'

'Aelfric was to come here, my lady? To live with you?'

'Come and sit down, my lord seneschal,' she relented. Her voice had become slightly less chilly, yet remained somehow devoid of life.

He stepped on to the dais and moved a heavy chair so that he could sit beside her. Lady Rowena turned in her seat and observed him as he settled himself. It was obvious that she was poor sighted and her embroidery must have been done more by feel than by sight. It perhaps explained, Nicholas considered, the reason for her ill temper.

'My father,' she began after a brief silence, 'was struggling.'

'No one's fault but his own,' commented the matriarch tartly.

'Kindly allow me to speak to the seneschal, mother. He has a job to do,' Rowena replied calmly. The old woman pressed her lips so tightly together that they almost disappeared into her bloodless face.

'My father Aelfric,' continued Lady Rowena, 'insisted on living in what was left of our family's holdings, but his only remaining servants were elderly and could no longer do much for him. My husband offered him a home here with us.'

'My son is a good man,' pointed out the old woman severely.

'Unfortunately,' continued Rowena, 'my father could not make up his mind. One moment he seemed keen on the thought of having a new home with us, the next he was dead set against it. Finally, perhaps because of the terrible winter we all endured this year, he decided he would come to us. On the day before the fire, we sent two of our serfs on horseback with a litter, to fetch him. They were to carry him back here on the litter because he was so frail, but he sent them back. It appears that he had changed his mind yet again. That night, either he or one of his servants must have knocked a rush light or a candle on to the floor rushes, and as you know, the whole place went up in flames. He is buried now at St Peter and St Paul's Church in Wisbech, one of the manors which our ancestors so carelessly handed over to the abbot in Ely...'

She paused. Nicholas heard the breath catch in her throat. For all her stony looks, Lady Rowena de Hurste had obviously cared about her father.

'Lady Rowena, do you remember there being a box of valuable items in your father's possession?'

'Ha!' She gave a bitter laugh. 'You think this was a bungled theft, do you? You think someone broke into my poor old father's home to steal his treasure and somehow started the fire? No, my lord seneschal, you should not listen to the idle gossip of my father's servants. They are simple folk and would consider any bright, shiny thing as treasure. That box, my lord, contained nothing but a few worthless trinkets. Anything of real value had been sold off years ago, to pay for life's necessities, such as tithes and rent. My father had nothing left of value. No one would have tried to steal from him. That fire must have been caused by one of the three old fools who lived in that house. I told my father he could no longer manage to live like that, that he must come here, and it seems after all that I was right.'

The seneschal nodded absently, his attention now focussed on a young woman who was stepping elegantly on to the dais. She curtseyed very correctly to the family elders and their visitor, looking as subdued as the older women were sour.

Lady Rowena stopped talking and she too watched the girl as she approached the group.

EIGHTEEN

Magan and Leof

'Come and sit with us, child,' said Lady Rowena. There was a hint of warmth somewhere within her almost expressionless voice. 'My daughter, Rose,' she continued, by way of introduction. 'This gentleman is the bishop's seneschal.'

Rose curtseyed again before sitting on the only other spare chair, next to her paternal grandmother. She busied herself for a short while with arranging the flowing skirts of her gown so that the toes of her small booted feet were covered. Her gown was of a pale shade of yellow that reminded the seneschal of the first primroses of the year and its neckline was one that he had only seen before on the most fashionable ladies of Ely. There was a small vertical slit following the line of her throat, trimmed with the same embroidered ribbon that decorated the hems of the wide sleeves and the skirt. Rose's hair was covered by the lightest of linen veils, leaving her young, pretty face on full view. The veil was so finely woven that the reddish tint of her fair hair showed through.

Her appearance was in direct contrast to her mother's, who seemed to have abandoned any interest she might once have had in dressing well. Lady Rowena's gown was dyed such a muddy shade of grey that any natural beauty she might still have possessed, and which was not hidden by the harsh lines of veil and wimple, was completely drained away. Her clothing made her appear old before her time. The other three women, however, presumably her sisters-in-law and mother-in-law, had taken drabness to the next degree, indulging themselves in the severest cut of gowns in the most depressing shades of brown.

'There is one more thing I should make you aware of, my lord seneschal,' continued Rowena. 'If you continue to waste your time on my father's lamentable but clearly accidental death, you may hear ridiculous claims concerning an old charter.'

Nicholas sat up straight in his chair. This was the first time the charter had cropped up in connection with the fire, the first hint that the constable's suspicions might be grounded in reality.

'The charter issued by your ancestors, Oswy and Leoflede, which gifted manors to Ely Abbey?' he asked to clarify. 'I am aware of it, my lady.'

'But have you heard the ludicrous story which accompanies it?'

'That nonsense!' barked her mother-in-law. 'I would hope an officer of the law ignored such fairy tales!'

'I am sure the seneschal will, mother. I am merely warning him about the matter before he hears of it elsewhere.' She raised her eyes and looked at the seneschal again. Once perhaps a clear blue, her eyes were cloudy and she was obviously still having trouble seeing him clearly. 'The charter is said to lead people to my father's house in the Old Market and to some sort of treasure, my lord seneschal. It is, as my mother-in-law states, nonsense. It is something made up years ago by people with too little to occupy their minds. I rather think, however, that my father enjoyed hearing about the legend. He even boasted about it, fool that he was. I believe he liked the fact that our family was still worthy of some small interest.'

While Lady Rowena was speaking, Rose lifted her head and peered curiously at her mother. She parted her lips as if to say something, but she seemed to think better of it and remained silent.

'Thank you, my lady,' said Nicholas as he rose from his seat. 'I must take my leave, but there is one more thing I would like to know. Did your father's two servants arrive here safely?'

'They did. They arrived last night and the steward sent them to work in the kitchen.'

'I would like to speak to them, in that case.'

Rowena raised her eyebrows in mild surprise, but summoned one of the servants from the lower part of the hall.

'Take the seneschal to speak to my father's villeins.'

The man bowed before accompanying Nicholas out through the hall and the main door to the yard outside. A few more paces took them past the bake house to the large kitchen next door.

The heat from the hearth in the centre of the room was overwhelming. This was the kitchen's main cooking fire and in such mild weather it was stifling. A saddle of pork was roasting on a spit, filling the kitchen and the yard outside with its aroma. It reminded Nicholas how long it had been since his early meal of bread and cheese. It also told him how well this family lived. Only the wealthy could afford to eat roasted meat, especially when there was no feast day to celebrate.

It did not take long to find Aelfric's old servants. Magan and Leof were standing at a large table in the corner, scrubbing earthenware cooking pots with sand and handfuls of straw. As the seneschal approached, they glanced up anxiously.

'I was glad to hear of your safe arrival,' he said. 'I need to speak to you both.'

They looked uncomfortable and made no response. Close behind the seneschal, one of the cooks was hovering, clutching a huge iron ladle. His broad, fleshy face looked like it had stuck years ago in an expression of anger and truculence. He opened his mouth, ready to warn the servants of the consequences of idle chatter, but one look at the seneschal, with his obvious authority and well tailored clothes, made him hesitate. He nodded his grudging assent as the villeins followed Nicholas out of the building and into the yard.

Once outside in the sun, the two elderly men seemed to relax a little. Magan leant against the warm kitchen wall and closed his eyes, as if in pain.

'Is all not well? You had a foul, rainy day for your journey yesterday,' the seneschal remarked. Leof took a deep breath before replying.

'We took a wetting, yes, sir, but soon warmed ourselves in the kitchen. We cannot expect things to be as before. We do our best with the kitchen work, but have never worked before in such a big place. There are so many cooks, all with their own tasks, and they are busy all the time. They have to keep this large household and its servants fed, and they are impatient with us. The steward seems a fair man, though. He understands our efforts would be better applied to the fields. We always enjoyed growing vegetables for the pot in our old master's garden. The steward says he will try to transfer us to work outside as soon as possible.'

'I am sure,' pointed out Magan, 'that the seneschal did not come here to listen to our troubles.'

'Maybe not,' said Nicholas, 'but I hope that your wishes are soon granted. I do not imagine Lady Rowena would want her father's faithful servants to be unhappy in her care.'

Neither of the men responded to the comment. Nicholas doubted that they had even seen the lady since their arrival.

'I came to ask you about the charter,' he stated. 'Did Aelfric ever refer to it?'

'The charter?' repeated Magan, looking puzzled. 'I do not think...'

'Do you mean the old scroll the master used to talk about, sir?' asked Leof. 'I don't know whether you'd call it a charter, but he talked about an old scrolled document of some kind. He said it had been written by his ancestors before the time of the Conqueror and that it contained some sort of riddle.'

'A riddle?'

'I think that was what he said, sir. We never knew much about it, just that it was connected in some way to the house in the Old Market. When the master lost all his other manors and land, he was determined to keep that one house and its garden. Perhaps it was because it was linked to that document, but I cannot be sure. After all, it was a private family matter and not for our ears, but towards the end, when just the three of us remained in the house, he spoke more often to us.'

Nicholas nodded.

'One other thing; were you aware of your master owing money to people? I mean for goods, services, small items?'

'He was an honourable man,' said Magan vaguely.

'Of course he was,' replied Leof. 'I'm sure he always meant to pay folk, but there was very little to pay them with.'

'Who did he owe money to?'

'That cobbler for one, and he never let the master forget it. Then I think there were a few pennies owing to the basket maker and a small amount outstanding to the baker.'

'It wasn't much,' insisted Magan.

'Nevertheless, thank you for telling me,' said Nicholas. 'I wish you both well in your new situation here. And now I must find my men-at-arms and take my leave.'

'But before you go, sir, will you not share some dinner with us?' offered Magan. 'We are about to eat and the steward will not see a visitor leave hungry. It would be an honour if you and your men joined us in the great hall. There is a fine galentyne sauce to go with today's pike fish. I know, because Leof and I helped to make it,' he added rather proudly.

Nicholas was happy to accept. Not only was he hungry, he was very thirsty. The ale flask he carried was almost dry and Lady Rowena had offered neither him nor his men refreshment.

He, Brithun and Ordgar soon found themselves seated at the very lowest end of the great hall. It was a novel and curious situation for Nicholas. As seneschal, one of the most important officials in the Isle of Ely, he should rightfully have been sitting as a guest of Sir Mortimer de Hurste and his lady.

If Nicholas leaned back slightly on the bench, he could see the lord of the manor sitting at the high table. The man was sneering about something but Lady Rowena, seated to his right, was making no reply. She looked stony faced and ill tempered and, beside her, Rose was staring down at her bread trencher, her expression hard to make out. The other women, members of Sir Mortimer's family whom Nicholas had had the dubious pleasure of meeting earlier, looked equally grim. On the rare occasions that they cast a glance at their peasants, the folk who toiled on their manor and filled its lesser tables at mealtimes, it was with a glare.

Nicholas had no inclination to join any of them. Despite the humility of his seating position, he was rather enjoying himself. Though the conversation that went on around him was doubtless stilted because of his presence, it was still merry. The lord of the manor and his cross faced family seemed powerless to suppress the good humour and banter that flowed back and forth across the table like a breath of fresh air, and Nicholas was glad to be a part of it. The food was good too. Magan and Leof might consider themselves ill suited to kitchen work, but they certainly knew how to make a good galentyne sauce.

By the time the seneschal, Brithun and Ordgar left Hurste Manor, they were well fed and watered and Nicholas had plenty to think about.

What he had learned about the charter was interesting. Rather than being an irrelevant, long forgotten document, it was something which even Aelfric's servants knew about. According to them, even to Lady Rowena herself, the document contained something which connected it to the house in the Old Market. The two servants had called it a riddle, but whatever it was, Aelfric had believed it to have existed.

Leof and Magan had also confirmed the cobbler's claim that Aelfric had owed him and others money, though whether any of that was related to the elderly man's death was impossible to tell as yet.

Lady Rowena's treatment of the subject of the charter had been strange. Having raised the matter, she had gone out of her way to warn him that any rumours of its connection to 'treasure', as she called it, were nonsense.

But if her intention had been to discourage his interest in the charter, she had failed miserably. Her words had only piqued his curiosity and now he was determined as never before to get to the bottom of this matter.

NINETEEN

Eric de Bourne

By late afternoon, Sir Nicholas Drenge and his men-at-arms were back in Wisbech. Leaving Brithun and Ordgar to take care of the horses, Nicholas went immediately to see the constable.

He found Sir Alexander de Astonne and his steward at the foot of the forebuilding steps. Judging by their heavy frowns, they were discussing matters of great import and the constable paused only long enough to give the seneschal a distracted greeting. Nicholas briefly explained what he needed.

'Simon is in the office,' said Alexander. 'He will be able to help you with that.'

Nicholas quickly climbed the steps to the forebuilding and strode through the anteroom towards the keep. Crossing the great hall, he skirted groups of officials gathered in ponderous and worthy debate, overdressed for the weather in their fur trimmed robes. He was soon ascending the narrow spiral stone steps and pacing along the passageway towards the constable's office. His knocking was answered straight away and he entered the room.

'Ah, Nicholas!' smiled Simon de Gardyn. 'Back so soon from Hurste? Alexander will be back soon, but if I can help in any way...'

'I have already seen him, thank you, Simon, and have only a small request. I need to have a proper look at Oswy and Leoflede's charter. It seems that wherever I go that document is mentioned.'

'Ah, yes, the charter. I have the key to the document chest right here.'

The deputy constable rose from his seat and lifted an iron ring of keys that was attached to the girdle of his long tunic. Selecting one of the smaller keys, he knelt before the iron-bound chest that stood beneath an ornate tapestry. He placed the key in the lock and turned it carefully. The old mechanism seemed to resist his first attempts, but at last something gave and he was able to lift the high, arching lid of the chest. He spent some time searching through the many scrolled documents inside, picking up one after another and examining them briefly before finally selecting one of the oldest and most dog-eared. He handed it to the seneschal.

Nicholas placed it on the desk and carefully unrolled it. The edges of the parchment were frayed and the whole document had become discoloured. It was badly stained in places, as if often and carelessly referred to in the past. The text was arranged in tight blocks of neat, tiny lettering and the lines were very close together. There was a lot of it, too, the opened document showing paragraph after paragraph of script. The ink had faded badly in many areas and Nicholas could hardly make sense of it at all.

'I thought it would be written in Latin,' he sighed. The deputy laughed.

'As did I! I looked at it briefly after that young fellow came here, trying to get hold of it. I could read none of it. I confess I am unable to read the old Saxon language.'

'I'm afraid it evades me too.'

Once more, Nicholas ran his eye down the long document. At fairly regular intervals, the paragraphs were broken up into sections beneath short headings.

pisbece

'I think this heading here reads "Wisbech", but the rest of the text escapes me. I shall have to take it to the chaplain's office and engage one of the clerks to translate it for me.'

'You need to take it away?' queried Simon. He looked shocked by the idea. 'I'm not sure what the... but of course, if you think it necessary. I must request, though, my lord seneschal, that the charter does not leave the castle and is kept locked away when not being studied. It is our only copy.'

Nicholas nodded impatiently and left the room, the ancient scroll tucked beneath his arm. Leaving the keep, he crossed the bailey to the small office next to the castle chapel, knocking once on the door and walking in without awaiting a reply.

The three young clerks seated at their writing desks paused in their work and looked up as one, like a nest full of baby birds greeting a parent in hope of food. The chaplain's head shot up too, but in his case it was with obvious annoyance. He could only have been in his thirties, but his face was already etched with lines of impatience.

'My lord seneschal?' he said tersely.

'Father Leofric, I have a document here, written in the Saxon language which I find difficult to interpret. Would one of your clerks be able to look at it for me? Could it be translated into modern English?'

The chaplain rose from his desk and joined the seneschal by the door. He took the scroll and unrolled it, frowning as he examined it.

'Get on with your work!' he barked at the three clerks, who were still watching, open mouthed with curiosity. The three heads went down again and the distracted scratching of quills on parchment began shortly afterwards.

'Much of the text is faded, but is just about legible,' Father Leofric commented. 'It will take time, but I am sure it can be done. Eric!' he said with a slightly raised voice. 'Come here, boy.'

Eric de Bourne put down his pen and left his desk with undisguised alacrity.

'You have a good knowledge of the old Saxon language, do you not, boy?'

Eric glanced uncertainly at the long paragraphs of tiny script on the scroll before him. Translating such a document would take many hours, but at least it would give him some respite from writing the castle's tedious letters and setting out long pages of accounts, which formed the main part of his work.

'I was taught the old language from the priest in Elm, father. I still have some memory of it.'

'So,' responded the seneschal, 'you could write it out in language easy enough for an ignoramus like me to comprehend?'

'Well,' began Eric seriously, not at all sure how he should be reacting to the seneschal's self depreciation. 'Yes, sir. I shall do my best.' He decided to add a slight smile, one which would offend neither the chaplain nor the seneschal.

'Then you will be given time between your other tasks to work on this document,' decided Father Leofric.

'Yes, father,' responded Eric meekly, returning to his desk.

'You must allow us a few days, my lord,' Father Leofric said to the seneschal. 'We have a great deal of other demands on our time at the moment, so this task will have to be fitted in whenever possible. I hope you are not in a great hurry for it.'

'No, father,' replied Nicholas. He knew it would make no difference even if he demanded urgent action; Father Leofric was never one to be hurried. 'I have the Hundred Court hearings to attend to, so can afford to wait a few days.'

The chaplain nodded in a way that the seneschal recognised as dismissal. Nicholas obliged by leaving immediately, feeling uncomfortably like a chastened school boy.

TWENTY

The Carpenter's Son

Weland, son of Godmund the carpenter of Ely, stood without moving a muscle in the deep shadow of the high wall. He hardly dared to breathe. The constable's men were still close by. He could hear snatches of their conversation as they moved about, but he knew if he stayed still and silent enough, he would evade capture for another night. Dusk was falling at last and darkness would soon follow, bringing the town search to a close for the day.

He was safe where he was for the time being, but knew he could not stay there forever. People would catch on eventually and he could not afford to be caught. It might, he thought, be best if he left town for a bit. He could always return later and try again. After they had given up looking for him.

From close by, out of the darkness rose the sound of singing, the soothing harmony of male voices. In St Peter and Paul's, the church just beyond the castle walls, people were attending Compline, the evening service. That would be the signal for the men-at-arms to end their day's search. And how many days after that would they bother to look for him? They could not go on forever.

The singing reminded Weland of the monks at home in Ely. He felt a sudden, unexpected wrenching of the heart, a surge of regret that for a moment almost robbed him of his common sense. He had never much valued the time he had spent with the monks, but it had been safe. He had not been full of fear then.

But he could never go back. He had walked away without a word and they would no longer trust him. Perhaps even his father would refuse to have him back.

If they found out what he had done, what he had been involved with, his life would be over anyway. And of all his most ridiculous thoughts, was that helping his father in his carpentry workshop had become oddly appealing. But it was too late now for anything like that. Such things were almost certainly lost to him forever.

With one bold move, one ill conceived plan, he had gambled away his future. He had been too easily carried away, too easily flattered. He had been a fool. But perhaps, perhaps there was still a chance.

He had only to lie low and wait.

TWENTY-ONE

Feast of St Edbert of Lindisfarne; Sunday 6th May

The search of the town had yielded nothing. The sergeant and his men had spent the whole of Thursday, Friday and Saturday, from first light to last, searching every workshop, attic, outbuilding and hearthside in the town and had found nothing. The sergeant had never believed that it would be anything but a waste of time and was glad when Sunday's day of rest arrived, so that his men could stand down and bring the search to a close.

It was only then that anything of interest had come to light. One of the seneschal's two men-at-arms, an Ely man whom the sergeant considered to be rather dim witted, had reported something that sounded worth pursuing. The soldier, who went by the name of Brithun, had joined the search late, having only just returned from some errand or other with the seneschal near Tydd St Giles. As was typical in life, it had been none of the sergeant's own hard working and long searching men, but this newcomer who had provided the breakthrough. It seemed to Baldwin yet another sign that the hardest toiling folk in life were the least rewarded.

Brithun, unaware of the sergeant's resentment, had informed him that a woman in the New Market had reported seeing an individual fitting the description of the wanted man.

'The goodwife says she has been away, visiting her family in Welle,' Brithun had told the sergeant. 'She wasn't here when you searched, sir, but came to tell us about someone she saw on her return to the town.'

'Go on,' the sergeant had grunted.

'The goodwife told me that she was on her way back from Welle yesterday afternoon when she encountered a stranger coming from the Wisbech direction and hurrying along the road. The weather being fine, the goodwife was hot from walking and, like everyone else she met along the road, had removed her cloak and hood. She had noticed this particular stranger because he was heavily overdressed. The hood of his long, black cloak was pulled forward to hide most of his face and his movements seemed furtive to her, as if he were trying to avoid everyone on the road. She said the man was tall and thin, sir, which matches the description of the individual we want.'

Baldwin the sergeant was beginning to forget his grudges and to take interest.

'The goodwife saw this man yesterday, you say.'

'Late afternoon, it would have been, sir. The goodwife says it was only later, when she found out about our search, that she thought she should tell us what she had seen.'

The sergeant had grunted again.

'It's most likely too late now to find this man. If he was leaving town at a good pace on Saturday afternoon, he could be well on his way to March by now. He won't know we've been alerted though, so if we set out immediately, we may be in luck. Get back to the castle and ready yourself to leave.'

And so, the sergeant-at-arms and a small band of men, including the seneschal's two Ely soldiers, set out on horseback at noon on Sunday along the Elm road out of Wisbech. The road that ran along the top of the river bank past Elm and on to Welle had dried out somewhat over the last few days of fair weather and the party made good progress. The few travellers they encountered along the way were duly questioned, but none of them admitted to having seen the man they sought. The soldiers overtook a few folk too, mostly tradesmen travelling from Wisbech, their goods loaded on to the backs of mules. None of them looked remotely like the man they were looking for.

They reached the manor of Welle with its church dedicated to St Peter and its cluster of homes and workshops that hugged the river bank, before they had any promise of success at all.

They had no luck in the Widgeon. The harassed looking inn keeper was single handedly attempting to serve his many customers and offered the sergeant nothing more than a distracted shaking of the head in response to his questions. The soldiers, having left their horses at the inn, spread out along the quiet back ways of the village, their intimidating mail-coated presence yielding nothing more useful than a few nervous denials and blank looks. Once more, it was Brithun the Ely man who eventually struck lucky. A baker delivering a basketful of loaves to the Widgeon thought he knew the person the sergeant and his men were looking for.

'You mean the tinker,' he said with a good natured smile. 'My wife bought a couple of ladles from him this morning. Seemed a pleasant enough fellow to me. He took one of my loaves as part payment and I gave him some ale for his journey. He won't be far away.'

They found him soon afterwards. He was sitting peacefully in the sun on the grassy bank in front of the new chantry chapel. He was eating his bread and drinking from a small flask and, despite the warmth of the day, was still wearing his hood. When he looked up to see the band of armed men bearing down on him, it was with curiosity, rather than fear or panic.

'Get up!' ordered the sergeant, his hand on the hilt of the short sword hanging at his side.

The man frowned in confusion, dropping the remainder of his bread as he staggered to his feet.

'You're coming with us!' the sergeant bellowed, his huge hand gripping the man's shoulder.

'But why?' the man managed to speak at last. 'Let me pick up my bag. I cannot afford to lose my things.'

He reached for the large, bulky canvas sack that had been lying in the grass and as he did so there was the sound of metal clanking against metal.

'What's in there?' the sergeant demanded.

'The things I have for sale, sir. I make my living selling things.'

One of the men-at-arms grasped the bag and peered inside, muttering something to the sergeant.

'What are skeins of wool doing in here?' demanded Baldwin.

'Payments I've received for my tin ware, sir. Some folk have no coins, but pay me with the wool they've spun in their homes. Once I reach Ely, I can sell the wool and have coins to pay my way with.'

Baldwin the sergeant gave him a disbelieving look and threw the bag back on the ground.

'You'll be a lot longer getting to Ely than you thought, then, won't you? The seneschal wants a word with you in Wisbech Castle,' he announced with satisfaction.

The man looked terrified. His hood slipped back from his head and hastily he pulled it up again. His hair was thinning and angry looking sores were clearly visible on his scalp and forehead. This brief glimpse was not lost on Brithun and Ordgar, the Ely men. The man's nose, they also noticed, was small and slightly upturned at the end. His features in general were nothing like the description they had been given. This situation was beginning to feel wrong to both of them. The tinker with his small nose and bad skin condition was not the man they sought. Anyone hiding from the law for so long would have panicked and tried to escape when approached by armed men. He had shown them nothing but curiosity.

For the tinker, it was a miserable trudge back to Wisbech, hands tied and forced to walk behind one of the horses. The seneschal's men-at-arms had picked up the man's canvas bag and it was now safe inside a saddle bag. They knew they were wasting their time with this wretched man and that the seneschal would be less than pleased. There was, however, nothing they could do about it. The sergeant clearly shared none of their misgivings. He whistled a tune as they rode back towards the castle with their prisoner, his face a picture of smug satisfaction.

TWENTY-TWO

Monday 7th May
The Chaplain's Office

Nothing much ever happened to disturb the air of quiet industry which prevailed in the chaplain's office. That morning, the silence was broken only by the sound of one of the clerks hiccoughing. Father Leofric was clearly displeased, but did his best to ignore it. He continued to work with almost saintly perseverance, but as the hiccoughs became louder and more frequent he could take no more and his patience snapped. He threw down his quill and glared at the offending clerk.

'What's *wrong* with you, boy?' he demanded. 'Could you not digest your morning ale in a more seemly manner? Get outside and sort yourself out!'

With a dismissive flick of the hand, the priest lowered his head over his work again as the boy rose from his seat and made his hasty way outside. Eric caught his eye and the two clerks exchanged a grin. Eric wished he could join him. Birdsong and the glorious scent of late spring flowers wafted in through the briefly opened door and seemed to be beckoning him outside. It was a joyful May morning, one of freshness and hope, the promise of a long summer. The last place Eric wanted to be was in this airless office with his listless colleagues and their irritable chaplain. He sighed heavily, instantly regretting it. Father Leofric heard him and lifted his head to stare at him. Eric hastily lowered his eyes and tried to concentrate on the document before him.

This morning, the chaplain had set him to work on the charter of Oswy and Leoflede for the seneschal, and it was not easy. The task of translating the document into modern English had not appeared difficult to start with. After all, Eric had been a diligent student as a boy and had learned with pleasure the old Saxon language from his tutor. He was familiar with its strange lettering, so that gave him no problems. What was causing him so much difficulty was the degree by which the old ink had faded. In places, the lettering had become totally illegible and he was having to leave long gaps in his translation. In other areas, old stains, perhaps from a carelessly placed ale or wine cup long ago, made an otherwise clear passage hard to decipher. Even when he did manage to make out a paragraph, he wondered why he had bothered. The charter's long winded descriptions of the land and manors gifted to Ely Abbey in ancient times seemed to Eric pointless in the extreme.

Each of the manors was given its own heading. Those for Walpole, Wisbech, Debenham, Brightwell and Woodbridge were clearly written, but the script beneath each heading was cramped and tiny. Described in bewildering and repetitive detail was every church, house, outhouse, workshop and stable. In frustration, Eric found himself wondering why the dung heaps and privies had not been included too. Translating the document felt like a huge waste of effort, yet at the same time the trivial nature of the descriptions made him want to laugh out loud. He dare not even smile, though. He knew Father Leofric was watching from the corner of his eye.

At the back of Eric's mind nagged the suspicion that the seneschal was expecting much more from this translation.

He felt he was missing something, that he was failing to pick up from the text whatever the law man hoped for.

He suppressed a yawn, longing for dinner time when he could enjoy some fresh air. As if trying its hardest to grant part of his wish, the door opened with apologetic slowness and admitted a breath of soft spring air. The previously banished clerk, looking pale and miserable, came in and reclaimed his seat.

Eric went on with his work, writing out a few more lines, but continuing to leave huge gaps where the ancient writing had faded too much to understand. He needed some help, he decided, another pair of eyes. He thought of his old friend, John of Tilneye. He had always been so much better at deciphering these things than Eric; quicker and brighter. If he could persuade John to come to the office and cast his eye over this document, there would be more hope of the job being completed to the seneschal's satisfaction.

No doubt Father Leofric would disapprove of John's presence, but he was unlikely to make a formal protest. The Tilneye family was well respected in the town. If the chaplain was told nothing about Eric's plan before being presented with a 'fait accompli' there would be little he could do about it.

Eric decided to walk to the Tilneyes' manor of Marshmeade as soon as his day's work was done. With any luck, the sun might still be shining.

TWENTY-THREE

Same Day, Monday 7th May
The Castle

'You set fire to Aelfric's home,' the sergeant was shouting.

The tinker, whose wrists were secured with a heavy pair of handcuffs, cowered in the corner of the seneschal's office in the Mote Hall. He had been forced to spend the night in a cell with two of the most unpleasant individuals he had ever had the ill fortune to meet. They were men charged with crimes that the tinker did not even wish to think about, men who waited only for their Assizes hearings and inevitable death. They had nothing to lose by making the tinker's life more miserable than it had already become.

It had been the sergeant's decision to put the prisoner in that particular cell. There had been no need. There were still empty cells in the gloomy depths of the keep, but he had hoped it would oil the wheels of justice to intimidate the tinker before he was questioned.

The seneschal was not impressed by the sergeant's actions. The sight of the tinker's black eye and the drying blood around his nose and mouth had incensed the Ely law man who now took his seat next to Baldwin, facing the prisoner across the desk. The sergeant had shown no remorse. He was confident in his own methods and considered the bishop's man too soft. The seneschal would soon be gone anyway, back to Ely, leaving the sergeant to get on with his work in the way he knew best.

The tinker's canvas sack had been thoroughly searched and found to contain nothing but a few cheap metal utensils and some skeins of wool.

'I did not, sir,' the tinker replied in a terrified voice.

'Why did you break into his house, then? Stealing's your game, is it?'

'Sir, I did not break into his house. I broke into no one's house. I just came to Wisbech to sell my things.'

'And laid low while my men were out, searching the town for you. Where were you skulking all that time?'

'I was not skulking and I did not hide. I saw your men, sir, but just carried on with my work, calling at a few houses. The soldiers took no notice of me, nor I of them.'

'But then,' said the seneschal calmly, speaking for the first time, 'you were seen hurrying away from town. Why were you leaving with such haste?'

The tinker frowned and looked thoughtful.

'I was not really hurrying, my lord seneschal. I had been quite successful in selling my pots and things in the town and was glad to be on my way to Ely. It is my way to walk quickly. The faster I travel, the sooner I can sell the wool in Ely and have some coins in my purse. I had quite a lot of wool this time from folk as payment.'

The seneschal nodded and was quiet for a moment. At his side, he could feel the sergeant bristling with impatience.

'Did you always wear your hood up while you were in town?' the seneschal continued.

The tinker looked puzzled.

'My hood? Well, yes, my lord. Mostly, anyway. Only if the day becomes extremely hot do I lower it. I have a skin condition and most folk would prefer not to see it. It is not a good idea to put people off when I am trying to sell to them.'

He raised his bony cuffed hands and with difficulty pushed back the dark folds of his woollen hood. His grey, greasy hair was very thin and the open sores which covered his scalp were clearly visible. Despite his good intentions, the seneschal felt himself recoiling from the sight. The last time he had seen skin so badly affected was on one of the poor souls seeking help at the leper house on the outskirts of town.

'God's teeth, man,' bellowed the sergeant, leaning back in his seat, 'You're a leper!'

'I will fetch a physician to see you,' the seneschal said quietly. 'You will no longer need to wander the lanes. You will have help now.'

The man had lowered his uncovered head into his heavily bound hands.

'I have feared for some time that I might have the disease,' he admitted, 'but tried to carry on with my work. I never minded the wandering life, but to live as a leper, with a begging bowl and a bell to warn folk to stay away from me... no, that is something I could not bear.'

'That should not be necessary,' the seneschal tried to reassure him. 'The Church takes good care of people who seek its help. There are good leper hospitals now. One of them is located close by, between Wisbech and Elm. You will be well cared for.' He paused and turned to look at the sergeant. 'Remove this man's handcuffs. He is no longer a prisoner.'

Baldwin was white faced with fury as he did as commanded. Nicholas watched without sympathy for the sergeant as the action of removing the cuffs brought his face uncomfortably close to the tinker's, exposing him for a moment or two to the disease.

'And what,' demanded the sergeant once he and the seneschal had left the room, 'about the break-in to Aelfric's house? What about the fire? The killing of a man?'

'What about them?' snapped the seneschal. 'The man in there had nothing to do with any of it. You arrested the wrong man, sergeant, and I would thank you to remember my status when addressing me.'

The sergeant muttered a grudging apology and plodded off towards the guard house. Nicholas turned towards the keep, giving orders for ale and bread to be sent to the tinker in the Mote Hall office and sending a messenger to summon the physician.

His hopes of catching the individual responsible for starting the fire that killed Aelfric had diminished almost to nothing. Yet, far more was going on here than a fire and a man's death. Everything was connected to the charter, that tedious document which cropped up so often in people's speech. The situation intrigued him, even though he was unsure how to continue from here.

Perhaps Eric de Bourne would show the way forward, discover some illuminating clue in the charter. Perhaps. The seneschal was not holding his breath.

TWENTY-FOUR

Marshmeade

As soon as Eric de Bourne was free of his duties in the chaplain's office, he left the castle and set out along the river road towards Elm and the manor of Marshmeade. It was early evening by then, and the sun that cast its glance on the water of the Well Stream was coppery now and lent less warmth to the air. Where it touched the river, it was sliced into tiny fragments by ripples on the wind-blown surface.

He strode along purposefully, soon leaving behind the last small dwellings of Wisbech. The orchards that reached down to the river bank were quiet now, their depths draped in the first shadows of evening. Even the birdsong had relented, softening to the weary chirpings that heralded the end of day. The fruit trees were fully clothed in leaf now, their blossom long faded, and the first tiny bead-like apples, pears and plums, were invisible to Eric from the bank-top road.

He was soon passing the low thatched roofs of the leper house. Catching the sunlight at the end of its avenue of willow saplings, the gates still stood open, welcoming any soul in need. Soon afterwards, the bank top road took Eric past the manor of Elm, the smoke from its hearth fires drifting tranquilly into the evening air. There was no one around, no one to remark on the traveller who strode along the bank, and Eric quickened his pace, moving on rapidly towards Marshmeade.

It was impossible to tell where the land belonging to Elm ended and where Marshmeade's acres began, but the pasture that stretched out from the river bank was fresh and verdant, the sheep that wandered there healthy and content.

Eventually, the first small buildings of Marshmeade came into view and soon Eric was making his way along the narrow lane that led into the centre of the village. There was nothing to set apart these simple, single-roomed homes from any he might see on other manors, except that they were neater than most. Their thatch was in good repair and the daub covering their low walls freshly applied. Here and there, a dung heap steamed lazily in the evening sun, the all too familiar odour filling Eric's nostrils as he hurried along. There were few folk about now. Most of them had retired from their day's labours on the manorial lord's demesne land and were settling down by their fireside to sleep.

The manor house was not yet shuttered for the night and Eric approached it hopefully, passing its stables, dairy, bake house and kitchen before reaching the high roofed great hall itself. There was a single, stone step that led up to the main entrance and tentatively he walked up to the door and knocked. The sound seemed hardly to carry at all, the door being so thick and solid, but instantly he was aware of movement on the other side of it.

A young girl opened the door to him. She looked no more than twelve or thirteen, but smiled in ready welcome, leading him into the great hall. She spoke to someone there who disappeared into the gathering shadows before Eric could catch a glimpse of him.

The hall was crowded. A good fire burned in the central hearth, even though the evening was far from cold and all food preparation was done across the yard in the kitchen. It was a far cry from simpler homes, where a single fire served all aspects of living; cooking as well as heating. Around this fire sat the Tilneye family, which would have been surprising to anyone unfamiliar with their ways. Unlike most families of their rank, who habitually took their seats on the elevated dais, the Tilneyes preferred the comfort of their fireside. It was, Eric remembered, more important to them than the need to remind their villeins and serfs constantly of their superiority in rank.

'Eric, my old friend! What brings you here?' called out John as soon as he caught sight of the visitor.

'I come in request of a favour,' replied Eric with an embarrassed half smile. He bowed apologetically to John's parents.

'Eric dear!' cried Lady Clare of Tilneye. 'We haven't seen you for far too long! How is your dear mother? Is she quite over the ague?'

'She is, thank you, my lady,' smiled Eric. John's mother had always been kind to him. He remembered the days when he and John had returned from their long, usually very dull lessons with their tutor and were welcomed with Lady Clare's cosseting. Her insistence on his joining the family to share their ale and honey cakes before returning to his own home in Wisbech was a happy memory that had always stayed with him.

'Husband, dear, do you not remember Eric?' she prompted when Sir Roland of Tilneye continued to regard the visitor with a total lack of recognition.

'Ah, young Eric de Bourne! So it is! It was the whiskers that threw me. The boy had a face as smooth as a ripe apple before. Very round, I seem to remember.'

Eric laughed good naturedly. He knew he was anything but good looking and was used to the odd uncomplimentary remark. John's two sisters looked up and giggled. They were both much younger than his friend and he remembered them from his earlier visits as little more than babies.

'A favour, you said,' prompted John in an attempt to change the subject. 'Let us take a walk and discuss it.'

He rose from the bench he had been sharing with his sisters and led Eric back across the hall and out into the dusk.

'My apologies for my father's comment. He does not always consider his words before he speaks, but he means no harm.'

'It is of no account,' smiled Eric. 'He was always good to me.'

'Well, yes. He means well. This favour, then. How can I help?'

'Sir Nicholas Drenge, the seneschal, has asked me to translate a document written in the old Saxon language. Some of it is straight forward, but there are faded sections which I can hardly make sense of at all. You were always much better at understanding the old language than I was, and I wondered whether you might take a look at it.'

'But if the ink has faded, how would I be able to interpret it any better than you?'

'You are more analytical than I. There are sections which could be put together from the words that are still legible. It needs a better understanding of the language than mine, though.'

'I rather think you flatter me, but, yes, why not? I could try, and two pairs of eyes are often better than one. Give it here and I'll take a look at it.' He held out his hand but then noticed the small dimensions of the scrip attached to Eric's waist. 'Where is it, then?'

'I'm sorry, but I couldn't bring it. The document has to be kept safe at the castle and is locked away at night. I wondered whether you might come to the office tomorrow and look at it. I'm sure Father Leofric would not object...'

'What? You mean you haven't even asked the old misery guts yet?'

'I thought it might be better to inform him once you've arrived. It would be too late for him to refuse by then. The Tilneyes command a lot of respect in Wisbech. He won't cross you.'

'I'm not sure that will be enough to stop him kicking my sorry backside out of his office, but yes, all right, but it can't be tomorrow. Too much going on with the spring sowing. How about the day after? I could finish my work here by midday and ride up to the castle.'

'Thank you. I am grateful.'

'It's nothing. Now, I'll get someone to fetch your horse...'

'I came on foot. It was too much bother to borrow a horse from the castle stables and I enjoy walking.'

'Well, you'd better take one of our horses. I'll walk to the castle on Wednesday and ride it back. I do wonder at your naivety sometimes, Eric de Bourne. You're not even armed! It'll be dark shortly and the river road between here and Wisbech is known for its footpads. There are too many lawless men about after dark. If the authorities took more interest in solving problems like that and worried less about worthless old documents, the world might be a better place.'

Eric was surprised to hear John speak in this way. He had changed since the old days, when he had been interested only in horses and eyeing up girls. He was beginning to sound more like his father, Sir Roland.

A girl crossed the yard in front of them, the same young girl who had answered the door to Eric on his arrival. As she passed John, she visibly altered her gait, swaying her hips in a way that was obviously provocative and anything but childlike.

'Goodnight, then!' John called to her, grinning.

Eric raised his eyebrows in disbelief. In some ways, his old friend had not changed at all.

TWENTY-FIVE

Feast of St Pachomius; Wednesday 9th May

John had been right about his lack of welcome at the chaplain's office.

All afternoon Father Leofric had been showing his disapproval with thunderous looks and loud harrumphing noises. Right from the start, things had not gone well. In order for an extra desk to be fitted in for John, it had been necessary for all the existing furniture in the small office to be moved. The extra desk had had to be fetched from the dustiest depths of the keep and time wasted in wiping it down to remove layers of ancient cobwebs. At long last, John had been able to take his seat and begin some work.

Throughout all this upheaval, Father Leofric had bitten his lip and passed no comment. As Eric had anticipated, the Tilneyes were so well regarded in Wisbech and the manors to the south of the town, that the priest had thought it best to say nothing. Instead, tension was allowed to simmer unpleasantly all afternoon. Occasionally, one of the younger clerks cleared his throat or sniffed and Eric sighed a lot on account of his struggles with a very long letter he was penning to the bishop. He was relieved to have someone else working on the charter, but could see that John was far from happy about it.

John straightened the long document as well as he could on the steep slope of his desk, allowing the top of the scroll to hang down the back of the desk. He had already succeeded in interpreting sections of partly faded script which Eric had failed to do. It was really not too difficult if you applied some logic. John had the sneaking suspicion that Eric had not tried very hard.

He had reached a badly stained section of the charter which referred to the manors of Walpole gifted to Ely Abbey and was working through a long description of a small piggery and a chapel with two altars and nine lights. It might, John thought with increasing impatience as he dipped his pen into the ink well, have saved everyone a lot of bother had such pointless detail been omitted. He tried to curb his frustration, continuing to add to the paragraphs that Eric had left unfinished.

There came a point when he could hide his irritation and boredom no longer. He yawned, and the yawn was so mighty that his jaws made a cracking sound.

'Since one of my clerks has displayed his ineptitude in bringing you here, boy, you could at least try to hide your disdain.' The chaplain's words, releasing some of his pent up anger and impatience, sounded as brittle as gravel falling on stone.

'I apologise, father.' John did not bother with excuses. There was no point. The sooner that peace reigned again, the better it would be for everyone.

Heavy silence resettled on the office and John bent his head once more over the document. After an hour or two, he had succeeded in deciphering most of it, but wondered why he and Eric had been put to so much bother. As his friend had found, there was nothing of great substance in the charter and the seneschal's interest was hard to understand.

He lay down his pen, having had quite enough of the office and its tedious atmosphere. He had done what Eric had asked of him and he was ready to leave. The horse he had lent to his friend a couple of days earlier was still in the castle stables. It was time to release him and ride home.

But then the door opened, and for John of Tilneye everything changed.

TWENTY-SIX

Rose

A young woman stood there, her slim form framed by the doorway. She looked at that moment as taken aback by the five pairs of male eyes regarding her as they were surprised to see her. The breeze lifted her fine linen veil so that it billowed out at the back as she stepped into the room.

'I apologise for the interruption, father,' she said, 'but I am looking for Eric de Bourne. I understand that he is working on my grandfather's charter.'

'Ah!' sang out Father Leofric, who had been instantly and miraculously transformed from a curmudgeonly middle aged priest to an avuncular, smiling personification of charm. 'You must be Rose de Hurste! Well, my dear lady, come in, come in. How may we be of service?'

Rose smiled, looking mildly embarrassed to be intruding. Nevertheless, the smile reached her blue eyes and widened to display neat, white teeth.

'I should have given my name to begin with, father. Again my apologies. I cannot stay long, but I need to speak to Eric if he is the clerk tasked with working on my grandfather's charter.'

Eric had been gazing at this vision of beauty as if in disbelief that such an exotic creature could walk the same earth as him. He realised too late that he was staring open mouthed and in his confusion found himself incapable of speech.

With an impatient grunt, Father Leofric spoke for him.

'Eric de Bourne has been working on your family's charter, but has passed the task to John of Tilneye. They studied together as boys and John has the better command of the Saxon language used in the charter.'

It was not difficult for Rose to tell which of the young men in the room was John of Tilneye. He was the one gazing boldly at her, apparently lacking the painful shyness displayed by the others. Rose's glance in his direction was quickly averted.

'Then, father, might I speak to John of Tilneye? It is important that I do so and I must be back at Hurste before nightfall.'

Father Leofric nodded indulgently, but John was already half way to the door.

It was then that his usual unwavering confidence did something it had never done before. It threatened to let him down. As he followed Rose out of the office, he suddenly found himself in the ludicrous position of being almost as tongue tied as Eric. Never before had he cared about not being particularly handsome. His good humour and easy charm had always made up for the way his pinkish complexion sometimes clashed with his fiery red hair. Now, however, he was aware with crushing clarity of his own limitations.

Rose was looking at him expectantly, apparently unaware of the effect she was having on him. He pulled back his shoulders, took a deep breath and tried to take control of himself.

'You wished to speak to me, lady? Let us find somewhere out of the wind to sit. May I fetch you some ale?'

'Thank you, but no. My companion and I have already been given refreshment in the great hall.'

She glanced across the bailey towards the imposing wall of the keep. Sitting by the steps to the forebuilding was a plainly veiled and wimpled young woman. She raised her head and looked soberly at her mistress. John found a bench close to the stables and out of the wind. He made sure it was well away from both the keep and the office. The companion, as far as John could tell, made no attempt to follow her mistress, but he had the feeling that she remained somewhere nearby, observing them.

'I came here today to see the seneschal,' began Rose as soon as they were seated. 'He came to visit my mother a few days ago and seemed determined to discover who was responsible for setting fire to my grandfather's house; for causing his death.' She paused, blinking and swallowing hard. 'Sir Nicholas also showed interest in certain items belonging to my grandfather which I assume have not been recovered since the fire. My mother told him that those things, which were important to my grandfather, were nothing but cheap trinkets. She then went on to tell the seneschal about the charter.'

'The Charter of Oswy and Leoflede.'

'Yes. My mother told the seneschal that any rumour he might hear about the charter leading to some sort of treasure was nonsense. The seneschal hadn't even raised the subject of the charter, so my mother's warning must have seemed strange to him.'

'I see,' replied John slowly, understanding at last why the seneschal had wanted the charter translated. 'And you, lady? Do you believe that the charter leads folk to something of value?'

'I do, sir. I believe it because my grandfather told me it is true. I was very close to him, though his own daughter, my mother, never was. He used to show me those old family treasures, and I can tell you, sir that they were not cheap trinkets, as my mother claims. Even as a child I could tell those things were very fine indeed. My father, Mortimer de Hurste, owns many beautiful things, but none are superior to those kept by my grandfather in that small box. I believe those treasures were what the charter was said to lead to.'

John frowned. This was all news to him and he was surprised that the lady was entrusting him with so much information.

'I also believe, sir, that someone tried to take that box from my grandfather. In doing so, they started the fire that caused his death. I am sure that they were led to his house by the charter...'

'I am sorry, lady, but I know nothing about the things you speak of. It is the seneschal himself you should be talking to.'

'That was my intention, but I was told he is absent today. I can afford to wait no longer. Please, sir, speak to the seneschal on my behalf. Tell him what I have entrusted to you. My mother misled him and I have no idea why.'

'I shall gladly do that. The seneschal is bound to be back soon; he has court hearings to preside over in a few days' time.'

He looked into her bright eyes and she looked hastily away, a slight blush colouring her creamy complexion.

'Thank you. There is, I am afraid to say, something else I must ask of you. Please study the charter carefully. There must be something there, something not immediately obvious. My grandfather told me that the document held some hidden clue. Please do your best to find it, sir, even if my grandfather's possessions are never recovered. The seneschal will see then that my grandfather was killed because of a search for treasure. Because of greed.'

She was looking at him earnestly, imploringly, leaning very slightly towards him on the bench. He nodded. It was impossible to refuse her.

'Have no fear, lady. I shall find whatever there is to be found. And now, you must start back for home. Where is your escort? Who travelled here with you and your companion?'

'No one. We had no escort, but shall be in no danger if we leave now and are home before nightfall. Before,' she added, 'my parents discover that we have ridden so far. They know nothing of my trip here today, and I would ask you and the seneschal to keep my visit a secret.'

'You have my word. But now we must leave.'

'We, sir?'

'Surely you don't think that I would let you and your companion ride home without an escort? Do not worry, none of your household will see me. Saddle your horses, lady, and meet me by the gate as soon as you can.'

Rose nodded and went to find her quiet companion. John went to saddle his horse, wishing that it was his own Albanac who greeted him as he entered the stable. The Marshmeade horse he had lent to Eric rewarded John with its own familiar whinny and, as John rode towards the gatehouse, his mind was more engaged with the thought of escorting Rose home than the quality of his mount.

As the three riders crossed the bridge over the castle dyke and made their way towards the Wysbeck, John spared no thought for the clerks or the chaplain whom he had neglected to notify of his departure. He would leave that problem for the morning. He would offer his apologies and return to the office. He was determined as never before to work on the charter. If the document hid any secrets, he would find them.

And it was all for Rose de Hurste. His desire to help her was as fervent as his appreciation of her charms.

TWENTY-SEVEN

Thursday, 10th May
Nobility

Sir Nicholas Drenge was hard at work in the Mote Hall office, writing as quickly as his pen would permit to fill the long pages of parchment before him.

People from out of town were beginning to arrive for the court hearings due to start on Saturday. Travelling from all parts of the Hundred, whether to defend their misdemeanours or to point the finger at erring neighbours, folk were gradually filling the back rooms and attics of all the hostelries and inns of Wisbech.

Dyke reeves representing manors from Thorney in the west of the Hundred to Welle in the east, were arriving too. Offences concerning the failure to maintain flood defences always featured heavily in the cases to be heard. The reeves frequently had to seek the backing of the law to force tenants to repair the river banks and dykes on their property. As the Hundred Court hearings drew closer, officials could be found in the town's inns, sharing an ale or two and shaking their heads over lamentable tales of rubbish dumped in dykes and pigs damaging river banks.

As for the seneschal, he had had precious little time to idle in ale houses recently, having dedicated so much of his energy to the charter situation. It had left him having to catch up with court work before the hearings and he was not, therefore, at all pleased when the Tilneye boy arrived to disturb him.

Having invited himself in, the youth stood there, looking rather full of himself, with an irritating grin on his face.

'Yes?' demanded Nicholas shortly. Already his eyes had lowered again and were refocusing on the page before him.

'Sir Nicholas?' persisted the visitor. 'I wonder if I might have a word? It concerns the translation of the charter which I have been helping Eric de Bourne with. My name is John of Tilneye.'

The seneschal looked up with reluctance but some curiosity.

'It appears that matters have moved on without my knowledge. I was unaware that Eric had sought help in the matter. And you, Sir John, I believe to be newly knighted, or so your father told me when I saw him last.'

'That is true, sir!' said John with another grin.

'Come and sit down, then. Wait while I complete this section and then we can talk.'

John did as invited, closing the door behind him and perching himself on a stool at the side of the large desk. He occupied himself with furtive glances at the seneschal, wondering how the man had managed to lose his hair so quickly. He looked youthful, but what was left of his fair hair clung to the lower part of his head and was bunched above his large ears, leaving a bald patch that would have made any monk proud. Sir Nicholas was clearly aware of being observed because he looked up crossly after writing only a few more words. He laid down his pen and regarded his visitor with obvious annoyance.

'What did you wish to say to me?'

'Eric and I have both been working on the charter, sir,' began John in a manner that was far more restrained than before. 'Eric had translated a lot of it, but asked me for help with some of the more stained and faded areas of the document. I made some progress but reached a point where I could do no more. But then,' he added with a smile, 'Rose de Hurste came to see me.'

'Rose de Hurste? Are you acquainted, then?'

'No, sir. In truth, she came to find you, but you were away from the castle. Someone must have told her that we were working on her grandfather's charter in the chaplain's office, so she came to seek us out. She entrusted me with what she needed to tell you and I gave my word that I would pass it on.'

'Very well, then, tell me everything Rose said.'

'She explained that some of what her mother had told you was misleading. Lady Rowena had apparently described items belonging to her father as cheap trinkets, but Rose says this is untrue, that those things were of great value. The lady then urged me not to give up with the charter. She seemed to believe that it contains clues leading to her grandfather's house and to items of great worth. I must admit, sir, that what she told me sounded nonsensical at first, but she urged me to repeat to you everything she told me.'

'Thank you, John,' Nicholas replied after a short pause. The young knight certainly had his full attention now. The seneschal had put to one side the half completed list of court cases and appeared to have forgotten its existence. 'What you have told me might well be of importance. May I second Rose's request? If you are willing, I would be grateful if you continued to work on the charter.'

'Of course, sir. I am happy to help.'

'Then I thank you. Look at it carefully. Try to see how it might have led someone to Aelfric's house.'

John frowned. Rose had not mentioned her grandfather's name and he had been too distracted by her charms to ask.

'Do you mean Aelfric the Saxon, sir? Was Rose's grandfather's house the one that burned down in the Old Market? She comes from a very old English family then.'

'And a very noble one. Her father, Mortimer de Hurste, was no fool when he married Rowena. Her family may by then have lost its wealth, but no one could take away their nobility.'

'So Rose is doubly blessed,' grinned John. 'Money and breeding. And such a beauty too!'

'If I were you,' said Nicholas darkly, in a way that reminded John of his father when displeased, 'I would concentrate on the charter and leave Rose in peace. Sir Mortimer will doubtless be considering several wealthy and worthy suitors for his daughter. His list is unlikely to include you.'

'Well not yet, anyway,' John retorted with another extremely annoying grin.

The seneschal shook his head as the youth stood up. He was too brash for his own good. He seemed bright enough, but his arrogance could well prove to be his downfall.

'Let me know, please,' Nicholas called to him as he reached the door, 'what progress you make with the charter.'

'Of course, sir,' John replied cheerfully. 'You may depend on that!'

John went straight from the Mote Hall to the chapel office. He knew there would be trouble. He was returning for the first time since his departure the previous afternoon when he had stepped outside to speak to Rose. Stony silence greeted him as he seated himself at his writing desk. He glanced surreptitiously around him. All the clerks looked uncomfortable, their heads bent over their work. No one, not even Eric, looked up to acknowledge his presence. The silence went on.

'Does it normally take so long,' came Father Leofric's growl once the silence had built to a pitch that was almost painful, 'to walk outside to see a young woman? Where are your morals, boy? Where are your manners? I did not want you here from the start, but I relented because Eric here was out of his depth. You have rewarded my condescension with appallingly poor conduct, boy!'

John's pinkish complexion had flushed a dark, angry red.

'Father, I...'

'I do not wish to hear it. Get on with your work and be quiet about it. I shall tolerate no further interruptions from you. I shall allow you to continue your work here only because you are helping the seneschal, but I hope your presence will be an extremely short one!'

John lowered his head and opened the long scroll once more on the desk before him. He knew the chaplain's anger was justified, but it made his ability to concentrate even weaker than usual. The silence gathered like dust once more around him, but at least it had lost its intensity now that Father Leofric had released some of his anger. Once, close to dinner time, Eric managed to turn his head towards John without being observed by the chaplain, and gave him a small smile. John was grateful for it as he continued to stare at the document before him.

If Rose was right, something was hidden there, but whatever secret the charter was hiding, it was doing it very well. It was giving nothing away, nothing but intolerably tedious descriptions of cesspits and tumbledown shacks. He suppressed a yawn, but then thought of Rose's eyes as she had appealed to him not to give up with the document.

He had to try harder. He bent his head once more over the Charter of Oswy and Leoflede and went on staring at it.

TWENTY-EIGHT

Same day; Thursday 10th May
Privilege

Brithun and Ordgar, the seneschal's men-at-arms, were once more keeping watch over the Old Market. As the days passed, the point of doing so was becoming harder to see, but they had had no orders to stand down and so the watch continued.

Though the constable's men also took their turn on watch, the seneschal's men found themselves more often on duty than most. Brithun and Ordgar, therefore, were becoming very familiar with the daily comings and goings in the Old Market.

The dilapidated riverside hostelry, with its broken wooden sign depicting a badly carved ship, always seemed to be doing a good trade. By day, the bench outside was occupied by the same drunken group of locals who kept up a rowdy commentary about everything that went on in the square. As the hours passed and they became increasingly incoherent, they attracted more and more attention from the waspish Goodwife Aswig and her sharp elbowed neighbour.

Around mid morning each day, the two women took a break from their housework and met on the corner by the screened off buildings. Glaring disdainfully at the drunks, they delved gleefully into their daily dissection of the latest gossip. Whatever work tool they had most recently been using was usually tucked under one arm while they nattered. Sometimes it was the long handle of a besom brush, other times a bucket or a wooden spoon. Nearly always, their hands were still white with flour from the morning's bread making. Folding their bony arms, they passed satisfying judgement on everyone and everything. Most of it was lavished on the noisy fools outside the Ship, but the women always had plenty to spare for the two men-at-arms.

'I'd like to know what that law man of yours is playing at,' Goodwife Aswig announced on an almost daily basis. 'Why don't you just arrest that cobbler and his two useless sons? I don't know why you don't just get on with it.'

Brithun and Ordgar rarely bothered to reply these days. They soon discovered that she went away more quickly when she saw she was getting nowhere. They rarely saw the cobbler himself, who remained out of sight in his workshop. They knew he was in there, though; the sounds of his hammering could usually be heard through the open shutters as he worked at his bench. His two sons, however, made regular appearances. Once or twice a day, one or the other lolloped across the square on some errand or other, sometimes glancing furtively at the sectioned off ruins, but never quite approaching them.

The business belonging to Burdo the basket maker was regularly busy. The goods displayed beneath the window of his workshop must have held some attraction because the womenfolk of the Old Market often stopped to look. Many of them went inside to buy, emerging with a useful looking basket in which to store their vegetables or linen. As far as the men-at-arms were concerned, Burdo was a good man. Anyone who so diligently and regularly crossed the square to bring them cups of ale had to be good. His thoughtfulness was particularly appreciated when the day was warm and their watch longer and more tedious than usual.

It was unfortunate that the soldiers happened to have been enjoying some of Burdo's ale when the sergeant had first come to check up on them. Though they were the seneschal's men, they were currently working in the sergeant's town and he considered it his duty to keep them in order.

Baldwin the sergeant had found them with the locals, having a good laugh and swigging ale as irresponsibly, in his opinion, as the half-wits outside the Ship. Brithun and Ordgar might have been mistaken, but they suspected he had relished the chance to catch them out. The seneschal had received his report concerning the men's conduct with astonishing speed. Sir Nicholas had duly reprimanded them, but it made no real difference. Burdo had just become more careful with his timing, the men more devious in hiding their cups, full or otherwise. Convenient rabbit holes were soon found for them in the river bank.

On that particular Thursday, the sergeant was spending far longer than was customary in the square. Brithun and Ordgar, who longed to retrieve their ale from the bank, stood outside the cobbler's workshop and watched Baldwin's activities with increasing frustration. He stood for a while and chatted to the raucous Ship regulars before strolling across the square to share what appeared to be a friendly word with the two resident gossips. The day was warm and Goodwife Aswig had the sleeves of her loose gown folded back to reveal her thin elbows. The men-at-arms heard her screech with laughter about something the sergeant had said before she and her companion made their way back to their houses.

Bringing themselves to attention, the men-at-arms braced themselves for the sergeant's daily inspection. The sergeant disappeared from view for a moment, but they went on waiting. The square was still quite busy, even with Goodwife Aswig and her friend back indoors, but there was no longer any sign of the sergeant. The men-at-arms moved further into the square, but still could not see him. Thinking at last that he may have walked out towards the open fields of Sandyland, Brithun and Ordgar considered sneaking back to their cups for a sip of ale.

But then they saw him. The sergeant was standing close to the tall screens surrounding the ruined buildings. He had been hidden by passersby, but now the soldiers had a clear view of him. He appeared to be detaching something from his girdle as he approached the gate set into the screens.

'He has a key,' remarked Brithun with a frown. In all their time of watching the square, neither of them had seen anyone entering the closed off area.

'His privilege, I suppose,' commented Ordgar.

The gate swung shut behind Baldwin as he disappeared inside the enclosure and the two men walked slowly towards the screens. The basket maker was standing at the door of his workshop and he too appeared to be watching. Apart from the seneschal's men, he seemed to be the only person in the square who was remotely interested in the sergeant's activities.

Baldwin was still inside the enclosure by the time Brithun and Ordgar arrived at the screens. As he made his exit, he came face to face with the soldiers. He scowled as he locked the gate.

Behind them, the basket maker went back inside his workshop and closed the door.

'Is something amiss, sir?' queried Brithun as the sergeant casually replaced the key on the ring attached to his girdle.

'Amiss? Why should there be?'

'Why did you enter the closed off area, sir?' asked Ordgar in a far more direct manner.

'It is not for you to query my actions, soldier.'

'But it is, sir,' persisted Ordgar. 'We have instructions from the seneschal to watch the square and so I must ask you your reasons for going into the burned out buildings.'

The sergeant made a low growling sound in his throat.

'Can a man not take a leak in peace?' he demanded. 'Mind your own business, soldier. Your seneschal will hear of this.'

'A leak?'

'Do you not understand English, or don't Ely men pee like ordinary folk?'

'You went in there for a *pee*?' queried Brithun with a disbelieving frown.

The sergeant threw the men an enraged look, refusing to engage any further in discussion. He strode rapidly across the square towards the river.

'I wonder why he can't pee on the river bank like everyone else,' commented Brithun as they followed him to the ford and watched him splash his way across the knee high water.

'I thought that myself,' agreed Ordgar, 'and now he'll be going to the great hall, close to all the privies any man could have need of.'

'Exactly. So why pee behind the screens?'

'How much would you wager, that the seneschal never receives this particular report from the sergeant?'

'The odds would not be worth the trouble. We could, however, report it ourselves.'

'We should consider it our duty,' remarked Ordgar with a grin.

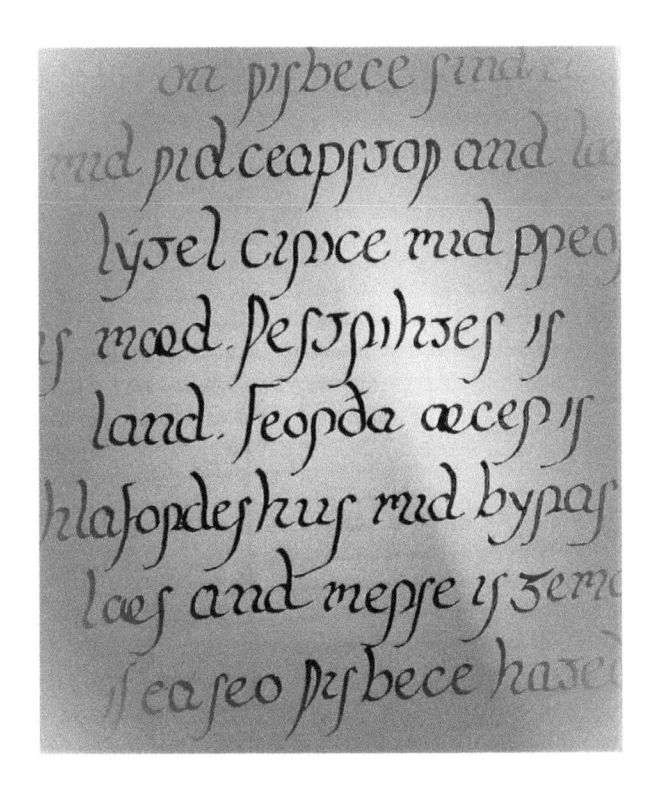

TWENTY-NINE

Feast of St Walter de L'Esterp; Friday 11th May

Sir Roland of Tilneye was heartily displeased with his son. Spring was a busy time of year, with the sheep shearing and the sowing of peas and beans to be seen to on the many acres of demesne land. Yet, it seemed that all the boy wanted to do was to pore over a pointless old document at the castle. And all because of some ill advised promise to a friend.

It was just as well that Sir Roland was ignorant of his son's real incentive. Whereas he understood, however grudgingly, that a promise should be honoured, he would have been far less impressed with a pursuit of romance. As far as Sir Roland was concerned, marriage for John would be considered only when he was mature enough to take on the responsibility. Until then, any courtship would be a waste of time, one which would take the young man's attention away from his training for his future manorial role.

Despite his father's disapproval, John returned to work at the chaplain's office on Friday. He was growing very familiar with the charter and knew by heart many of its antiquated terms, yet still it held on to whatever secret it was hiding. John was at a loss to see how he would ever achieve a breakthrough.

Outside, the May weather continued to be fine; perfect conditions for working in the fields. He fully understood his father's frustration and had to admit to himself that he shared some of it. He knew he should be outside, working with the villeins and serfs, but he had made a promise to Rose and could not give up with the charter. With increasing regularity, however, his attention wandered as he listened to the birdsong that reached him through the single lancet window on the south-east wall. Through that window too shone a golden beam of sunlight that seemed determined to taunt him about all he was missing outside.

As the long morning hours stretched by, John watched the steady progress of the sunbeam across the office. It was like a sundial, he thought, a measurement of time that mocked his lack of progress while informing him how long remained before dinner. He was hungry as well as bored and dinner time would bring a welcome break from his labours, as well as food.

At least the atmosphere in the office had improved on the previous day. The chaplain was engrossed in a huge tome that overlapped his desk and looked, from the single glance John had had of it, even more mind-numbingly dull than the charter he was working on. Though the tension of yesterday had lessened, John still found the silence uncomfortable. Even worse than the silence, though, was when it was broken by a sigh, sniff or cough. He found those interruptions increasingly irritating and he wondered how Eric tolerated working there, day after day.

He put his head down again and continued to work on the most faded parts of the text. If there truly was a message hidden there, John reasoned that it had to be in the sections which so far had eluded him and Eric. By holding the document towards the strip of sunlight that angled its way in through the narrow window, he had managed to make out a few more words, but they had turned out to be describing nothing more exciting than a cow shed in Debenham. He had barely managed to stifle an exasperated curse at that point and Father Leofric had peered around the slope of his desk and scowled darkly at him. After that, John had discovered hardly anything else, though a few more of the gaps left by Eric on the translation sheet were now filled. His friend's neat handwriting, which still formed the great majority of the work, was now defaced by John's untidy additions.

He suppressed a yawn, noticing that the sunbeam had reached the slope of his desk. Idly, he turned the charter so that the light fell on it, forming a neat, bright stripe down the centre of the page. His stomach had started to rumble and he was sure that Father Leofric would remark on it soon. He longed even more for his dinner.

But then something caught his eye. It seemed nothing much at first, just a happy accident that the heading of 'Wisbech' found itself in the centre of the band of sunshine. He followed the illuminated stripe down the page, noticing how a narrow column of words had become highlighted. They were suddenly so brightly lit that everything written on either side was rendered practically invisible.

The word 'ceapstow' or 'market place', he noticed, was written immediately below the heading of 'Wisbech'. And just below that, he read 'cirice' or 'church'. Curiously, his eye followed down to the next line, reading 'Þestrihtes' or 'to the west' beneath the word 'church'. Below that, was written 'feorþa' or 'fourth' and on the line beneath that he found 'hus' or 'house'. His eye continued to follow the script down the page, but after 'hus', no further words stood out clearly.

wisbece

ceapstop

cirice

westnihtes

feorða

hus

He frowned and lined up the highlighted words in his head;

Wisbech

market place

church

to the west

fourth

house

He sat back and stared. Could it really be so simple, so obvious? After all the long hours that he and Eric had laboured over this ridiculously tedious document, could the directions to Aelfric's house really have been written in such plain sight? Yet, it was likely that those words would have remained hidden from his eyes had that ray of sunshine not illuminated them and set them apart from the rest.

He realised that Eric had turned his head and was looking at him curiously. Even Father Leofric was peering around his desk again and was regarding him steadily.

'What is it, boy?' the priest enquired without his usual crossness. 'Have you discovered something?'

'I think I may have done so, father.'

'Then go and see the seneschal straight away. After that, you can come back and remove the desk that had to be lugged in here for you. We shall all benefit from having room to breathe again.'

John grinned, though the chaplain was perfectly serious. He left his desk and, clutching the scrolled charter and its translation, made a quick exit from the room.

John of Tilneye was not quite ready to see the seneschal, however. He had to make sure first that he was right, that what he had found fitted everything that had been going on in Wisbech over the past few weeks. He walked through the gatehouse and over the bridge, turning along the main street into town. He kept walking until he reached the New Market place then stood on the southern edge of it, looking across the square.

Midday had brought its usual bustle to the New Market, but there were considerably more folk about than usual. They were filling the market place and crowding into the hostelries. John had never seen the place so busy. The craftsmen seemed to be doing a good trade too. A carpenter working outside his shop on a fine carved chest was attracting a lot of attention from would-be purchasers while a small crowd had assembled to look at the iron monger's new display of knives and spoons on the rack by his door. On the western side of the square outside the Swan, a dour looking peasant was unloading sacks of wheat from a cart, attracting a flock of pigeons that landed with cautious grace to peck at a few spilled grains.

John tried to ignore the crowds, directing his gaze towards the northern edge of the square. He studied the long row of mismatched buildings that made up that side of the market place. Most of them were in good repair, though others looked like they stayed upright only by leaning against each other. He counted them, right to left. He smiled. He was right.

He turned and walked back through the New Market and past the castle gates. Fording the shallow river, he entered the Old Market. He stood with his back to the river, looking towards the square's northern side. This time, however, there was no satisfied smile. He thought for a while, then took to walking around and speaking to a few of the folk gathered outside the basket maker's workshop and the Ship. Most of the hostelry's clientele were too befuddled with ale to be of any help, but one of the eldest spoke some sense and told him what he needed to know.

With an air that was almost smug, John strode back towards the castle. He needed to see the seneschal, but even more importantly, he had to eat. Entering the bailey, he went straight to the great hall.

THIRTY

Noon
In Plain Sight

'As grateful as I am that you've found something in that document,' Eric was saying while chewing on a hard lump of gristle in his pottage, 'if you don't get that desk out of the way soon, he'll blame me. And if you'd ever had one of Father Leofric's cuffs round the ear, you'd know what I'm talking about.'

'Don't worry,' promised John as he removed an indigestible piece of meat from between his teeth. 'I'll see to it straight after dinner. What *is* this stuff we're eating? Castle food is usually excellent. This is terrible.'

Eric laughed as he persevered with another chewy mouthful.

'Your trouble is you're too used to fine living. You're accustomed to sitting up there at the high end of the hall, enjoying the kind of dishes the constable and his guests eat. We lowly clerks have to sit back here at the low end of the hall and put up with grub like this. You're far too pampered, it strikes me, John of Tilneye.'

John grinned.

'Maybe you're right. Lucky to have meat at all, I suppose. Many poor wretches never have a taste of it. What sort of meat is this anyway?'

Eric shrugged.

'No one ever asks. It's just meat.'

As soon as they had finished eating, John and Eric carried the offending desk out of the chaplain's office. Once it was standing outside, John would have delegated its removal to the keep to the castle servants, but Eric would not hear of it. Such idleness, he warned, never went down well with Father Leofric, and he would be bound to find out. Eric and John therefore lugged it as far as the forebuilding steps, but after they had hauled it awkwardly up one or two of them, Eric made no further protest when John hailed two passing serfs. Ordered to heft the desk up the rest of the steps and into the keep, the serfs obligingly put down the bundles of laundry they were carrying and obeyed.

Brushing dust from his tunic, John made his way to the Mote Hall. He had only just entered the building, however, when he came to an immediate halt. The main hall and office were heaving with people. Though they were all decked out in their best clothing, John could tell from their strange accents and awkward manners that they were country folk. They looked oddly out of place in the formality of the Mote Hall.

John had forgotten all about the Hundred Court hearings, which were due to begin the next day. They were, he realised, the reason for all the strangers he had seen in town. He swore under his breath. He could hardly have picked a worse time to speak to the seneschal, but he was unwilling to leave his news to another time and so he waited. He leant against the back wall of the office and watched as the country folk registered their attendance. There was a clerk, he saw now, sitting at the seneschal's side, who was recording the arrival of each defendant and accuser whose cases were listed before him.

When at last the crowd had dispersed, Sir Nicholas bent his head over the lists with the clerk as they discussed the following day's hearings. They both seemed unaware of John, who was now standing right in front of the desk.

While he waited, he unbuckled his scrip and pulled out the scrolled charter and its translation. The ancient document had not fared well from being shoved into the scrip and was now badly bent and squashed. Hastily, he smoothed out some of the worst creases.

At long last, the clerk rose from his seat, making a small bow as he left the room.

'John of Tilneye,' said the seneschal flatly when he finally noticed the youth. 'How may I be of assistance?'

'I hope, sir,' replied John cheerfully, 'that I may be of assistance to you. I think I have found what Rose de Hurste believed was hidden in her family's charter.'

The seneschal was beginning to look less inconvenienced.

'You've found a connection between the charter and Aelfric's house in the Old Market?'

'I have, sir.'

'Then tell me, but don't be long about it. I fear I can spare little time...'

'I know sir. The Hundred Courts and all that...'

John unrolled the crumpled charter and laid it across the desk. The seneschal's desk was not of the high sloping kind used by scribes and many clerks, but was wide and flat and of far more use to a man who spent more time in perusing documents than in writing them.

'You see here, sir, the heading for Wisbech,' John began. 'Beneath it are listed the buildings and land being gifted as part of the manor to Ely Abbey. All this detail distracts the eye from the message which is actually written in plain sight. If you look straight down the centre of the page and simply read the words directly in a line beneath the heading, the message becomes clear. Wisbech, market place, church, to the west, fourth and house. Beneath that, the line is broken and no further words are obvious.'

'God's eyes!' groaned Nicholas. 'Is that it? Is that what everyone has been alluding to? But how does it fit Aelfric's house? There is no church in the Old Market.'

'That's what I thought too at first, sir, so I went to the Old Market and talked to some of the older folk there. They told me they remembered a dilapidated, timber built church standing by the river many years ago, on the north-eastern corner of the square. They'd been told as children that it had fallen into disrepair when the Normans built their church next to the castle. Everyone in the town had to attend the new one, leading to the church in the Old Market being abandoned. Eventually, I suppose, it just fell down.'

'So,' said the seneschal, 'anyone finding these words in the charter, who knew the Old Market's history, could follow the directions to its market place. Then, starting from where the old church used to be, they could identify the fourth house to the west of it. That would be on the northern-most side of the square.'

'Yes, and I counted,' said John. 'The fourth building along that side of the square, after a grain store and two small dwellings, was indeed the Big House, where Aelfric lived.'

'Whoever broke into and burned his house must, therefore, have seen this charter, or taken directions from someone who had.'

'Yes, sir, but that's not all. I went to the New Market place too. Starting from St Peter and Paul's Church and looking westwards, anyone trying to work from this charter could either count the houses along the northern or southern sides of the square. I tried both. The southern side leads to nothing significant. However, the fourth building along the *northern* side just happens to be the home of an elderly and impoverished widow which Baldwin told me a few weeks ago was broken into.'

Nicholas frowned.

'I do remember the constable telling me about that. The break-in seemed pointless, as the poor woman had nothing worth stealing.'

'Perhaps that break-in,' replied John, 'was the first attempt of whoever was following the instructions in the charter to find the treasure reputed to lie inside "the fourth house". It would have been an easy mistake to make, because anyone seeing the word "church" would naturally think of St Peter's and assume the wording applied to the New Market. They probably forgot that when the charter was written Wisbech consisted only of what we now call the Old Market. No New Market would have existed back then. The culprit must presumably have realised their mistake and turned their attention to the Old Market.'

'An excellent point. But what about this "treasure", as Lady de Hurste called it? Is it mentioned in the charter?'

'Not that I could see, sir, so that remains a puzzle.'

'Even so, you think logically, John of Tilneye. You've gone to a considerable amount of effort.'

'Thank you, sir. I wonder whether whoever caused all this grief found what they were looking for.'

'I have queried that myself. Nothing of value has been found in the ruins of Aelfric's house. If the thief managed to take what he was looking for, he will have left town long ago. However, if he failed, he might still be somewhere close. The Old Market is watched night and day in case he returns to search the ashes of the Big House.'

He looked pensive for a moment but suddenly seemed to remember the day's priorities and brought the conversation to a close.

'Thank you for your persistence,' he said with a smile. 'I greatly appreciate what you have done, but now I must continue my preparation for tomorrow's hearings.'

He sat back in his chair as John, accepting his dismissal, began to roll up the document and take it away.

'And you can leave that here!' demanded Nicholas, more harshly than he had intended. 'It needs to be locked away again before you do it any further damage.'

The young knight placed the scroll back on the desk, looking somewhat deflated as he made his exit. Nicholas had no time to think about the charter now. He had to concentrate on the Hundred Court hearings. Only when they were done, could he afford to think about what John had discovered.

THIRTY-ONE

Feast of St Pancras; Saturday 12th May

The first day of the Hundred Court hearings was relentless. The seneschal heard and passed his well considered judgement on a whole host of cases, ranging from the more serious charges of assault and theft to the more trivial, such as women accused of being scolds and the inconvenient placement of dung heaps.

Nicholas dealt severely with the scolds. In each case he gave the woman a stern order to restrain herself from inflicting further misery on her long suffering husband and neighbours. Any recurrence of bad behaviour, he warned, would result in a considerable fine of ten pence. Regarding the cases involving the placement of dung, entrails and other obstacles in roadways or ditches, he ordered the perpetrators to pay an amercement of three pence to the court. They were warned that a further fine would follow should the blockage not be removed immediately.

The seneschal listened carefully to several cases concerning the wrongful appropriation of land, though some seemed hardly worthy of his time. In one situation, a man had been reported by his neighbour for enclosing and taking possession of six square feet of common land opposite his house. Most cases of purpresture, the illegal annexing of land, concerned acreage of more significant size. Nicholas decided to treat this case, however, in the same way as those involving larger areas; such perpetrators needed to be discouraged from taking greater liberties in future. He issued an order to distrain and an amercement of six pence. The distraining order would simply result in the tiny plot being returned to its previous use as common land.

The cases went on and on, interrupted only by a short break at midday, and the day passed quickly for the seneschal. The clerk seated at his side worked tirelessly, scratching away with his quill as he noted down the details of each case. He would later write up his notes to be kept as official court records.

Nicholas was kept too busy to think about John of Tilneye's findings in the charter. It was not until mid afternoon, when he was trying to concentrate on a particularly tedious case concerning animal entrails dumped in a stream, that his attention began to wander.

The neighbour presenting his complaint against a March butcher who had fouled a watercourse was extremely long winded. He described in fulsome detail how the sheep's entrails had spoiled the water supply so that it could no longer be used for brewing. The seneschal agreed with all he said and was ready to pass judgement on the butcher, but the neighbour, who was enjoying being the centre of attention, was hard to stop. Nicholas found his thoughts straying more and more to the charter, a subject he found infinitely more interesting than offal. Curtly, he stopped the complaining neighbour in mid flow and pushed the charter to the back of his mind.

On Sunday he was at last at liberty to think. The Hundred Court would not sit again until Monday, leaving free this day of rest. He attended Mass in the small castle chapel where Father Leofric officiated. The familiar Latin words drifted peacefully through the chapel, but even as Nicholas uttered the responses he had known since childhood, his thoughts were straying on to other things.

He knew that John of Tilneye, for all his arrogance, was right. Whoever had broken into the house in the New Market had soon realised their mistake and had turned their attention to Aelfric's home. Therefore, they had to be aware of the words hidden in the charter. That meant that they had either read those words themselves, or had spoken to someone who had.

As far as Nicholas was aware, only two copies of the charter existed; one in Ely Abbey, the other locked inside the chest in the constable's office in Wisbech Castle. He knew how securely the Wisbech copy was stored, that only the constable and his deputy had access to it, but what of Ely's? Although he was confident that the document there would be safe in the care of the armarius, it would be a good idea to find out who might have seen the document in the past few months.

The seneschal sent a message to Ely as soon as Mass was over. His note to his deputy was carefully worded, requesting that he visit the scriptorium and library at the abbey. He needed his deputy to find out all he could and emphasised the need for immediate action. The messenger Nicholas chose rode the swiftest of coursers and would waste no time in reaching Ely.

Monday in the Mote Hall brought a fresh list of cases. He listened to each and every one with proper consideration, trying to be fair, however hard his patience was tried. For now, these hearings were keeping him in Wisbech, but once they were over he had a decision to make.

It was no longer likely that the miscreant who had burned Aelfric's house and caused his death would be found. The seneschal's most sensible course of action, therefore, would be to return to Ely. He would still be able to keep a distant eye on the situation in Wisbech, leaving things in the capable hands of the constable.

Yet something was holding him back. He was finding more reasons for staying than for leaving and he decided to delay his return at least until he received a reply from his deputy. It was just possible that something useful would be discovered in Ely.

THIRTY-TWO

Subterfuge

On the same Saturday that Sir Nicholas Drenge was presiding over hearings in the Mote Hall, John of Tilneye was on his way to Hurste Manor. He had been to oversee work on his family's demesne land north of Wisbech and on impulse, having finished there early, had decided to continue along the road towards Hurste in the northernmost part of the shire.

He passed a good number of travellers on the road, all taking advantage of the fair weather, and his palfrey Albanac ambled along at a satisfactory pace. John was enjoying the ride, especially now that Rose and Hurste Manor lay at the end of it. Only when he had passed Tydd St Giles and was drawing close to his destination did he begin to think things through properly.

When the idea had first occurred to him, he had imagined going straight to the manor house and asking to speak to Rose. It now dawned on him that doing so would bring her a lot of trouble. She had ridden to Wisbech to see the seneschal without her parents' consent and circumstances had led to her placing her trust in John. He could hardly betray that trust now through his own rash stupidity.

This sudden realisation slowed his progress considerably. When he finally arrived at Hurste, it was hesitantly, not at all as boldly as he had originally intended. He passed the first small homes of the village, hardly hearing their barking dogs or seeing the women who fed livestock or carried heavy baskets of linen to dry on low trees and bushes. He was puzzling over what to do while gradually becoming aware of the attention his fine palfrey and expensive clothes were drawing. Men on their way to the fields, children who played at the side of the road and the women with their laundry were all pausing to stare as he passed by.

They would expect him to ride straight to the manor house. Any stranger dressed as well as he invariably did just that, yet circumstances dictated that he would have to conduct himself in quite a different way. He understood at last how irrationally he was behaving. If he were to speak to Rose at all, he would have to wait until she left the house and hope that she did so without the rest of her family.

Quite apart from simply wishing to see her again, he wanted to let her know that he had succeeded in doing what she had asked of him. He had found the hidden words in the charter and had informed the seneschal. Although the law man was temporarily distracted by court hearings, John had no doubt that he would act on the information as he saw best.

As he drew nearer to the manor house, he was relieved to find a hostelry situated conveniently close to the manor's gates. He led Albanac into the run-down stable at the back of the hostelry, removing the horse's bridle and making sure he had a plentiful supply of oats and drinking water. John knew that he might have a considerable wait ahead of him and it was helpful to have his horse safe and out of sight, attracting less attention.

The ale house was as shabby as the stable and it was dark, its single window still half shuttered to admit only the narrowest shaft of daylight. Unbothered by such minor inconveniences, he found himself a bench just inside the doorway, a position which provided a clear view of the manor house gates. He settled himself with his ale to wait.

And the wait was long. People left the manor house and people entered. Carts and riders passed through the gates, but there was no sign of Rose. In fact, no one of her rank left the house at all. Perhaps, he was beginning to think, the Hurste family disliked fresh air. He thought briefly of his mother, about how on a day like this she would be out, visiting the cottagers on the manor and overseeing work in the bake house and kitchen. She loved to feel the sun on her face. As did he, he acknowledged.

But still the only folk to pass through the gates were tradesmen and the occasional dour looking visitor. John drank more ale, ate some of the day old bread and hard cheese on offer and chatted idly with the hostelry keeper. His hopes of seeing Rose were gradually seeping away, along with his good humour. If the wait went on for much longer, he thought, he would end up as dour as the house's visitors.

It was well past noon when Rose de Hurste, accompanied by the same young woman as before, finally appeared at the gates of the manor and turned into the narrow lane.

John set down his cup and sprang to his feet. With a brief farewell to the hostelry keeper, he made his cautious exit. Rose had not seen him. She was looking straight ahead as she strolled along, every so often addressing a remark to her companion. Whenever they met people in the lane, however lowly their status, Rose either nodded or called out a greeting. John was having trouble keeping the ladies in sight without drawing attention to himself, and it was not until Rose had passed a long threshing barn and had reached a quieter part of the lane that he risked catching up with her.

'Lady!' he called quietly just before he reached her. She turned abruptly and looked at him with a mixture of astonishment and annoyance. Her companion looked disgruntled.

'Sir John of Tilneye! What brings you here?'

It was not quite the greeting he had been hoping for, but he was still smiling as he fell into step beside them.

'I came to tell you,' he said, 'about the work I have been doing at your request. On your family's charter.'

'Ah.' She hesitated, some of the crossness falling away from her voice. 'As I explained, sir, my family know nothing of my trip to Wisbech. I have to take care.'

'I understand and have no wish to bring you trouble. Is there nowhere we can speak safely?'

Rose's companion began to speak at that point, but she might as well not have done so. Her muttering was so quiet and incomprehensible that she could have been speaking in another tongue. She was also doing her best to avoid looking at John, her eyes darting about nervously and focussing on anything but him.

'Matilda is right,' said Rose after a lengthy, inaudible exchange. 'There is a workshop no one has used for a while. My father has not yet found a new tenant for it. Come this way and please be quick.'

John dropped back and walked some distance behind the two ladies as they continued along the lane, so that no chance encounter with a villager would result in idle gossip. They soon reached the workshop. The place was heavily shuttered and the door had to be pushed with some force to allow them inside. The workshop appeared to have been abandoned for some time. It smelled of dust and animal droppings and the earthen floor was bare of any covering.

'What is it that you wished to say to me, sir?'

Rose was still looking annoyed, but there was something else in her manner which John was quick to detect. He was sure she was enjoying the subterfuge. Her eyes were sparkling, however cross and inconvenienced she was pretending to be.

'I finally found something in your family's charter,' he said as soon as the door was firmly closed behind them. 'There are just a few words, nothing much at all, but they direct anyone finding them to your grandfather's house in the Old Market.'

Her face broke into a dazzling smile. She seemed unable to stop herself.

'Then my grandfather was right! There really *are* clues of some sort leading to his house! Thank you, sir. You are very good to have dedicated so much of your time to helping me and I wish I could have received you better today than in this shameful way.'

'No, the fault is mine. I should not have come here like this, but I wanted you to know about the progress that's been made and I...'

'And now you must go. I am grateful for all you have done, but now...'

'There is still something I am puzzled by, the seneschal too,' he persisted. 'Nothing in the wording I discovered referred to anything of value to be found in the house. No mention of treasure, in other words.'

'I believe you are right. I think the "treasure" silliness was always hearsay, perhaps someone's idea of a game. Long ago, when that legal document was drawn up, it appears that either its author or its scribe included a few clues that led to one of the properties being gifted to the abbey. Maybe it was just for their own entertainment. Then, perhaps they spread rumours of treasure to go along with it, and those tales have remained in people's minds for decades. In the end, it seems that someone followed those clues to my grandfather's home in search of that treasure and my grandfather died because of it.'

'And I am very sorry for what happened to him. Might I...'

'It is time for you to leave, sir. It is best that you do not come again, however grateful I am.'

'At least call me John, lady. My name is John.'

'Go, sir, and thank you.'

But it was Rose who departed, turning elegantly with a swishing of her long skirts on the earthen floor. She was followed wordlessly by Matilda, her companion. John was left alone to breathe in the stale air of the abandoned workshop and to kick the dust beneath his feet. When eventually he emerged into the lane, the ladies had disappeared from view.

THIRTY-THREE

Tuesday 15th May
Father Godweard

The town was quieter now. Everyone with cases to be heard, complaints to be made and grudges to be satisfied were now leaving the manor of Wisbech Barton. That was perhaps why the commotion coming from the riverside just after Mass on that Tuesday morning carried so very clearly to the ears of Father Godweard.

His small, solidly built church that was dedicated to Saints Peter and Paul had been full again that day, a good number of townspeople attending Mass before the start of their working day. There had, of course, been the usual nuisances, but he had dealt with them in his customary unflappable manner. The deacon had been sloppy when preparing for Mass, forgetting to cover the chalice immediately with the purificator. As a consequence, the chalice had been targeted by one of the many pigeons that roosted in the ancient thatch. The bishop, Father Godweard knew, would be horrified at the thought of birds fouling the chalice, but such was life. As he reminded himself, there were many more terrible things in the world than an absent minded deacon and incontinent pigeons.

Father Godweard was proud of his church, despite its modest size. The nave, with its narrow windows set into the thick stone walls, benefitted from very little natural light. Even on the brightest of summer days, the arrow slit shaped windows let in only the merest hint of sunshine. And yet, St Peter's invariably glowed with the honeyed light of many candles.

Beeswax candles were a luxury, yet the little church was blessed with an almost unending supply of them. They lent their flickering light to every corner of the building, illuminating the beauty of the wall paintings that covered the lime washed walls. Behind the altar, set neatly into the rounded apse at the eastern end of the nave, was a painting of the Last Supper. The disciples were depicted in lifelike detail, their robes painted in shades of red and green, their eyes reaching up to heaven.

The candles, as well as many other gifts and endowments, had been generously donated to St Peter's by the wealthier members of its congregation. Such gifts were made in the belief that their donor would be assured a swift transition to heaven when their earthly toils came to an end. Wealth brought the ability to show repentance for sins by means of generous contributions to worthy causes. Such payments reduced the need, as far as many rich folk were concerned, for the more tedious acts of repentance, such as fasting and excessive prayer.

As grateful as the priest was for these gifts, it was the poor of the town with whom he spent most of his time. While the rich gave orders and rested on their backsides, making grants to the Church in the hope of salvation, the poor laboured and suffered. However little they possessed, and however much they struggled, they still had to pay their tithes to the Church. But tithes, like taxes and servitude, were inescapable facts of life. For the poor, life was extremely tough.

With Mass over for the day, Father Godweard was preparing to visit Father Leofric at the castle chapel. He was slow in his movements, the almost constant damp having stiffened his joints, making speed next to impossible. He still had not removed his chasuble, the richly embroidered garment he wore over his alb during the Eucharist, when the noise from the river bank reached his ears.

Loud, shrill voices, mostly those of women, seemed to rise in a wave of panic. He abandoned his disrobing and walked as quickly as he could out of the church, gathering up the skirts of his long alb as he went. His legs, so long unused to speed, refused at first to move any faster, but after a few painful knee clicks he managed to break into a slow trot.

The commotion was coming from the vicinity of the ferryman's hut, a tiny cottage that nestled at the foot of the river bank and housed the ferryman and his wife. The Well Stream was the main river running through the town and, unlike the feeble Wysbeck by the Old Market, could not be crossed at high tide without a ferry.

A group was gathered outside the cottage, apparently trying to comfort the goodwife who stood in their midst with a soot blackened face. As Father Godweard drew closer, the members of the group noticed him and fell silent, turning their heads to watch his approach. Then, almost in unison, they started talking again, even more loudly than before. This time, however, their comments were addressed to him. Each voice tried to drown out the others, making their combined effort completely incomprehensible.

It was not difficult, though, for the priest to understand the gist of what had happened. As soon as he entered the cottage through its low doorway, the harsh tang of burned grasses and smoke assailed his nostrils and the scene before him told its own story. The floor rushes had been reduced to a few glowing stalks on the dried earthen floor. A charred bench and the remains of a board had been pushed into one corner. Near the central hearth lay a small leather purse, its drawstring pulled open and spilling its meagre contents on to the earthen floor. There were six or seven coins, halfpennies and farthings, which were cut segments of silver pennies. There was one whole penny too, which caught the gleam of light from the door. The pots on the hearth had been tipped over, spilling the pottage that had been cooking on the embers. Its herby scent, now mingled with smoke and burned debris, made the priest feel queasy as he examined the timber corner posts of the building. They were singed in places, but still looked sturdy enough.

The fire appeared to have been put out before it had had chance to destroy the building, and the damage was thankfully slight. It was nothing a good clean, fresh floor rushes and a new mess of pottage would not put right.

'What happened here?' he asked as he lowered his head again to leave the dwelling. The goodwife and her neighbours were watching him expectantly and, all at once, they began another discordant chorus of information. He put his hand up to silence them.

'Let the goodwife speak.'

The woman's sooty face was streaked with tears. One of her elderly male neighbours arrived with a stool from one of the other houses and she sank gratefully on to it.

'I caught a man in the house,' she said in a shaky voice. 'I'd been up on the bank, looking to see if my husband was coming back. He's gone out, you see, to visit the husbandman in Walsoken we buy our grain from. When the tide's out, he often goes wandering. No one needs the ferry to cross the Well Stream until the water's high again. No doubt he's holed up somewhere now with an ale or two. What he'll say when he sees this mess, I dread to think.'

She covered her face with her hands and began to weep noisily. Another neighbour, a kindly looking woman, handed her a cup of ale and the goodwife thanked her, but seemed to have forgotten all about answering the priest's question.

'The goodwife's in no fit state to talk, father,' said the neighbour. 'If I may, I shall tell you what happened.'

'Please do,' said Father Godweard, who was feeling in need of an ale or two himself.

'Goodwife Brona says she caught a stranger in her house when she returned from the bank top. He'd found the purse the ferryman keeps his earnings in and was about to make off with it. Brona was having none of that; she needed the money to pay for food from the market this Saturday, as well as the grain from Walsoken. So, she took her broom and swung it hard, knocking the purse out of the devil's hands and striking him around the head, didn't you, Brona?' The goodwife did not appear to hear, having buried her tear streaked face in the skirt of her gown, so the neighbour continued. 'He began to holler at her and she thought he would run. Well, she was right about that. He ran away like a coward, but not until he had knocked the rush light from the shelf on to the floor rushes. Before Brona had time to think, the place was on fire, but she took the pan of water from the hearth and managed to put some of the flames out with that. By then, we'd heard all the goings-on and could smell the smoke, so we ran and filled buckets with river water. We managed to put out the fire before any real damage was done.'

'I have good neighbours, father,' sobbed the goodwife.

'That is very true, Goodwife Brona,' smiled the priest, 'and I am sure they will help you to put the house right. The ferryman will, I suppose, fetch you fresh floor rushes when he returns?'

No one replied. The ferryman was not known for his gentleness and the priest suspected that the goodwife's tears were as much out of fear of her husband as they were from the shock of what had just happened.

'If there's trouble later,' he said quietly to the woman who had explained the situation, 'please come and tell me. I shall have words with the ferryman.'

'I hope that won't be necessary, father, but thank you. I shall make sure they have something to eat today. That pottage is well and truly wasted.'

'You are indeed a good neighbour. While you are seeing to that, I shall speak to the sergeant. This incident should be reported.'

The neighbour nodded and watched as Father Godweard made his way back to the church. When the priest turned back to glance at the group, they were still standing there, looking at him, as if not quite sure what to do next.

THIRTY-FOUR

The Ferryman

Father Godweard was enjoying a cup of ale and a simple meal in his room in the church tower when the seneschal arrived.

Sir Nicholas Drenge had heard about the fire in the ferryman's hut from the sergeant. Quite how much he could trust the sergeant, he was no longer sure. His men had reported Baldwin's suspicious behaviour behind the screens in the Old Market a few days earlier and, quite apart from that, the sergeant had been completely wrong about the tinker.

The seneschal had not, therefore, given Baldwin much of his time when he had come to report the fire on the riverside. Nicholas had pointed out that house fires, being fairly commonplace, did not require the attendance of the bishop's seneschal. The sergeant, he had stated, should see to the matter himself. But then Baldwin had told him of his hunch, that this fire was connected somehow with that far more serious incident a few weeks earlier in the Old Market.

Though unwilling to indulge the sergeant, Nicholas, since he was anything but overloaded with work, decided to go and look for himself.

Father Godweard was just about to bite into a piece of soft, fresh bread when he heard the south door opening in the nave below. The door always screeched as it opened, being swollen from years of damp, and it tended to drag itself over the stone flags. The priest did not move. People entered the church at all times of the day and usually they required nothing from him. As often as they came to pray, the townsfolk used the church as a meeting place, even somewhere in which to do business. Sometimes, they came in just to shelter from the rain.

The priest went on eating, glad of the chance to rest after the morning's panic. His accommodation on the first floor of the church tower was very simple, but it gave him everything he needed. It was just far enough below the bells that rang out regularly from the top of the tower to prevent early deafness, yet elevated enough to provide a good view of the town from its single, narrow window. He had a small brazier in the corner of the room which, together with a pile of woollen blankets, stopped him freezing in winter. During those long months of seemingly endless snow and frost, he spent much of the day by the fireside in the Swan in the New Market. The hostelry always kept a good fire going and its host had no objection to the priest toasting his toes on the hearth stones while enjoying a plentiful supply of ale, bowls of steaming pottage and freshly baked bread.

He was just cutting himself a slice of sheep's cheese and anticipating its creamy flavour, when he realised that someone was calling him.

Whoever he had heard entering the church had now reached the small door at the western end of the nave that led into the tower. The priest heard the door latch click. Then there was a voice calling up the stairway. Father Godweard heaved a sigh, sorely tempted to stay silent and pretend he was out. Yet the voice did not give up. It went on calling his name until the priest laid his wooden board and the remains of his meal on the floor and went downstairs.

'Ah, Father Godweard!' stated the visitor rather unnecessarily as the priest rounded the last turn in the narrow stairway.

The seneschal had a business like air about him, pleasant enough in his bearing, but he was clearly not someone who would fall for a priest's trick of pretending he was out.

'I suppose, my lord seneschal, you have come about the ferryman's cottage?' enquired the priest with what he hoped was an accommodating look.

'I understand you reported it to the sergeant earlier, father.'

'I did, sir, but regret I can add very little to what I told him earlier. I did not witness the fire; I arrived after it had been put out. Perhaps it would be better if you spoke to the goodwife herself? If you wish, I can take you there.'

Nicholas nodded.

'That would be helpful; thank you.'

As they left the church, the warmth and light of the May morning greeted them, reminding the priest how chilly the church was with its thick stone walls and narrow windows. The seneschal's two men-at-arms seemed to emerge from nowhere, accompanying the priest and seneschal across the small churchyard towards the river. It seemed to Father Godweard rather heavy handed for the law man to have brought armed men on such a venture.

Perhaps, he considered as he walked along, he should no longer be surprised by such precautions. These days there seemed to be danger and violence everywhere. The law did its best to keep the peace, but it was always wise to be alert. Even he, a priest, carried a knife when out alone after dark.

He was not sure he would know how to use it, but its presence gave him some reassurance.

They found the ferryman's cottage in a calmer and more organised state than when Father Godweard had been there earlier, though the smell of smoke still hung in the air. The neighbours had dispersed and the ferryman had returned, looking sour and angry about the state of his home. His wife sat on the charred bench in the corner, her face pale and puffy, as if she had only just stopped weeping. Father Godweard cast the ferryman a stony look and enquired when he planned to fetch new rushes for the floor.

'Once the floor is made good again,' he pointed out, 'there will hardly be any reminder of the fire.' He looked around and saw that the pots had been set upright again on the hearth. One of them, thanks no doubt to a kindly neighbour, even contained a fresh supply of pottage which cooked slowly on the embers.

'Tide's coming in again,' grunted the man. 'Folk will be needing the ferry. No time for house repairs today. One of the neighbours will do it. They love sticking their nose into our affairs.'

It was a good thing they did, thought Father Godweard.

'This,' he said coldly, 'is my lord seneschal. He needs to speak to you and your wife about the intruder and the fire.'

The ferryman, who had so far ignored the tall, well dressed stranger who was stooped uncomfortably beneath the low roof of the cottage, belatedly tried to improve his behaviour. He attempted a smile, but it looked more like a sneer.

'Good of you to come to see us, my lord seneschal,' he said begrudgingly. 'This felon might have taken my wife's life, all for a few pennies. He needs to be caught. You can see how upset she is.'

Nicholas doubted that the man cared much about his wife's state of mind. He moved across the room and crouched beside her in the corner.

'Sit here on the bench, my lord,' she said, recovering her manners and moving to make room for him, 'you too, father. This seat was not too badly spoiled by the fire.'

'I'll leave you to it,' stated the ferryman, having dropped his temporary veneer of politeness. 'I have work to do.'

'I too shall go,' said Father Godweard, but in a much gentler way. 'You will be in good hands with the seneschal, Goodwife Brona.'

The seneschal thanked him and perched himself on the end of the bench. The goodwife had visibly brightened up, he noticed. He suspected it had a lot to do with her husband's departure.

'Tell me what happened,' he prompted her gently.

'I was up on the bank and had left the door open, the weather being so fine,' she began in an agitated way. 'It was silly of me, but I trust the folk around here and didn't expect strangers to call, not with the ford being passable and there being no need for the ferry. When I walked back in, there he was. I saw him holding the purse we keep our takings in. The coins in that purse are all we have and I needed the money for grain and the market this week. Yet this stranger was standing there, bold as you like, in our home and about to take our money.

'I didn't think about it, just picked up the broom and swung at him. It took him by surprise, knocked the purse clean out of his hands. He started shouting and by then I was hollering too, hoping the neighbours would come to see what was happening. With so much racket going on, I thought he'd give up and run while he could still get away. But then he made things far worse. He deliberately knocked over the rush light I had burning in the corner there,' she said, pointing towards the darker end of the house. 'Before I knew it, the floor rushes had caught and then there were flames everywhere. I started to stamp them out and used water from the pot on the hearth, but the fire was getting out of control. I didn't see the devil leave, though he must have escaped while I was trying to put out the flames.'

'You did well, Goodwife Brona. You saved the house and stopped him taking your money.'

She shook her head.

'Without the help of my neighbours, we'd have lost the house. They were here in no time and helped me put out the fire.'

'What did this intruder look like?'

'He was tall like you, sir. He had to stoop while he was standing there with the purse in his hands. But thinner than you, sir, much thinner. I couldn't see much else of him on account of the long cloak and hood he was wearing. Dark like a monk's, it was, but he was no monk. The good brothers I have come across do not steal from poor folks' houses.'

'Did you see his face?'

'Not much of it. He kept his head down. Didn't want me to see him, that much was obvious, but coming to think of it, he had a big, broad nose. Nasty looking, he was.'

'Thank you, goodwife. Your description helps me a great deal.'

'Will he be caught, sir?'

'I shall do my best to make sure he is. And now, as Father Godweard said, you need to make your home comfortable again. What about floor rushes? Will one of your neighbours help?'

The woman sighed.

'I expect one of them will help me go and cut some fresh rushes. There's a good growth of them upriver. It's on common land and we're entitled to cut as many reeds and rushes as we need for this small house.' She looked at the seneschal nervously as she said this, as if in fear that he might challenge that right. When he said nothing, she continued, 'I don't know what I would do without my neighbours.'

Nicholas noticed that she made no mention of her husband at all. It seemed that no one in the neighbourhood, not even his wife, expected him to pull his weight. Nicholas hoped that the neighbours, as good hearted as they were, did not grow tired of helping her.

His men-at-arms were still waiting outside when he left the cottage. For them and for the seneschal there would be no immediate return to Ely. The seneschal agreed with the sergeant's hunch; there was certainly a link between this fire and the one in the Old Market. The man the goodwife had just described sounded very much like the one Burdo the basket maker, and indeed the deputy constable weeks before, had spoken of.

The man the seneschal sought was still in town. He could still be caught. It was clear that the seneschal's work in Wisbech was far from finished.

THIRTY-FIVE

Feast of St Carantoc; Wednesday 16th May

Micah was clearly happy to be ridden out that morning, even though the sky had clouded over and was threatening rain. After too many days of inactivity in the castle stables, the horse trotted along in an animated way, sharing his rider's cheerfulness.

Knowing that the felon he pursued was still close by had given the seneschal fresh hope for his investigation, but it also presented new queries. Since the man had not left town, it seemed fair to assume that he had failed to steal Aelfric's box of treasures when he had broken into the house. And that begged a significant question; if he did not have the treasure, where was it?

A second question too played on the seneschal's mind, one that concerned the work John of Tilneye had done on the charter.

The break-ins that had occurred in both the New and Old Markets now appeared to be attempts to follow the directions hidden in the charter. However, as far as he knew, no mention had been made in the document of the ferryman's cottage. If it were true that this latest fire and attempted theft was the work of the same man, how did it fit in with his other crimes? It was this question that had urged Nicholas that morning to visit the manor of Marshmeade and speak to John again.

He was riding along the bank road out of town and was just passing Elm when it began to rain. It was merely a shower, nothing much at all, but it brought a chill that changed the nature of the day. A gust of cold wind blew along the river, sending shivers through the banks of tall grasses and bright outcrops of blue flowered brooklime. Nicholas pulled his fashionable but inadequate cap further down about his ears and urged Micah more swiftly along the road.

Though Nicholas was acquainted with Sir Roland of Tilneye and came across him occasionally when business took the manorial lord to Ely, he had never visited his manor of Marshmeade. Now, seeing it for the first time, he was impressed with its neatness and general good repair. Everywhere he looked, the manor's peasants were hard at work, either on the patches of land behind their homes, in the fields or repairing ditches and hedgerows. There was no sign of neglect; no raggedy or sickly children or the worn down hopelessness of older folk, which the seneschal often saw elsewhere.

The manor house itself, set within its well maintained palisade fence, had a pleasing appearance, even in the rain. A groom appeared with impressive efficiency to take Micah to the stables and the seneschal's first knock on the heavy front door yielded an instant response. The girl who answered the door was welcoming and cheerful. In fact, if Nicholas had to find anything at all to criticise, she was a bit *too* welcoming and cheerful. The way she looked him up and down with eyes that were far from bashful, was going to get her into trouble one day. And, he surmised, that day was not far away.

It was Sir Roland himself who greeted him as soon as he entered the great hall.

'Ah! So what brings the bishop's law man here?' enquired the manorial lord as they greeted each other. 'Has my ne'er do well of a son sinned again? Another father complaining? Wouldn't be surprised if...'

Nicholas smiled.

'Sir John is not in trouble, Sir Roland,' he said, 'but I would like to speak to him.'

'Ah, he'll be here somewhere, since he's not yet come up with an excuse for wasting his time in town today. He'll be out in the west field, I expect. We're sowing some late peas and beans and he'll be hanging around, watching everyone else work, I'll wager. There'll be no danger of him doing much himself.'

Nicholas laughed, understanding some of the frustration Sir Roland felt with his son. He found the youth pretty irritating himself.

By the time Nicholas left the house, the rain had stopped, though the sky remained overcast. He walked along the lane in a westerly direction and, after a longer trek than he had expected, came to the field which Sir Roland had mentioned. As he drew nearer, figures in the distance came gradually into focus. There were four workers in the west field. Each of them carried a basket of pea seed that was supported by a strap over one shoulder. They were walking in straight lines across the freshly prepared soil, casting the seed to their right and left. One of the workers was John himself. He appeared completely engrossed in the task and Nicholas had to wait until the men had walked the furlong length of the field and had turned to make their way back, before John saw him.

He was wearing a plain hood that had been dyed so long ago that it had faded to something between a dull green and a dusty brown. The hood and his plain tunic were wet from the recent shower, but John looked anything but complaining as he laid down his basket and made his way towards the seneschal. Sir Roland, Nicholas realised, had been unjust in his assessment of his son's character.

'My lord seneschal!' John greeted the visitor with a wide smile. 'Come to help with the late spring sowing?'

'Not exactly, no,' laughed Nicholas. 'It is more a case, I fear, of once more racking your brain.'

'Then you'll be bitterly disappointed, sir. There's not much worth racking.'

'John,' went on Nicholas, 'do you remember the charter you worked on making any mention of a cottage by the Well Stream? The ferryman's hut?'

John screwed up his face as he thought back over the wording he had found.

'No, nothing at all. Anyway, would a ferry have existed on that part of the river in those days? The original Saxon manor, where our Old Market is now, would have been quite a distance from the modern ferry. Why do you ask, sir?'

Nicholas hesitated. It had not been his intention to tell John any more than he needed to, but the person who stood before him, with dirt on his hands and a muddy smudge across his nose where he had wiped it, who worked alongside his father's peasants, was not the idle, foolish youth he had mistaken him for.

'There was another house fire yesterday,' he said, 'at the ferryman's cottage near St Peter's Church. The goodwife there found a man in her home who was about to steal a purse of money. As the man escaped, he deliberately set fire to the house, though he failed to steal anything. The woman's description of the intruder fitted an earlier one of the man who burned Aelfric's home in the Old Market.'

'He's still around then,' concluded John.

'But no longer restricting his activities, it seems, to what was written in the charter.'

'He must be hungry,' pointed out John. 'Wherever he's hiding, it's been for some time now. He must be getting desperate. Not much of a thief, is he? I reckon I could do better than that myself!'

'I'd rather you didn't try,' Nicholas replied wryly. 'You are right, though; he must be getting hungry and desperate. If he's still around, chances are he's still looking for what he missed at Aelfric's house and he won't want to waste much more time about it.'

'We need to draw him out,' said John. 'We need to make him try again to take what he came here for.'

'We?'

'I thought you'd come to request my help, sir, and I am happy to give it. The peas and beans are almost sown now and I shall soon have a little more time on my hands.'

'Though not,' Nicholas smiled, 'if your father has anything to do with it.'

John gave an amiable shrug.

'So, what can I do?'

'As you say, we need to draw this man out. If he really is waiting for an opportunity to search the Old Market for what he failed to take the first time, we ought to give him an incentive to try again.'

'You mean we should let it be known that Rose's grandfather's valuables have never been found, which is true, is it not? We could say they're believed still to be in the ruins of his house.'

'Something like that, yes, but we must be more subtle. If items of value are mentioned, every crook in the shire will head for the Old Market. The castle gaol will be at breaking point and I shall be no nearer to clearing up this matter. We need to attract the right person only and then catch him.'

'So how...?'

'I assume you are no stranger to the town's hostelries?'

'Not exactly...'

'Good. Frequent them, if you will. Befriend people. Talk about the Old Market fire, like the well spread gossip it is. Mention that whatever the would-be thief was looking for is said to be there still, in the ashes. And it might be useful to add that the site is soon to be cleared ready for rebuilding. It will be obvious to everyone who hears you that anything still hidden in the ashes will be discovered at that time. If anyone is to act, they will know they have to do so immediately.'

'How about a time limit?' suggested John. 'Perhaps I should mention that the site's to be cleared within a week?'

'Yes, do that. And then we hope that the rumour you spread reaches the right pair of ears. And quickly.'

John grinned. The idea obviously appealed to him.

'I shall start as soon as I can. And is it true, sir, that the treasure has never been found?'

'Yes, it's true, so you won't be telling much of a lie. You must involve no one else in this matter. You must tell no one what I have told you.'

'You do not have to explain that, sir. You can trust me.'

Nicholas nodded. In spite of his previous misgivings, he had a strong conviction that the youth was right. He could trust him.

'Thank you. I shall continue to work in the Mote Hall office. If you need anything, or have anything at all to report, find me there.'

John was still smiling as he bade the seneschal farewell. When Nicholas looked back, the young knight had picked up his basket again and had resumed his work on the land.

THIRTY-SIX

Feast of St John; Friday 18th May

John of Tilneye was in the Swan in the New Market place. No one would have seen anything unusual in that and he was already well acquainted with the regulars. The hostelry was busy that night and among the familiar faces were a few lesser known ones. As was usual on a Friday evening, traders and customers had travelled in from the fen ready for the next morning's market. Those able to afford it, would share the modest accommodation on offer in one of the hostelry's attic rooms.

Conversation that night was mostly of the light hearted kind. The late spring weather that had followed a long and bitter winter was steadily improving and the early crops were showing promise. With less worry on their minds, the drinkers were more inclined to laughter than during past times when they had drunk to drown their sorrows and humour had been scarce.

Though John found the banter entertaining, there had been no opportunity for him to air the subject he needed the drinkers to talk about. One of the regulars, old Ned, looked like he was about to fall off the end of his bench, having enjoyed a copious supply of strong ale. He had dominated the conversation for quite some time, discussing his pigs and other livestock and John, being insufficiently well versed in porcine matters, had been unable to join in. There had then followed plenty of drunken jokes which had lost their punch lines in the general clash of voices and interruptions from newcomers.

In the end, it had been one of the other regulars who had done John's work for him. John had been ordering another cup of ale when, amongst the general hubbub, one quiet yet distinct voice reached his ears.

'What's going on in the Old Market now, then?' asked the voice. 'The constable's men never leave the place. Night and day, they're out there, keeping their eye on everything. I was minding my own business the other day when I...'

'Yeah, something's up,' broke in another voice. 'Far too much interest in a few burned out buildings for my liking. Something's definitely afoot. If you get too near the fences round Aelfric's old place, they want to know your business. Got me by the scruff of the neck, one of them did.'

'Well, if you will go creeping around, sticking your nose into other folks' business,' pointed out a third drinker, 'what do you expect?'

John turned round on the bench to face the speakers. There was a group of them seated just behind him. He recognised a few of them from other ale houses, though he had not seen them before in the Swan.

'That happened to me,' he lied. The men looked at him expectantly and he continued, encouraged. 'The place is always watched, but I'd noticed that the guards always let things slip around supper time each day. They're too interested in their stomachs then to care about anything else, and I was curious. I just wanted to...'

'You want to take care, young John,' warned one of the older men in a friendly manner. 'Doesn't do for a young lord to be arrested for snooping around.'

'You're right,' he grinned, 'but I couldn't help having a look. They're saying it's not been found yet.'

'What hasn't?'

'Not sure exactly. Whatever it was he was looking for. You know, whoever it was who burned Aelfric's place down. What he was looking for.'

'They reckon it's still in there, then? You mean whoever set fire to the place never found it?'

'That's what's being said.'

'How do you know all this?' enquired another voice.

John realised that all the talk around him had quietened now. Everyone seemed to be listening. He shrugged and drank from his refilled cup before replying. He could feel their eyes on him as they waited, cynical yet interested.

'I asked the guard who was threatening to arrest me,' he said. 'They're not such a bad lot once you get talking to them.'

One of his listeners gave a harsh bark of a laugh.

'Maybe not when your old man's lord of the manor up the road. Bet the guard was worried when he realised who you were! Things are not quite the same for the rest of us.'

There was a general murmur of agreement.

'Seems to me,' said one of the others, 'if they're saying that whatever it is hasn't been found, they must be expecting someone to break through those barriers and search the ruins. To nick what the other bloke missed.'

'So what is it?' asked another drinker. 'What is this thing that's so precious that the Old Market has to be watched day and night?'

'No idea,' said John, 'but it must be pretty important. And whoever's after it needs to hurry up. They'll be clearing the site in a week's time, apparently, ready to rebuild. Anything left in the rubble then is certain to be found by the authorities.'

'Yeah,' added yet another man, 'making the constable even richer.'

'True,' acknowledged John. 'Let's hope it falls into more deserving hands.'

He turned round again on the bench and drained his cup. He placed a coin on the table in front of him and the hostelry keeper brought over his jug of ale once more to fill John's cup. Behind him, the discussion about the Old Market continued. More and people were joining in and John smiled to himself.

Suddenly, there rose a great roar of laughter from the whole company. Old Ned had fallen off his bench.

THIRTY-SEVEN

Feast of St Godric of Finchale; Monday 21st May

St Godric, though he had travelled widely during his lifetime, was remembered fondly in Wisbech and its surrounding manors because of the saint's local connections. He had been born in nearby Walpole, where he spent his early years, and beside his many good deeds, was known for his kindness to animals. Such dedication and care was respected and venerated, both locally and countrywide, by people who relied so heavily on the good health and wellbeing of their livestock. Today was St Godric's feast day and on this day every year people remembered the saint in their thoughts and prayers.

Burdo the basket maker, however, had forgotten all about the saint and his feast day this year. He was far more concerned about the continuing presence of the men-at-arms who kept watch day and the night in the Old Market.

It had not been too bad at first. In the first few days following the fire, the soldiers' presence had been mostly friendly and they had allowed folk to come and go unchallenged. Lately, though, the mood in the market square had changed. There was hardly a moment now when its residents did not feel scrutinised. Life had become very uncomfortable.

Even the two gossips, Goodwife Aswig and her friend, had curtailed their daily meetings in the square. They objected to being stared at, they said. Their daily round up of news and hearsay was confined these days to the privacy of one or other of their homes.

Burdo was sitting at his bench by the open window that morning, as was his usual habit. He was working on a large laundry basket, a sturdy, practical item which every household needed. He enjoyed making his baskets as pleasing to the eye as possible, even the everyday essential things. The base and sides of the laundry basket were now completed and he was finishing the item with a firm rim that would keep it in good order for years to come. Once he had added the handles, the basket would be ready for display outside his workshop.

He had become completely engrossed in his work and he started a little when someone knocked loudly at the door. Normally at this time of year, his door would have been propped open to welcome his customers, but the air that morning was a little too fresh for comfort. He rose from his bench and stretched his back, readying himself to greet his first customers of the day. He unlatched the door and pulled it open, smiling in anticipation of a cheery conversation and possible sale.

But the individual standing there did not look like one of his usual customers. Heavily cloaked and hooded, the man darkened the doorway by more than just his physical presence. He was tall and quite well built, but Burdo could see very little of the face which was hidden by the hood. The man was far too heavily dressed for a May morning, even a chilly one.

'A quick word, if I may,' the stranger said. His voice sounded like a low growl.

From behind him, Burdo heard his dog's swift patter of paws across the floor rushes. The animal let out a growl of his own. It was guttural and threatening and Burdo sensed the stranger's apprehension. He seemed to move backwards slightly from the doorway.

'Steady, Foxtail,' murmured Burdo as he placed one hand on the animal's head. 'What do you want?' he demanded of the man. He felt significantly bolder with Foxtail beside him, but was still fervently wishing that the stranger would go and leave them in peace. He wondered where the men-at-arms were. Surely, they should be here, questioning this interloper? Surreptitiously, he peered through the gap between the man's cloak and the door frame, hoping to catch sight of one of the guards, but could see neither of them. Typical, he thought angrily. Now that I have need of them...

'I know you saw me,' growled the man.

The voice was still menacing, yet somehow familiar. Burdo could not understand how that could be so. His fear was blocking his ability to think. Despite Foxtail's presence, his heart was beating so loudly that he could hardly hear his own thoughts. There was a pause before the man spoke again.

'You saw me, but will say nothing. Do you understand?'

The stranger's hands had emerged from the folds of his cloak and a knife blade gleamed in the light. Burdo nodded, though nothing made sense. Surely this man knew that it was too late? Burdo had already told the seneschal about the stranger he had seen fleeing from the fire.

Still he said nothing. After what seemed an eternity, the stranger's dark bulk moved away from the doorway.

'Just remember,' he uttered as a final warning.

The basket maker slammed the door shut, leaning against it in relief. Foxtail, still growling, began to sniff at the ground just inside the workshop.

'It's all right now,' Burdo said, burying his fingers in the thick, coarse hair on the top of the dog's head. 'Good boy.'

The pair of them stood by the closed door for a long time. Neither of them seemed to possess the power to move, though gradually the dog and man became calmer. The door would remain shut for the rest of the day, Burdo decided. He would take a good look at any callers through the window before he let them in. There had been enough trouble for one day. He wandered through to the back room and poured himself a cup of ale. It was only as he stood there, looking at the small vegetable patch behind his premises, that he realised why the man had seemed familiar.

The heavily cloaked and hooded figure walked across the square just as Brithun and Ordgar, the men-at-arms on duty that morning, emerged from behind the corner of the cobbler's workshop. They had not been missing for long, only for enough time to visit their secret ale supply and take a sip or two. Now, however, it looked like they had been caught out.

They approached the man guiltily as he strode towards them, but he said nothing, merely nodding as he passed them. He had reached the steps cut into the river bank before turning back and calling over his shoulder.

'Everything in order?' he enquired.

'Yes, sir,' they replied in unison.

Curiously, they climbed to the top of the bank once he had gone and watched the sergeant-at-arms as he made his way over the river towards the castle.

THIRTY-EIGHT

Feast of St Bede the Venerable; Friday 25th May

Sir Nicholas Drenge was once again returning from the Old Market. The constable's men on duty there still had nothing to report and the days were dragging by with the same irksome lack of progress. He was playing a waiting game, one which by its very nature could not be hurried, but each passing day felt like time wasted. He could not delay his return to Ely for much longer. His work there was piling up and he could not expect his deputy to deal with it all.

John of Tilneye was still spreading rumours in the town's hostelries and Nicholas suspected that he was enjoying the task rather too much. He certainly seemed in no hurry for his nightly round of ale houses to end. He had visited them all, from the smarter ones such as the Swan and the Mitre, to the truly down at heel like the Ship in the Old Market and the Boar close to the confluence of the Wysbeck and Well Stream.

The seneschal was walking through the gatehouse arch towards the castle bailey when he heard someone hailing him. A castle servant was hurrying towards him, a small sealed scroll in his hand. He bowed before presenting Nicholas with the scroll.

'The messenger from Ely has already departed, my lord, but left this for you. He said it was urgent, but required no reply.'

Nicholas thanked the man, heading straight for his Mote Hall office. The scroll, he was glad to see, had been sealed in his own office in Ely, so must have been sent by his deputy. The seneschal had come to expect speed and efficiency from his second in command, but was still surprised to receive a reply so soon.

Nicholas seated himself in the chair behind his desk and broke the seal on the scroll, unrolling and smoothing out a single, small sheet of parchment. As was his deputy's habit, he had crammed as much of his neat, diminutive handwriting as possible into the available space. Nicholas had to squint to make some of it out, but he read with increasing interest.

The deputy had been to the abbey, the location of the only other known copy of the Charter of Oswy and Leoflede. He had spoken to the abbot who had taken him to see the armarius, the brother in charge of the library's books and documents. The armarius had told him that few of the brethren had had access to the charter in the past few months, since the document was safely locked away with other charters and manuscripts. On further questioning, the armarius had admitted that, despite the charter's secure location, its contents were familiar to many. The story attached to the charter, whether credible or not, had created something of a legend around it.

The deputy had then related the story with which Nicholas was already familiar, that of hidden clues and treasure, but then the report became more interesting. When asked whether any of the brethren or abbey servants had shown particular interest in the document, the armarius had been quick to tell him about the youth who had gone missing.

Weland, the son of Godmund the carpenter, had worked in the abbey library for a few months. His work had been satisfactory and the brothers had found his curiosity about some of the books and documents pleasing. It had only been after his sudden and unexplained disappearance that the brothers recalled Weland's obsession with a certain document; the Charter of Oswy and Leoflede.

The seneschal's deputy had then visited Godmund, the youth's father. He stated that he had last seen Weland in March, when he had left home on foot with grand ideas about making his fortune. He had never shared his plans with his father who had heard no word from him since. Godmund the carpenter had given up his son for dead.

Nicholas read to the end of the report then sat back in his seat and thought about what he had just learned. Weland's disappearance from Ely in March fitted the timing of both the break-in in the New Market and the burning of Aelfric's house.

This individual, then, was highly likely to be the one Nicholas was searching for. His knowledge of the charter, its legend, as well as timing, fitted very neatly. The youth named Weland must have been living on his wits in Wisbech for two months or more. Somehow, he had evaded capture, despite the town being searched. It could be that he had friends in the town, allies who were hiding him.

But such a situation could not go on indefinitely. In time, Weland would hear the rumours John was spreading in the ale houses and, unless he was brighter than the seneschal gave him credit for, would soon fall into the trap set for him.

THIRTY-NINE

Vespers

The seneschal's men-at-arms had just been relieved of their watch over the Old Market that evening when things had finally started to happen. And because of the timing, those things were almost missed.

The night watch had not yet taken up their posts and the day watch were still in the process of handing over, when it occurred. This brief lapse in security came each day about supper time and John of Tilneye had taken care to promote it as part of his rumour spreading. By the time the new guards had noticed anything amiss, the lock on the gate between the barriers around the ruined buildings had been broken.

Even then, it had only been because one of the guards had noticed the tall gate moving in the breeze that he had decided to investigate. He had wandered across the square with more curiosity than anticipation of trapping their long hunted quarry. Grasping the gate and snatching it fully open, he had been rewarded with the sight of a man searching with bare hands through the heaps of ash and scorched timber. He was clad in the dark robes and hood of a Benedictine abbey servant.

Before the man even knew he was being watched, the man-at-arms had seized him from behind, pulling his arms behind his back and securing his wrists with iron cuffs. The other guard had arrived by then and together they had marched their captive through the square. The Old Market's residents had appeared en masse in their doorways, following the guards and their prisoner across the square and to the top of the river bank, jeering and catcalling. The loudest of them all was Goodwife Aswig, who had not had so much fun in ages.

Weland, son of Godmund the carpenter of Ely, was taken to an empty cell in the castle gaol. After the disastrous wrongful arrest and crowded imprisonment of the tinker, the sergeant was careful not to make any further mistakes. Though the gaol was steadily filling up due to the approaching summer Assizes, he made sure that adequate space was found for the new captive. Weland would remain there until the seneschal was ready to question him.

The bells for Vespers were sounding out from the tower of St Peter and Paul's as the seneschal climbed the stairs towards the constable's office. His tread was considerably lighter than it had been in the past few days. Though he had not yet seen the prisoner, news of the arrest had brought him renewed optimism and he strode energetically along the passageway. His knock was answered immediately and he entered the office to find the constable and his deputy in conversation.

'Nicholas!' cried Alexander warmly. He looked pleased to be interrupted. His discussion with Simon seemed to have brought neither man much cheer. 'Do you have news?'

'An update at least,' replied Nicholas as he seated himself in the proffered chair at the large desk opposite the other two men.

'I'm hoping it's positive, then,' commented Sir Simon de Gardyn, the deputy constable. 'We could do with some good news.'

'The guards in the Old Market have made an arrest,' Nicholas stated. 'They caught a man breaking into the enclosure around the ruins of Aelfric's house. I have not yet questioned him, but he fits the description we had. The Old Market is still under observation, though, and will remain so until I am sure we have the right man in custody.'

'Sounds very promising,' acknowledged the constable. 'Your determination has paid off then, Nicholas.'

Alexander sounded extraordinarily cheerful and the seneschal noticed for the first time that he was looking even better dressed than usual. His dark hair and beard were neatly trimmed and his tunic, dyed a dark blue and edged with elaborate embroidery, looked as fresh as if it had been made for him yesterday. Perhaps it had, thought Nicholas. Alexander was known for sparing no expense when it came to his wardrobe.

'The felon could not have been caught without the men you provided, and I have to admit that the young Sir John of Tilneye has proved to be unexpectedly helpful.'

'You doubted his abilities, then,' smiled Alexander.

'I confess that I did. The young knight goes to great lengths to disguise his good qualities and I was slow to see them. It was he who discovered the connection between the charter and the fire in the Old Market, as well as a previous theft in the New Market.'

'The charter?' questioned Simon with raised eyebrows. Nicholas realised that he had not brought the constable and his deputy up to date for some time with the progress he had been making.

'Yes,' he replied. 'John found wording in the charter which could have led anyone with the ability to interpret it to Aelfric's house.'

'But that's ridiculous!' objected Simon. 'That charter is nothing but an endless list of the most tedious detail. How could it be of any use to anyone?' His Adam's apple was bobbing up and down in his pale throat, adding emphasis to his words.

'If John is right,' said Alexander, ignoring his deputy, 'it would explain the attempt back in the spring to relieve us of our copy of the charter. Fortunately, Simon was not fooled. But this man you have in custody, how could he have seen the charter? In order to follow the wording you say is there, he must have seen it, and few people are able to do so. There are only two copies in existence, ours here and the one in Ely.'

'I cannot be sure until I have questioned the man, but I believe he either saw the document in Ely or spoke to someone already familiar with it.'

'Well, then, Nicholas,' said Alexander, 'I hope you find out all you need to know. Let us hope that this concludes this long drawn out matter.'

'Indeed,' added Simon. 'Let us hope so.'

FORTY

Saturday 26th May
Mistake

The hood of his Benedictine robe no longer covering his face and hair, the tall, young man who occupied the seat in the corner of the seneschal's office looked thin, pale and hungry. The descriptions given by both the deputy constable back in March and Burdo the basket maker more recently, had been quite accurate. Weland's face was broad, but not in a fleshy way. His brow and jaw were wide and heavily defined and his nose was bony and large, giving him a truculent look. The only thing to have changed about him since his early sightings in Wisbech was the straggly growth of a dark beard, evidence of weeks of rough living.

'It would appear,' began the seneschal calmly, 'that you have been staying as an uninvited guest in our town for some time. Where were you hiding when the town was searched?'

Weland appeared to find this question amusing.

'It wasn't difficult. If the soldiers went one way, I went in the other direction. Brainless, the lot of them. Didn't use their eyes either.'

'And where did you find shelter?'

Weland hesitated.

'Here and there. Stables sometimes, workshops, anywhere out of the way. And right here. Under your very nose; in the great castle itself!' He was laughing, clearly enjoying his moment, even though he must have known it would be one of his last.

'You can shut your lying mouth!' bellowed the sergeant who had remained quiet up to that point. 'If you'd been anywhere within the castle walls you would have been seen!'

'Is that right, sergeant?' the man said sarcastically. 'Searched and got nowhere, did you?'

The sergeant glared at him.

'How did you feed yourself?' asked the seneschal.

'Easy to take food from market stalls when you're hungry. No one seems to notice. Getting quite good at that, I am. Even took coins sometimes, though that was harder. Was nearly caught once or twice.'

'As you were in the ferryman's cottage.'

The man shrugged.

'Why did you break into Aelfric's house in the Old Market?' continued the seneschal.

'Who's Aelfric?' asked Weland with an arrogant, dismissive look. 'I have no idea who he is.'

'Aelfric is the man you killed!' Nicholas retorted, anger threatening to rob him of his calm. 'Aelfric is the man whose life you took when you set fire to his home!'

Weland was clearly unmoved.

'Wasn't my fault. Didn't mean to start the fire. I knocked over his lamp by accident. Silly old duffer got in my way. I only wanted to...'

'What?' Nicholas demanded. 'What was it you wanted?'

For the first time Weland looked unsure of himself.

'They say there's treasure there,' he said after a pause. 'Everybody was talking about it. It's in the legend, you know...'

'Perhaps you could tell me,' replied the seneschal stiffly.

Weland looked impatient, as if he were trying to explain to a slow person how to peel an apple.

'It's in an old charter. You look for certain words and they lead you to that house in the Old Market where there's supposed to be treasure. Only at first I got it wrong and...'

'You went to the wrong house, by God's teeth,' shouted the sergeant. 'You stole from a poor old woman in the New Market and injured her servant. You're obviously as stupid as you are incompetent!'

'Easy mistake to make,' Weland smirked, 'but I got it right the next time.'

'So you found what you were after in Aelfric's house, did you?' continued the sergeant. 'You found the loot you went in there for?'

'If I had, I'd have been long gone from this dump of a town, wouldn't I?'

The sergeant let out something resembling a growl.

'Tell me,' demanded Nicholas, 'how you knew about the charter.'

Weland frowned.

'They were all talking about it at the abbey. Where I used to work. The brothers used to tell me about it and I wondered why no one had ever tried to take the treasure, or whatever it was. I thought it had to be worth a try, but I needed to look at the charter myself, find the words that were meant to be hidden in it. But I couldn't get hold of it. They kept it locked away.'

'So you understand the old Saxon language, do you?' asked Nicholas. 'If you had been able to see the charter, you would have been able to read it, would you?'

Weland frowned again, looking confused.

'But you came to Wisbech anyway,' continued the seneschal, 'and invented that dim witted tale about acting for the bishop, in an attempt to get hold of the castle's copy of the charter.'

Weland said nothing.

'But you failed, so you still hadn't seen a copy of the charter. How, then, did you know how to find the right house?'

'Well, as your sergeant pointed out, I went to the wrong house the first time.'

'Yes, you made a mistake, but only because you misinterpreted the directions in the charter,' pointed out Nicholas. 'By that time, you had clearly found out what those directions were. So, if you'd never seen a copy of the charter, how did you know what it said?'

Weland opened his mouth to speak but then shut it again. He reminded Nicholas of a landed pike fish, his mouth opening and shutting as if short of breath. His smirk had faded completely.

'Who told you about the words hidden in the charter? Who was helping you?' demanded Nicholas. 'You've not been acting alone, have you? You're just not clever enough!'

Still Weland said nothing. His cheeks were burning and his eyes glinting, his heavy jaw set in angry defiance. A stubborn silence filled the room and went on building, enough to crack the sergeant's patience. He lunged suddenly towards the prisoner.

'No, sergeant,' shouted the seneschal just before Baldwin's fist made contact with Weland's nose. 'Let it be for now.'

'This fire you claim to have started by accident,' the seneschal continued, 'was useful for you, wasn't it? It allowed you to escape after Aelfric found you in his house. Is that why, when you later failed to steal from the ferryman's house, you started a fire there too?'

Weland looked up at him for the first time in a while and nodded.

'Worked out it was a handy thing to do,' he said. 'Just knock over a lamp or a candle and no one stops you getting away.'

'Because you're such a useless excuse for a thief,' growled the sergeant. 'You've failed every time, haven't you? You're pathetic!'

'So I return to the same question,' said the seneschal. 'Who have you been working with? Who has been helping you? Who has been hiding you?'

The man closed his lips firmly and said no more. Nicholas let the silence run on before opening the door and bringing in the guards.

'Let him fester in his cell for the night. We shall resume this enlightening conversation in the morning.'

The seneschal and sergeant waited as the guards took the prisoner away. Nicholas knew he would have to be patient, but was confident that Weland would tell him in the end what he needed to know. The man was going to hang anyway; he had nothing to lose by telling the truth now.

Nicholas walked out into the late afternoon air. It was cool and fresh and the earthen surface of the bailey was damp beneath his feet. It must, he realised, have been raining while they had been in the Mote Hall.

Visitors to the castle were beginning to thin out now, but still gatherings of strangers and horses lingered in various stages of departure. Nicholas had to weave his way between them in order to reach the keep. A group of noblemen and women, who were making hard work of mounting their horses, were blocking his way ahead. The seneschal tried to keep a straight face at the sight of one of them, a particularly corpulent nobleman who was having to be assisted on to his finely bred and unamused palfrey. The man's overfed belly and broad backside were refusing to obey his short, stocky legs which flailed impotently until his servant gave him a shove from behind.

Nicholas moved swiftly out of the way. As he did so, he caught the briefest of glimpses of someone else in the crowd who was enjoying the spectacle. She was laughing and it struck him as unusual; he had only seen her looking cold and haughty before. He began to make his way towards her, moving out of the path of several horses as he did so.

He could no longer see the lady, but continued towards the place where she had been standing. He looked for her amongst the crowd, but to no avail. He went on walking and searching, but could not find her anywhere.

Perhaps, he had to conclude after a fruitless search, his mind was playing tricks on him. He doubted it, though. He had been convinced in that moment that Lady Rowena de Hurste had been standing there.

If so, she was gone now. She had completely disappeared.

FORTY-ONE

Feast of St Augustine; Sunday 27th May

John of Tilneye was waiting outside the small church dedicated to St Giles in the manor of Tydd. He had seen the Hurste family entering the church earlier, having narrowly avoided bumping into them on his way to Hurste Manor. This early sighting had saved him a fruitless journey to Hurste, though he now had to endure a long wait while the good folk of Tydd St Giles performed their Sunday devotions.

It was well past noon now. Having attended early Mass in Elm, he had been seized by the urge to ride to Hurste and see Rose. The sensible, easily overridden part of him failed to understand why he was persisting with her. The lady gave him no encouragement and he knew his behaviour had become laughable. In the past, he would have sneered at any man acting as desperately as he was now. He was not proud of his actions, yet was somehow unable to prevent them.

He was keeping well out of sight of the church door, standing behind the high fence that enclosed the Tydd blacksmith's yard. Thankfully, on this day of rest, the yard was deserted and there was no one to witness his skulking and shameful behaviour.

He had left Albanac in the care of the hostelry keeper near the church and a few coins had ensured that the palfrey would be well fed and watered while he waited. It was easier for John to keep a low profile without a well bred horse for company and this time he had toned down his clothing so that he would stand out less amongst the locals.

The service going on inside St Giles was an extremely long one. Every so often, the priest's voice could be heard as it rose in song, followed by the more discordant and fractured response of the congregation. John wondered if they were as eager for the Mass to end as he was. Sunday or not, many of these folk had animals to see to and land to be worked. There really was little time for rest.

The Hurstes, along with the principal families of Tydd, were the first to leave the church. John watched as they processed elegantly along the path from the north door. Leading his family group, Sir Mortimer de Hurste paused to bid farewell to one of the Tydd families. His haughty expression hardly changed; he merely inclined his head now and then in polite acknowledgement of whatever was being said. His displeased air reminded John of someone who was permanently offended by the pong of a ripe dung heap.

His wife, Lady Rowena, walked beside him. She might, John decided, have been handsome once, but dissatisfaction with life seemed to have faded her prematurely. Her gown, though, was well cut and fashionable, the pale blue cloth fitting her neat waist and falling to the ground in generous folds. Behind the couple walked two men of around John's age whom he assumed were Rose's brothers. They were both shorter in stature than their father but shared his imperious bearing. One of them was glancing over his shoulder and his proud face broke into a smile. It was hardly surprising, John thought, considering that the person he was looking at was his sister. She was walking swiftly to catch him up, having been delayed by speaking to someone in the doorway. Rose, concluded John, would make any man smile; brother, father or lover.

John had but the briefest glimpse of her before his view was blocked by the three crones who followed the young siblings. He had no hesitation in calling them crones, even though they might have been Rose's beloved aunts and grandmother. Their faces were so shrivelled by decades of disdain and disapproval that they resembled dried out and forgotten plums left unplucked on the tree.

As the Hurstes reached the lichgate and paused to pass through it, the family group broke into single file, allowing John another glance at Rose. He smiled to himself. She was as beautiful as ever. She too was smiling as she chatted to the more amiable of her two brothers, completely unaware of John who waited, just out of sight in the blacksmith's yard.

He moved as soon as the family reached the lane. They would, he assumed, be going to the hostelry to fetch their horses. He sprinted through the yard and out to the back lane, turning down an alley between a pig sty and a carpenter's workshop. He emerged further along the church lane and saw the Hurste family behind him. They were still strolling along, perhaps enjoying the warm May air, though few of them looked capable of finding pleasure in anything.

The rest of the congregation had left the church by that time, most of them overtaking the leisurely ambling gentry, and John was able to lose himself in the crowd. Turning to look over his shoulder, he found himself almost face to face with Rose. He saw her register surprise, then annoyance.

She shook her head at him, willing him away.

'Who's that fellow?' asked one of her brothers. He sounded petulant.

'No one,' John heard Rose reply. 'I thought I recognised someone, but I was mistaken.'

It was not, he had to admit, the most encouraging of exchanges to take place right in front of him. Not encouraging at all.

He watched the family go, watched as they disappeared into the hostelry. After a while, he saw them leave on horseback. Rose was riding the pretty grey jennet she had taken to Wisbech on the day that John had first seen her.

It was time, John told himself, to stop this foolishness. He was popular with women and it was pointless to pursue this one reluctant girl who was so closely guarded by her unpleasant looking family.

He hardly noticed the ride home, so immersed in his thoughts was he. He rarely stayed out of sorts for long, however, and by the time he reached Marshmeade he was already thinking of brighter things, successfully burying thoughts of Rose beneath them.

He knew that his obsession with Rose would not disappear overnight. Thoughts of her would remain, nagging away at the back of his mind and emerging when he was careless enough to let his guard down.

He was not off the hook yet.

FORTY-TWO

Sunday 27th May; early morning, the same day
The Darker Realms

Nicholas had been awoken early by the usual sounds of activity coming from the castle kitchen below, but had allowed himself to drift in a half slumbering meditation about the day that lay ahead.

In the end, he had been later than usual in rousing himself. He was dressing in a hurry, pulling his hose on to one leg, not having started on the other one, when he heard someone calling him. He ignored it at first, cursing its inconvenient timing, and continued to struggle with his hose. But then the voice was accompanied by a hammering on the door and he felt obliged to hop over to it, a stocking still dangling from his partly clad leg. He unfastened the door latch, cursing under his breath.

It was Brithun. The man-at-arms appeared not to notice the seneschal's state of undress, being too focussed on the news he had come to deliver. As the soldier's words began to sink in, Nicholas forgot his annoyance and returned to his bedside only to complete his dressing. He finished putting on his hose, tying the tops to the drawstring of his breeches. He pulled a long tunic over his linen undershirt and breeches and was still tying a girdle around his waist by the time he was descending the spiralled stairs, close on Brithun's heels. Once on the ground floor, they ran to the back stairs and continued to descend, down to the undercroft where the prison cells were located.

The door to Weland's cell was wide open and Ordgar stood there in the darkness, his face illuminated by a single tallow candle.

The prisoner lay on his back in the centre of the small cell, his hood thrown back and his eyes closed. Taking the candle from Ordgar, Nicholas knelt down beside the body. Spread across the black habit that covered Weland's chest was an ugly stain, the blood encrusted, as if all that had happened in the night was already old history.

'He was stabbed just once, in the abdomen,' came a voice from the corner of the cell. Nicholas raised his eyes from Weland's body to seek out the speaker and noticed for the first time the physician sitting there in the gloom. 'Whether whoever struck the blow was experienced in these things or simply lucky, I cannot tell, but he caused heavy and unstoppable bleeding. This poor soul would have died quite quickly, which is something to be thankful for, but death would still not have come immediately. He would have had time to cry out, and it surprises me that none of the guards heard him.'

The elderly physician crossed himself, his thin, white fingers where they emerged from his dark robes looking eerily detached from the rest of his body. He was the same physician as had attended the wrongly arrested tinker a few weeks earlier and had diagnosed his leprosy. The seneschal respected his opinion and wondered how long the man had been sitting there with Weland's body. He must have been cold.

'Thank you, sir,' said Nicholas. 'Leave this to me now. Please take some refreshment from the hall before you leave.'

The man nodded, giving the seneschal a small bow as he left. Nicholas remained where he was for a while, feeling unable to move away, a sense of hopelessness engulfing him. He felt, rather than heard, his two men-at-arms moving to stand behind him.

'He would have told us more,' said Nicholas quietly.

'Only then to die on the scaffold,' remarked Brithun. 'Perhaps to him it was all the same in the end, sir.'

'But not to us. There was more we needed to know,' pointed out Nicholas. 'And someone knew that. Someone wanted to make sure that Weland had no chance to tell us more. Someone who has been helping him and keeping him hidden all this time.'

The seneschal rose at last from his knees.

'Get this boy to the church. I will write to my deputy in Ely, so that this miscreant's father can be informed. It will be up to him whether he fetches the body or leaves the boy to be buried here. I must go and speak to the constable.'

'We'll have a litter brought for Weland, sir,' said Ordgar, 'so that he's carried with some dignity to the church.'

Nicholas nodded and left the cell, making his way along the damp, chilly passageway to the stairs which would take him up to the lighter realms of the castle.

FORTY-THREE

Evil

The deputy constable was alone in the office when the seneschal arrived. Sir Simon de Gardyn was grey faced and there were dark patches underlining his watery eyes. He was unshaven and his clothes looked as hastily thrown on as Nicholas's.

'This is a very bad business, Nicholas,' he stated dismally. 'How could such a thing have happened?'

'I have to wonder that myself,' replied the seneschal as he sank into the seat on the visitor's side of the desk. 'Is the constable here?'

'He has just returned from Murrow and I was obliged to greet him with these grave tidings. He knows he must take full responsibility for the death of one of our prisoners and it sits very heavily on his shoulders.'

The seneschal nodded.

'Constables have lost their living over smaller matters than this,' he agreed.

The door opened as they were speaking and the constable himself entered the room. If possible, he looked to be in an even worse state than his deputy. The sweat from riding was still visible in dark patches beneath his arms and the neckline of his tunic looked greasy. In normal circumstances, he would have gone straight to his rooms on return to the castle to remove his dusty travelling cloak and change his stained clothing. The news he had just received had cast all such niceties from his mind.

'I see you have been apprised of the situation, Nicholas,' Alexander stated bleakly. He sank into his usual seat beneath the pair of windows, next to the one occupied by Simon.

'I fear so,' replied Nicholas, 'and can afford to waste no more time in rooting out this evil. I shall need the names of all the guards on duty last night and of everyone who had access to Weland's cell at any time.'

'The sergeant will help you with all that,' nodded Alexander. 'He was on duty until dawn and will be back in the guard room by late afternoon. I shall make sure he assists you in every way possible. Had you been able to discover much from questioning the prisoner yesterday?'

'Not as much as I wanted to,' replied the seneschal, 'and whoever killed Weland clearly wanted the situation to remain that way.'

'So it would appear,' agreed Alexander. 'Find this devil, Nicholas. Simon here will make sure you have everything you need. Meanwhile, I must go to Ely and see my lord bishop. The disgrace of this breach... I have always taken pride in the castle's security. I have done everything I could to keep our prisoners secure and there have been no escapes from custody under my watch. The shame of such a thing happening would have great enough, but a death in custody? The killing of one of my prisoners? This is infinitely worse. What occurred last night is unspeakable and the responsibility for it lies at my door. Look after things here, will you, Simon? I may be some time in Ely.'

'Of course, sir,' replied Simon mournfully, 'but my lord bishop is a good and fair man. Surely he will understand that it was I who was on duty in your absence. If anyone is at fault, it is I.'

Alexander shook his head.

'As constable, the responsibility is mine. The sooner I arrive in Ely and make my report to the bishop, the better. There are things I must see to here first, but shall leave first thing on Tuesday morning. I wish you good fortune with your investigation, Nicholas.'

'And the best of fortune to you, too, Alexander.'

The constable rose wearily from his seat and left the room. Silence seemed to sweep in and fill the space he had left.

'God help him,' muttered Simon after a pause. 'The bishop, the chancellor of England himself, is considered to be a fair man. I hope he can see beyond this terrible business and allows the constable to remain in his post here.'

'I certainly hope so,' agreed Nicholas.

He took his leave. He would not be able to begin questioning the guards until the sergeant was back on duty, but felt the need to do something positive. Drearily discussing the constable's prospects with the deputy was not going to help anyone.

FORTY-FOUR

The Day Watch

The church of St Peter and St Paul was basking in the warmth of late May. The oaken panels of the south door were patterned with sunlight that filtered through the fronds of the old yew trees overshadowing the path.

On that Sunday, the nave of the small church was filled with townspeople. Morning Mass was over, yet people were staying to chat, forming small groups engaged in lively discussion. This for many was their only weekly social interaction. Goodwives discussed children and the latest scandals while the men aired their views on business and working the land.

At a respectful distance from the crowd lay the body of Weland the carpenter's son. Wrapped in a woollen shroud, it rested on a bier before the altar in the rounded apse at the eastern end of the church. Father Godweard was there as the seneschal approached, standing quietly and perfectly still beside the boy's body. Only when Nicholas's footsteps brought him right up to the bier did the priest raise his head.

'It is strange,' said the priest, 'how such a troubled soul can gain the look of innocence and peace in death. This boy caused so much pain, yet now...'

'It is good of you to keep him here until his father arrives,' replied Nicholas.

The shroud had been left open to show the boy's face and, as Father Godweard had pointed out, there was no longer any hint of the violence that had haunted then ended his short life. Death could be very deceptive.

The seneschal left the priest to his work and walked slowly back to the castle. By then it was dinner time and he enjoyed a fine meal with Simon in the great hall before attending to a few administrative matters. As soon as the sergeant-at-arms was back on duty in the guard house, the seneschal went to speak to him.

'I fail to see what all the panic is about,' objected Baldwin gruffly. 'We needed the wretch caught, to stop his burning and killing. He was a menace and now he's gone and it's saved the expense of a trial and a hanging.'

'As a man of the law and the officer in charge of the constable's men, you must realise how irresponsible your remarks are,' protested Nicholas. 'Weland was killed to prevent him telling us everything he knew. Does that not concern you, sergeant?'

Baldwin was clearly not concerned at all, but made an effort to wipe the sneer from his face. It was perhaps finally dawning on him that his future at the castle might depend on how he conducted himself now.

'Yes, my lord,' he replied without conviction.

'You were on duty until dawn, were you not?'

'Yes, sir, on the night watch with two of my men.'

'Did anything occur during your watch that was at all unusual?'

'No, sir, nothing. It was a quiet night.'

'I need the names of all the guards on duty last night, both on the night watch with you and on the day watch which relieved you.'

'Yes, sir, the guard changed at dawn. There were two men on duty with me, then three men on the day watch which relieved us at dawn. It was one of them who found the body. They've only just come off duty, but I'll send them to answer your questions before they go to their beds. They'll only be stuffing themselves in the hall.'

The sergeant reeled off the names from both shifts and Nicholas committed them to memory. Baldwin could neither read nor write and Nicholas had nothing on which to note down the names.

Having dismissed the sergeant, the seneschal went to his office in the Mote Hall and awaited the arrival of the guards to be questioned. The first man he spoke to went by the name of Alaric and was the most senior of the men on the day watch.

'The prisoner was alive and well when we arrived on duty this morning,' Alaric told the seneschal. 'Always, when we start our shift at dawn, we go to check on the prisoners. That's on the constable's orders. Outside, it was just getting light, but down in the cells you would never have known it. The windows high in the walls are so small that the cells stay dark for most of the day. As I always do, I carried a rush light and could see well enough to tell that all the prisoners were alive and as well as could be expected. There's a cut-out, a small window, on each cell door for us to look through. It's too risky to open the door unnecessarily. We even pass food through there sometimes. They'll jump you, some of them, if you're not careful, and no one wants an escape on their hands. It wasn't until later that I went to check the prisoners again and realised that something was wrong.'

'How much later?'

'Hard to say, but it wasn't quite so dark by then. As soon as I peered through that window I could see him. He wasn't playing dead. This was no trap, and believe me, sir, I know all about the traps some of the devils set. They lure you over to them, playing dead, then they catch you by the throat and get away. No, this was no trap. This was real.'

'Weland was attacked with a knife while you were supposedly watching his cell,' pointed out Nicholas. 'So how did someone get in there carrying a knife? How did someone enter the cell and kill your prisoner without one of you hearing or seeing? Were you asleep? Or were you just very easily distracted? Perhaps one of you assisted the killer by turning a blind eye. Perhaps one of you carried out the deed yourself.'

Alaric shook his head vehemently.

'No, sir, no! None of us can understand how it happened! The men I work with are honest and decent. The constable insists on a high level of security, as well as fair treatment of the prisoners. No one could have slipped past any of us on duty. If anyone had tried to visit the cells without the proper authority, they would have been stopped.'

'And did anyone without the proper authority come down to the cells this morning?'

'No, sir. No one. As soon as I found the dead man, I called out the alarm. I ran upstairs and found one of your men in the great hall. He said he would alert you and the constable immediately.'

Nicholas nodded.

'When you came on duty at dawn,' he continued after a pause, 'did you see anyone loitering in the castle, anyone close to the steps that lead down to the cells, who should not have been there?'

'No, sir. The only thing I should say, though, is that...'

'What is it?'

'Sometimes, sir, the change of guard at dusk and dawn leaves the cells unwatched for a short period. Usually, the changeover is quick and efficient; a transfer of keys, a brief report, and all done very quickly. However, at times, if the incoming watch is slightly late in arriving, the men about to be relieved walk up the steps to wait for them. In my opinion, sir, that's a weakness in our security, one which leaves the cells unwatched for a very short interval.'

'And did such a sloppy changeover occur this morning?'

'Well, yes, sir. Not as bad as it sometimes is, but we arrived a little late. By the time we reached the steps leading down to the cells, the night watch was already coming up.'

'The sergeant too?'

'Yes, sir. I think he was following behind the others. But it can't have been then that anyone slipped into the prisoner's cell, because, as I said, Weland was still alive when I checked at the start of our watch.'

'And the keys to the cell doors? Were they handed over to you without delay?'

'Oh, yes, sir. That was done correctly. No one without authority could have unlocked any of the doors. Nothing like that happened and, as far as I know, there has never been a breach of that kind.'

Nicholas dismissed him without further delay. The next watchman, as well as the one who came after him, was clearly ready for his bed and did more yawning than speaking. Neither of them had anything useful to add. They both reported hearing Alaric crying out in alarm when he found the dead man, but had apparently seen nothing untoward themselves.

The seneschal noted down what he had learned so far and awaited the arrival of the night watch, the soldiers who had been on shift before dawn.

FORTY-FIVE

The Night Watch

The guards who had been on the night watch with the sergeant had benefitted from a day's sleep before going back on duty at the end of the afternoon. They were therefore noticeably more alert when they faced the seneschal's questions than their day watch colleagues had been. Even so, the first man to arrive in Nicholas's office was white faced and drawn. He was clearly nervous.

'I swear to you, my lord, nothing untoward happened on our watch. We checked the prisoners before going off duty at dawn, as we always do, and all was as it should have been.'

'And the changeover; did it go smoothly?'

'Well, yes, sir, fairly smoothly.'

'Fairly smoothly? The new guards arrived on time, did they? They came down to the cells to take the keys from you?'

The man hesitated.

'Well, sir. They were a little late and we did walk up the steps to meet them. It sometimes happens like that, though I don't suppose it ought to. There was no real delay, though. The day watch arrived as soon as we'd reached the top of the steps. We handed over the keys, the sergeant gave them a brief report and that was that.'

'So, there was a short interval during which the doors to the cells were not watched.'

'Well, yes, sir, but it was hardly any time at all and it would have been difficult for anyone to have slipped down to the cells because there's only one way down to them and that was by the stairs we were standing on. No one could have made their way down there without us knowing.'

'Yet someone killed your prisoner. Someone unlocked his cell door and was in there long enough to stab him to death. He then locked the door and left again, all without the guards on duty noticing.'

'I don't understand how it could have happened, my lord. It is very mysterious.'

'More like impossible. One of you on duty last night, either on your shift or the one that followed, knows something. Without the compliance of one or more of you, Weland would still be alive.'

'My lord,' the man protested desperately, 'I swear I do not know how it could have happened!'

Nicholas dismissed him, feeling exasperated. The next man was no more helpful. He repeated the account of the less than perfect change of guard but declared a similar wonderment about how Weland's stabbing could have taken place.

'Was there anything at all out of the ordinary that occurred on your watch? Think carefully.'

'No, my lord. It was a quiet night. When we arrived on duty yesterday at dusk, we took the prisoners bread and ale, as usual. After that, there was very little to do. There were no disturbances. Some nights, one of the prisoners is troubled. Sometimes they call out; nightmares and such like, and who can wonder at that? All of them know they face the hangman's rope sooner or later. But nothing of the sort happened last night. All was quiet. And Weland was still safe and well by dawn, I swear. I know that because we checked on him and all the other prisoners before our shift ended.'

'And were there any visitors to the cells during the night?'

'No, sir, no one during the night. Even after dawn, no visitors as such, as far as I know.'

'What do you mean by "as such"?'

'Well, my lord, it's quite usual for the constable to come and check that all is well. Not every night, but often enough. Sometimes he comes just before the end of our shift, other times at the start of the next one.'

'And did he call last night?'

It would have been nigh on impossible for him to do so, added Nicholas in his thoughts, since the constable claimed to have been in Murrow until early morning.

'No, my lord, the constable was away last night, but I believe the deputy came. I saw him heading for the gaol steps just after we'd come off duty. If you talk to the guards on the day watch, they'll confirm it.'

Yet they had not mentioned it at all.

'So, the deputy constable arrived just as the new watch was beginning.'

'Yes, sir.'

'Return to your duties, then, but before you do so, kindly wake the guard called Alaric from his slumber and send him back here. He has more questions to answer.'

Because Alaric, though he had had plenty to say, had failed to mention the deputy constable's visit. The seneschal waited with mounting impatience. He disliked intensely being lied to.

FORTY-SIX

Alaric

Alaric did not keep the seneschal waiting for long. He arrived wearing only the long linen shift that served both as underwear and for sleeping in. He had fallen asleep earlier as soon as he had settled down on his mattress, but being so rudely awoken to face more of the seneschal's questioning had quickly sharpened his mind again.

'I shall keep this simple as I know how eager you are to return to your bed. Why did you make no mention of the deputy constable's visit to the cells early this morning?'

For the very slightest of moments, the seneschal detected a look of relief that flickered over the guard's features. It was quickly controlled and turned into something that looked more like thoughtfulness.

'My lord seneschal, if I omitted to mention the deputy's visit, it was only because it is such a normal occurrence. Most mornings at an early hour, the constable or his deputy calls in. Sometimes it's just before the night watch ends, other times just after the day watch has begun. They like to check that everything is in order.'

'And this morning's visit? What did Sir Simon de Gardyn do when he visited?'

Alaric frowned, as if recalling the incident cost him a great effort.

'He wasn't there for long. I seem to remember he took a quick glance through the windows in the cell doors, had a word or two with us, and then he left. I'm sorry I forgot to mention it earlier, but finding Weland's body pushed everything else to the back of my mind.'

'Is there anything else,' Nicholas asked, 'that was pushed to the back of your mind? Anything you would like to mention now?'

'No, sir.'

'Then I need to ask you one final thing. When you checked the prisoners' cells after you had arrived on duty, when you say Weland was still alive, was that before or after the deputy's visit?'

'Afterwards, sir. Sir Simon arrived just after the change of guard. We were still settling ourselves in, so it wasn't until he'd gone that I had chance to check the cells.'

'And you can definitely state that all was well?'

'Yes, sir, all was well.'

'And did you see the deputy constable leave?'

'Yes, sir, I did. I remember thinking I was glad he had gone, so that I could get on with the usual checks of the morning. I'm sorry if that sounds disrespectful, sir.'

Nicholas made no comment, merely dismissing the guard back to his rest. He knew he had still not been told everything. At least one of the guards had to know something they were keeping to themselves.

And they were not alone in that. He needed to speak to Simon de Gardyn again.

FORTY-SEVEN

The Deputy Constable

Sir Simon de Gardyn was just leaving the constable's office as the seneschal reached it. It was long past supper time and it appeared that the deputy constable, like Nicholas, had been too busy to think about eating. He was a little out of breath and there was a sheen of sweat on his brow. His hair was damp and he was using the back of his hand to push it away from his face.

'Have you been out, Simon?' asked Nicholas.

'Just a quick journey to Newton in the Isle, but it took rather longer than I expected and I am in need of supper. I'm going down to the hall,' he said pleasantly. 'Why don't you join me, Nicholas? I'm sure one of the cooks will find us some leftovers. This terrible business has left none of us time to think about our stomachs. Come along and we can talk while we eat.'

The great hall was empty but for a few kitchen boys who were wiping down the long trestle tables. On the dais, the high table had already been cleared and covered with a fresh white linen cloth, ready for the morning. Simon appeared not to notice, seating himself at the table as one of the boys approached. Nicholas followed and pulled out a chair, thanking the lad who promised to bring bread and ale. If the boy felt at all aggrieved at the prospect of clearing up a second time, he hid it well.

Until the food arrived, the seneschal and deputy spoke of general things, but as soon as a platter of fresh bread and sheep's cheese had been set before them and their cups were filled with good, strong ale, the seneschal quickly changed the subject.

'When we spoke earlier, why didn't you mention your visit to the cells at dawn this morning?'

Simon looked up from his trencher in surprise, but finished chewing his mouthful of bread before replying.

'Did I not mention it?' he asked with a shrug. 'I apologise if not, Nicholas, but it's such a normal part of my routine. I'm an early riser and whenever the constable is away and I am left in charge, I like to go down to the cells round about the time the shift changes, just to make sure all is in order. I suppose it didn't come to mind as anything worth saying, when we spoke earlier.'

Nicholas looked thoughtful.

'And was it?'

'Was it what?' replied Simon as he bit into another piece of bread.

'All in order?'

'Ah, yes. Everything was as it should have been. I spoke to the three men on duty, had a quick look through the cell door windows, and then went up to the office. It wasn't long afterwards that I received the report that one of the prisoners had been killed in his cell. And then I had to tell Alexander, of course, as soon as he returned from Murrow.'

The seneschal left Simon to his cheese and ale, having eaten enough supper to keep him going until the morning. He climbed the two flights of steps to his rooms and lay down on the bed fully clothed. Daylight was fading now, gently retreating with the dusk. He did not bother to get up and light a candle, finding the gathering darkness peaceful. He closed his eyes and thought through what he had learned so far in connection with this investigation.

He knew now that it had been Weland who had broken into the Wisbech houses and started fires in two of them, killing Aelfric in the process. Now Weland himself had been killed, but not before he had said enough to make it obvious that he was not working alone.

Someone had been helping him. He or she had left the youth to do the dirty work and take the blame. That person must also have been sheltering him, keeping him safe from the town search. And that person had killed him, to prevent him giving them away.

Weland had not struck the seneschal as being capable of much on his own. He had failed to steal the treasure from Aelfric's house as well as the coins from the ferryman's cottage. He was one of life's failures, even making a mess of his criminal activities. Therefore, it made sense that someone else was involved. And, since everything seemed to be based on the charter, whoever had been behind these incidents had to be familiar with that document.

So, who was it likely to be?

Someone in Ely? Someone there who had seen the copy of the charter held in the abbey? It could not be ruled out.

A member of the Hurste family? They were all aware of the contents of the charter, though Lady Rowena had tried hard to explain it away as nonsense. He had also seen her at the castle on the afternoon before Weland's death.

The officials in Wisbech? The constable, deputy, even the sergeant, knew about the charter, however much or little they had studied it themselves. The sergeant had perhaps never seen it, but could easily have learned about it over the years. As for the constable and his deputy, they both had free access to the document. However unthinkable it was that anyone responsible for upholding the law could be guilty in this matter, their involvement could not simply be dismissed.

The Old Market residents? They all seemed to know plenty about Aelfric and his family history, and not all of them liked him. Although people like the cobbler and Burdo the basket maker had benefitted from next to no education and were unlikely to have seen the charter themselves, they could have heard about its secrets from others.

But no, Nicholas decided. Whoever had orchestrated the hunt for Aelfric's treasure, who had therefore been behind the fires and the deaths of Aelfric and Weland, had to be someone in authority. Whoever it was, had enough influence to persuade an impressionable, wayward miscreant like Weland to act on their behalf.

Nicholas needed to return to Hurste manor. He needed to speak this time not only to Lady Rowena, but to Sir Mortimer, Rose and her brothers. This investigation needed to be brought to a close now. He needed to find Weland's killer and return at last to Ely.

FORTY-EIGHT

Feast of St Augustine of Canterbury; Monday 28th May

Sir Mortimer de Hurste was clearly not pleased to see the seneschal, but Nicholas doubted that such a stony faced individual showed much delight in anything.

The lord of this fine manor, with its pasture, arable land and extended acreage in neighbouring Lincolnshire, had just finished his dining. He sat alone at the table in his great hall and, judging by the clutter and debris left on the table, his family had only just left his side. A small army of kitchen boys arrived just after Nicholas and proceeded to clear the table, earning themselves a scowl from their lord.

'Let us find a more congenial place to speak,' grunted Sir Mortimer.

He rose from his seat and walked away from the long table, knocking against it as he went. Too much fine wine, thought Nicholas, or perhaps something else was ailing him. Sir Mortimer left the dais and walked through the hall, seating himself on a bench near the fire. On such a fine day, it was unusual to see a fire burning which was not needed for food preparation. Sir Mortimer appeared to feel chilly, though, and looked like he relished the warmth. The seneschal sat down next to him and began to speak as soon as they were settled.

'Sir Mortimer, I do not doubt that you are familiar with the charter which...'

'So you want to know about that ludicrous gift, do you?' Sir Mortimer interrupted wearily. 'That ill conceived donation of good manors to the Church? That gift which ultimately reduced my wife's family to beggars?'

'The Charter of Oswy and Leoflede, yes. Your wife's ancestors. Have you ever seen it? Have you read it yourself?'

The man frowned with a mixture of irritation and puzzlement.

'No, of course not! Why should I want to see it? I believe it's held at the castle or some such place. Talk to my wife, if you must. She may have seen it when she was young. I really do not know and cannot be bothered with such trivialities. You will find my wife soon enough. She likes to take a stroll with our daughter after dinner, but will be back here soon to get on with her stitching. Why she bothers with needlework I do not know. Blind as a bat, the silly woman, yet still she persists. It's all pride with her. Always has been.'

Nicholas could think of nothing else to say. He was more interested in the man's apparent lack of knowledge about the charter than his dismissive attitude towards his wife. Nicholas thanked him and left him to warm himself by his fireside.

The courtyard was warm with dappled sunshine, the young trees before the great hall providing a canopy of vibrant, fresh leaf. A serf was busy sweeping the well trodden path to the door and he bowed his head in deference as the seneschal walked by. Nicholas had only just passed the stables when he saw Lady Rowena and Rose entering the courtyard through the main gate.

Lady Rowena frowned and squinted, as if having trouble in recognising him, but Rose gave him a broad smile. Nicholas could fully understand why John of Tilneye found this young woman so appealing.

'Sir Nicholas!' Rose called out when they were still some distance apart. 'Have you come to tell us how your investigation is going?'

'Might we speak?' asked Nicholas, and Lady Rowena, perhaps relieved that her daughter had solved the mystery of their caller's identity, nodded coolly.

'Come inside, Sir Nicholas,' she said. 'They will have finished clearing the hall after dinner by now.'

There was, Nicholas thought, something different about Lady Rowena today. It made him recall the laughter he had seen on her face during that brief glimpse of her on Saturday afternoon at the castle. The gown she was wearing now was well fitted and of a becoming shade of pale green. A few tendrils of fair hair escaped her fine linen veil and there was brightness in her eyes, more colour in her cheeks. Some of the beauty with which Rose was blessed could once more be seen in her mother.

As Lady Rowena had predicted, the manorial servants had finished their work in the great hall and the high table had been relieved of its soiled linen cloth and remnants of dinner. The lord of the manor, however, remained at his fireside. His wife and daughter inclined their heads towards him as they passed and continued towards the dais where they sat with the seneschal at one end of the table.

'Would you like some wine, sir?' asked Rose as soon as they were seated. Nicholas, who was still hot and thirsty from his ride and who had been offered no refreshment by Sir Mortimer, accepted gladly. He doubted that Lady Rowena would have thought to offer him anything.

Once the wine had arrived, Nicholas told the two ladies about Weland's capture and his subsequent death. Rose expressed relief that the man had been caught, then dismay on learning that he had soon afterwards met his end. Lady Rowena hardly reacted at all to the news, simply giving absent minded nods now and then, as if her thoughts were elsewhere.

'But how?' demanded Rose. 'How could someone have killed him in his cell? Surely there could be no safer place!'

She took a sip of wine, obviously savouring it. It was good white Rhenish wine, imported from the Rhine Valley and expensive. The cost might explain, thought Nicholas, why Rose's parents were so sparing with it. Rose, perhaps lacking the need to consider such things, was far more generous to their guests.

'That is one of the questions I am trying to find an answer to,' replied the seneschal as he enjoyed a sip of wine himself.

'Then surely,' said Lady Rowena coldly, 'you should be at the castle, seeking your culprit. What do you want from us?'

'Speaking of the castle, my lady, I saw you there on Saturday. I was disappointed not to be able to speak to you, but you must have had to slip away.'

If it were possible, Lady Rowena's glare became even frostier as she met his eyes.

'You are obviously mistaken, my lord. I was not at the castle on Saturday.'

He held her eyes for a moment without replying. He no longer had any doubt that he had seen her there, that she was lying, but decided not to pursue it for now. Rose was looking curiously at her mother, but Rowena appeared not to notice.

'My reasons for coming here today, Lady Rowena, were to inform you of Weland's capture and to request a little more information from you. Weland's death has raised several questions. Please tell me how familiar you are with the wording of your family's charter, the Charter of...'

'Yes, I am fully aware of its title, thank you,' she interrupted crisply. 'What do you mean by how familiar I am with it?'

'Have you ever read the document?'

'I have not, neither have I seen it. The document is ancient, my lord seneschal, around two hundred years old and has to be stored safely. I believe it is kept at the castle. However, my father did tell me about it when I was a child.'

'And did he tell you about certain words hidden within the charter, clues which led to your father's house in the Old Market?'

'Yes,' she replied impatiently. 'He told me all about that myth and I thought I had already told you so. Such a lot of nonsense! Who would want to find that broken down old place? And once there, what were they meant to find? A box of cheap, nasty, gaudy trinkets?'

'But mother,' protested Rose, 'grandfather's house was not always broken down. It was once the principal residence of the Manor of Wisbech which was gifted to the abbey by our ancestors. In their day, the house would have been very fine and might have contained many treasures.'

Her mother gave a scoffing sound and scowled at the table cloth.

'I still see no point in your questions, Sir Nicholas. You have caught your killer and have even been saved the bother of an execution. Perhaps you should be thankful that someone took that out of your hands when they broke into his cell with a knife.'

'Mother!' objected Rose. 'These things cannot simply be ignored! The seneschal has to find out who killed Weland, despite all the man has done.'

Nicholas could not help wondering how Rose had managed to inherit such a sunny and sensible nature. Her grandfather, he thought, must have been a good influence on her character. Aelfric, by most accounts, had been a pleasant and popular man.

'Then perhaps you will excuse me?' he said as he finished his wine. 'I need to speak to your sons, Lady Rowena. Are they at home today?'

'Why must you bother them?' she demanded. 'They are busy, my lord. Kindly leave them undisturbed!'

'They are in the north field, sir,' said Rose, ignoring her mother's exasperated look. 'Just follow the lane out of the village, past the threshing barn and the carpenter's workshop.'

'Thank you,' he smiled, nodding politely to Lady Rowena as he took his leave. He thought he could feel the lady's eyes on his back as he walked away from the dais and out through the great hall. Perhaps her poor sight caused her to stare more than other folk. Whatever the reason, it made him feel uncomfortable and he was glad to leave the hall and to be back again in the warmth of the May afternoon.

HURSTE MANOR

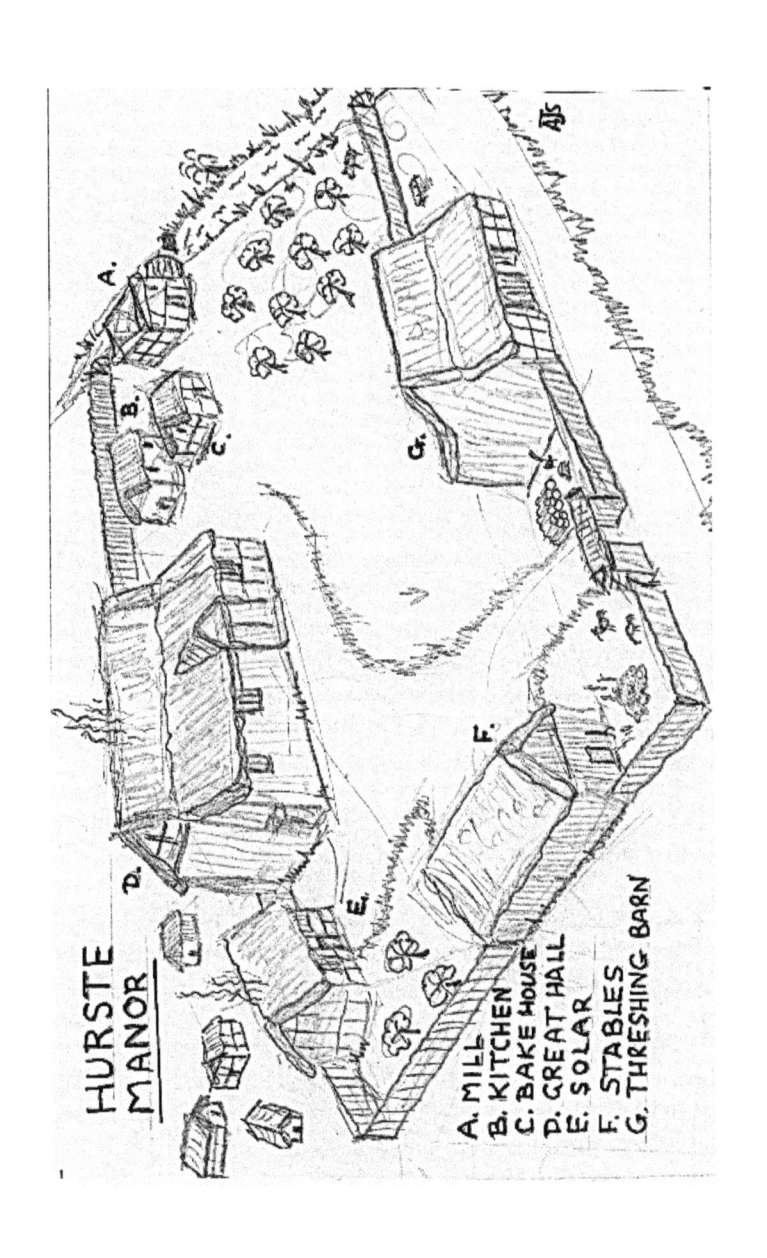

A. MILL
B. KITCHEN
C. BAKE HOUSE
D. GREAT HALL
E. SOLAR
F. STABLES
G. THRESHING BARN

FORTY-NINE

Leonard and Wallace

The sun was hot on the seneschal's back as he followed the dusty lane out of the village. It was not a long walk, certainly not one which warranted taking his horse from the manor's stables. After a short while, he could see the distant forms of peasants working in the fields. As he drew closer, he recognised two of them as Aelfric's old servants, Leof and Magan. They lifted their heads as he approached and as soon as they recognised him, greeted him warmly.

'I see you've been granted your wish, then,' he hailed them with a smile. 'Out of the kitchen and into the fields!'

'Yes, my lord,' confirmed Magan. 'I think our efforts were so lacking in the kitchen that they were glad to be rid of us. The steward had no trouble in finding us work out here.'

The men looked without doubt much happier than they had been in the kitchen. They lowered their heads again and went back to work with their long handled hoes. They were gradually working their way across the field, uprooting the many weeds that had sprung up between the tall bean plants.

'Where might I find Leonard and Wallace de Hurste?' the seneschal enquired.

Leof looked up from his hoeing again and grinned.

'Hard to miss them, sir. Leonard is on horseback in the barley field, giving orders. Wallace is more likely to be getting his hands dirty.'

'Keep your voice down, I keep telling you,' hissed Magan. 'You'll land us both in trouble with that mouth of yours.'

'But no one can hear us out here!' objected Leof. 'We're furlongs away from everyone!'

The seneschal nodded his thanks and continued along the edge of the field in the direction indicated by Leof. He could see the soft green haze of the barley field straight ahead and made his way towards the only man on horseback he could see.

'Leonard de Hurste?' he called out. The man turned round in the saddle, looking down at him.

'And who might you be...sir?'

Leonard had added the 'sir' as an afterthought, having belatedly noticed the newcomer's bearing, as well as the quality of his clothing.

'Nicholas Drenge, seneschal of the Isle of Ely. I would be obliged, sir, if you dismounted, so that we could speak without shouting.'

Leonard grimaced as he begrudgingly obeyed.

'I suppose you're here about my grandfather's death.'

Now that the man had lost the advantage of being on horseback, Nicholas saw that he was rather short in stature and had to raise his chin to look the seneschal in the eye. He soon tired of doing this and focussed his eyes instead on the distant horizon as they spoke.

'You suppose correctly,' replied Nicholas. 'I offer you my condolences.'

'Why?' queried Leonard, looking genuinely puzzled. 'I hardly ever saw the man. As far as I was concerned, he was a silly old fool and we had nothing in common.'

Nicholas was not surprised to hear it.

'How well did you know Weland of Ely?'

'Who?' he demanded. 'I know of no such fellow!' He pulled a face, as if assaulted by a nasty smell.

'You appear to find the thought of someone you do not know surprisingly repugnant. Are you unaware that Weland of Ely is a man of considerable standing?'

'Then I apologise. I meant no disrespect to him.'

Nicholas tried a different approach. His attempt to trick Leonard into admitting to know Weland had failed completely.

'I assume you know about your mother's family charter?'

'Oh, yes, we all know about that,' he said sarcastically. 'It was quite a smart move, wasn't it? One that turned a worthy, noble family into a wretchedly poor one overnight.'

'I believe other factors were involved,' said Nicholas. 'How well do you know the wording of that charter?'

'These are strange questions, my lord seneschal!' retorted Leonard. 'I do not believe I have ever seen the document. Surely an old thing like that rotted away years ago! Does it still exist, then?'

Leonard's curiosity had wiped the haughtiness from his face, but it had been replaced by a mocking smirk. The seneschal doubted that he would learn any more from him.

'Where is Wallace, your brother? I need to speak to him also.'

Leonard laughed, but not pleasantly.

'If you wish to find Wallace, my lord seneschal, look for the most stupid worker of those you see before you. The one who is sweating the most. My brother has not yet learned that the lord's sons do not labour with peasants.' He raised his voice suddenly and yelled, 'Wallace! Come here and answer this nice man's questions!'

He seemed to find his own words very amusing. Nicholas turned away as the man remounted his horse.

Wallace de Hurste was inspecting the green barley that was rapidly gaining height, its progress hampered only by the strangling hold of bindweed and other invasive weeds. Unlike the workers who sweated over their hoes, he did not appear to be greatly exerting himself. Leonard had been exaggerating his brother's involvement, but at least Wallace was showing genuine interest in the work. Wallace looked up in response to Leonard's call and began to make his way towards the two men. His brother muttered something and Wallace turned to speak to the seneschal.

'You wish to speak to me, my lord?'

Wallace was as short and unsmiling as his brother, but there was no obvious arrogance about him. Nicholas began by offering his condolences on the death of the young man's grandfather.

'Ah, yes. I was sorry to hear what happened. It was a terrible business. I was fond of my grandfather. We used to visit him as children and he told us tales about the old days, when the family was wealthy. They owned most of the land around here and plenty more in Suffolk, according to him.'

'He was quite right about that,' said Nicholas. 'Did your grandfather also tell you about the gift his forebears made to the abbey?'

'The charter and all that. Oh, yes, he certainly told us about that! Sometimes, it was all he wanted to talk about. With that charter the family gave away land and manors, but it took far more than that one act of misguided generosity to reduce the family to poverty. King William the Conqueror, though few will admit it these days, was no friend to his new English subjects. He destroyed them. He took their wealth and land and gave it to his own people. Everywhere you look now, Normans own English land.'

'You are half Norman yourself, though, Wallace.'

The man's face suddenly broke into a wide grin and he looked much better for it.

'You are right. I am, but there is Saxon blood in me too, and I hate the way the old English families were treated. My grandfather had lost everything, but he still had his pride. He kept going on about that charter and how it was supposed to lead to his house and some sort of treasure. I thought he was asking for trouble, keeping a silly legend alive like that, and it seems I was right.'

'Have you ever seen the charter?'

'Oh, no, my lord. It's locked away in the castle, I believe. I'm not sure why. It's of no use to anyone these days.'

'Did you ever see your grandfather's "treasure", as it is sometimes referred to?'

'Yes. He was very proud of those little trinkets and showed them to us all; my brother, sister and me. I believe he even gave a few items to Rose. If he had continued to give pieces away like that, there would soon have been nothing left.'

'Do you think that was why the treasure was stolen? To prevent your grandfather giving any more items away?'

Wallace frowned.

'I don't know. Was it, then? *Was* it stolen? Do you think my grandfather's killer took it?'

'It has never been found,' is all Nicholas said.

'But you caught the man, did you not? He died in the cells; stabbed, I believe. Surely, though, you had already found out from him whether or not he found the treasure?'

Nicholas did not reply immediately, hearing again in his head the words Lady Rowena had used earlier. He realised now that she had already known about Weland's death, though she had not admitted to it. She had given herself away by mentioning the knife. Nicholas had disclosed nothing about the manner of Weland's death. Now her son too was showing that he knew far more than he should have done.

'Wallace, how did you know about Weland's death? It happened only yesterday and one of my reasons for coming here today was to inform you all of it.'

'How did I know? My mother told me this morning! She must have been informed by someone else in authority. I did see a visitor's horse in the stables before supper yesterday. A fine beast it was, too. No commoner's horse, for sure. Perhaps someone else was doing your work for you, my lord.'

Nicholas was trying to control his anger. He did not like to be tripped up by those he was attempting to question. Wallace, seeing that the conversation was at an end, gave a shrug and returned to his work in the barley field.

The seneschal walked away, back between the fields and down the lane towards the manor house, thinking about what he had just heard. Someone had gone behind his back. Someone had visited Lady Rowena on the day of Weland's death and told her things which should have been kept, at least for the time being, confidential. Whoever it had been was wealthy enough to ride a good horse and influential enough to know all that was going on at the castle.

Lady Rowena too was being far from honest with him, and he did not like it at all.

He strode back to the manor house and hammered on the door. The young girl who answered his knocking was left in no doubt about his insistence on seeing Lady Rowena, but was unable to help. The lady, the girl replied, her eyes big and frightened, had retired to her bed.

'Then tell her to get up again!' Nicholas ordered. 'Inform the lady that the seneschal of the Isle of Ely demands that she speak to him!'

'My lord, I cannot,' protested the girl, close to tears. 'She says she is ill. She has a terrible pain in the head. She is too ill to see anyone!'

Nicholas withdrew angrily from the doorway. He knew he was being lied to once more, that the lady was making sure she would not have to face him again that day. In truth, there was nothing he could do about it. Mere suspicions about the lady's conduct and truthfulness were insufficient reason to break into her bed chamber and demand answers to his questions.

He strode towards the stables, both to find his own horse and to question any groom or stable lad he might find there. Someone, he reasoned, must know whose finely bred horse had visited the stables the previous evening.

There were, however, no grooms to be found in the stables. The neatly swept out stalls, with their peaceful equine occupants, were overseen by only one human being, and she could not have looked less like a stable lad if she had tried.

He wondered how long Rose had been there, speaking softly to her pretty grey mare while waiting to speak to him.

'I am glad to have caught you before you left, my lord,' she said quietly as soon as she saw him. Her sunny disposition seemed to have abandoned her and she looked pale and anxious.

'Rose? Is something the matter?'

'Sir Nicholas,' she whispered. 'I need to speak to you. Weland was wicked and I despise him for the callousness with which he caused my grandfather's death, but I have had time to think about things since we spoke earlier. I can see that you're linking Weland's death to my grandfather's, so I understand why you have to find out who killed him. I want you to know that I'll help in any way I can. Just let me know how I can be of assistance.'

'Thank you,' he said with a smile. 'There is something I hope you can help me with straight away. A visitor called here late yesterday afternoon and left his horse in these stables. It was a fine, well bred animal. Who was its rider? Who came to visit?'

She looked puzzled.

'Yesterday afternoon? I do not recall seeing anyone at all, sir.'

'What about the horse? Did you notice a stranger's horse in the stables?'

'No, sir, but I do not believe I came out here after midday. I am sorry, but I saw neither the visitor nor his horse.'

Nicholas cursed inwardly, but continued.

'When your mother was speaking to me earlier, was she telling the truth?'

'As far as I can tell, sir, but something feels wrong. My mother has not been herself lately. She disappears sometimes for hours and when I speak to her she seems hardly to hear me. Her mind is elsewhere most of the time. I would not betray her; she is my mother and has not had the easiest of lives, but...' Rose paused and seemed to think carefully over her words. 'All I am saying is that, if whoever killed Weland had a hand in my grandfather's death, they should be caught. Whoever they are!'

The seneschal nodded in agreement.

'Rose, you should go to your mother now. I understand she is unwell. If there is some way in which you can help, I promise I'll let you know.'

Even after he had ridden out of the courtyard, Rose remained where she was. She was in no hurry to move. She knew he was right, that she should go to her mother, but Lady Rowena's headaches and strange behaviour were becoming very frequent of late and very tiresome. Rose was not at all sure what to make of it.

FIFTY

Monday Twilight

The upper storeys of the castle keep were quiet as Nicholas reached them, most of the day's activity fading away with the twilight. The constable's office was still occupied, however, and its door was ajar. He pushed it cautiously open to find the deputy constable working there alone.

'Ah, Nicholas!' Simon exclaimed with a friendly look. 'I thought you were Alexander. He is due back at any moment and I need to discuss something with him.'

Nicholas regarded the deputy without speaking for a moment. He was recalling his appearance on the afternoon following Weland's death, the last occasion on which Nicholas had seen him. Simon had been late for supper, sweaty and dishevelled, explaining that he had just ridden from Newton in the Isle. The timing fitted rather well with Wallace's account of the unidentified visitor to Hurste that same afternoon. And Newton was not at all far from Hurste.

'How much did you tell her?' demanded Nicholas, breaking his own silence. He declined the offer of the usual chair, standing instead and staring down at Simon.

'I beg your pardon?' Simon looked perplexed. Nicholas had the impression that the man's confusion was genuine, but still he continued.

'Lady Rowena de Hurste had a visitor from the castle yesterday afternoon. Whoever that visitor was informed her of Weland's death in the cells.'

'Lady Rowena?' queried Simon looking astonished. 'Why by God's teeth do you assume I paid her a visit?'

'Because someone in authority did. Someone who, despite the need for discretion, chose to ride to Hurste and tell Aelfric's daughter all about Weland's killing!'

'Well, sir, it most certainly was not I!'

Simon de Gardyn had pulled himself up straight in his chair and had grown pale, his prominent Adam's apple bobbing up and down as he spoke. It occurred to Nicholas that someone of Lady Rowena's supreme dignity was unlikely to want to spend much time with this unprepossessing individual.

The door behind Nicholas slowly opened.

'I believe,' said Alexander de Astonne as he entered the office, 'that you need to ask me about that.'

'You, sir?' asked Simon. He looked aghast as he rose to his feet to allow the constable to take the principal chair. 'You went to see Lady Rowena yesterday? Why?'

'It is true that I was there,' replied Alexander with enormous weariness as he lowered himself into his chair. 'As you know, I must go to Ely early tomorrow and I wanted to see the lady before I left, to let her know that I shall be missing for a few days. She and I have known each other since long before her marriage, and for a considerable time we stayed in touch. We knew the nature of our friendship was wrong and, quite apart from the immorality of it, I began to fear what might happen to her if that thug of a husband found out about our meetings...'

The constable seemed to lapse into his own private thoughts and both Simon and Nicholas continued to look at him in expectation.

'So, did you stop meeting her?' prompted Nicholas after a considerable silence.

'Yes, for a time I did, and immediately regretted it. I began to reason that a virtuous life isn't necessarily a good one. And so, a short time ago, I returned to see her and it seems she is as happy as I for things to continue.'

'And the thug of a husband?' queried Nicholas.

'If things went wrong, I would take her away. There would be nothing else for it. There would be hell to pay, but...'

Nicholas looked mildly surprised. The constable's words, however, explained the recent improvement in Lady Rowena's appearance, as well as the changes in behaviour which Rose had told him about.

'And you visited her yesterday,' stated the seneschal, 'and told her about the killing of your prisoner in the cells.'

'I should not have done that. I realise that by telling her so much, I made matters more difficult for you,' replied Alexander with a deep sigh. 'Weland's death weighs heavily on my conscience and I found myself telling her everything. I could not help myself. I am sorry, Nicholas.'

Simon was staring in horror at the constable.

'And did you, by any chance,' asked Nicholas, 'see the lady when she visited the castle on Saturday afternoon?'

'Saturday afternoon? Why would you think that? I had left Wisbech by then. I was on my way to Murrow.'

Nicholas did not pursue the point, though he had to wonder why Lady Rowena had been there. If she had hoped to see the constable, his absence would have been a disappointment for her. If she had been there for another reason, however...

Now was not the time to think about that.

'Well, Alexander,' he said after another awkward silence, 'again I wish you good fortune for your visit to the bishop tomorrow.'

'Thank you, Nicholas. I fear I shall be away for at least two or three days. I hope I shall return still as constable, but if I am forced to step down...'

Nicholas nodded, not without sympathy.

'Then I shall leave you both in peace.'

The constable and his deputy bade the seneschal sober, rather embarrassed farewells as he left the room.

Though nothing quite fitted into place as yet in the seneschal's reasoning, he had a strong feeling that he was close to the truth, to knowing who had been controlling things since the beginning and was responsible for the deaths of Aelfric and Weland.

He hoped that the constable would not be away for long.

FIFTY-ONE

Tuesday, 28th May
Serpents

Tuesday morning brought rain, a change in the weather that was welcomed by almost everyone. The early summer warmth had brought on growth everywhere, the fields and vegetable plots showing green with abundant life, but the recent patch of dry weather was beginning to take its toll. Now, great soaking drops of rain were darkening the thirsty soil and refreshing the wilted green of leaves and shoots.

The seneschal would have been grateful for a different kind of refreshment. Though he still sensed he was not far from the truth, his next move was anything but clear. That morning, for want of anything more positive to do, he walked from the castle towards the Old Market, pulling his cap more snugly around his ears as the rain continued to fall.

There was one thing, he contemplated as he walked, which had largely been neglected in his thinking. That one thing lay at the root of everything that had occurred, and it was Aelfric's box of treasures.

Whether the items it contained were valuable, as Rose believed, or worthless trinkets, as Lady Rowena insisted, it had been their promise of riches that had lured Weland to Aelfric's house. The treasure had been linked verbally to the words hidden in the charter for longer than anyone remembered and had led to the deaths of Aelfric then of Weland himself. So what had happened to that treasure?

Weland had failed to find it and it had not been unearthed from the ashes of the Big House in the Old Market. The site had now been cleared and nothing of significance had been found. The Old Market had been watched continuously. If anything had been removed from the site, it had either to have been done before the seneschal's arrival or right in front of the guards on duty.

The water in the Wysbeck reached no higher than the tops of the flat stones that lined the river bed that morning and the seneschal forded it easily, climbing the far bank towards the main square of the Old Market. He stood for a moment on the bank top and looked out over the square before beginning to walk down the steps. He soon had to give up and find another way down. The steps cut into the bank were already eroded in places and the morning's heavy rain had filled the hollows, making each step an obstacle to be negotiated. Nicholas moved to one side and began to make his way down through the partly trampled grass. His booted feet swished through the wet growth, parting tall weeds and dispersing the seeds of a dozen or more dandelion heads as he went.

About half way down, his foot struck something hard in the grass and he bent down to toss the object away. It was a small off cut of limestone, too insignificant for any practical use and probably discarded decades ago. As he picked it up, he almost missed the tiny object that lay beside it. It was almost completely hidden amongst the yellow dandelions and grass, but it had the unmistakable gleam of gold.

Nicholas carefully eased the small item from the earth. It had been half trodden into the soil and much of it was encrusted with earth. He cleaned it as well as he could using the edge of his cloak and was then able to take a proper look at it. It was a brooch.

It was, he could see at once, of very high quality. The seneschal recognised good workmanship when he saw it and the small piece of jewellery he held in his hand was a fine example of that. It was of an old design, more likely Saxon than Norman, and had been expertly worked by a goldsmith. Circular in shape, it was no larger than a silver penny. Within an intricately decorated rim was an openwork pattern of entwined serpents, their eyes glowing with the light of miniature rubies. In the centre was a single, beautifully cut emerald.

The seneschal gave the brooch another polish on his cloak and turned it over. The pin that had once fastened it to a tunic or gown was bent out of shape and would no longer serve any purpose. Apart from this small flaw, the brooch was in good condition and clearly valuable. What was more, the seneschal had found it no more than a furlong or so from where Aelfric's house had stood only weeks before.

Surely his eyes could not be deceiving him? He had been thinking of Aelfric's treasure only seconds before he had chanced on this thing and it seemed too much of a coincidence, too good to be true.

Yet, the tiny brooch that sat in the palm of his hand was real enough. Was it too great an assumption to consider it as part of Aelfric's collection? Its age, quality and location certainly led to that conclusion. Whoever had stolen Aelfric's treasure could only have left the Old Market by one of two routes; either north along the river towards Newton in the Isle, or across the Wysbeck towards the castle and the New Market.

Having chosen the castle direction, the thief would have forded the river at this spot. He would have been in a hurry, needing to reach somewhere safe in which to hide his loot. If he had run up the steps cut into the bank, it was possible that he dropped an item or two into the grass. The place where the brooch had been found was but a pace away from the steps on the right hand side.

If Nicholas was right in his assumptions, this small object was the first evidence that some of Aelfric's treasure had been found and stolen. If Weland had not succeeded in taking what he went into the house for, someone else must have found this brooch in the ashes. But who?

Perhaps the brooch could be used to identify that person. Whether or not they had also been behind the killing and destruction, it was too soon to tell. Finding out who had dropped this brooch, though, was certain to bring the seneschal closer to the truth.

He placed the brooch safely inside his scrip then climbed back up the bank and crossed the river. He needed to think things through.

FIFTY-TWO

Tuesday Afternoon
Fine Mist

The rain had hushed the manor of Hurste. The earlier downpour had softened to heavy drizzle by the time Nicholas reached the village, yet still its lanes and paths were becoming a slippery mess. Most folk had retreated indoors and the bustle which had been evident everywhere on his previous visit had diminished almost to nothing. Even the pigs and poultry, rather than wandering the lanes in contented curiosity, were huddled into sties and pens and were notably subdued. Only the distant barking of a dog broke the rainy quiet, and even that sounded half hearted, as if the animal would rather be sleeping.

The doors of the manor house and outbuildings were closed but their shutters remained half open, showing at least some willingness to admit the world outside. Through the kitchen windows drifted the usual sounds of clattering pans and servants' banter. Now and then, the voices rose to a torrent of laughter, quietened only when a harsher, more commanding tone cut in to chastise them.

The seneschal's knocking was answered almost immediately and he was led into the great hall. The place was full to capacity and the noise of fifty or more different conversations resounded from the high roof beams. It felt like the whole manor, with its freemen, villeins and serfs, had escaped the rain and was packed into this one large hall. The fire in the centre was lit as before, making the place hot and stuffy, and the combined smells of sweat, smoke and left over food from dinner time were overwhelming. Kitchen boys were moving amongst the throng of people, attempting to clear away the last of the long trestle tables and resettling their occupants to groups of seats around the walls and fire.

Sir Mortimer de Hurste was sitting alone at the high table on the dais and, despite the heat, looked as chilly as before. The fingers of his right hand were wrapped around a thickly potted cup from which he occasionally sipped, seemingly unaware of doing so. He looked completely detached from the rest of the company and, as the seneschal approached, he looked up in surprise, as if caught taking a nap. His long, lugubrious face nodded his assent as Nicholas joined him at the table. Drawing another cup towards him, he poured some ale for the seneschal. Though not so refined as the Rhenish wine Nicholas had enjoyed before, the ale was more refreshing after his damp ride and he was glad of it.

'So you wish to speak to Rose,' the manorial lord concluded after hearing the seneschal's request. 'I do hope it's not as a suitor. Far too many of them already, all with spotty faces and some with scarcely an acre to their name. Why they think I should marry my daughter to any one of them, I fail to comprehend. Not a mote, not a flicker of intelligence between the lot of them!'

Nicholas smiled and Sir Mortimer responded with a look of dry humour. Nicholas found himself wondering whether he had misjudged this man. What had appeared at first to be hostility looked more like world weariness to him now.

'I assure you, sir, that my need to speak to your daughter is purely in connection with my current investigation.'

'Ah, yes. That business. My father-in-law and all that. Well, go ahead. She'll be off on one of her walks with her mother, I should think. Rain or shine, they always wander off as soon as dinner is done with. Wait around and you'll find them soon enough.'

Nicholas finished his ale and rose from the table.

'Do you have a wife, Sir Nicholas? Or a daughter?' asked Sir Mortimer just as the seneschal was leaving.

'A wife, yes, but no daughter. A son only.'

'Ah, then, you'll know at least some of my anguish,' said Sir Mortimer with something faintly resembling a laugh. 'Women are such peculiar things. Tantrums, tears... especially a daughter's. A daughter is a penance, Sir Nicholas, as much as she is a treasure.'

The seneschal smiled as he took his leave, walking back through the crowded hall towards the main entrance. Just as he reached the door, Rose and her mother walked in from the rain. Rose greeted him warmly, though Lady Rowena stared at him with no perceptible change in her expression.

'My lady. Rose,' said Nicholas. 'Lady Rowena, might I have a word with Rose?'

Lady Rowena shrugged as a servant began to lift the wet cloak from her shoulders.

'Do as you must.'

There was nowhere private in which they could speak. Normally, they could have found a quiet corner in the great hall, but today it was far too crowded. The manor house was typical of its kind; apart from the large communal hall, there were only the family's private solars and work spaces for servants. It was nothing like the castle with its ante rooms and offices.

'Let's go outside,' Rose suggested. 'The rain will not harm us.'

Nicholas, though not keen on another wetting, accompanied her into the courtyard. Fortunately, the rain had lessened by then to no more than a fine mist and they hardly noticed it as they walked through the gates and into the lane. Once they had walked far enough and he was sure that they could not be observed, the seneschal took from his scrip the brooch he had found by the river. Rose's sudden intake of breath told him instantly that she recognised it.

'That was my grandfather's,' she confirmed. 'I looked at it often as a child. It is very old and of the finest Saxon craftsmanship. Have you seen how each of these serpents is fashioned? Each has his own individual face, each one slightly different to the others, if you look closely. That was what fascinated me whenever I looked at it. Grandfather used to say that they all had their own personalities. It was a sort of game for us. He told me that this brooch had been passed down through many generations of our family. It was kept in the box with all his other treasured family pieces. May I?'

He nodded and she took the brooch from the palm of his hand.

'The pin at the back has been broken,' she observed after a moment or two of examining it. 'It was in perfect condition before. I know because Grandfather used to let me wear it sometimes, so long as it was back in the box before I went home.'

'There's no real damage,' replied Nicholas. 'The pin has only been bent out of shape and could easily be repaired. Rose, if your parents gave you leave, would you come to Wisbech and help me? I'd like you to wear this brooch while we speak to people, so that I can test the reactions of a few individuals.'

'I am not sure that my father...but if Matilda came too....yes, of course, Sir Nicholas. I will gladly help if I have permission to do so. Let's go and speak to my father!'

'But first, I need a smith!' declared Nicholas.

The blacksmith of Hurste Manor was far more accustomed to working with iron than with gold and was unused to dealing with objects as tiny as the Saxon brooch, but the task took very little of his time. He straightened the pin sufficiently to allow the brooch to be fastened securely to Rose's gown.

'It's the best I can do, lady,' said the smith apologetically as he looked fondly at Rose. He had known her since she was a child, had watched her grow up and regarded her as kindly as he would one of his own children.

'It's perfect,' she assured him with a broad smile. The seneschal, glancing at the man's large, calloused hands that were used to heavy work, agreed wholeheartedly with Rose's assessment. He thanked him warmly as he paid for the work.

'Now,' he said as they emerged from the smithy, 'we need to speak to your parents.'

Rose had pinned the brooch to the front of her gown, just beneath the rounded, embroidered neckline. Once they were back indoors and her cloak had been removed, she arranged the skirts of her dove grey gown and looked at the seneschal for approval. The red of the rubies and the gleam of gold stood out boldly against the pale grey background. The brooch would be hard to ignore.

They walked into the great hall, dodging their way through the crowds to reach the dais where Lady Rowena sat with her husband. None of the more senior members of the family were present. Sir Mortimer broke off from what he had been saying to his wife and watched his daughter approaching with the seneschal. Lady Rowena lifted her head, peering hard at them both.

'Sir Mortimer; Lady Rowena,' said the seneschal. 'I have a request to make of you concerning my investigation into the death of Aelfric and of Weland of Ely. It would do me a great service if Rose could spend a day or two in Wisbech. She would be accompanied, of course, by her companion and by whomever else you considered appropriate...'

'Certainly not!' exclaimed Lady Rowena. She looked cross and suspicious. 'And what is that ridiculous bauble you are wearing, girl? It has the look of one of those toys your grandfather used to hoard. Is it?'

'Yes, mother,' replied Rose demurely, clearly ready with her answer. 'My grandfather gave me a few pieces of family jewellery when I was younger.'

'So I recall,' sniffed her mother disapprovingly. 'Take it off at once! If you wish to wear jewellery, there are better pieces you can wear, gifts from your father and me.'

Rose's hands hovered over the brooch, uncertain whether or not to obey her mother. In the end, perhaps noticing that Rowena had turned her attention to Sir Mortimer, she let her hands fall and left the brooch where it was.

'How would my daughter's presence in Wisbech be of benefit?' asked Sir Mortimer calmly.

'Rose is wearing her grandfather's brooch, as my lady has observed,' replied Nicholas carefully. He was sure of no one yet and was unwilling to give too much away. 'It would be helpful to see people's reactions to it.'

'As part of Aelfric's hoard,' said Sir Mortimer thoughtfully.

'Of course Rose cannot go with you!' persisted Rowena. Her voice was becoming shrill and her husband turned and gave her a long, expressionless look.

'You have no wish for whoever was behind your father's killing to be caught?' he asked her in the same level voice.

She was becoming flustered, far less confident of facing down Sir Mortimer than she was the seneschal.

'Naturally, he must be caught,' she conceded, her face reddening, 'but I am unwilling for Rose to be paraded around Wisbech like a dancing bear at a fair and...'

'My lady,' said Nicholas when her words ran away to nothing. 'I assure you that no such thing will happen. Rose can keep her companion with her at all times, her own men-at-arms too, if you wish. She will only need to stay in the town for a day, two at the most, and she will be treated with the greatest honour as the constable's guest.'

'When will this be?' asked Sir Mortimer,

'It is likely to be in a week's time, sir. I will send word shortly before Rose and her party need to set out for the castle.'

There was no point in doing any of this, Nicholas knew, until the constable was back from Ely, and that would not be for several days yet.

'I do not like it,' stated Lady Rowena through pursed lips.

'Very well,' stated the lord of the manor. 'Rose will ride to the castle as soon as we hear from you. We must,' he added pointedly, turning to look at his angry wife, 'assist the law whenever we can. Is that not so?'

Lady Rowena nodded stiffly and reluctantly, refusing to look at the seneschal as he made his exit. Rose too hurried out of the hall, close on Nicholas's heels, eager to avoid any attempt of her mother's to talk her out of what had been agreed.

Rose and Nicholas spoke briefly before he left. He made sure that she understood the role she was to play.

'And take care of the brooch until then,' he added. 'Don't let it out of your sight.'

She nodded soberly as she bade him goodbye, looking in that moment a lot like her father.

FIFTY-THREE

Feast of St Justin; Friday 1st June

The fields belonging to the manor of Marshmeade were waist high with growing crops. The rain that had fallen over the last few days had swollen the ditches and reinvigorated growth. The crows, wood pigeons, rabbits and deer were doing well from all this bounty, helping themselves to anything they fancied. There was a limit to how much bird scaring the village children were able or prepared to do. The young ones threw themselves daily into their duty of running around, making a lot of noise and waving their arms at all the unwelcome wildlife. It had become a game for them, but as with all games, there inevitably came a time when they grew tired of it. No sooner had the adults turned their backs, the children began to wander off in search of other entertainment.

On the first day of June, John of Tilneye was out in the fields. He was wading through the great sea of barley, the fresh, green, bearded heads standing tall and healthy and moving gently in the summer breeze. He knew that one day, when his father was no more and John became lord of the manor, all of this land and its people would become his responsibility. He was in no hurry for that day to come, satisfied that for now it was Sir Roland who made the decisions, leaving John a measure of freedom with which to please himself. He would be ready when the time came, though, and was gradually taking over the responsibility for the manor's agricultural acres, seeing to their ploughing, sowing and harvest.

The wheat and barley harvests promised to be good that year. If all continued to go well, there would be enough grain in the stores to keep the people of Marshmeade fed through the winter and into the next spring. There was the wool, too, and that had great value. The spring had brought plenty of new lambs to swell the flocks, meaning increased wool production for the future. There was already enough to supply the manor's needs, leaving a considerable surplus to be sold. The wool trade was very lucrative. The demand for good, clean fleeces was huge and the market was buoyant as never before.

Marshmeade was not a large manor. It was not blessed with the acreage enjoyed by many of its neighbours, but the land it had was good. The rich, dark soil produced abundant crops year after year and the pasture that lined the bank of the Well Stream supported healthy flocks of sheep. As well as all this, there was the manor's area of fenland. Untamed and uncontrolled, it was a natural source of wildfowl, fish and eels, as well as willow, reeds and rushes for building homes.

So productive was the manor of Marshmeade that it supported its lord, his family and all his people, leaving plenty to spare. Sir Roland saw no need to acquire other manors through marriage or by favours to those in higher authority. This lack of ambition was sometimes seen as laziness and excessive complaisancy. There were times when he attracted criticism and sneering comments from his richer neighbours who sought constantly to increase their wealth and standing in the world by expanding their acreage.

This was most likely the reason, John thought as he stood and looked out over the fields, why families like the Hurstes never took the Tilneyes seriously. It was perhaps why Rose was disinterested. One of the reasons, anyway.

Once more, he tried to push Rose away from his thoughts. He had vowed to think no more of her, to go on enjoying the freedom he cherished. Ever since that last uninspiring trip to Hurste, he had thrown himself back into his old ways. He had spent even more time than usual in the hostelries and bestowing his charm on the local women, but it was beginning to pall. And it had failed to dislodge Rose from his mind.

But he would not go back on his vow. There would be no more trips to Hurste, no more hiding and spying in the hope of scavenging some crumb of Rose's attention. He would forget her in the end. He was capable of most things, so that too was possible.

He turned abruptly on his heel and headed for home.

FIFTY-FOUR

Feast of St Boniface; Tuesday 5th June

The constable returned to Wisbech Castle on the feast of St Boniface, following an absence of seven days. He was grey faced and exhausted as he walked into his office.

'Alexander!' exclaimed his deputy. 'I am heartily pleased to see you.'

Sir Alexander de Astonne smiled grimly as he removed his cloak, throwing it on to a bench by the wall. He dropped gratefully into his usual seat beneath the windows.

'I am truly glad to be back, Simon.'

'And how did you find my lord Bishop William de Longchamp?'

'All things considered, his grace was good to me. I would not have blamed him had he removed me as constable, but he did not. No, the worst I endured was the interminable delay before being able to see him. When I first arrived, his return from Winchester was still awaited. As chancellor, affairs of state take up much of his time, and his journey back to Ely this time was hampered by poor weather and even poorer roads. It meant, of course, that I had to wait. And while I waited I was held in judgement by the eyes of men from all over the shire. They appeared to have learned with miraculous speed about my failings towards the prisoners in my care. It is most surely a fact, Simon, that bad news travels more quickly than good. The spreading of ill tidings seems to be done with particular relish.

'When at last I was able to speak to my lord bishop,' Alexander continued, 'I stated the facts of the case without embellishment. I made no excuses and his grace, after asking a few pertinent questions, withdrew to consider the matter for two long days. I kept to my lodgings for most of that time, awaiting my summons and fearing that my time here as constable was at an end. At last, early yesterday morning, I was called to the bishop's office and informed that I was to be punished with a fine. Just a fine. I was greatly relieved.'

'Well, sir,' acknowledged Simon warmly. 'That sounds like a very good outcome!'

'Indeed it is. I have only to pay half my yearly salary and all is forgiven!' he replied with a wry smile. 'Ten marks! Ten marks for dereliction of duty. For being so slipshod that a man was killed in my custody. I deserved far harsher treatment, Simon, and no fine is going to ease the remorse I feel.'

'But sir, if my lord bishop has not judged you more severely, why do that to yourself? Perhaps you should accept his greater wisdom?'

'I fear that will be easier said than done,' remarked Alexander.

'I must let the seneschal know of your return,' said the deputy after a short pause. 'He needs to know, apparently.'

'I shall send word to him myself. The man has a job to do and I hope he sees it through to the end now. Then we can draw a line under this matter and the seneschal can relieve us all of his presence.'

Simon nodded.

'And perhaps then we can have some peace again.'

'Until the next time,' added the constable under his breath.

FIFTY-FIVE

Thursday, 7th June
The Swan

Rose de Hurste arrived shortly after noon, two days after receiving the seneschal's message.

On her parents' insistence, she was accompanied by two men-at-arms and her usual silent companion, Matilda. Sir Nicholas Drenge, who had been awaiting her arrival with ill disguised impatience for more than a day, went straight to the castle bailey to greet Rose. Her men-at-arms were sent to stable the horses and, though dinner was finished, to beg some food from the kitchens. Rose's companion, however, was not so easily dismissed.

Matilda, having received strict instructions from Lady Rowena not to leave Rose alone at any time, refused to leave her side. She stuck out her already prominent chin and folded her arms defiantly.

Her lady, she insisted, needed her.

'All will be well,' Rose assured her. 'Go with the men to the kitchens. You haven't eaten in a while and must be hungry. I shall see you later, but I need to speak to the seneschal alone.'

Matilda went at last and with obvious resentment. As soon as she had disappeared from sight, the seneschal led Rose out of the castle towards the New Market place. He needed to speak to her before anyone else at the castle saw her, and she made no objection as he hurried her away. She even seemed to be enjoying herself and was perhaps relieved, thought Nicholas, to be free of Matilda's joyless company for a while.

Like the rest of her party, Rose had not eaten since early morning. Their journey had taken longer than expected, mainly because Matilda was such a poor rider and could manage nothing faster than a snail's pace. Rose therefore accepted the seneschal's offer of late dinner in one of the town's hostelries, and she did so with undisguised enthusiasm.

The problem for Nicholas was that, having neglected to think through the situation beforehand, he was unable to think of any ale house that might be suitable for a young lady of Rose's standing. Most of the town's hostelries were as terrible as the Ship in the Old Market, places for men to drown their sorrows in. Their regular customers cared nothing at all about stale floor rushes, filth, vermin, or the stink of unwashed bodies.

Nicholas was racking his brains, trying to think of somewhere suitable for them to go to, while Rose chattered about her journey. Women did, of course, visit inns and hostelries, especially when travelling. Where there was a religious house on the route, travellers were normally accommodated there, but Wisbech had no such place. Official visitors were put up at the castle, but that was the place he most needed to avoid for now.

It was with relief that he remembered the Swan in the New Market. It was the most respectable hostelry he could think of. In a manner that he hoped made it appear that he had intended to go there all along, he guided Rose towards its door. At this time of afternoon, the place was relatively quiet. A few of the older regulars sat in one corner, speaking now and then in a drowsy tone that suggested they might doze off at any moment. Nicholas took Rose to sit in the opposite corner where the floor rushes looked the least trodden and where they were less likely to be overheard.

She was looking around with interest, smiling as she took in the well worn yet comfortable scene before her with its aromas of ale and baking bread.

'Is it always like this?' she asked. 'I mean, so pleasant? I had heard that hostelries were squalid, foul places.'

She was squinting a little as she took in her surroundings, raising her hand to shield her eyes from a beam of bright sunshine that stole in through a high window.

'You've not been in a hostelry before?' Nicholas asked, astonished. For all his care in finding the best place for her, he had not expected her to be quite so new to them.

'No. My parents do not permit it and I have never travelled, so there has been no need. This is very pleasing.'

She might not be so keen, he reflected, if she saw the place closer to midnight. Late at night, even the finer qualities of the Swan were overwhelmed by drunkenness. It would be no place for a lady.

The hostelry keeper came out from the back room, wearing a pleasant but mainly toothless smile.

'Any of your fine pottage available today?' enquired the seneschal. 'The lady has missed her dinner.'

'Indeed there is,' lisped the man, 'and a new batch of bread is just out of the oven.'

'Sounds perfect,' Nicholas replied, seeing Rose's face light up even more.

The man hurried away and Nicholas lowered his voice. It was time to discuss the work ahead.

'We should go to the Old Market first,' he began. 'Nothing could be more natural than you wishing to visit the site of your grandfather's home. No one will query your presence there. In fact, I rather fear that seeing the square as it is now will cause you some pain.'

'I am prepared for that, my lord seneschal,' she said. 'I do not expect it to be easy and any sadness I show will add conviction to our charade. People might be less on their guard, so it should be easier for us to catch them unaware and lead the guilty into giving themselves away.'

He nodded. Rose's common sense was making his job far easier than he had expected. She appeared to need very little guidance from him and looked more than equal to the task.

'If you put the brooch on just before we leave here, we can walk to the Old Market and spend some time there, chatting to people. It will be up to me to watch their reactions. You can just concentrate on being charming and...'

He paused as the door opened and, taking his cue, Rose too fell silent. They watched as the newcomer made his entrance, looking around as if deciding, in the almost empty ale house, where to sit. He started to head for the group of regulars by the far wall, then hesitated.

He turned to look at the seneschal and Rose, but seemed to be having trouble seeing them clearly. He was blinded by the beam of sunshine that cut across the room, almost dividing the place into two. As Rose had done earlier, he shielded his eyes to look properly at the two figures seated in the corner.

'My lord seneschal!' he announced, then more incredulously, 'lady!'

His surprise hardly disguised his obvious delight in seeing Rose. She peered up at him, as if undecided whether his arrival was a good thing.

'Sir John of Tilneye!' she responded with immaculate courtesy. Nicholas tutted. With them about to start work in the Old Market, the last thing they needed was company.

John appeared not to notice the lack of warmth in their welcome. He pulled out a stool and seated himself opposite them at the small board table, smiling broadly.

'Are you about to eat?' he asked. 'I'm pretty hungry myself.'

'Yes,' replied Rose politely. 'The pottage will be here in a moment.'

Nicholas, in spite of his frustration, listened with interest to their simple exchange. John was clearly trying to curb his puppy-like zeal. He sounded slightly nervous. It was Rose, though, who surprised him. Beneath her cool and faultless delivery, he sensed a degree of suppressed excitement.

'You're planning something, aren't you?' John observed after a short pause. 'Let me help.' Neither Rose nor Nicholas made any reply. Rose looked down at her hands while Nicholas glared at John across the table. 'My lord seneschal,' the young knight continued, 'you have already involved me in your work, so please allow me to continue. Besides, there is only so much a man can do on his manor. I can't make the barley grow any faster.'

The hostelry keeper appeared with a tray and began setting out bowls of pottage and a large platter of rye bread on the table. The savoury aroma increased John's hunger.

'Do you have any more of that? And some of the bread would be welcome.'

The hostelry keeper replied with another of his gaping smiles and bustled away to fulfil the order.

'So,' continued John cheerfully, 'how can I help?'

Nicholas sighed heavily in exasperation. The youth's self confidence, though somewhat checked by his obsession with Rose, was as overwhelming as ever. The seneschal opened his mouth to deliver a dismissive remark when Rose began to speak.

He tried to stop her, but in a few blurted sentences she had told John all about the brooch and what they intended to do. Nicholas had credited her with far more sense, and his disappointment as she breathlessly uttered all that should have been kept quiet, was considerable.

Suddenly, and far too late, she appeared to realise that she had broken some unspoken promise and she slumped back against the wall in dismay.

'I am sorry, my lord,' she said quietly. 'I have let you down before we've even started.'

Nicholas said nothing, though his annoyance was obvious. John, surprisingly, looked far from honoured to have been told so much. In fact, he looked rather unimpressed with what he had heard.

'So, Rose de Hurste is going to be led around Wisbech by the seneschal of the Isle of Ely, in the hope that someone forgets him or herself and blurts out their secrets,' he stated cynically.

'No, it wouldn't be like that,' Rose objected hastily, thinking that he sounded a bit like her mother. She fell silent as the hostelry keeper returned with John's food. The group remained quiet until the man had retreated into the back room, though it took him an infuriatingly long time. They could still see him hovering close to the door and they took the opportunity to eat. The pottage, made with turnips, leeks and a good selection of herbs, was excellent, as good as its aroma had promised. Mopped up with rye bread, it was filling too.

'Rose will not be "led around", as you put it, at all,' the seneschal pointed out coldly, as soon as he was confident they could no longer be overheard. He wondered why he was justifying his decisions to this arrogant young knight.

'Poor choice of words,' acknowledged John in a slightly humbler tone. He had taken the time while he ate to rethink his approach. 'However, I wonder whether the people Rose speaks to be would be less guarded if, instead of being with a law man, she is an accompanied by an old family friend. One who is looking after her while she revisits the site of her old family home.'

'And I suppose,' said Nicholas sarcastically, 'you just happen to know one such old family friend who is happy to oblige.'

'Well, for all anyone around here knows, the Hurstes and the Tilneyes could have been friends for years.'

'But that simply is not true,' pointed out Rose crossly. 'We hardly know you at all.'

John appeared a little taken aback by her response.

'I meant no offence, lady. I simply meant that if you were walking through the town with me, people who you wanted to catch out might respond a little better than if...'

'All right,' cut in the seneschal impatiently. 'You have made a good point. We will try out your idea in the Old

Market, but I shall not be far behind. Neither will Rose's companion, nor her men-at-arms. I gave my word to her parents that she would be well protected and I do not intend to break that promise.'

'But, sir!' protested Rose.

'It will be all right,' he assured her. 'John will accompany you, as he proposes. As a family friend. There will be no one to contradict you, but I shall keep a close eye on you, so have no fear.'

She nodded reluctantly, removing the Saxon brooch from the purse that hung from her girdle and fastening it to the front of her gown. She was wearing clothes of a deep scarlet today and the brooch sat neatly below the neckline, its rubies blending with the colour of her gown. Far from being lost, they sparkled from the mellow gold of their setting. Outside in the sunlight, they would be even more remarkable.

As she stood up, John's wide smile showed his appreciation. Nicholas had to admit that the colour of her gown set off her pale features beautifully, but he kept his opinion to himself.

'Now go,' he ordered. 'The Wysbeck should be easily fordable for a while. Take as much time as you need in the square. Make sure you speak to both Burdo the basket maker and the cobbler. And use your eyes, John. I shall not be far behind you.'

FIFTY-SIX

The Old Man's Debts

Rose did not have high hopes of John's company. She was expecting him to be rather pleased with himself for having persuaded the seneschal to do things his way, boastful even. Instead, as they walked from the New Market towards the ford over the Wysbeck, he hardly spoke at all. When she surreptitiously turned her head to glance at him, he looked serious and focussed on the task ahead.

'Take care, now,' he said as they descended the bank to the ford. 'The water is low, fortunately, and if you look, you'll see there's a crossing marked out with stones. Follow those and the water will hardly touch your shoes.'

She laughed, but not unkindly.

'You are very good to be concerned, Sir John, but perhaps you forget that I've visited the Old Market many times, to visit my grandfather. I know this feeble little river as well as you.'

His serious face broke into a grin.

'I shall follow you across, then, lady, since you know what you're doing.'

As they were descending the slippery steps cut into the bank on the Old Market side, he lent her his hand, but she dropped it like a lump of hot iron as soon as they had reached level ground.

And there she stopped. As she saw for the first time the blackened end of the square and the flimsy screens hiding the place where her grandfather's house had stood, he heard her gasp. It was almost a whimper. Whatever she had expected to see, the scene before her had come as a considerable shock.

'Come on,' he said gently, 'let's look at what Burdo has for sale. We can take as long as we like there; he always has a good display of baskets outside his workshop.'

She nodded, battling to recover her composure as they walked to the workshop. As John had anticipated, Burdo had made the most of the fine weather and had set out a fine display of his wares. The baskets were arranged on a set of planks joined together like steps. Ranging from the smallest for bread to the largest for fishing and laundry, they were all there to be admired and purchased. Rose picked up a small, prettily woven item and examined it, taking her time as the seneschal had instructed her to do. She wanted as many folk in the square to notice them as possible.

'This is for wool,' she informed John, turning the basket around in her hands.

'I shall buy it for you,' he smiled. When she began to object, he added in a low voice, 'for are we not old family friends?'

Burdo appeared in the doorway, glad to welcome the customers to his shop.

'Sir John,' he said, regarding the young knight with a deferential lowering of the head. Then, as he began to greet the lady, his eyes crinkled in recognition and delight. 'Rose!' he exclaimed. 'How good it is to see you again! I hardly knew you at first; you are so grown up and quite the lady! I was very sorry about what happened to your grandfather. He was a good man and the square is not the same without him.'

'And I am glad to see you, Burdo,' she smiled. 'I wanted to thank you for caring for my grandfather's peasants before they came to us at Hurste.'

'There is nothing to thank me for,' he added sorrowfully. 'They were good company and I miss having them around. How are they faring at Hurste?'

'They are working on the land now and much more content than when they were in the kitchens.'

'Ah, yes, that's understandable. Though I was grateful for their help, they were perhaps not the most skilled with the cooking pot!'

As she chatted with the basket maker, John noticed that she was standing with her shoulders back, so that the brooch pinned to her gown was in full view. Burdo, however, did not appear to have noticed it.

'I will take the basket for the lady,' said John, earning himself a wide smile from the craftsman.

'A good choice, sir! How glad I am that this fine young lady is taking a small reminder of Wisbech home with her!'

John gave him a coin and the man slipped it into his purse.

'I wish you both a good day. Do come back to see us again, Rose. How good it has been to see you! You look even more like your dear grandfather these days.'

They left Burdo outside his shop and continued along the eastern side of the square. Glancing back, Rose saw her companion Matilda walking a short distance behind them. Outside the Ship, a larger group than usual was gathered.

Among them were the seneschal and the two Hurste men-at-arms. All three were cloaked, their heads lowered over their ale, but John did not doubt that the seneschal had witnessed everything about their conversation with the basket maker.

'Burdo didn't even notice it,' remarked Rose in a quiet voice, her hand straying to touch the brooch at her neckline.

'No,' replied John. 'I don't think it meant anything to him.'

'So where next?'

'I think,' he replied as he caught sight of Goodwife Aswig hurrying across the square towards them, 'you'll find people come to you now. Starting with...'

'Oh, no,' Rose murmured, 'not one of grandfather's favourite neighbours...'

'Bless you, dear!' called out the goodwife when she was still several paces away from Rose and John. 'And thank the good lord that they caught the wastrel who set fire to the Big House and killed your poor grandfather! We can sleep safely in our beds now, though I still think the cobbler was behind it all. I do not trust him. It's the way he looks at you. All piggy eyes, he is, him and his two sons...'

'Good afternoon, Goodwife Aswig,' said Rose, trying hard to look pleasant.

'And to you, lady. Your grandfather was a good man. I never had a bad word to say about him.'

'I am greatly reassured to hear that,' said John with a grin. It was common knowledge that Goodwife Aswig rarely had a good word to say about anyone and could utter falsehoods with a perfectly straight face.

The goodwife barely acknowledged his presence, continuing to address her comments to Rose and lavish praise on Aelfric. John stood back and observed the woman. Her greying hair was scraped back from her thin face with the usual linen barbette. Her rather small eyes darted about as she spoke, taking in the fine cut of Rose's clothing, the rings on her fingers and the brooch on her gown. She was obviously impressed by all of it, yet at no point did her eyes appear to settle on any detail in particular.

Suddenly, it seemed, there were people all around them. Neighbours had seen the goodwife out in the square and, when they realised who she was speaking to, flocked to join her.

'Lady!' they were crying in a disharmonious chorus of voices, completely drowning out Aswig's monologue.

'How good it is to see you again, young Rose!' one elderly man's voice rose above the rest to greet her. 'We were truly sad about what happened to your grandfather.'

More and more voices joined in and Rose tried to acknowledge each and every one of them, clearly moved that her grandfather had been so well regarded. After a while, John touched her arm and led her politely away. As pleasant as this neighbourliness was, it was not helping them to achieve what they were there for.

As they moved away, John noticed a man standing alone and perfectly still on the corner by the ford. Apart from the group drinking outside the Ship, he was the only person in the square who had not hurried to greet Rose, and his solitary stance was very noticeable.

'Good afternoon, Will cobbler,' nodded Rose as they approached him. The man folded his thick muscular arms and gave her a surly look.

'Come to pay the old man's debts, have you, lady?' His tone was sneering and John felt his hackles rise.

Rose regarded the cobbler steadily.

'Did my grandfather owe you money, Will?' she asked. Her voice was neither friendly nor cold. She sounded more mature than her years and more than capable of facing down a man like him.

'You could say that. Good at sending his shoes for repair, not so good at paying the bill.'

'Very well, have a note made of the debt and take it to the castle today. I shall make sure that you are paid as soon as I am home.'

'Or,' he said, exhaling heavily and releasing a miasma of bad breath, 'you could just pay me with that brooch of yours.'

John watched as the man leered at Rose's neckline, obviously more interested in the gemstones than the beauty of her figure. To his surprise, Rose laughed.

'What, this little thing? You would be disappointed, Will cobbler. My father bought it for me recently and told me I can safely wear it without fear of losing it, because it is nothing more than glass and copper!'

The man looked confused for a moment and John was sure he was about to say something, either to contradict or persuade her, but he seemed to think better of it.

'Have what you are owed written out,' Rose repeated as they turned away. 'One of the clerks will help you. The debt will be paid.'

'Cleverly done,' said John in an undertone as they began to climb the river bank. 'You manage falsehood with as much ease as Goodwife Aswig, and I've long admired her talent for spinning a yarn. The cobbler showed considerable interest in the brooch, did he not?'

'Yes,' she replied, ignoring his back-handed praise, 'but perhaps no more than any greedy man does if he sees something he thinks is valuable.'

'You could be right,' he acknowledged. 'We shall let the seneschal know, anyway, and let him decide.'

'Keep your voice down,' warned Rose, reaching the top of the bank before him. 'The sergeant is crossing the ford. Should we speak to him too?'

'Why not? I always enjoy a chat with the old boy!'

Baldwin hailed John in his usual friendly fashion as he climbed the bank to join them.

'What brings you to this part of town, Sir John?'

'Escorting an old family friend,' replied John with a smile. 'Rose de Hurste.'

Baldwin inclined his head politely towards Rose.

'I didn't know your families were so well acquainted.'

'Oh, we go back years!' lied John. 'Rose wanted to come here, to see what remained of her grandfather's house. It has been a sorrowful time for her.'

'I am truly sorry, lady,' said Baldwin as he turned to descend the steps towards the square. 'Aelfric is sorely missed. I wish you both a...'

He seemed to have lost track of what he was saying. His eyes were riveted on the brooch Rose wore.

'How did you...I thought...' His words trailed away to nothing. He was obviously making a huge effort to control himself.

'What did you think?' prompted John.

'I thought,' began the sergeant once more, clearly checking each word before uttering it, 'that Aelfric's treasure was lost, that it has never been found. Was that just a tale, then? A ruse of the seneschal's to catch the killer?'

'I am not sure I understand you,' said Rose reasonably. 'Why do you doubt that my grandfather's possessions are still missing?'

'Because of *that*!' he exclaimed, pointing at Rose's chest. 'Because of that which you wear, lady!'

'And what makes you think,' asked John, 'that the lady's brooch has anything to do with her grandfather's lost items?'

'Well...' replied the sergeant more hesitantly, 'it has the look of Saxon work. Very distinctive. The serpents, the way they are arranged like that. Very distinctive...'

He fell silent. Rose and John said nothing more but stared at him like members of the jury in an Assize hearing. Baldwin dropped his head abruptly and hurried down the steps to the market place.

'Something at last to report to the seneschal,' John said quietly.

'He knew exactly what this brooch is,' whispered Rose. 'Could he have had something to do with my grandfather's death?'

'I do not know, but the seneschal may have thoughts on that. Come on, let's return to the castle and find you some refreshment. Your companion, the seneschal and your men-at-arms will doubtless soon follow.'

Rose nodded her agreement and started across the river. It was not long before Matilda caught up with them and began to teeter nervously across the water with her lady. The river was higher than earlier, wetting Rose's elegant boots to their tops. Matilda tutted and fussed, complaining about the trouble she would have later with cleaning the leather, but Rose dismissed each comment with an impatient smile. She seemed, John could not help noticing, to be enjoying herself.

He followed the ladies across the water, gratified to have something worth reporting to the seneschal. He had elbowed his way into this role and his motives had been far from sincere. He knew how clearly the seneschal saw through his protests and understood his true reason for wanting to work with Rose. Yet, having taken on the work, John had begun to take it seriously. He was relieved not to have made a mess of things. At least not yet.

FIFTY-SEVEN

Pokerounce

The great hall was quiet, almost empty, which pleased John. It was still not quite supper time, but one of the kitchen boys went cheerfully enough to fetch Rose and John a jug of ale and a platter of pokerounce. This sweet dish was one of John's favourites; he loved the exotic flavour of honey and spices soaked into small slices of toast. He was just biting into his second piece when the seneschal joined them. Rose reached for the jug and poured ale for them all. She had dismissed Matilda, who had left with obvious reluctance, and Rose knew she would not be gone for long.

'Well, then?' began Nicholas. 'You spoke to practically the whole of the Old Market. Do you have anything to report?'

Rose was the first to speak, since John's lips were stuck together with honey. She recounted their various conversations with folk, going into a little more detail when it came to Burdo and Goodwife Aswig. She then told him about the cobbler.

'He certainly noticed the brooch,' she remarked, 'but I don't think he recognised it as any particular piece of jewellery. He just thought it might be valuable and when I pretended it was only made of glass and copper he did not contradict me. It was the sergeant's reaction which was really interesting.'

'Ah, yes, Baldwin. What did he have to say for himself?'

John took over the narrative.

'He could hardly take his eyes off the brooch,' he said. 'From his reaction, I'm sure he knew it was from Aelfric's collection. Before he had time to think, he questioned why the treasure was said to be lost when my lady was clearly wearing part of it.'

'And when John picked him up on that,' added Rose, 'asking Baldwin why he assumed the brooch had anything to do with my grandfather, he looked like a rat caught in a trap. He tried to back out from what he had said and came out with some foolishness about the workmanship being typically Saxon. It was obvious that he was lying.'

The seneschal nodded thoughtfully, cutting into a slice of pokerounce and putting it into his mouth. Not having tasted it before, he was surprised. He had expected so much honey, cinnamon and ginger to be cloying, but the pepper gave the mixture some bite and it was very good indeed. So generously coated was the toast, that some of the honey dribbled down his chin. He wiped his face with the back of his hand and washed down the sweetness with a swig of ale. Rose was looking at him with undisguised impatience. He had been silent for quite some time.

'So, who, sir,' she asked, 'do you most suspect? Who could have been involved in all this business? Who could have killed Weland in his cell? I have to ask because I know you have doubts about my mother. I accept that she appears unfeeling at times, but she cared about her father, my grandfather.'

'Tell me, then,' replied Nicholas, 'why Lady Rowena insists that Aelfric's collection of family jewellery was worthless. You said yourself that you knew that to be untrue.'

'I confess, sir, I do not know. I find it very puzzling indeed. Perhaps it is because of her shame about our family's dwindling fortunes. My grandfather, when he was left with almost nothing, clung to his one remaining house in one of the family's old manors, Wisbech. He was even obliged to pay rent for it, because his ancestor had gifted the whole manor to the Church. What an indignity that must have been for him! That box of treasures, as he called it, was his single reminder of past greatness and my mother despised his regard for it. She refused to look at it, so grandfather shared his memories with me instead. He spoke to my brothers too, but they were never as interested as I was. However, despite my mother's obstinacy, she would never have hurt her father. I do not believe she would have done anything to harm him.'

Perhaps, though, thought Nicholas, the intention had never been to harm him. Perhaps it had been merely to take what valuables he had and for the thief to escape undetected. The fire had, according to Weland, been started by accident.

In spite of Rose's protest, Nicholas believed Lady Rowena to be perfectly capable of plotting and of persuading others to do the nasty work for her. He kept these thought to himself, merely acknowledging Rose's words with a nod before claiming another slice of pokerounce. He had to be quick because John was indulging himself so much. Apart from the one slice Rose had eaten and the two Nicholas had taken, John had managed to empty the platter by himself.

'Your grandfather had been giving you items of family jewellery over the years, had he not?' queried Nicholas once he had finished his second slice of toast.

'Yes, a few pieces,' she agreed, 'a ring or two and a golden chain.'

'And what did your mother think of that?'

'She did not like it at all. She remonstrated with my grandfather, then later I heard her complaining to my father that Aelfric was offloading his rubbish on to me.'

'What was your father's reaction?'

Rose frowned, trying to remember.

'I think he told her not to worry about it, that it was harmless. I don't believe he took her complaints very seriously. But all of this was years ago, my lord seneschal. I was just a child then.'

'And my lord constable, Sir Alexander de Astonne; he visits your parents regularly, does he not?'

She looked astonished.

'The constable? I am not aware that he...well, I suppose I have seen him there once or twice, but why is that of concern?'

'Why are you questioning Rose?' demanded John suddenly. He was paying more attention now that all the pokerounce had gone. 'She is here to help, not to be treated like one of your suspects, sir.'

'John of Tilneye, kindly keep your objections to yourself,' Nicholas said sternly. 'You insisted on pushing your way into this, so allow me to work unmolested. Rose offered her help to find the person behind her grandfather's killing, so please let her do that!'

John scowled and fell silent, lifting his cup to take another swig of ale. Nicholas turned back to Rose.

'Is your father always present when the constable calls?'

She took a swift intake of breath.

'Of course he is! What are you suggesting sir?'

'Is he *always* present?' he insisted calmly.

Rose looked flustered.

'How can I tell? If my father is away on business when the constable calls, it could be that one of my brothers is there instead. Whatever the situation and whoever is there, my mother could hardly refuse a guest refreshment before starting his homeward journey, could she?'

Nicholas almost smiled. Lady Rowena's conscience had never appeared troubled over her neglect of *his* thirst.

'It would be very helpful, Rose, if you could stay for a little longer and speak to the constable, much as you did today with the people of the Old Market. Both he and his deputy are away until tomorrow morning, unfortunately, but would you stay with us until then? You will have well appointed chambers, so you and your companion will be comfortable.'

'Yes, sir,' she agreed. 'I did understand that this might take more than one day.'

'You did well today, Rose, as did you, John. I am grateful for your help, both of you,' smiled Nicholas. 'I think it best, John, if it is I who accompanies Rose tomorrow when speaking to the constable. It would appear unusual otherwise.'

'Of course,' said John with some reluctance, 'but might I join you both afterwards? Now that I am part of this, even though I pushed my way in, I would like to know what you discover.'

Nicholas grinned.

'Meet us here for dinner tomorrow, then.'

John smiled. As he looked up, he saw Matilda hovering in the doorway.

'I believe you are wanted,' he told Rose, 'but perhaps I may accompany you to the door, if the seneschal has no more questions?'

Nicholas nodded his assent as Rose and John left him to his ale. They walked slowly towards where Matilda waited.

'You called me "John" when you were talking to the seneschal,' he said.

'And you stopped calling me "lady". Perhaps we shouldn't make a habit of it, though. I'm not sure Matilda would approve.'

They were both laughing as they reached the disapproving companion in the doorway. John bade them both a courteous farewell and went whistling to the stables to saddle his horse. He was feeling extremely cheerful.

FIFTY-EIGHT

Matilda

'This was not how it was meant to be, and you know it,' Matilda grumbled as she untied the laces that secured the back of Rose's gown. Her hands tugged at the ties with what felt like unnecessary force, jerking Rose backwards with every stroke. 'I gave your mother my word,' continued the companion, 'that I would stay by your side wherever you went in this town, yet you continually push me away. Lady Rowena would not approve of you swanning around the market square with that boy!'

Rose heaved a long sigh.

'I am sorry you had to follow behind, but the seneschal knows what he is doing and it will not be for much longer. By tomorrow afternoon we will be on the way back to Hurste.'

'That is not the point I was making. It's not decent, the way you walk around and sit to eat with the Tilneye boy.'

'He has the rank of knight. Have some respect, Matilda.'

'Knight or not, it is not seemly. And what am I to tell your mother?'

'You need tell her nothing. I promised to help the seneschal and I am doing so. My men-at-arms are never far away, so there will be no danger and no impropriety of any kind.'

'I meant, lady, what am I to tell your mother in my own defence? She gave me strict instructions and through no fault of my own I am disobeying her. Have you forgotten the beating I suffered last time this sort of thing happened? You slipped away and pleased yourself, leaving me to take the blame.'

'Of course I have not forgotten! How many times must I say I am sorry? Do not fear. I shall tell my mother that we have been together throughout the whole of this visit. I know how to tell a falsehood when I have to. I will not let you down.'

'Yet you did before.'

'I was little more than a child then. I was selfish and wilful, too keen on running off without thinking about the consequences for you. Things, I assure you, are very different now.'

'So you will lie to protect me?'

'Yes, Matilda, I shall tell a white lie, I suppose you would call it,' said Rose. 'I shall say whatever is necessary.'

She was relieved when at last her companion left for her bed in the adjoining chamber. Matilda had been with her since early childhood. The daughter of the steward of one of Sir Mortimer's smaller manors, she was probably as dissatisfied with her role as Rose was to be saddled with her. Despite this, a bond had developed between the two women over the years, and Rose had come to understand the value of Matilda's loyalty.

Left alone in her pleasant chamber with its brightly painted walls, Rose lay in her bed and tried to make sense of her thoughts. They were as tangled and confused as they were surprising, and she relished the time and solitude to try to sort them out.

Unfortunately, she fell asleep long before she managed to make sense of anything.

FIFTY-NINE

Feast of St Edgar the Peaceful; Friday 8th June

The constable's voice, loud and confident, could be heard from half way along the passage as Rose and the seneschal approached the office that morning. Every so often, the quieter tones of Simon de Gardyn's voice broke in as the two men exchanged scraps of news and prepared for the day's work.

'Ah, Nicholas!' exclaimed the constable when the seneschal's tall shape filled the doorway. 'Come in! Ah, how charming, Rose de Hurste too, I see! Simon and I are just back from our travels. He's come from Newton and I from Guyhirn; business for my lord bishop, trouble here and there. So much to attend to these days; scarcely time to catch up, but what brings you here, Nicholas?'

'The same matter as has occupied me for the past few weeks,' replied Nicholas pleasantly. He wondered when he had last heard Alexander talk so much or so rapidly. The constable looked anxious, though he was trying hard to cover it up with bonhomie. It had not been lost on Nicholas how keenly Alexander had made it known that it had been Simon, not he, who had just returned from Newton in the Isle, in the vicinity of Hurste. Guyhirn, where Alexander had been, was nowhere near Lady Rowena's home. The constable was clearly making the point that he had not been to see the lady on this occasion.

As for Simon, he had hardly cracked a smile throughout the constable's monologue and now looked rather bored. The seneschal stepped further into the room and Rose moved to his side, wearing her most winsome smile and making sure the brooch could clearly be seen.

'I do not wish to disturb your work,' said the seneschal, 'merely to let you know that Rose is currently our guest at the castle. She has kindly offered to assist me in the final stages of my investigation.'

'Ah!' said Nicholas again, smiling benignly at Rose. 'Well you are a most welcome guest indeed, my dear. It must be terribly distressing for you to be back in the town where you spent so many happy years with your grandfather.'

'Yes, sir, but I am glad to help my lord seneschal. I wish to see justice done.'

'Quite right, my dear. Very commendable,' said Alexander. His eyes had been moving from Rose to Nicholas and back again throughout the conversation, but did not appear to have noticed anything in particular about Rose's appearance or her costume.

'So you found one killer,' said Simon, 'only to discover there's another to hunt down. I do not envy you at all, Nicholas, and hope you soon get to the bottom of this troublesome matter.' He managed a small, sympathetic smile and for a moment his eyes lingered on Rose. He seemed far more interested in the beauty of her face, however, than in the jewellery she wore.

The seneschal and Rose made their exit soon afterwards, leaving the door open, as they had found it. They passed the two guards stationed outside the office and a cloud of oppressive silence seemed to follow them along the passageway. It felt like a deep, nervous breath taken before the delivery of a speech, except that no speech came. The jovial mood between the constable and his deputy, which Nicholas and Rose had interrupted, seemed to have been completely broken.

Nicholas waited until they were a good distance along the passage before he spoke, and even then he kept his voice to a whisper.

'I'm not sure what's amiss there, but something certainly is.'

'Yet neither of them took the slightest interest in this brooch,' Rose whispered back. She was fingering the piece of jewellery as if she would have liked to remove it from her gown.

'Let's get away from here, go down to the hall where we can speak freely,' replied the seneschal.

And then, from behind them in the constable's office, came the bellowing of a curse. Loud and guttural, it was muffled only by the distance covered by the two visitors along the stone passageway.

'Sounds like we upset someone,' whispered Rose.

It was then that they ran into John and the sergeant.

SIXTY

The Stairway

John of Tilneye had arrived early at the castle that morning. Though he was not due to meet Rose and the seneschal until dinner time, he had found it impossible to settle down to any work on the manor. After seeing to a few essential duties, he had saddled Albanac and set out for the castle.

Having stabled the palfrey, John found himself with far too much time on his hands. He strolled idly through the bailey, chatting here and there to a few folk he knew, spending far more time than usual in polite enquiry after their families and livestock. Unfortunately, he had no chance of bumping into his old friend Eric, since, like the other clerks he would be hard at work in the chaplain's office.

Having run out of people to chat to in the bailey, John walked up the steps and into the forebuilding on his way to the great hall. Dinner was still some time away, a fact made obvious by the kitchen boys who were only just starting to set out the long trestle tables. There was a promising aroma in the air of savoury sauces and roasting meat, and he was looking forward to a good dinner almost as much as he was to seeing Rose again.

Though he was still early, he decided to make his slow way up to the constable's office. With any luck, he considered, he might meet Rose and the seneschal on their way down.

He walked between the kitchen boys and the long boards they were carrying to make up the tables. As he dodged between two boys, a trestle and a large dog who had awoken from his nap in the corner, he caught sight of someone slipping from the hall into the passageway beyond. There was something curious about the man's movements. He was moving so furtively, in so obvious an attempt not to be seen, that he was achieving the very opposite. He was unwittingly drawing attention to himself. With a frown, John realised that it was Baldwin, the sergeant-at-arms.

Baldwin was heading towards the stairs and, since John was going that way himself, he followed. By the time John had reached the opening of the passageway leading to the stairway, the sergeant was more than half way along it. John saw him glance over his shoulder and he stayed back, determined to follow unobserved.

Baldwin must have felt the presence of someone behind him because he continued to cast backward glances at regular intervals. Once he reached the stairs, though, he was easier to pursue. Each twist of the stairway allowed John to stay hidden as he climbed and the soft leather of his boots made hardly a sound on the stone.

He could hear the sergeant's heavy breathing as he climbed the steps ahead of him. The effort seemed almost too much for the older man, but he continued upward. Suddenly, close to the top, he came to a halt. John had to descend a few steps hastily to remain out of sight. He held himself rigid, afraid that his own breathing had betrayed him.

He was half expecting the sergeant to turn back and grasp him by the throat, but nothing happened. The wait went on and the silence was almost unbearable. Then, at long last, the slightest of sounds reached John's ears. Rather than the heavy footfall he had anticipated, it was light and metallic, like something very small falling on stone. He froze, expecting whatever it was to bounce down the stairs and bring the sergeant in pursuit of it. Yet nothing further happened.

After what seemed an impossibly long time, he heard the sergeant moving upwards again, his panting and heavy tread carrying him to the top of the stairs. John rounded the turn in the stairway and saw immediately what the sergeant had dropped.

He picked it up, giving it a brief glance. It was a brooch similar to the one Rose had been wearing, but was far plainer. A single serpent coiled its long tail around a central ruby, its eyes shining with tiny gemstones which John could not immediately identify.

'Hey! Baldwin!' he called loudly up the stairs. 'You dropped something!'

He could no longer hear movement. The sergeant would by now have reached the stone passageway which led to the constable's office. John leapt up the rest of the stairs and came face to face with Baldwin.

'Did you not hear me?' John asked with his usual friendly expression. 'You dropped something on the stairs! Looks valuable to me. Don't you want it back?'

'It wasn't me!' claimed Baldwin weakly. 'I didn't drop it. Why would I have such a thing in my possession?'

'That's what I was wondering,' came the seneschal's voice. He had appeared in the passageway behind Baldwin, Rose at his side, having just come from the constable's office. 'How did such a valuable thing come to be in your possession, sergeant?'

John realised that the seneschal had no way of seeing what John held in his hand. He was simply following John's lead, and that felt good.

Baldwin knew that he could not argue his way out of the situation. He dropped his shoulders and gave up his protest. Before he could blink, the guards from outside the constable's office had grasped him by the arms.

'In there,' the seneschal ordered, pointing to a disused room on the opposite side of the passage from the constable's office. The men-at-arms relieved the sergeant of his sword and knife and manoeuvred him into the room.

'Alert the two Ely men, if you will, John,' asked Nicholas, 'and then make sure this lady is given a fine dinner.'

John grinned ear to ear and went gladly to fetch the seneschal's men-at-arms and take Rose to the great hall.

SIXTY-ONE

The Other One

The small chamber into which the constable's men-at-arms, the sergeant and the seneschal crowded benefitted from no natural light. Its only illumination stole in through the open doors of better lit rooms on the opposite side of the passage. It was hardly bigger than a garderobe, probably left windowless because the castle's builders had considered it too insignificant.

It appeared always to have been used for storage. An old trestle table dominated the centre of the room, its supports bowed under the weight of a multitude of heavy boxes containing long forgotten and apparently useless items. One of the guards carried in a couple of stools while Nicholas cleared a space on the table and lit a candle. The sergeant, red faced with humiliation, took his seat between the wall and the table while the seneschal seated himself at the opposite side of the table. The two men-at-arms stood rigidly with their backs against the closed door.

'How did you come to be in possession of the brooch, sergeant?' the seneschal began.

Baldwin cleared his throat nervously. His rickety stool creaked loudly as he leant forwards to support his elbows on the table. The candlelight brought every feature of his flushed, heavily jowled face into unsympathetic focus.

'I found it, sir,' he muttered, 'down by the river in the Old Market. It was when we were keeping watch there soon after the fire. I happened to look down, and there it was, between my feet in the grass by the ford.'

'And you knew it to be Saxon, presumably of great value,' stated Nicholas. 'You displayed your knowledge when you spoke to Rose de Hurste and Sir John of Tilneye when you encountered them yesterday by the river.'

'Not what I'd call knowledge. More like a guess, maybe.'

'But you neglected to share that knowledge, or guess, or whatever it was, with me, sergeant. You failed to inform me of your discovery, even though you knew that items of value were missing from Aelfric's house. Even though you knew that those items played a vital part in my investigation.'

'I should have reported it, sir, but a brooch like that would have been my pension. It would have meant that I wouldn't be forced to work until the day I dropped dead, as my old father did, as all poor folk do.'

'And now it looks like you will work no more, sergeant. The Assizes will decide your fate now.'

The sergeant clenched his jaw but said nothing as the door behind Nicholas opened. Brithun and Ordgar made their entrance, relieving the constable's men-at-arms, who went to resume their watch in the passage outside. There was a brief silence before the sergeant spoke again.

'Would have been better if I'd taken off while I could,' he said quietly. 'I knew I should have, but I couldn't resist staying around and looking for more. I searched everywhere; in the ruins, in the dust, everywhere. And I wasn't the only one doing it.'

'Not the only one doing what?' asked Nicholas icily.

'Searching, of course.'

'So, who else was searching?'

Baldwin leered.

'My lord seneschal, how badly you must wish to know!'

Nicholas decided to change tack.

'So why suddenly decide to rid yourself of this valuable Saxon item? As you point out, it would have provided you with a decent pension. Why not simply hide it until this investigation was over?'

The sergeant's shoulders drooped. His swagger had quickly faded to nothing.

'Because Weland was caught and stabbed in his cell and suddenly things felt a lot more dangerous. Nobody understands how the killer entered a locked cell, yet he did just that. There was no telling what else somebody as clever as that might be capable of. We were all a bit on edge after that, I don't mind saying so. Then there was you, my lord seneschal. If you'd found out that I had the brooch, you'd have thought I was the killer. I had to get rid of it.'

'And were you? Were you that clever individual who entered a locked cell and killed Weland?'

'No, sir! I could never do such a thing! I knew you'd think that, but no!'

He looked terrified now and Nicholas sat back, allowing the room to fall silent for a moment.

'So why drop the brooch on the steps? Why here, of all places?'

'Because,' replied the sergeant in a voice heavy with loathing, 'because I wanted to see *him* punished. Seeing that would almost have made up for losing the brooch.'

'Him?'

'Yes, *him*, my lord seneschal!' He pointed towards the door where Brithun and Ordgar stood, motionless and expressionless. 'He who so smugly lords it over us, day in, day out. I *saw* him. I saw him looking everywhere for that jewellery, and by the look on his face I bet he found some too. I reckon he's nothing but a thief. A thief who makes out he's better than the lot of us put together. I wanted him caught. I left that brooch on the steps near his office, to lead you to him.'

'I presume you are not referring to one of my men-at-arms, sergeant? You appear to be pointing at them.'

'What? No! I mean the one sitting high and mighty in his office right across the passageway there.'

'The constable,' muttered Nicholas.

'No, sir. The other one. His deputy. I saw him, clear as day!'

Nicholas sat up straight on the stool. One of its legs was shorter than the others and it rocked sharply to the left.

'If you knew this, sergeant, why did you not just tell me?'

'Because he would have denied it and blamed me in return. Who would you have believed; the aristocratic Sir Simon de Gardyn or a humble free peasant risen to the rank of the constable's sergeant? The deputy saw me looking for those treasures, just as I saw him, so it seemed neither of us could tell on the other. But now that I *have* told you, I hope my prison cell keeps me safer than it did Weland.'

'Do you believe, then, that the deputy constable killed Weland?'

Baldwin leaned back again, resting his head on the wall behind him. He shook his head.

'In truth, sir, no. He wouldn't be capable of such a thing. A pimply, despicable weed like that would never have the guts! And besides, I saw him working in his office early on the morning of Weland's death when I went up there to check on the guards. It's something I always do at the end of my shift. Because I had suspicions of my own about him, I later spoke to the guards on duty outside his office. They assured me that he remained in his office from the time he returned from checking the cells at dawn to when he was brought news of Weland's death. He cannot have killed anyone, sir, though I'd like to say otherwise.'

Nicholas nodded.

'You will be taken to the cells now. You will be tried for theft at the next Assizes to be held later this summer. I will speak in your defence, sergeant, because you merely found the brooch. Since you did not take it from anyone, it could be argued that you did not know to whom it belonged. I can promise nothing; my words may have no effect. The Hurste family may well see things differently, but I will try on your behalf.'

'Thank you, sir,' the sergeant grunted as Brithun and Ordgar led him away.

Left alone, Nicholas put his elbows on the table and rested his chin on his hands. It seemed that no discovery he made took him any closer to the whole truth. He was merely treading a circle around it.

And he was very hungry.

SIXTY-TWO

Pottage

By the time the seneschal had joined his younger companions in the great hall, John had already finished off a huge bowl of pottage and a good portion of the bread he was sharing with Rose. She was still nibbling thoughtfully on a piece of white bread when Nicholas sat down beside them. They were obliged to wait for any news until the seneschal had finished his pottage, and it seemed to take a very long time, but at last he looked up from his bowl. He picked up a piece of bread and still said nothing.

'Did you find out anything useful from the sergeant, sir?' asked John when he thought he had waited long enough.

Nicholas used his bread to mop up the last of his pottage. It was a simple concoction of beans and peas, but a generous addition of herbs and garlic had produced a rich flavour.

'I made some progress, but I fear the sergeant will have to pay dearly for his actions. He found one of your grandfather's things, Rose, a brooch, but confessed to nothing else.'

Rose nodded, having already heard from John about how he had followed the sergeant.

'It would appear,' continued the seneschal, 'that the sergeant has been searching for some time for pieces of the treasure. He named someone else too, someone he claims was also hunting for pieces, but I only have his word for that at the moment. We still do not know whether the main bulk of Aelfric's treasure has ever been found, let alone who has it now. More importantly, I still do not know who killed Weland. Whoever it was, killed Weland to stop him naming them, because this person has been involved from the start; behind the fires, the thefts and the death of Aelfric. That person therefore has both influence and standing. Weland was obviously in awe of them too. He was very reluctant to name them.'

'Influence and standing,' said John. 'That certainly narrows the field. The sergeant's hardly influential, is he? The poor bloke just found a bit of gold. Hardly makes him a mastermind, does it?'

'I agree your point, though to someone like Weland, the sergeant may have seemed to have great authority. However, he does not strike me as having enough intelligence to be behind a sequence of events like this. I do not believe he is who we are looking for.'

'Could it be someone from Ely?' suggested Rose. 'Weland worked in the abbey where a copy of the charter was held. Someone there could have encouraged him to come to Wisbech and use the words hidden in the charter to find my grandfather's treasure.'

'I did consider that,' replied the seneschal, 'but if that had been the case, I think Weland would have taken the road back to Ely as soon as he messed up breaking into your grandfather's house. The fact that he did not, that he remained in Wisbech and managed to evade the town search, suggests that someone here was protecting him.'

'It could hardly be my mother either, then,' added Rose hastily. 'If she had been involved, Weland would have fled to Hurste.'

'I am sorry, Rose, but your parents have both friends and influence in Wisbech, and Hurste is close enough for anyone to come and go from at will. The fact that Weland remained in Wisbech does not exclude anyone from your home manor from being involved.'

'But their involvement would make no sense. Why would my mother want her father's possessions stolen?'

Nicholas was beginning to query his own wisdom in involving Rose in any of this.

'You said yourself, Rose, that your grandfather had been giving away items from his collection. You have some pieces and perhaps others have some too. It is possible that Lady Rowena wanted the treasure removed from her father's house before he gave any more of it away. Although she speaks scornfully of Aelfric's treasures, she must be aware of their monetary value. Had Aelfric moved to Hurste Manor, as planned, your mother could have been sure of keeping his possessions safe. His last minute refusal to leave his home may have frustrated your mother, prompting her to take what was left of the valuables into safety. I am not saying any of this is true; I am merely setting out possibilities.'

'I understand,' she said quietly. 'I know you have to think like that, but...'

'Shush!' hissed John. Behind them, kitchen boys were clearing away and a couple of them were hovering closely. Rose blushed and lowered her head.

'So,' said John quietly, once they were free to speak again, 'what about the constable and his deputy? You can't get much more influential than that!'

Nicholas reached for the last piece of bread and crumbled it thoughtfully between his fingers.

'There is nothing to tie Sir Alexander to Weland's killing, any more than there is Sir Simon. The constable was away from the castle on the night of Weland's death, apparently in Murrow. As for the deputy, after his usual checks at dawn, he was seen leaving the cells by the guards on duty. According to the sergeant, the men stationed outside the constable's office confirmed that Sir Simon returned to the office straight after checking the cells and remained there until Weland's killing was reported to him.'

'Could he have used someone else to do it?' suggested John. 'One of the guards?'

'It is possible, but doubtful. Whoever started all this made a mistake when they involved Weland. He was a disaster and he came close to giving his master away. I doubt that they wanted to risk involving anyone else. Somehow, in a way I have yet to understand, that person killed Weland without help from anyone.'

'What about the constable's claim that he was in Murrow?' continued John. 'We only have his word for where he was. For all we know, he could have returned early and done the killing himself.'

The seneschal did not reply. He too had wondered whether the constable had been anywhere near Murrow that night, but his suspicions were very different to John's. He believed it more likely that the constable had been in Hurste. He could hardly say so in Rose's presence, but she seemed to read his thoughts and looked uncomfortable.

'What about blood?' she asked hurriedly to change the subject. 'Surely there would have been blood on the clothes of whoever stabbed Weland.'

'Yes, I'd wondered about that myself,' added John.

'The physician who attended Weland told me that he had been stabbed once in the abdomen,' replied Nicholas. 'The knife wound caused very heavy blood loss, so yes, the assailant's clothes would have been stained. If he wore dark clothing, however, the blood may not have shown up clearly. Also, this happened just after dawn when few folk were about. It would still have been dark down in the cells.'

'But wouldn't Weland have cried out as he was attacked?' asked John. 'Wouldn't one of the guards have heard him and come running? It all sounds wrong to me. I still think one of the guards was in on it.'

'I agree it makes no sense,' said Nicholas.

'So what, then, can we do?'

'Perhaps,' began Rose hesitantly, 'there's another way to snare the killer. I'm thinking I could...'

But whatever Rose was about to suggest had to remain unheard for the time being. The group fell silent as Alaric, one of the senior guards Nicholas had questioned after Weland's death, approached the table. He looked fearful as he came to stand at the seneschal's side.

'Might I have a word, sir?' he asked quietly.

SIXTY-THREE

Ale

Alaric followed the seneschal towards the long table and benches at the back of the hall. The table there was one of the few which remained in place all of the time and it had already been cleared following the midday meal. They were able to speak there in privacy and, without delay, Alaric launched into what he had come to say. His words seemed like a heavy burden which he badly needed to shed.

'My lord seneschal, there is something I omitted to say when we spoke before. I have tried to push it out of my mind, but can no longer do so. I am afraid that if I don't tell you about our dereliction of duty, someone else will. To put it simply, sir, on the night that Weland was killed, I fell asleep on duty.'

'You'll hardly be the first man to have done that!' retorted the seneschal, disappointed with such a modest revelation.

'No, sir, but on that night of all nights! I swear that everything else I told you was the absolute truth. I checked the prisoners' cells as soon as we arrived on duty, and all was well. When I next checked them, I discovered Weland's body, as I told you. That second check, though, was made later than I led you to believe. I had awoken with a jolt, realising that I'd dropped off and the morning was advancing. Daylight was already showing through the high windows in the cells.'

'But the others? The guards on duty with you? Why didn't they wake you?'

'Because they too were sleeping, sir. We suspect we were given something, the way we all dropped off so heavily like that. It's shameful none the less and we dared not tell the sergeant, because that would have meant our dismissal. Yet, now we hear that the sergeant himself has been questioned, and...'

'It sounds very much as if you were drugged, soldier. You should have reported it immediately. How could this have happened? Did you all drink from the same cup or jug before you came on duty?'

'Yes, sir, as is customary. Before each watch comes on duty, the men always come here, to this table at the back of the hall, for their bread and ale. It is always laid out right here, ready for us. There was nothing different about it that morning, nothing that we noticed anyway. Maybe we were still too sluggish to think about it. It was before dawn and we had only just come from our beds.'

'So, there was nothing unusual about the taste of the ale?'

'Not really, sir, though as I said, we were barely awake. Yet, now that I come to think about it, the ale was slightly bitter and had a bit of a smell about it. It wasn't different enough for any of us to bother mentioning, though. We'd all tasted worse in our time. The bread was good, nothing wrong with that at all.'

Nicholas sat back and took a deep breath, exhaling noisily in exasperation.

'So someone drugged you all, came down to the cells while you slept, and killed Weland. Not very mysterious after all, is it? If you had just said so from the beginning...'

'I am sorry, my lord. I know I should have...'

'Where were the keys to the cells while you slept?'

'Attached to my belt, sir, as they always are while on duty. I was not aware of anyone taking them and when I awoke they were still in place.'

'So anyone could have killed your prisoner! Anyone at all!'

'Yes, sir.'

'Your failure to report this immediately has wasted a great deal of my time. I am ordering you now to keep this conversation to yourself. Tell no one. Do the other guards know you have come here today?'

'No, sir, I came on impulse. I couldn't stand hiding the truth any longer.'

'Good. Let the others speak to me if they wish, but tell no one what you have told me.'

'Yes, sir,' grunted Alaric as he took his leave. Nicholas was as confident as he could be of his silence. The seneschal remained on the bench at the back of the hall for a while, reassessing the facts as he understood them now.

It was the oldest trick of them all, and as simple as it was callous.

For Nicholas, everything had taken a step backwards. In theory, anyone in or close to the castle could have drugged the guards' ale that night and killed the prisoner.

Anyone at all. In his mind's eye, Nicholas saw once more the face he had glimpsed in the crowd on the afternoon before Weland's death; the face he was certain belonged to Lady Rowena.

SIXTY-FOUR

Gratitude

'There is something else I could try,' said Rose as soon as the seneschal returned to the table where she and John sat. Neither she nor John asked him about his conversation with Alaric and his face gave nothing away.

'I regret to say, Rose, that it is time for you to leave us,' replied Nicholas. 'I gave your parents my word that you would be here for a couple of days at most. If you are to arrive at Hurste before nightfall, you should soon be back on the road.'

'But there's one last thing which Rose is keen to try and it wouldn't take long at all,' said John. Rose turned to him with a grateful look. The glance was not lost on Nicholas who saw more in it than mere gratitude. Hastily, she lowered her eyes and studied her hands which were demurely folded in her lap. 'Either my lady's plan works or it doesn't,' continued John, 'and she will still be able to set off in time to be home before dusk.'

Mindful of the need to waste no more time, Rose quickly explained to the seneschal what she wanted to do. It was simple indeed.

'And this time, I believe it would be best if Matilda accompanied me. As before, my lord seneschal, I doubt you will be far away.'

Nicholas gave a thin smile.

'Then I suggest you organise yourselves quickly. He is due to leave the castle by mid afternoon and might be away for some time. It would be a pity to miss this opportunity.'

They stood up and Rose made her way back to her chambers to prepare for departure. The seneschal and the young knight watched as she walked away.

'She will be safe, won't she?' asked John with a look of uncharacteristic concern.

'She is hardly entering a den of lions, John. And we shall not be far behind her.'

SIXTY-FIVE

Emerald

Waiting around out of sight, while trying to think up excuses for doing so for Matilda's sake, was something which Rose found unexpectedly difficult. What she was doing was hardly fitting behaviour for someone of her rank, yet Rose was determined to carry out what she had planned.

They were standing just outside the castle stables and when Matilda's complaints became particularly irksome, Rose sent her inside to saddle the horses. Even then, Rose's wait was long and tedious as she continued to watch the steps leading to the keep's forebuilding. Matilda had just rejoined her when at last she was rewarded with the sight of the constable. He was walking swiftly down the steps, pulling on his gloves as he descended.

It felt quite natural, the way she stepped forward to meet him as he approached the stables.

'My lord constable!' cried Rose in her most winsome voice. 'I am glad to see you before I leave, to bid you farewell and thank you for your hospitality.'

Sir Alexander's face lit up at the sight of her.

'Rose, my dear!' he said with obvious delight. 'You are leaving us too soon!'

'Yes, my lord. My parents are expecting me home by this evening.'

'Ah, then you must not keep them waiting. I have scarcely seen you at all during your brief visit, but I expect Sir Nicholas has been keeping you busy.'

He was looking at the open door to the stables and Rose could see that, despite his gallantry, he was eager to leave.

'Farewell, then, my lord,' she added hastily, trying to keep his attention for a little longer. 'Perhaps we might see you at Hurste when business brings you our way?'

'I do hope so, my dear, but in the meantime, please give my kindest regards to your father and mother.'

She offered her hand and he took it in his, raising it to his lips which lightly brushed her fingertips, avoiding the heavy rings she wore. Matilda had criticised her earlier for her ostentation and foolishness in wearing large gemstones on her fingers when they were about to travel. It was inviting trouble, she had warned. She was right, but Rose had ignored her, as she often did.

'Goodbye then, my dear,' said the constable.

And then he had gone, ducking as he entered the low stable building. Rose's disappointment was obvious and she stood motionless for a moment or two, unsure of what to do next.

'What's the matter?' chided Matilda with a sour laugh. 'Thought he was going to propose marriage, did you?'

Rose refused to answer, turning her head with great reluctance towards the chapel where the seneschal and John were waiting.

'Alexander!' called a voice loudly from the foot of the steps. Rose glanced over her shoulder to see the tall figure of Sir

Simon de Gardyn striding purposefully towards them. The constable emerged from the stables, looking irritable.

'What is it, Simon? I shall be late!'

'Lady!' exclaimed the deputy constable, noticing Rose for the first time. He bestowed on her a broad smile and a courtly bow, ignoring the constable's protests.

'What is it?' repeated Alexander with growing impatience and between gritted teeth.

'You neglected to finish the bishop's report, sir, and his grace expects it by tomorrow.'

'You deal with it, Simon. I must be off,' replied Alexander curtly as his horse was led out of the stable for him. He mounted without further delay and was soon riding towards the gatehouse.

'Surely you aren't leaving us so soon, lady?' Simon said, turning his attention back to Rose.

'I am, sir. I must be home by nightfall.'

She smiled and offered her hand. Simon grasped it, lifting it awkwardly towards his mouth, as if not really sure what to do with it. And then he stopped, her hand still in his, raised half way to his lips.

He was staring at her fingers, or rather at the rings that sparkled so beguilingly in the afternoon sun. He frowned in confusion and indignation, as if about to protest against some unspoken insult. He swallowed hard, his Adam's apple bobbing.

'How did you...' he began, staring at Rose.

'How did I what?' asked Rose sweetly, wishing he would let go of her hand.

'That ring. How did you...'

'How did my daughter do what?' demanded the woman who stepped out of the stable and stood before them.

'Mother!' cried Rose in astonishment. 'Mother, I was about to leave. Surely there was no need to come and check up on me!'

Lady Rowena ignored her.

'Leave Rose alone,' she demanded, glaring at Simon. 'I do not trust you. I never have.'

The deputy constable, who had looked taken aback at the sight of Lady Rowena, quickly recovered himself.

'It is quite natural, my lady, for you not to trust me,' he replied smoothly. 'Why would you feel comfortable with someone who sees so clearly through you? I know what you are about, why you sneak your way into the castle. I know what you and Alexander have been up to, feathering your love nest. I saw Alexander only the other day with this very ring!'

'The ring appears to have upset you, Simon,' said the seneschal. He and John had gradually been making their way from the chapel and had heard most of what had been said. 'What is the matter? Are you afraid someone's taken something from your hoard?'

Simon stared balefully at the seneschal.

'Do not be ridiculous,' he replied indignantly. 'I am merely surprised. I saw this very ring in the constable's possession only a few days ago and was wondering how Rose had managed to take it back.'

He had released Rose's hand at last, but still his eyes lingered on the large emerald ring on her middle finger. He seemed mesmerised by it.

'This is all nonsense,' protested Rowena, but the usual icy control had gone from her voice. She sounded afraid and dangerously close to tears.

'Of course it is!' added Rose in support, but she sounded confused and uncertain, worried by the look on her mother's face.

'I think, my lady,' said the seneschal quietly, 'that we should speak in private.' Rowena nodded miserably as he led her away, towards the steps and the keep.

John of Tilneye stood with Rose as the seneschal and Lady Rowena disappeared through the high door of the forebuilding.

'I would never,' Rose began tearfully, 'have proposed trying that trick with the ring if I'd thought it would put my mother at risk.'

John hardly knew what to say, so remained silent. They had both turned their backs on Simon and seemed to have forgotten him.

'This emerald ring was one of a pair and they were identical,' Rose continued as she turned the jewel on her finger. 'My grandfather gave it to me when I was very young, long before I was old enough to wear it. He kept the other one and told me that one day I would inherit it and keep the pair. The rings were very precious, he said, made by the finest Saxon goldsmith of his time and set with emeralds of considerable value. Because of that and my mother's strong aversion to the family jewellery, I hardly ever wore it, even when my fingers had grown.

'Lately, it occurred to me that whoever had stolen Aelfric's treasures would most likely have the other ring of the pair. If so, they would be bound to appreciate its value. The trick we played with the brooch failed. Perhaps it did not stand out enough, or was too similar to others. However, the pair of emerald rings is exceptional and very hard to ignore. I thought that if anything could draw out the thief and the killer, it would be this ring. I never imagined my mother would be caught out by it.'

'It could just be a misunderstanding. The seneschal will sort it out. Your mother will be proven innocent. You'll see.'

'I very much hope so,' she replied faintly.

'Your father should be informed. He will be concerned when Lady Rowena does not return home immediately.'

She gasped, as if just returning to her senses.

'You are right. I must find my mother's escort and send them to inform my father of the delay. I do not think,' she added, 'that I need to tell him any details yet. As you say, my mother is bound to be proven innocent and my father should not be troubled needlessly. He is a good man. He is considered by many to be cold and calculating, moved only by the thought of land and money, but he has a good heart.'

'Might his good heart move him to speak to me if I asked courteously enough?'

Rose looked at him curiously.

'What would you need to speak to him about?'

'About you, Rose. Apparently you have an army of suitors lined up, awaiting your father's selection. I might as well line up with them. Or is this just the wrong time to mention such a thing?'

'It is absolutely the wrong time,' she replied tartly. 'I cannot imagine a worse one.'

He nodded, accepting the reprimand. Yet, when he stole a glance at her lowered face, he could have sworn that there was the faintest glimmer of a smile there.

SIXTY-SIX

Poise

Nicholas took Lady Rowena to the back of the great hall, to the table where he had spoken to Alaric earlier. There were no guards. His men-at-arms were engaged elsewhere and he saw no reason for their attendance.

Lady Rowena had recovered some of her poise by the time they sat down and he ordered wine for her. She sat up straight on the bench and faced him in the direct manner which he was becoming used to.

'I apologise for my conduct, my lord seneschal,' she began. 'It was a shock, hearing Simon talk about Alexander in that way and to suggest he knew about...'

She flushed, much to her obvious annoyance. She took a sip of wine, as if to calm her nerves.

'About your friendship with the constable?' Nicholas prompted.

'Friendship, yes,' she nodded. 'It was because of that friendship that I came here today. I have hardly seen Alexander over the last ten days or so, and his absence concerned me. He usually contrives to see me every few days, so this long silence has been worrying. However unwise it was, I decided to come here today and seek him out. I saw him going towards the stables and pausing outside to speak to Rose, so I went in through the back of the stables and met him there. He was flustered and in a great hurry to leave. It was clear that he did not wish to speak to me.'

It had been around ten days ago, Nicholas remembered, that Alexander had told him about his relationship with Lady Rowena. Perhaps that conversation had triggered a change of heart in the constable.

'And the day I saw you at the castle? The afternoon before Weland's death?'

'I should not have lied to you, my lord seneschal,' she replied uncomfortably. 'Similarly to today, I came here hoping to see Alexander, only to find he had already left the castle. On that occasion, however, I did see him later. It turned out that he was in Murrow and came to see me that night.'

'The constable called to see you at Hurste the night before Weland's death? I have to ask you; how long did he stay?'

Lady Rowena closed her eyes, pressing the lids closely together, as if to block out her shame.

'Until dawn, sir. My husband was away in Lincolnshire. I need not tell you how little I wanted to confess to this.'

Nicholas nodded. It was as he had suspected. If the lady was telling the truth, neither she nor Alexander could have killed Weland.

'And so, perhaps you could tell me about Simon's accusations concerning Aelfric's treasure?'

'That, sir, is complete nonsense. Alexander is no thief and he has no love nest to feather, as Simon so crudely put it. He is wealthy and, even if he wished to take me away, he has manors in plenty to give us a safe haven. However, no such thing will occur. I shall remain with my husband and Alexander knows that. I've had the feeling lately that he is relieved to hear it.'

'And you, Lady Rowena? Were you ever involved in the theft of Aelfric's treasure, as it tends to be called? Were you ever, in any way, involved in your father's death or that of Weland?'

'No, my lord, absolutely not! Whoever has those hideous pieces of jewellery is welcome to them. And no, of course I did not harm my father. Or anyone else.'

'And you were not involved in those deaths in any way?'

'No, my lord. Such an idea is as ridiculous as it is repugnant.'

'Thank you, my lady. Perhaps it is time now for you to take Rose home.'

SIXTY-SEVEN

Trickster

The seneschal's men-at-arms had been quick to follow orders. No sooner had Lady Rowena been taken into the castle had they cornered Sir Simon de Gardyn and escorted him to the Mote Hall. Some of the constable's men had been sent to the de Gardyn manor close to Newton in the Isle, leaving the seneschal time to speak to Simon at leisure.

Lady Rowena had reached Rose and her escort in time to stop them riding to Hurste with bad news. It was with a far more seemly pace that the whole party, including a disgruntled and resentful Matilda, set out on their journey home.

By the time the seneschal joined Simon in the Mote Hall office, the deputy was seething with indignity. He objected strongly to having been kept waiting and had been airing his views loudly to the obstinately unresponsive Brithun and Ordgar who were stationed with their backs to the door.

'How dare you treat me in this manner, Nicholas?' Simon demanded as the seneschal entered the office. 'The constable will have plenty to say when he returns and my lord bishop will be less than pleased with your outrageous conduct.'

Nicholas made no response. Rather than taking his usual seat at the desk, he remained on his feet, taking a few steps backwards and forwards, as if deep in thought.

'When was it that you first decided to use Weland to carry out your plans?' he asked after a long silence.

'What? What by God's teeth are you talking about? Weland the carpenter's son? Why would I have anything to do with that excuse for a human being? You are being ridiculous!'

With an exaggerated gesture, Simon folded his arms and lifted his chin defiantly. His hands were not bound. The presence of Brithun and Ordgar by the door had been considered enough to keep him safely contained for now.

'You were alone in the constable's office when Weland first came to the castle back in March this year. Sir Alexander was away,' stated Nicholas.

'That is true,' agreed Simon confidently, though much of the colour had drained from his face. 'I told you so at the time.'

'You did. You explained that Weland came to you with a feeble tale about the bishop needing the castle's copy of the Charter of Oswy and Leoflede and that, quite correctly, you refused to hand the document over.'

'Of course I refused! The man was an obvious fraud!'

'But what you failed to tell me was that your curiosity about the man's motives led you to seek him out later and speak to him, to find out what he was really up to.'

'What makes you assume that?' Simon laughed. 'Actually, you're right. No harm in saying so. I went down to the bailey, found him taking that nag of his out of the stables and demanded to know what his game was.'

'Because that charter fascinated you. You told me at the time that you couldn't understand a word of it because it was written in the old Saxon language. On a later occasion, however, you commented on the content of that charter, betraying the fact that you had read parts of it at least. You lied to me, Simon. You understand Old English perfectly well, do you not?'

Simon made a dismissive gesture with his hand.

'I understand bits of it. Not much. I should have explained more clearly.'

'You understand enough to have given Weland the information he needed from that charter. I rather think you'd had designs on Aelfric's house, and the items of value said to be hidden there, for some time. You'd had plenty of time to work on the charter, had you not? Whenever the constable was away, all you had to do was remove it from the chest behind you and study it.

'Your problem was that alone you could do nothing about seeking those riches, since you enjoyed a position of trust in this town. So, when a poor fool like Weland came along, he presented the perfect solution. That clumsy youth, who was already hell bent on seeing the charter and finding the legendary treasure, was the very person you needed to carry out your unpleasant work for you.'

'You're simply making this up!' protested Simon, his Adam's apple working hard to keep up with his indignation.

'Did you intend to have Aelfric's house burned down?'

'No! I...' The deputy constable drew in a sharp breath, realising he had reacted too hastily.

'What did you intend, then, Simon? Before we go on, I think it's only fair to inform you that I've sent men to search your house and outbuildings in Newton. We shall find the valuables you took from Aelfric's house.

'This morning,' continued the seneschal, 'when I spoke to the constable, he was keen to inform me that he had just returned from Guyhirn, to make it clear that he had not been visiting Lady Rowena in Hurste again. He also mentioned that you had been to Newton in the Isle. That, I understand, is where your main residence is situated. With this investigation closing in around you, you must have wanted to move the stolen items from wherever you'd hidden them in the castle to the safety of your own estate. It is only a matter of time before my men find those things, so you might as well tell me everything.'

'Nicholas, your confidence in your wild assumptions is admirable, but you have no evidence and I...'

'I know you stole Aelfric's family treasure and I know you returned to look for the pieces you dropped as you fled with them. You were observed, Simon.'

'That damned sergeant, I suppose. Takes a thief to know one.' Simon sounded less confident now. 'It's true I found the odd piece lying around, but ...'

'Yes?' encouraged the seneschal. 'As I said, you might as well tell me everything. What you've hidden will soon be found.'

'You think so, do you? But what if I've outsmarted you, Nicholas?' Simon smirked. The seneschal looked back at him, stony faced.

'I doubt that, but I'm sure your cleverness knew no bounds when outsmarting poor Weland.'

'Poor Weland? That peasant was a born thief and trickster. It took no effort at all to persuade him to work for me. I went to see him in Ely and he didn't hesitate to come back here with me. He could hardly wait to get started! He bought my promise, to share the bounty with him at the end, so very easily.

'I did not ask much of him. All he had to do was to break into that mouldering house in the Old Market, find the old man's loot and get out again. It was that simple. But the imbecile managed to set fire to the place and Aelfric died and suddenly it was no mere theft that might soon have been forgotten, but a death. Then you were called in to investigate. That fool of a boy ran to me, said he had nowhere to go, that his father would beat him to a pulp if he dared show his face back in Ely. I said I'd keep him hidden until things quietened down and then he'd be on his own.'

'So you hid him. Would you oblige me by saying where?'

Simon grinned.

'In the castle. In any unoccupied chamber. You could easily have spotted him many times, but you really aren't that observant, are you? On one occasion, the boy was in the empty court room next to your office. If he'd sneezed, you'd have heard him.'

Simon allowed himself a little chuckle.

'And what of the treasure?'

'I didn't have it. Not then, because Weland had failed to find it. I had to wait until the screens were put up around the ruins of the house before I could look properly. I found it eventually. The wooden box that had contained the jewellery had burned away to nothing, of course, so I had to pick the individual items out of the ashes and carry them in my scrip.'

'And you dropped a few pieces on your way back to the castle.'

Simon shrugged, but said nothing.

'So, after that you kept going back to look for the missing items. Baldwin beat you to it on one occasion and soon realised what you were doing. Then I too found one of the brooches you'd dropped. So, what about Weland? I'm sure that, being the honourable man you are, you did as promised and shared the loot with the boy.'

'I did not. He deserved nothing after failing to steal from Aelfric. By then, he hardly needed me anyway. He'd acquired a taste for theft and was starting to run wild with his house breaking and burning.'

'That must have been worrying for you, Simon. You must have known that he'd eventually be caught and give you away. When at last we had him in custody, you must have been terrified that he'd name you. You had to shut him up, so you killed him.'

Simon vigorously shook his head.

'No, no, no. Theft, all right, I admit to that, but killing...no.'

The seneschal nodded and spoke to his men.

'Put him in the cells for the night. Give him an idea of how that feels. I shall speak to him again in the morning, once I have enjoyed a good night's sleep. The evening is advancing and I believe I have missed my supper.'

SIXTY-EIGHT

Feast of St Columba of Iona; Saturday 9th June

The cells beneath the keep of Wisbech Castle were full to capacity. The summer Assizes were fast approaching and it was no longer possible for anyone to be given a cell to himself. Prisoners were being delivered from all over the Isle of Ely in readiness for the court hearings later in the month.

Sir Simon de Gardyn had spent a miserable night, having, according to him, shared a cell with two of the foulest smelling human beings in existence. They had apparently been quick to point out his error in hogging all of the meagre bed space, and by the time he appeared before the seneschal early that morning, he had a black eye and a swollen right cheek to show for it.

Nicholas chose not to comment, beginning his questions without preamble.

'You managed your timing very well on the night you killed Weland. I cannot help but be impressed with that.'

'As I told you, I did not kill anyone. I stole. Let the courts punish me for that and let's leave it there...'

'But Simon, I believe you did kill Weland. You went down to the cells just as the new guards arrived on duty, before they had begun their normal routine. You knew they wouldn't have had time for their first check of the cells, so they would have to do that as soon as you'd left. They would find everything in order, therefore clearing you of any suspicion later when Weland's body was found. But, instead of returning to your office where your arrival and leaving again would be noticed, you waited somewhere. Then, shortly afterwards, you returned to the cells and stabbed the prisoner.'

'That makes no sense at all,' pointed out Simon. 'The guards would have seen me if I'd returned, would they not?'

'I agree its puzzling, but I have to hand it to you, Simon; you achieved it. Somehow, unobserved and unheard, you returned. You clearly have experience in using a knife. You made sure that Weland would be quick about dying, that he made as little fuss about it as possible. What you were less careful about was keeping him quiet until the end, to make sure that he didn't betray you. Instead of waiting, you left the cells as quickly as you could, to change your clothing and return to your office. From then until you received the report of Weland's death, you presented a very convincing picture of the law abiding deputy working calmly at the constable's desk. I did, however, notice when I called to see you later, how hastily your clothes seem to have been thrown on, how poorly presented you were.'

Simon laughed, but it was a stunted, painful sort of laugh. His bruised face must have been hurting him.

'Nicholas, you spin a good story, but that's all it is, now...'

'If it's that good, kindly let me finish it. In your haste to leave the cells, you did not hear your victim crying out in anguish. Weland's last words, I am given to understand, were largely incoherent, but he spoke your name quite clearly. The guards all heard it.'

'They can't have! They were all s...'

Simon stopped abruptly, wincing painfully, knowing he had blurted out too much. He glanced wildly around the small room, as if searching for an escape route, but saw only the inexpressive faces of the two men-at-arms by the door. He hung his head and his shoulders slumped.

'Sleeping, yes,' said Nicholas, finishing Simon's utterance for him. 'The guards were asleep because you drugged their ale before they went on duty. Perhaps you were unsure of the dose because they didn't sleep for long, but long enough to suit your purposes. Why did you do it, Simon? Why risk your position in this town and the Isle of Ely? Why destroy the bishop's trust in you with theft, then allow things to escalate to killing?'

Simon raised his head just enough to glance at the seneschal. He exhaled loudly before speaking.

'I never intended to harm anyone. All I wanted was to keep those English treasures, those beautiful examples of Saxon craftsmanship, in Saxon hands. Lady Rowena has no respect for her roots. She married a Norman and is proud of it. She rarely visited her father or the house in the Old Market where she had grown up. The place was no longer good enough for her once she was enjoying the refinement of Hurste manor. But we all know why these Normans are so prosperous, don't we? It's because they stole from our countrymen when they came here with the Conqueror. They took our land and robbed us of our possessions and status. The manor at Hurste was stolen from a noble Saxon family. Did you know that?'

'I didn't know that about Hurste, but of course it is true of manors all over the country. But what's all this about,

Simon? You are as Norman as I am. Your name is unmistakably Norman. Are you not a descendant of one of the Conqueror's men?'

Simon de Gardyn smiled bitterly.

'No, my lord seneschal, I am Saxon and proud of it. My grandfather changed our family name when he grew tired of having to prove himself to our Norman overlords. Having a Saxon name was a disadvantage. In those days, we went by the name of Wyrtgeard; the Old English word for a garden. He normanised it, you could say, by changing it to Gardyn and adding a "de" for good measure. It was all rather cynical, but it worked for us and made us sound like respectable Normans. Yet, I loathe everything that is Norman. I cannot forget how our land has been plundered and our people massacred. You noticed, Nicholas, that I slipped up in admitting to being able to read the charter. In fact, I can read our old language with ease. I have made it my business to become conversant with it.

'I found the words hidden in the charter years ago. I knew of the legend which connected the house in the Old Market with a priceless collection of Saxon jewellery. Those treasures were, quite rightly, in the hands of Aelfric. However, I knew that on his death his possessions would pass to his daughter. Or rather, in accordance with Norman law, everything would go to that husband of hers.

'It was necessary, therefore, to remove those treasures from that house and keep them in safe Saxon hands. When that eager and greedy little brat, Weland, came along, I decided to let him do the job for me and save myself a lot of trouble. As we all know, the idiot made a monumental mess of it all. Poor Aelfric died in the fire and Weland failed to take what he had gone in there for. When I heard about Aelfric's death I was horrified. A good, noble man of Saxon lineage dying like that!'

'So Weland became a liability,' said Nicholas. 'He was caught and you feared he would name you.'

'He was a thorn in my side,' admitted Simon. 'He had to be shut up. He'd had enough warnings. I'd told him time and time again to leave town, but he was enjoying his light fingered life by then. He refused to go and I had little choice but to continue hiding him. He was becoming more and more arrogant, believing he could push me around because of what he could tell the bishop about me.'

'A brazen kind of blackmail,' observed Nicholas drily.

'After you'd questioned him, I realised with relief that he hadn't yet mentioned my name. I was safe so far, but I knew he'd drop me in it in the end. I had to prevent that happening. I knew that the guards' ale and bread is always left ready in the great hall before each new shift and it was easy to add a sedative to the ale. At that early hour, there is never anyone around. Poppy juice is easy to obtain, but I had to guess the dose, not being versed in the use of medicines and such like. I had no wish to harm the guards; I just needed them to fall asleep.'

'While you stabbed their prisoner. The keys, I assume, you took from Alaric's belt.'

Simon nodded.

'As you said, I had already been down to the cells and made sure that the guards all saw me leave. Then I went to the stables and waited for what I hoped was long enough for the sedative to take effect. When I returned to the cells, all three guards were slumped like drunks on a bench. Alaric didn't even stir when I took his keys and unlocked Weland's cell.

'There was nothing satisfying about the act itself; I did not enjoy killing the boy, but it had to be done. I just wish he hadn't woken and seen me standing over him. The terror on his face, the horror of it all, are things I shall never forget. I see his face at night when I try to sleep, however much I try to blank it out. He cried out then, but I carried out the deed quickly and left, knowing that his death would come quickly. I could hear him still trying to speak, but I didn't stay to listen. I left that stinking place as soon as I could, returning the keys to Alaric's belt. He never even knew they had gone and I was sure that he and the other guards were still soundly asleep. It seems now from what you say that I was wrong, that they were beginning to awaken. I must have used too small a dose of poppy. Who heard Weland cry out, Nicholas? Which of the guards was it?'

'None of them. The guards were still sleeping and heard nothing. As you say, Simon, I spin a good story.'

Simon cursed under his breath, wincing again with pain as Brithun and Ordgar hauled him to his feet.

'The Assizes will be held later this month,' said the seneschal. 'At least your wait will not be long and I shall try to give you better company in your cell this time. The treasure you stole has now been retrieved from its burial pit behind your stables in Newton in the Isle. It will all be handed over to Sir Mortimer de Hurste, its new and rightful owner. Perhaps he will be generous enough to allow his daughter to keep some of it. If so, you can rest assured she will value the jewellery highly and continue to honour her Saxon heritage. Knowing that will perhaps bring some small comfort to you.'

Simon Wyrtgeard raised his head and looked at Nicholas, giving him an almost imperceptible nod as he was taken away. The seneschal remained alone in the Mote Hall office for some time, knowing that his work was done, but feeling bereft of the total satisfaction that such knowledge usually brought him.

He had tricked Simon in order to gain a confession, and he never liked having to do that. Yet without such a ploy, he doubted he would ever have learned the truth.

Nicholas did not much like Simon, but he would at least do the man the honour of using his true family name of Wyrtgeard at his trial.

SIXTY-NINE

Feast of St Barnabas; Monday 11th June

The Assizes were, as Nicholas had reminded Simon, fast approaching. Already the time had come for the seneschal to start his preparation for them. The half yearly Assizes were far more complex affairs than the Hundred Courts and demanded a lot more of his time. There was a jury to be summoned and plans to be made for the arrival of the Justice who would preside over the court hearings.

Having finally completed his investigation, it was too late for Nicholas to return to Ely before the Assizes. It was with regret, therefore, that he wrote to his wife explaining that he would be delayed for a while longer in Wisbech.

For most of the time, he was left to work in his Mote Hall office in peace. The constable, newly bereft of a deputy, rarely seemed to leave his office. Whether it was due to the disgrace of all that had befallen the castle through Simon's arrest, or simply volume of work, Nicholas neither knew nor very much cared.

By dinner time on St Barnabas Day, the seneschal was sufficiently satisfied with the progress he had made to allow himself time for a good meal. He left the Mote Hall and made his way across the bailey. It was as lively and busy as always at that time of day. There was the usual medley of visitors to the town, many of them proclaiming their high status with elegant garments and fine horses. They mingled disdainfully with the ordinary folk; the tinkers, townspeople and husbandmen, as well as the usual army of castle servants who weaved their way from task to task across the open bailey.

Nicholas walked as quickly as he could through the crowd, disregarding the noise and bustle, focussed only on reaching the great hall. In the middle of the mass of people, and causing most of the congestion, was a superior looking party consisting of a high ranking man on a fine palfrey and an escort of lesser mounted men-at-arms. Nicholas tutted to himself and manoeuvred his way around them, but just as he was dodging past the nose of one of the horses, its rider dismounted. Nicholas found himself face to face with the lofty visage of Sir Mortimer de Hurste.

'Sir Nicholas!' exclaimed the manorial lord. He was as unsmiling as ever, but there was unmistakable warmth in his voice this time. He looked to be in better health than when the seneschal had last seen him. Perhaps the fresh air was doing him good.

'Good day to you, Sir Mortimer,' replied Nicholas as he thought of his dinner.

'Well, it is and it isn't,' considered Sir Mortimer. 'I've just bumped into the constable. Seemed distracted, poor chap. He'd quite forgotten we'd agreed to meet this afternoon. Business, you know. Poor fellow's in quite a state without his deputy. Seems he relied on the chap a great deal. Quite a blow, this arrest. Are you sure about all this? Seemed a decent enough individual, though a bit wet. Can't imagine him having the nerve to sink a knife into anyone. Anyway, I'm glad to see you, my lord seneschal. Since business has brought me to this neck of the woods today, I've been persuaded to pay a visit to a manor close by. My daughter insists on it, as daughters do. Can you tell me how I find the place? Marshmeade, I believe it's called. '

'Indeed I can!' smiled Nicholas, leading the knight through the crowd towards the gatehouse. 'The Tilneye family have held the manor of Marshmeade since the time of the Conqueror and are well respected, good people.'

'Glad to hear it,' acknowledged Sir Mortimer unconvincingly. 'My daughter, Sir Nicholas, as I'm sure I've told you ad nauseam before, has a string of suitors as long as my arm. Some are, quite frankly, hopeless cases, but others are worthy individuals of good standing. Yet, she gives none of them the time of day. Not one of them! Then along comes this young fellow who is so full of himself and has the cheek to ask for her hand! Dismissed him straight away, of course. Damned lucky not to have my boot up his backside. Never even heard of this Marshmeade place he claims to hail from, but my daughter begged me to reconsider. Now why, by God's wounds, would I do that? I want Rose to marry well, to be connected with the best families. Yet here I am, at her command, as usual, dutifully riding off to see this place in the middle of nowhere...'

'But the Tilneyes of Marshmeade are well known and respected in these parts,' Nicholas broke in to assure him. 'And the young Tilneye knight is of good character, however arrogantly he may present himself on first acquaintance. He has been of great help to me with my work here.'

Sir Mortimer looked unimpressed.

'Well, I shall do as Rose begs of me and go to see the father. Sir Roland, I think the name is. The sooner I get this business over and done with, the better. My daughter will be wed into a good Lincolnshire family and will learn to be content. Just as her mother did.'

Nicholas led Sir Mortimer through the arch under the gatehouse and over the bridge. The two men looked down the road that led past the church and along the river towards Marshmeade.

'The ride will not take you long,' Nicholas said. He spent a little time describing the local area and landmarks the party should look for on their way. When he had finished, Sir Mortimer thanked him with a great deal more enthusiasm than he had shown before.

Nicholas lingered by the gatehouse as Sir Mortimer made his way back to the keep for his meeting with the constable. And then the seneschal went at last to enjoy his dinner.

SEVENTY

Saturday, 30th June
Market Day

At last he was going home.

Though the early morning was breezy, the sun was warm on Nicholas's face as he raised it towards the sky. The Assizes were over for another six months and all was done but for the hangings and other punishments.

He would not stay for them. He would not stay to see the gallows erected by the castle gate or to witness Simon Wyrtgeard's execution by axe. He had seen enough death in his time and had no need to watch more men die. He had done his job and the Justice and jury had done theirs. It was time to move on.

It was a good day for riding, dry and warm. He and his men would travel as far as their horses could go, then sleep under canvas or find a wayside inn if one was conveniently situated.

In the New Market square the booths had been set up for the weekly market. At this early hour it was already well attended. Nicholas stood and viewed the activity as he chewed on his morning bread and sipped from his ale flask. Two country women were lifting a large wooden cage of hens from a cart, setting it gently on the ground. The birds squawked and scampered about in protest, keeping up their discordant complaint as the women set up their stall. On a wobbly trestle table, they spread out a cloth on to which they placed their newly harvested peas and beans alongside bunches of onion, rosemary, purslane and parsley.

Elsewhere, stallholders were setting out sacks of wool, woven cloth, bags of flour, dairy products and metal goods. The seneschal idled for a moment by a pen of piglets while he finished his bread, amused by their frantic activity and squealing playfulness.

'Don't even consider it,' came a voice from behind him. 'You'll never balance a pig on your saddle all the way to Ely.'

Nicholas laughed, recognising the voice, and turned to see John of Tilneye dismounting from his horse.

'I'm glad I caught you, sir,' said John. 'They told me at the castle you'd already left and I wanted to thank you.'

'Thank me? It is I who should be thanking you. No one else's bladder could have withstood all that drinking while you were spreading rumours for me in the ale houses.' He could hardly hear himself speak above the din of squealing piglets and he pointed towards a booth selling ale. 'Come on,' he added. 'We can speak more comfortably over there and I can have my flask refilled.'

They settled themselves on a rough bench inside the small enclosure. Neither John nor Nicholas was a stranger to this market booth and the corpulent brewer greeted them both cheerfully. He hefted a huge jug of ale from a board in the corner and filled cups for them. He had a small brewery in Elm and brought his ale on a cart to the market place every Saturday morning, setting up his simple enclosure of canvas with its well worn benches. It was always worth his while. He regularly did as much business on a Saturday as any of the town's hostelries, his jovial manner and free flowing gossip attracting plenty of customers, both regular and new. Already, though the day was young, the benches were almost fully occupied, and John had to lower his voice to avoid being overheard.

'First of all,' he began, 'I want to pass Rose's thanks to you for sending Aelfric's treasures to Hurste Manor. Without you, they would never have been recovered and, though Lady Rowena regards them with as much scorn as ever, Rose and Sir Mortimer appreciate their value.'

Nicholas looked at him curiously.

'You appear to be extraordinarily familiar with the thoughts and sentiments of the Hurste family.'

'That, sir, is because I have spent rather a lot of time there lately, trying to convince Sir Mortimer of my worth as a suitor for Rose. But that's another story, one which I may bore you with in a moment. Firstly, though, I thought you would be pleased to hear that Sir Mortimer, having received the goods as Aelfric's legal beneficiary, has gifted the whole lot to Rose.'

'All of it?' asked Nicholas in surprise.

'Indeed all of it, including the pieces you and the sergeant found in the Old Market. I have to admit his lordship has his good points. The old boy seems to have recovered his health, too, less yellow about the face these days, so I suppose he can afford to make the odd decent gesture.'

'I confess that I misjudged him,' said Nicholas.

Perhaps, he thought, Lady Rowena's disillusionment with the constable was making her a little more attentive at home. He too had noticed an improvement in Sir Mortimer's demeanour and well being when he had seen him last.

'Oh, don't be too generous, sir. He's still as hard as nails and as unyielding as an ox. However, he told Rose that by right she should have what her grandfather left. It is her Saxon inheritance. And there is more pleasing news. When Rose found out about the damage Weland inflicted on the widow's house over there,' he said, pointing to the shabby house on the northern side of the market place, 'she was quick to make amends. Weland's actions were connected to her family's charter, so she considers it only fair to pay for the widow's home to be repaired. Work is about to start and she has already replaced all the items he destroyed. Also,' he added with a laugh, 'she made sure that her father paid that miserable cobbler in the Old Market the amount he says Aelfric owed him.'

'It appears that Rose de Hurste is as generous as she is charming,' acknowledged Nicholas.

John agreed with a lingering smile. Both men sipped their ale in silence before the seneschal changed the subject.

'So come on,' he urged. 'I believe you have more to tell me.'

'I do, sir, and this is what I wish to thank you for. As I said, I have been spending rather a lot of time at Hurste, mostly out of Sir Mortimer's sight, because it was obvious that he had no regard for me. I asked for Rose's hand in marriage during my first visit, only to be laughed at. Rose had warned me that it would be far from easy. Some of her suitors were truly wealthy, with manors and land promised to them on marriage by their prosperous families. The fact that none of those men were in any way pleasing to Sir Mortimer's daughter was, of course, considered to be of no importance whatsoever. Rose had accepted that she would be married off to one of them and would have to make the most of it.

'So,' continued John, 'it was hardly surprising that Sir Mortimer laughed at my plea and sent me away like a beggar. Rose, though, was not content to leave it at that. She told me how she pleaded with her father and how, in the end, he agreed to pay a visit to Marshmeade. Sir Mortimer has a soft spot for his daughter, but even so, I do not believe she had much hope for his final decision.'

'I chanced upon Sir Mortimer at the castle, just before his visit to Marshmeade,' said Nicholas.

'Yes, sir, I rather believe you did,' said John with a grin. 'And the strangest thing, the most curious thing, was that on his arrival Sir Mortimer was all smiles. I was at home when he arrived and could hardly believe the change in his attitude. I had not believed his frosty old countenance capable of contorting itself into anything better than a grimace. I feared he would do himself an injury. Yet there he was, this noble, amiable visitor, accepting my parents' hospitality with the smoothest of manners and the most gracious compliments about our humble manor. I could hardly believe what I was seeing or hearing. And then he mentioned seeing you at the castle. I had to wonder what miracle you had worked to change his mind so profoundly.'

'What are you suggesting, John of Tilneye?' asked Nicholas with a very straight face. 'That the seneschal of the Isle of Ely could use guile to sway a man's opinion?'

'Well, sir, no, but...'

'Perhaps I do have a small confession to make,' Nicholas relented, 'but this is for your ears alone, John,' he added meaningfully, looking the young knight in the eye. 'I admit that when giving Sir Mortimer directions to Marshmeade, I took care to mention all the good pasture attached to the manor and the number of sheep it supported. Perhaps I emphasised a little too heavily the land lining the river bank between Elm and Marshmeade and between Marshmeade and Welle.'

'But, sir!' exclaimed John, his eyes wide with disbelief. 'That acreage does not belong to us!'

'Does it not?' asked Nicholas innocently. 'Well, it's an easy mistake to make. There's no way of telling where one man's pasture ends and the next man's begins. I can see no point in correcting my misunderstanding now. I take it from your lack of misery that Sir Mortimer's decision was positive in the end?'

'Oh yes, and now I know why! No doubt he believes we are profiting very handsomely from the wool trade!' John was laughing as he held out his cup for a refill from the brewer's jug.

'Well, you are, surely?'

'Yes, sir, but hardly as well as we would be if we owned all the land between Elm and Welle!'

The seneschal merely smiled and sipped his ale.

'We are to be wed at the end of the summer,' John continued. 'Rose's father told her that he was happy to compromise for the sake of her happiness and that he was glad to have found such a worthy family for her to wed into. Even my own father caved in! He'd been adamant that I delay marriage until there was some sense in my head, but mother talked him round.'

'I am truly glad for you, John. Your wedding will be a very happy conclusion to this sorry time.'

'Thank you, sir. There is but one fly in the happy ointment in which I find myself.'

Nicholas looked at him curiously.

'Matilda, Rose's doleful companion, insists on moving with her mistress to Marshmeade. Lady Rowena, I am disappointed to learn, took no persuading at all to let the girl go.'

Nicholas laughed.

'Ah, well, you can't have it all your way. The sooner a man learns that, the better!'

The seneschal rose to his feet, handing his travelling flask to the brewer for refilling.

'I must go,' he said. 'I am already late in setting out, but glad to have seen you and heard your news. I wish you and Rose the very best of health and happiness.'

'Thank you, sir. Thanks for everything.'

John watched as Nicholas made his way back through the market towards the castle and its stables. Already the early morning freshness was surrendering to warmth, the flimsy enclosure of the ale booth cheered by the first advances of sunshine.

It was going to be another hot day.

Original Norman pillars c.1111 in St Peter and Paul's Church, Wisbech. With the kind permission of the parish church

AUTHOR'S NOTE

The first undisputed reference to the tiny settlement of Wisbech dates from around AD1000. At that time, the manor of Wisbech was a Saxon village situated roughly where the Old Market is today. It had developed from a community of wildfowlers and fishermen living on the banks of the old Wysbeck River. Not much is known about that village, but in fairly recent years a couple of Saxon brooches have been unearthed close to the Old Market. Crafted from a copper alloy and circular in form, they were decorated with an intricate pattern of intertwined serpents. Though not of a precious metal, they were clearly the work of a skilled craftsman and gave historians a small clue about the people who lived in Saxon Wisbech.

The manor of Wisbech was one of many held by a high ranking couple called Oswy and Leoflede. (Under Saxon law, women as well as men could own property in their own right. The Normans later changed that, reducing women to little more than appendages to their fathers and husbands). When the couple's young son Aelfwine became an oblate of the Church of Ely, that is to say he vowed to follow the rules of the Church though not yet becoming a monk, Oswy and Leoflede marked the occasion by making a generous gift to Ely Abbey. In the presence of witnesses, they gifted Walpole, Wisbech (with its outlying hamlets), Debenham, Brightwell and Woodbridge (the last three being in Suffolk), to the abbey. Aelfwine later went on to become the Bishop of Elmham (in Norfolk), so it seems his parents' generosity was justified.

Saxon nobles, such as Oswy and Leoflede, would later suffer an abrupt decline in their status and fortune under the Normans. When William I, known as the Conqueror, defeated King Harold Godwinson at the Battle of Hastings, he began a brutal campaign of subduing the English and making this land his own. Saxon manors, land and riches were taken and placed into Norman ownership, the 'right' to do so protected by new laws.

This very early part of our local history has interested me for a long time. Lately, it occurred to me that it would make a good basis for a story. Whether the gift made by Oswy and Leoflede was set out in a formal document is not known for sure, but it is highly likely. A written record would have been essential to settle any disputes about ownership that might arise in the future.

The idea for the book quickly developed and has grown into another Fenland Mystery, this time set in 1190. Once more, a seneschal, the bishop's law man for the Isle of Ely, appears as the solver of riddles.

Members of the fictitious Tilneye family, who appeared in both 'In The Wash' and 'The Lazar House', are here again too. John of Tilneye, who assists the seneschal this time, will eventually become the father of Ralph and Rufus from 'In The Wash'. I have become so used to writing about the rather unassuming Tilneyes and their imaginary manor close to Elm, that I catch myself wondering whether any trace of Marshmeade remains. I suppose that's how completely unsubstantiated tales and rumours spread!

The manor of Hurste near Tydd St Giles is another product of my imagination, as are most of the hostelries that appear in the book. However, the Swan in the New Market did exist. It would eventually become the Rose and Crown which still holds a prominent position in the market place today. It is not certain when this ale house first started trading in the town, but it is thought to have originated around the time of King John. This book is set a little earlier, in 1190, during the reign of Richard I, but I hope it is not too great a stretch to think of its earliest incarnation being there at the time.

As for the Old Market of the 1190s, practically nothing is known of its layout, so I have had to use imagination. Once the Norman castle was constructed in the 1080s, it became the centre of a new, fashionable part of town. It was known as the New Market to differentiate it from the original Saxon quarter, the Old Market across the Wysbeck River. From then on, the Old Market was pushed somewhat into the shade.

I feel I should add a brief note about the title of 'seneschal'. Since the seventh century, the Isle of Ely had been given the right to have its own jurisdiction. This brought the shire certain benefits, among which was the freedom for the bishop to appoint a chief bailiff. This officer had equivalent status and responsibility to those of a High Sheriff of any other shire. The bailiff's full title was 'Seneschallus Insulae Eliensis', or seneschal of the Isle of Ely. As the word 'bailiff' was used to cover a variety of posts at that time, the title of seneschal seemed preferable.

On a more national theme, I couldn't resist including the snippet of news about King Arthur's body allegedly being found inside a hollow oak tree by the monks of Glastonbury. At a time of such violence and bloodshed, it is somehow reassuring to know that curious, even trivial, things could still make the headlines!

The more I write about Wisbech's early history, the more fascinated I become by it. To help with the plot this time, I started to learn Old English and I'm finding it very interesting. Our old language gives considerable insight into the past we share yet about which so little has been written.

Though I keep saying it, we are so very fortunate to share this heritage, this long, rich history. It continues to be a privilege to write about it.

THANK YOU

As ever, I am very grateful for the support I've had from local people, both in the research for this book and the local history talks I give all around the Isle of Ely.

Once again, I thank my husband Tony for his clever maps and illustrations, as well as his proof reading and unwavering kindness and support. Especially when I hit a rocky patch.

I would also like to thank:

Wisbech and Fenland Museum and the Friends of the Museum,

St Peter and Paul's Church, its clergy and all my friends there,

Wisbech Library,

Ely Library,

Wisbech Eco Hub and Heritage Centre,

Geoff Hill, Karen Scarr and Bridget Holmes for the loan of articles and books,

Michelle Lawes, who has very generously given me a huge treasury of local history books,

And everyone who reads this book. I truly hope you have enjoyed it.

BIBLIOGRAPHY

'An Historical Account of the Ancient Town and Port of Wisbech in the Isle,' by William Watson

'An Introduction to the Old English Language and its Literature,' by Stephen Pollington

'English Local Administration in the Middle Ages,' by Helen M Jewell

'First Steps in Old English,' by Stephen Pollington

'Food and Cooking in Medieval Britain,' by Maggie Black

'Historical Costumes of England,' by Nancy Bradfield

'Learn Old English with Leofwin,' by Matt Love

'Liber Eliensis, a History of the Isle of Ely,' translated by Janet Fairweather

'Subversive Scribes and Killer Rabbits,' article by Johanna Green (BBC History Magazine)

'The Building of England,' by Simon Thurley

'The Chronicle of Britain and Ireland,' edited by Henrietta Heald

'The Court Rolls of Ramsey, Hepmangrove and Bury, 1268-1600,' edited and translated by Edwin DeWindt

'The Legend of Hereward,' by Mike Ripley

'The World of the Luttrell Psalter,' by Michelle P Brown

'Webbed Feet and Wildfowlers,' by Diane Calton Smith

Ingram Content Group UK Ltd.
Milton Keynes UK
UKHW010001250423
420706UK00005B/82